DRAGONLANCE®

THE LOST CHRONICLES

VOLUME THREE

DRAGONS OF THE HOURGLASS MAGE

Margaret Weis & Tracy Hickman

The Lost Chronicles

DRAGONS OF THE HOURGLASS MAGE

©2010 Wizards of the Coast LLC

Published by Wizards of the Coast LLC

DRAGONLANCE, WIZARDS OF THE COAST, and their respective logos are trademarks of Wizards of the Coast LLC in the U.S.A. and other countries.

Printed in the U.S.A.

Cover art by Matt Stawicki
Original Hardcover First Printing: August 2009
First Paperback Printing: May 2010

9 8 7 6 5 4 3 2 1

ISBN: 978-0-7869-5483-4
620-25357000-001-EN

The Library of Congress has catalogued the hardcover edition as follows:

Library of Congress Cataloging-in-Publication Data

Weis, Margaret.
  Dragons of the hourglass mage / Margaret Weis and Tracy Hickman.
    p. cm. -- (The lost chronicles ; v. 3)
  ISBN 978-0-7869-4916-8
  1. Dragons--Fiction. 2. Krynn (Imaginary place)--Fiction. I.
Hickman, Tracy. II. Title.
  PS3573.E3978D7535 2009
  813'.54--dc22

                                                                2009007817

U.S., CANADA,   EUROPEAN HEADQUARTERS
ASIA, PACIFIC, & LATIN AMERICA   Hasbro UK Ltd
Wizards of the Coast LLC   Caswell Way
P.O. Box 707   Newport, Gwent NP9 0YH
Renton, WA 98057-0707   GREAT BRITAIN
+1-800-324-6496   Save this address for your records.

Visit our web site at www.wizards.com

By Margaret Weis and Tracy Hickman

CHRONICLES
Dragons of Autumn Twilight
Dragons of Winter Night
Dragons of Spring Dawning

LEGENDS
Time of the Twins
War of the Twins
Test of the Twins

The Second Generation

Dragons of Summer Flame

THE WAR OF SOULS
Dragons of a Fallen Sun
Dragons of a Lost Star
Dragons of a Vanished Moon

THE LOST CHRONICLES
Dragons of the Dwarven Depths
Dragons of the Highlord Skies
Dragons of the Hourglass Mage

This book is dedicated to the memory of our friend, editor and mentor, Brian Thomsen, who would have appreciated the irony.

Canticle of the Dragon
By Michael Williams

Hear the sage as his song descends
like heaven's rain or tears,
and washes the years, the dust of many stories
from the High Tale of the Dragonlance.
For in ages deep, past memory and word,
in the first blush of the world
when the three moons rose from the lap of the forest,
dragons, terrible and great,
made war on this world of Krynn.

Yet out of the darkness of dragons,
out of our cries for light
in the blank face of the black moon soaring,
a banked light flared in Solamnia,
a knight of truth and of power,
who called down the gods themselves
and forged the mighty Dragonlance, piercing the soul
of dragonkind, driving the shade of their wings
from the brightening shores of Krynn.

Thus Huma, Knight of Solamnia, Lightbringer, First Lancer,
followed his light to the foot of the Khalkist Mountains,
to the stone feet of the gods,
to the crouched silence of their temple.
He called down the Lancemakers, he took on
their unspeakable power to crush the unspeakable evil,
to thrust the coiling darkness
back down the tunnel of the dragon's throat.

Paladine, the Great God of Good, shone at the side of Huma,
strengthening the lance of his strong right arm,
and Huma, ablaze in a thousand moons,
banished the Queen of Darkness,

banished the swarm of her shrieking hosts
back to the senseless kingdom of death, where their curses
swooped upon nothing and nothing
deep below the brightening land.

Thus ended in thunder the Age of Dreams
and began the Age of Might,
when Istar, kingdom of light and truth, arose in the east,
where minarets of white and gold
spired to the sun and to the sun's glory,
announcing the passing of evil, and Istar,
who mothered and cradled the long summers of good,
shone like a meteor
in the white skies of the just.

Yet in the fullness of sunlight
the Kingpriest of Istar saw shadows;
At night he saw the trees as things with daggers, the streams
blackened and thickened under the silent moon.
He searched books for the path of Huma,
for scrolls, signs, and spells
so that he, too, might summon the gods, might find
their aid in his holy aims,
might purge the world of sin.

Then came the time of dark and death
as the gods turned from the world.
A mountain of fire crashed like a comet through Istar,
the city split like a skull in the flames,
mountains burst from once-fertile valleys,
seas poured into the graves of mountains,
the deserts sighed on abandoned floors of the seas,
the highways of Krynn erupted
and became the paths of the dead.

Thus began the Age of Despair.
The roads were tangled.
The winds and the sandstorms dwelt in the husks of cities,

The plains and mountains became our home.
As the old gods lost their power,
we called to the blank sky
into the cold, dividing gray to the ears of new gods.
The sky is calm, silent, unmoving.
We had yet to hear their answer.

Then to the east, to the Sunken City
scarred in its loss of blue light,
came the Heroes, the Innfellows, heirs to the burdens,
out of their tunnels and their arching forests,
out of the lowness of plains, the lowness
of huts in the valleys,
the stunned farms under the warlords and darkness.
They came serving the light,
the covered flames of healing and grace.

From there, pursued by the armies,
the cold and glittering legions, they came
bearing the staff to the arms of the shattered city,
where below the weeds and the birdcall,
below the vallenwood, below forever,
below the riding darkness itself,
a hole in the darkness called to the source of light,
drawing all light to the core of light,
to the first fullness of its godly dazzle.

FOREWORD

his book, *Dragons of the Hourglass Mage*, concludes the *Lost Chronicles* series. Our goal in these books has been to tell the previously untold and unknown stories of the Innfellows during the War of the Lance, a period covered by the *Dragonlance Chronicles*. Although these books can be read on their own, readers will find that they will have a far more complete idea and understanding of what is happening to whom and where and why it is happening if they read the complete series of *Dragonlance Chronicles* before reading the *Lost Chronicles*.

The end of the War of the Lance was chronicled by Astinus of Palanthas in a volume that came to be known as *Dragons of Spring Dawning*. In that book, we follow the adventures of the Heroes of the Lance: Tanis Half-Elven; Flint Fireforge; Tasslehoff Burrfoot; Caramon Majere; and their friends Laurana, the Golden General; Tika Waylan; Riverwind; and Goldmoon; and we recount how they finally defeat the Queen of Darkness.

1

This book deals with one of the heroes of the Lance, Raistlin Majere, whose story was never told, but without whom the other Heroes could never have succeeded.

If you would like to follow the complete tale, Astinus suggests that you read *Dragons of Spring Dawning* first then read this book after. If you would just like to share Raistlin's dark and perilous adventures, then simply keep on reading.

At the time this book begins, the Heroes of the Lance have been separated by the war. Tanis; Caramon and Raistlin; and Tika, Riverwind, and Goldmoon travel to the nightmare land of Silvanesti and from there to Flotsam. Laurana, Sturm Brightblade, Flint, and Tasslehoff travel to Icewall and from there to the High Clerist's Tower, where Sturm sacrifices his life for the cause of Light. Laurana helps defeat Kitiara and her dragonarmy at the battle of the High Clerist's Tower. She, Flint, and Tas travel to Palanthas, where Laurana is made the Golden General, in charge of the human and elf forces now battling Takhisis.

Once in Flotsam, Tanis meets his former lover, Kitiara, and is shocked to discover that she is now a Dragon Highlord in Takhisis's evil army. But though she is on the side of evil, he cannot resist her dark eyes and crooked smile. The two again become lovers.

Kitiara urges Tanis to join her army. He cannot abandon his friends and the cause of Light. Torn by guilt, he leaves Kit and joins his friends on a ship fleeing Flotsam. On board the ship is also Berem Everman, sought by the Queen of Darkness. Hearing the Everman is on this ship, Kitiara flies her dragon in pursuit. Desperate to escape, Berem steers the ship into a maelstrom.

Raistlin Majere believes the ship is doomed, and he uses the magical dragon orb he obtained in Silvanesti to save himself, leaving his twin brother and friends to die. His magic carries him to the Great Library of Palanthas. The spellcasting proves too much for him. He is on the verge of death when Astinus accidentally provides Raistlin with the key that will not only restore him to life, but unlock the mystery of his divided soul.

Raistlin arrives in Palanthas on the twenty-sixth day of the month of Rannmont. We take up his story several days later, on the first day of the month of Mishamont.

Astinus, Chronicler of the History of Krynn, writes:

On the Twenty-sixth Day of the Month of Mishamont, Year 352 AC, in the city of Neraka, the Temple of Takhisis falls. The Dragon Queen is banished from the world. Her armies go down to defeat.

Much of the credit for this victory is given to the Heroes of the Lance, who fought valiantly for the Forces of Light. History should note, however, that the Light would have been doomed to failure if not for one man who chose to walk in Darkness.

PROLOGUE

wo legends of Krynn are essential to the understanding of the plot. Many variations of these
legends can be found. Every bard tells them
somewhat differently. We have chosen these versions
as being the closest to what actually occurred, though,
as with most legends, the truth of the matter will likely
never be known.

Excerpts from "A Child's Garden of Tales of Krynn,"
translated from the Elvish by Quivalen Soth:

The Story of Berem and Jasla
A Tale of Love and Sacrifice

Long ago, at the end of the Second Dragon War,
the valiant knight, Huma Dragonsbane, drove Queen
Takhisis into the Abyss. He forced her to swear an oath
before the High God that she would not return to the

world to upset the delicate balance between good and evil. The gods believed that an oath taken before the High God was so powerful that not even the Queen of Darkness would dare break it. Sadly they were mistaken.

Time passed. The Kingpriests of Istar, acting in the name of the Gods of Light and with their blessing, rose in power. The world was at peace. Unfortunately a man may be blinded by light as well as by darkness. The last Kingpriest looked into the sun and saw nothing but his own glory and dared to proclaim himself a god.

The Gods of Light realized to their sorrow that *they* were now threatening the balance that causes the world to keep turning. They sought the help of the other gods, including Queen Takhisis. The gods determined that in order to restore the balance and teach mankind humility, they would cause a great Cataclysm. Before they acted, they sent the Kingpriest many warnings, urging him to change. The Kingpriest and his followers turned a deaf ear, and the gods, greatly grieving, hurled a fiery mountain down upon Krynn.

The blast leveled the city of Istar and cast it into the sea and destroyed the Temple of the Gods of Light. Or so the gods believed. But although the Temple of Istar lay in ruins at the bottom of the sea, the Foundation Stone upon which the Temple was built remained intact, for that stone is the foundation of faith.

After the Cataclysm, the gods hoped men would acknowledge their faults and seek out the gods. To the gods' sorrow, men blamed the gods for their suffering. Word spread that the gods had abandoned their creation. The world erupted into chaos. Death stalked the land.

Takhisis, Queen of Darkness, was still imprisoned in the Abyss. All the exits were guarded. If she tried to break free, the other gods would know and they would stop her.

Still, she never quit seeking a way back into the world, and one day, in her restless roaming, she came upon a great prize. Takhisis discovered the Foundation Stone. The other gods did not know it still existed. She realized that she could use the stone to return to the world.

True, she would be breaking her oath to the High God. But she was cunning and she counted upon the fact that the world was already in peril. Men had lost hope. Plagues, pestilence, famines, and wars had killed millions. Takhisis could enter the world and wake her evil dragons and launch her war. When she conquered Krynn, she would be so powerful that the other gods would not dare to punish her.

Takhisis, cloaked in darkness, slipped into the world through the gate left open by the Foundation Stone. She woke her evil dragons and ordered them to steal the eggs of the good dragons, who slumbered in their lairs. She prepared to prosecute her war with all her might and power. Then she discovered one day that her way into the world through the Foundation Stone had been blocked.

A man named Berem and his sister, Jasla, were walking together when they came upon the Foundation Stone. They could not believe their good fortune. Rare and precious gems, embedded in the stone, sparkled and shone in the light of creation. Berem was a poor man. One gem could relieve his family's poverty. One gem, one perfect emerald, out of so many would not be missed. Berem began to pry the emerald loose.

His sister, Jasla, was horrified by the theft. She grabbed hold of her brother to try to stop him. Berem flew into a rage and flung her away. She fell and struck her head on the stone and died, her blood staining the Foundation Stone.

Berem loved his sister, and he was appalled at his crime. And he was afraid. No one would believe him

7

when he said that killing his sister had been an accident. He would be executed for murder. Instead of confessing his sin and seeking forgiveness, he turned to flee. As he did so, the emerald that he had been trying to steal sprang from the Foundation Stone and embedded itself in his chest.

Berem was frantic with terror. The spirit of his sister grieved for him. She assured him she still loved him, but he refused to listen. He tried to tear the gem out with his fingers. He was so desperate, he sought to cut it out of his own flesh with a knife. The emerald remained a part of him, the everlasting reminder of his guilt. Berem covered up the gem with his shirt and fled, closing his ears to the pleas of his sister to seek forgiveness even as she had forgiven him.

Takhisis had been witness to this tragedy and had reveled in Berem's downfall . . . until she tried to cross the Foundation Stone. She found her entrance barred by a chain forged of love. Jasla's spirit blocked her way. Now only the Dark Queen's shadow could be cast over Krynn. Her power over man was reduced; she would have to rely on mortals to prosecute her war.

Takhisis had to find Berem. If she could destroy him, his sister's spirit would depart and the Dark Queen would once more be free. She had to be careful in her search for him, however, for if he returned to his sister and redeemed himself, her entry into the world would be blocked for good.

She sent secret word out to her most trusted servants to seek a man named Berem who had a green gemstone embedded in his chest. A man with an old face and young eyes, for the gem gave him immortality. He could not die until he was either redeemed or his soul was utterly lost.

Berem was always on the move, running not only from the Forces of Darkness, but also from his own guilt. Time and again, Takhisis was thwarted in her efforts to capture him. She launched her war, which became known as the War of the Lance, and still Berem had not been found. But by now, his tale was becoming known to more and more people and, eventually, was bound to come to the attention of those fighting Queen Takhisis.

Berem Everman would become men's greatest hope. And their greatest fear.

---

*The Story of Fistandantilus
A Cautionary Tale*

Long ago there lived a powerful wizard named Fistandantilus. He was so powerful that he came to believe that the rules and laws, which governed other, lesser men, did not apply to him. These included those laws of his own order of magic, that of the Black Robes. Fistandantilus left the order and became a renegade, subject to death at the hands of his fellow wizards.

Fistandantilus did not fear his fellow wizards. He had amassed such knowledge and skill in magic that he could destroy any who came to try to bring him to justice. Such was the fear and respect in which his fellow wizards held him that few tried.

Fistandantilus flaunted his power in the face of the Conclave, even taking on apprentices. What no one knew was that he was feeding off his pupils, sucking out their life-forces and using that to extend his own. He had created a magical gem, a bloodstone, for this purpose. He would press the stone to the heart of his victim and drain him of life.

9

As Fistandantilus's power grew, so did his arrogance. He decided to enter the Abyss and overthrow the Queen of Darkness and take her place. To this end, he crafted one of the most powerful and complex magical spells ever created. His arrogance proved his downfall. No one is certain what happened. Some say Takhisis found out and her wrath brought down his fortress on top of him. Others say that his spell escaped his control and blew the fortress apart. Whatever the cause, Fistandantilus's mortal body died.

His soul, however, did not.

His soul refused to leave Krynn, and the evil wizard remained on the ethereal plane. His existence was tenuous, for he was constantly under siege from Takhisis, who continued to try to destroy him. He kept himself alive by leeching off the life-forces of his victims, even as he hoped someday to find a living body he could inhabit and return to life.

Fistandantilus had managed to retain his bloodstone and, armed with that, he lay in wait for victims. He sought out young magic-users, particularly those who were leaning toward darkness, for they would be most likely to succumb to temptation.

The Conclave of Wizards knew Fistandantilus was searching for prey, but they were powerless to stop him. Whenever a young magic-user took the dread Test in the Tower of High Sorcery, the Conclave knew there was a chance that Fistandantilus would seize him. Many who died taking the Test were thought to have been his victims.

Five years prior to the start of the War of the Lance, a young mage and his twin brother came to the Tower of Wayreth to take the Test. The young man had shown great promise in his studies. Foreseeing a time of war and evil

10

coming to Krynn, the head of the Conclave, Par-Salian, hoped that this young mage would assist in defeating the darkness.

The young mage was himself arrogant and ambitious. Although he wore the red robes, his heart and soul tended toward darkness and his own choices led him to strike a bargain with Fistandantilus.[1] The evil wizard did not intend to keep his side of the deal; he meant to drain the young man of his life.

Raistlin Majere was not like others before him. He was in his own way as skilled in magic as Fistandantilus. When the evil mage came to seize the young man's heart and rip it from his body, Raistlin grasped hold of the heart of Fistandantilus.

"You may take my life," Raistlin told Fistandantilus, "but you will serve me in return."

The young man survived his Test, but he was shattered in body, for Fistandantilus was continually draining him of life in order to sustain himself on his magical plane. In return, however, Fistandantilus had to keep Raistlin alive and would come to his aid by feeding him knowledge of magicks that were far advanced for such a young wizard.

Raistlin did not remember any of his Test, nor did he remember his bargain. He thought the Test had ruined his health, and Par-Salian did not tell him otherwise.

"He will know the truth only when he comes to know the truth about himself, confront and admit the darkness within."

Par-Salian spoke those words, but not even he in his wisdom could foresee how the dark and strange alliance would, in the end, be resolved.

---

1 The story can be found in *The Soulforge* by Margaret Weis, published by Wizards of the Coast.

BOOK I

I

A ROll of the dye.
An unexpected encounter.

2nd Day, Month of Mishamont, Year 352 AC

he city of Palanthas had been awake most of the night, bracing for war. The city had not panicked; ancient aristocratic grand dames such as Palanthas never panicked. They sat rigid in their ornately carved chairs, holding tight to their lace handkerchiefs and waiting with stern countenances and straight backs for someone to tell them if there was going to be a war and, if so, would it be so rude as to interrupt their plans for dinner.

The forces of the feared Blue Lady, Dragon Highlord Kitiara, were rumored to be marching on the city. The Highlord's armies had been defeated at the High Clerist's Tower, which guarded the pass leading down from the mountains into Palanthas. The small group of knights and foot soldiers who had held the Tower against the initial assault were not strong enough to hold out against another attack. They had left the fortress and the graves of their dead, retreating to Palanthas.

The city had not been pleased at that. If the militant, warmongering knights had not entered her walls, Palanthas would have been left in peace. The dragonarmies would not dare to attack a city so venerable and revered. The wise knew better. Almost all other major cities in Krynn had fallen to the might of the dragonarmies. The baleful eyes of Emperor Ariakas were turned to Palanthas, to her port, her ships, her wealth. The glittering city, the jewel of Solamnia, would be the most magnificent gem in Ariakas's Crown of Power.

The Lord of Palanthas sent his troops to the battlements. The citizens hunkered down in their houses, shuttered their windows. Shops and businesses closed. The city believed she was prepared for the worst, and if the worst came, as it had come to other cities, such as Solace and Tarsis, Palanthas would fight valiantly. For there was courage in the heart of the old grand dame. Her rigid spine was made of steel.

She was not tested. The worst did not come. The forces of the Blue Lady had been routed at the High Clerist's Tower and were in retreat. The dragons sighted that morning, winging toward the city's walls, were not the red fire-breathing dragons or the lightning-crackling blue dragons people feared. The morning sun sparkled on shining silver scales. Silver dragons had flown from their homes in the Dragon Isles to defend Palanthas.

Or so the dragons claimed.

Since war did not come, the citizens of Palanthas left their homes and opened their shops and surged out into the streets, talking, arguing. The Lord of Palanthas assured the citizens that the new dragons were on the side of Light, that they worshiped Paladine and Mishakal and the rest of the gods of Light, that they had agreed to assist the Knights of Solamnia, protectors of the city.

Some people believed their lord. Some didn't. Some argued that dragons of any color were not to be trusted, that they were there simply to lull the people into a state of complacency, and that the dragons would attack in the dead of night and they would all be devoured in their beds.

"Fools!" Raistlin muttered more than once as he shoved his way through the crowds, or rather as he was bumped and jostled and nearly run over by a careening horse cart.

If he had been wearing his red robes that marked him a wizard, the people of Palanthas would have eyed him askance, left him severely alone, gone out of their way to avoid him. Clad in the plain gray robes of an Aesthetic of the Great Library of Palanthas, Raistlin was trampled and pushed and trod upon.

Palanthians were not fond of wizards, even those of the red robes, who were neutral in the war, or the white, who were dedicated to the side of Light. Both Orders of High Sorcery had worked and sacrificed to bring about the return of the metallic dragons to Ansalon. The head of their order, Par Salian, knew that the sight of the spring dawn glistening on silver and golden wings would come as a punch in the gut to Emperor Ariakas; the first blow that had been able to penetrate his dragonscale armor. All during the war, the wings of Takhisis's evil dragons had darkened the skies. Now the skies of Krynn shone with brightening light, and the Emperor and his Queen were starting to grow nervous.

The people of Palanthas did not know that the wizards had been working to protect them and would not have believed such a claim if they heard it. To their minds, the only good wizard was a wizard who lived somewhere besides Palanthas.

Raistlin Majere was not wearing his red robes because they were wrapped in a bundle tucked under his arm. He wore the "borrowed" gray robes of one of the monks of the Great Library.

Borrowed. Thinking of that word brought to mind Tasslehoff Burrfoot. The light-hearted and lighter-fingered kender never "stole" anything. When caught with purloined goods upon his person, the kender would claim to have "borrowed" the sugar basin, "stumbled across" the silver candlesticks, and "was just coming to return" the emerald necklace. Raistlin had "stumbled upon" the Aesthetic's robes lying folded neatly on a bed that morning. He had every intention of returning the gray robes in a day or two.

Mostly people, absorbed in their arguments, ignored him as he fought his way through the crowded streets. But occasionally some citizen would stop him to ask what Astinus thought about the arrival of the metallic dragons, the dragons of Light.

Raistlin didn't know what Astinus thought and he didn't care. Keeping his cowl pulled low to conceal the fact that his skin shimmered gold in the sunlight and that the pupils of his eyes were the shape of hourglasses, he would mutter an excuse and hurry on. He hoped sourly that the workers at his destination were actually doing some work, that they were not out gossiping in the street.

He regretted thinking of Tasslehoff. The memory of the kender brought back memories of his friends and his brother. He should say his *deceased* friends, *deceased* brother: Tanis Half-Elven, Tika, Riverwind and Goldmoon, and Caramon. All of them dead. He alone had survived, and that was because *he* had been smart enough to have foreseen disaster and planned a way out. He had to face the fact that Caramon and the others were dead and quit obsessing over it. But even as he told himself he should stop thinking about them, he thought about them.

Fleeing the dragonarmies in Flotsam, he and his brother and their friends had sought to escape by taking passage aboard a pirate ship, the *Perechon*. They had been pursued by a Dragon Highlord—his half-sister, Kitiara, as it turned out. The crazed helmsman had steered the ship deliberately into the Blood Sea's feared Maelstrom. The ship was being ripped apart, spars falling, sails being torn to tatters. The wild water was breaking over the decks. Raistlin had a choice. Either he could die with the rest of them or he could leave. The choice was obvious to anyone with a brain—which excluded his brother. Raistlin had in his possession the magical dragon orb that had once belonged to the ill-fated King Lorac. Raistlin had used the magic of the orb to escape. True, he might have taken his friends with him. He might have saved all of them. He might at least have saved his brother.

But Raistlin was only just learning about the powers of the dragon orb. He was not certain the orb had the ability to save the rest, and therefore, he had saved himself—and the other. The other who was always with him, who was with him even as he pushed his way through the streets of Palanthas. Once this "other" had been a whispered voice in Raistlin's head, unknown and mysterious and maddening. But the mystery had been solved. Raistlin could put a hideous face to the disembodied voice, give the speaker a name.

"Your decision was logical, young magus," Fistandantilus said, adding with a sneer, "Your twin is dead. Good riddance. Caramon weakened you, diminished you. Now that you are free of him, you will go far. I will see to that."

"*You* won't see to anything!" Raistlin retorted.

"I beg your pardon?" said a passerby, halting. "Were you speaking to me, sir?"

Raistlin muttered something and, ignoring the man's offended stare, kept on walking. He had been forced to listen to the yammering voice all morning. He had even fancied he could see the black-robed, soul-sucking specter of the archmage dogging his footsteps. Raistlin wondered bitterly if the bargain he had made with the evil wizard had been worth it.

"Without me, you would have died taking the Test in the Tower at Wayreth," said Fistandantilus. "You came out of our deal well enough. A bit of your life in exchange for my knowledge and power."

Raistlin had not been afraid he would die. He had been afraid he would fail. That was the true reason he had made the bargain with the old man. Raistlin could not have borne failure. He could not have endured his brother's pity or the fact that he would have been dependent on his stronger twin for the rest of his days.

Just thinking about the undead leech of a wizard sucking the life out of him as one sucks the juice from a peach brought on a coughing fit. Raistlin had always been frail and sickly, but the bargain he had struck with Fistandantilus, which allowed the spirit of the archmagus to remain alive on his dark plane of tortured existence in return for Raistlin's escape, had exacted its toll. His lungs seemed to be always filled with wool. He felt as though he were being smothered. He was subject to fits of coughing that almost doubled him over, as happened at that moment.

He had to pause and lean against a building for support, wiping the blood from his lips with the gray sleeve of the purloined robe. He felt weaker than usual. Using the magic of the dragon orb to transport him across a continent had taken far more out of him than he had anticipated. He had been half dead when he had arrived in Palanthas four days earlier, so weak that he had collapsed on the steps of the Great Library. The monks had taken pity on him and carried him inside. He was recovered somewhat, but he was still not well. He would not be well ever . . . not until he ended his bargain.

Fistandantilus seemed to think that Raistlin's soul was to be his reward. The archmagus was going to be disappointed. Since Raistlin's soul was finally his own, he was not going to meekly hand it over to Fistandantilus.

Raistlin considered that the archmagus had done well out of the deal he'd made with Raistlin in the Tower. Fistandantilus was, after all, leeching part of Raistlin's life-force in order to cling to his miserable existence. But as far as Raistlin was concerned, the two of them were even. It was time to end their bargain. Except Raistlin couldn't figure out how to do that without Fistandantilus knowing about it and stopping him. The old man was constantly lurking about, eavesdropping on Raistlin's thoughts. There had to be a way to shut the door and lock the windows of his mind.

Raistlin finally recovered enough to be able to resume his errand. He continued through the streets, following directions that were given to him by people he met along the way, and soon left the central part of Old City behind and, with it, the crowds. He entered the working part of the city, where streets were known by their trade. He passed Iron-Mongers Avenue and Butchers' Row and the Horse Fair and Goldsmith Lane on his way to the street where wool merchants plied their trade. He was searching for a particular business when he glanced down an alleyway and saw a sign marked with the symbols of three moons: a red moon, a silver, and a black. It was a mageware shop.

The shop was small, a mere hole in the wall. Raistlin was surprised to find such a shop at all, surprised that someone had even bothered to open a shop dealing in objects related to the use of magic in a city that despised those who wielded magic. He knew of only one wizard who resided in the city and that was Justarius, head of Raistlin's own order, the Red Robes. Raistlin supposed there must be others. He'd never given the matter much thought.

His steps slowed. The mageware shop would have what he sought. It would be costly. He could not afford it. He had only a small sum of steel, hoarded up and hidden away over months. He had to save his steel for lodging and food in Neraka, his destination, once his health was restored and his business in Palanthas was finished.

Besides, the owner of the mageware shop would be bound to report Raistlin's purchase to the Conclave, the body of wizards that enforced the laws of magic. The Conclave could not stop him, but he would be summoned to Wayreth and called upon to explain himself. Raistlin didn't have time for all that. Events were happening— momentous, world-shaking events. The end was coming. The Dark Queen would soon be celebrating her victory. Raistlin did not plan to be standing on the street corner cheering as she rode past in triumph. He planned to be leading the parade.

Raistlin walked past the mageware shop and came at last to the place he'd been seeking. The stench alone should have guided him, he thought, covering his nose and mouth with his sleeve. The business was located in a large, open-air yard filled with stacks of wood to stoke the fires. Smoke mingled with steam rising from the huge kettles and vats and reeked with the odors of the various ingredients used in the process, some of which were not at all pleasant.

Clutching his bundle, Raistlin entered a small building located near the compound, where men and women were hauling wood and stirring the contents of the vats with big, wooden paddles. A clerk on a stool was writing figures in a large book. Another man sat on another stool, studying long lists. Neither took any notice of Raistlin.

Raistlin waited a moment; then he coughed, causing the man looking over the lists to raise his eyes. Seeing Raistlin waiting in the entrance, the man left his stool and came over to inquire how he might serve one of the honored Aesthetics.

"I have some cloth to be dyed," said Raistlin, and he brought forth the red robes.

He kept his hood over his face, but he could not very well hide his hands. Fortunately the building was shadowy, and Raistlin hoped the man would not notice his gold-colored skin.

The dyer examined the color, running his hands over the cloth. "A nice wool," he pronounced. "Not fine, mind you, but good and serviceable. It should take the dye well. What color would you like, Revered Sir?"

Raistlin was about to reply when he was interrupted by a fit of coughing so severe that he staggered and fell back against the doorframe. He missed his brother's strong arm, which had always been there to support him.

The dyer eyed Raistlin and backed up slightly in alarm. "Not catching, is it, sir?"

"Black," Raistlin gasped, ignoring the question.

"I am sorry, what did you say?" asked the dyer. "It's hard to hear with all that jabbering."

He gestured to the compound behind him, where women engaged in dunking the cloth in the kettles were yelling back and forth or exchanging barbed comments with the men who stoked the fires.

23

"Black," Raistlin said, raising his voice. He generally spoke softly. Talking irritated his throat.

The dyer raised an eyebrow. Aesthetics who served Astinus in the Great Library wore robes of gray.

"It is not for me," Raistlin added. "I am acting for a friend."

"I see," said the dyer. He cast Raistlin a quizzical glance, which Raistlin, overtaken by another fit of coughing, did not notice.

"We have three types of black dye," stated the dyer. "Our cheapest grade uses chromium, alum, and red argol, logwood and barwood. This produces a good black, though not very durable. The color will fade with washing. The next grade dye utilizes camwood and copperas and logwood. This grade is better than the first I named, though the black can turn slightly green over a long period of time. The best grade is done with indigo and camwood. This provides a deep, rich black that will not fade no matter how many times the cloth is washed. The latter is, of course, the most expensive."

"How much?" Raistlin asked.

The dyer named the price, and Raistlin winced. It would considerably diminish the number of coins in the small leather pouch he had hidden in a conjured cubbyhole in the monk's cell he was occupying in the Great Library. He should settle for the less costly dye. But then he thought of appearing before the wealthy, powerful Black Robes of Neraka, and he cringed as he imagined walking among them in black robes that were not black but "slightly green."

"The indigo," he stated, and he handed over his red robes.

"Very good, Revered Sir," said the dyer. "May I have your name?"

"Bertrem," Raistlin replied with a smile that he kept hidden in the shadow of the cowl. Bertrem was the name of Astinus's long-suffering and harried chief assistant.

The dyer made a note.

"When may I return for these?" Raistlin asked. "I am—that is, my friend is in a hurry."

"Day after tomorrow," said the dyer.

"Not sooner?" Raistlin asked, disappointed.

The dyer shook his head. "Not unless your friend wants to walk the streets dripping black dye."

Raistlin gave a curt nod and took his leave. The moment Raistlin's back was turned, the dyer spoke a word to his assistant then hurried out of the building. Raistlin saw the man hastening down the street, but exhausted from the long walk and half suffocated by the choking fumes, he paid no heed.

The Great Library was located in the Old City. The hour being High Watch, when shops normally closed for lunch, more people thronged the streets. The noise was appalling, dinning in Raistlin's ears. The long walk had taxed Raistlin's strength to such an extent that he was forced to stop frequently to rest, and when he finally came in sight of the library's marble columns and imposing portico, he was so weak that he feared he could not make it across the street without collapsing.

Raistlin sank down on a stone bench not far from the Great Library. Winter's long night was drawing to a close. The dawn of spring was near. The bright sun was warm. Raistlin closed his eyes. His head slumped forward onto his chest. He dozed in the sun.

He was back on board the ship, holding the dragon orb and facing his brother and Tanis and the rest of his friends . . .

"... using my magic. And the magic of the dragon orb. It is quite simple, though probably beyond your weak minds. I now have the power to harness the energy of my corporeal body and the energy of my spirit into one. I will become pure energy—light, if you want to think of it that way. And becoming light, I can travel through the heavens like the rays of the sun, returning to this physical world whenever and wherever I choose."

"Can the orb do this for all of us?" Tanis asked.

"I will not chance it. I know I can escape. The others are not my concern. You led them into this blood-red death, half-elf. You get them out."

"You won't harm your brother. Caramon, stop him!"

"Tell him, Caramon. The last Test in the Tower of High Sorcery was against myself. And I failed. I killed him. I killed my brother . . ."

"Aha! I thought I'd find you here, you doorknob of a kender!"

Raistlin stirred uneasily in his sleep.

That is Flint's voice and that is all wrong, Raistlin thought. Flint isn't here. I haven't seen Flint in a long time, not for months, not since the fall of Tarsis. Raistlin sank back into the dream.

"Don't try to stop me, Tanis. I killed Caramon once, you see. Or rather, it was an illusion meant to teach me to fight against the darkness within. But they were too late. I had already given myself to the darkness."

"I tell you, I saw him!"

Raistlin woke with a start. He knew that voice as well.

Tasslehoff Burrfoot stood quite close to him. Raistlin had only to rise up from the bench and walk a few paces and he could reach out his hand and touch him. Flint Fireforge was standing beside the kender, and though they both had their backs to Raistlin, he could picture the exasperated look on the old dwarf's face as he tried arguing with a kender. Raistlin had seen the quivering beard and flushed cheeks often enough.

It can't be! Raistlin told himself, shaken. Tasslehoff was in my mind, and now I have conjured him up whole.

But just to be safe, Raistlin pulled down the cowl of the gray robe, making sure it covered his face, and he thrust his gold-skinned hands inside the sleeves of his robes.

The kender looked like Tas from the back, but then all kender looked alike either from the front or the back: short in stature; dressed in the brightest clothing they could find; their long hair done up in outlandish topknots; their small, slender bodies festooned in pouches. The dwarf looked the same as any dwarf, short and stocky, clad in armor, wearing a helm decorated with horsehair . . . or the mane of a griffon.

"I saw Raistlin, I tell you!" the kender was saying insistently. He pointed to the Great Library. "He was lying on those very stairs. The monks were all gathered around him. That staff of his—the Staff of Maggots—"

"Magius," the dwarf muttered.

"—was on the stairs beside him."

"So what if it was Raistlin?" the dwarf demanded.

"I think he was dying, Flint," said the kender solemnly.

Raistlin shut his eyes. There was no longer any doubt. Tasslehoff Burrfoot and Flint Fireforge. His old friends. The two had watched him grow up, him and Caramon. Raistlin had wondered frequently if they were still alive, Flint and Tas and Sturm. They had been parted in the attack on Tarsis. He now wondered, astonished, how they had come to be in Palanthas. What adventures had brought them to that place? He was curious and he was, surprisingly, glad to see them.

Drawing back his cowl, he rose from the bench with the intention of making himself known to them. He would ask about Sturm and about Laurana, the golden-haired Laurana . . .

"If the Sly One's dead, good riddance," Flint said grimly. "He made my skin crawl."

Raistlin sat back down on the bench and pulled the cowl over his face.

"You don't mean that—" Tas began.

"I do so too mean it!" Flint roared. "How do you know what I mean and don't mean? I said so yesterday, and I'll say it today. Raistlin was always looking down that gold nose of his at us. And he turned Caramon into his slave. 'Caramon, make my tea!' 'Caramon, carry my pack.' 'Caramon, clean my boots!' It's a good thing Raistlin never told his brother to jump off a cliff. Caramon would be lying at the bottom of a ravine by now."

"Ah, I kind of liked Raistlin," said Tas. "He magicked me into a duck pond once. I know that sometimes he wasn't very nice, Flint, but he didn't feel good, what with that cough of his, and he did help you when you had the rheumatism—"

"I never had rheumatism a day in my life! Rheumatism is for old people," said Flint, glowering.

"Now where do you think you're going?" he demanded, seizing hold of Tasslehoff, who was about to cross the street.

"I thought I'd go up to the library and knock on the door and I would ask the monks, very politely, if Raistlin was there."

"Wherever Raistlin is, you can be sure he's up to no good. And you can just put the thought of knocking on the library door out of your rattle-brained mind. You heard what they said yesterday: no kender allowed."

"I figured I'd ask them about that, too," Tas said. "Why won't they allow kender into the library?"

"Because there wouldn't be a book left on the shelves, that's why. You'd rob them blind."

"We don't rob people!" Tasslehoff said indignantly. "Kender are very honest. And I think that's a disgrace, kender not being allowed! I'll just go give them a piece of my mind—"

He twisted out of Flint's grasp and started to run across the street. Flint glared after him; then, with a sudden gleam in his eye, he called out, "You can go if you want to, but you might want to listen to what I came to tell you. Laurana sent me. She said something about you riding a dragon . . ."

Tasslehoff turned around so fast that he tripped himself and tumbled over his own feet, sprawling flat on his face on the street and spilling half the contents of his pouches.

"Me? Tasslehoff Burrfoot? Ride a dragon? Oh, Flint!" Tasslehoff picked up himself and his pouches. "Isn't it wonderful?"

"No," Flint said glumly.

"Hurry up!" Tasslehoff said, tugging on Flint's shirt. "We don't want to miss the battle."

"It's not happening right this minute," Flint said, batting away the kender's hands. "You go on. I'll be along."

Tas didn't wait to be told twice. He dashed off down the street, pausing at intervals to tell everyone he met that he, Tasslehoff Burrfoot, was going to be riding a dragon with the Golden General.

Flint stood long moments after the kender had left, staring at the Great Library. The old dwarf's face grew grave and solemn. He was about to cross the street, but then he paused. His heavy, gray brows came together. He thrust his hands in his pockets and shook his head.

"Good riddance," he muttered, and he turned and followed Tas.

Raistlin remained sitting on the bench a long time after they had gone. He sat there until the sun had gone down behind the buildings of Palanthas and the night air of early spring grew chill.

At last he rose. He did not go to the library. He walked the streets of Palanthas. Even though it was night, the streets were still crowded. The Lord of Palanthas had come out to publicly reassure his people. The silver dragons were on their side. The dragons had promised to protect them, the lord said. He declared a time for celebration. People lit bonfires and began dancing in the streets. Raistlin found the noise and the gaiety jarring. He shoved his way through the drunken throng, heading for a part of the city where the streets were deserted, the buildings dark and abandoned.

No one lived in that part of the great city. No one ever went there. Raistlin had never been there, but he knew the way well. He turned a corner. At the end of the empty street, surrounded by a ghastly forest of death, rose a tower of black, silhouetted against a blood-red sky.

The Tower of High Sorcery of Palanthas. The accursed Tower. Blackened and broken, the crumbling building had been vacant for centuries.

None shall enter save the Master of Past and Present.

Raistlin took a step toward the Tower, then stopped.

"Not yet," he murmured. "Not yet."

He felt a cold and corpselike hand brush his cheek, and he flinched away.

"Only one of us, young magus," said Fistandantilus. "Only one can be the Master."

2

The last of the wine.

2nd Day, Month of Mishamont, Year 352 AC

he gods of magic, Solinari, Lunitari, and Nuitari, were cousins. Their parents formed the triumvirate of gods who ruled Krynn. Solinari was the son of Paladine and Mishakal, gods of Light. Lunitari the daughter of Gilean, God of the Book. Nuitari was the son of Takhisis, Queen of Darkness. From the day of their birth, the cousins had formed a strong alliance, bound together by their dedication to magic.

Eons earlier, the Three Cousins gave to mortals the ability to be able to control and manipulate arcane energy. True to form, mortals abused their gift. Magic ran amok in the world, causing terrible destruction and loss of life. The cousins realized that they must establish laws governing the use of the power, and thus, they created the Orders of High Sorcery. Ruled by a conclave of wizards, the order established laws regarding the use of the magic that strictly controlled those who practiced the powerful art.

The Tower of High Sorcery in Wayreth was the last of the five original centers of magic on Ansalon. The other three towers, those located in the cities of Daltigoth, Losarcum, and Istar, had been destroyed. The Tower of Palanthas still existed, but it was cursed. Only the Tower of Wayreth, located in the wayward and mysterious Forest of Wayreth, remained active and very much alive.

Since people tend to fear what they do not understand, wizards trying to live among ordinary folk often found life difficult. No matter whether they served the God of the Silver Moon, Solinari, or the God of the Dark Moon, Nuitari, or the Goddess of the Red Moon, Lunitari, wizards were generally reviled and mistrusted. Small wonder that mages liked to spend as much time as possible in the Tower of Wayreth. There, among their own kind, they could be themselves, study their art, practice new spells, purchase or exchange magical artifacts, and enjoy being in the company of those who spoke the language of magic.

Before the return of Takhisis, wizards of all three orders had lived and worked together in the Tower of Wayreth. Black Robes had rubbed elbows with White Robes, waging debates related to magic. If a spell component required the use of cobweb, was it better to use cobweb spun by spiders in the wild or those raised in captivity? Because cats pursued their own secret agendas, did they make untrustworthy familiars?

When Queen Takhisis declared war upon the world, her son, Nuitari, broke ranks with his cousins for the first time since the creation of magic. Nuitari loathed his mother. He suspected her flatteries and promises were lies, yet he wanted to believe. He joined the ranks of the Dark Queen's army, and he took many of his Black Robes with him. The wizards of Ansalon continued to present a united front to the world, but in truth, the orders were being torn apart.

The wizards were ruled by a governing body known as the Conclave, which was made up of an equal number of wizards from each order. The head of the conclave during such turbulent times was a white robe wizard named Par-Salian. In his early sixties, Par-Salian was deemed by most to be a strong leader, just and wise. But given the rising disorder among the ranks of the wizards, there were those who began to say that he had lost control, that he was not fit for the job.

Par-Salian sat alone in his study in the Tower of High Sorcery at Wayreth. The night was cold, and a small fire burned in the grate—a real fire, not a magical one. Par-Salian did not believe in using magic for the sake of convenience. He read by candlelight, not magical light. He swept his floor with a plain, ordinary broom. He required everyone living and working in the Tower to do the same.

The candle burned out, and the fire dwindled, leaving Par-Salian in darkness, save for the glow of the dying embers. He gave up trying to study his spells. That required concentration, and he could not concentrate his mind upon memorizing the arcane words.

Ansalon was in turmoil. The forces of the Dark Queen were perilously close to winning the war. There were some glimmerings of hope. The meeting of the Whitestone Council had brought together elves, dwarves, and humans. The three races had agreed to set aside their differences and unite against the foe. The Blue Lady, Dragon Highlord Kitiara, and her forces had been defeated at the High Clerist's Tower. Clerics of Paladine and Mishakal had brought hope and healing to the world.

Yet for all the good, the mighty force of the dragon-armies and the terrifying threat of the evil dragons were arrayed against the Forces of Light. Even now, Par-Salian waited in dread for the news that Palanthas had fallen . . .

A knock came on the door. Par-Salian sighed. He was certain it was the news he feared to hear. His assistant having long since gone to bed, Par-Salian rose to answer the knock himself. He was astonished to find his visitor was Justarius, the head of the Order of Red Robes.

"My friend! You are the last person I expected to see this night! Come in, please. Sit down."

Justarius limped into the room. He was a tall man, strong and hale, except for his twisted leg. An athletic youth, he had been fond of participating in contests of physical skill. All that had ended with the Test in the Tower, which had left him permanently maimed. Justarius never spoke of the Test and he never complained about his injury, other than to say, with a shrug and a half smile, that he had been most fortunate. He might have died.

"I am glad to see you safe," Par-Salian continued, lighting candles and adding wood to the fire. "I thought you would be among those battling the dragonarmies in Palanthas."

He paused in his work to look at his friend in dismay. "Has the city already fallen?"

"Far from it," said Justarius, seating himself before the blaze. He positioned his injured leg on a small footstool, to keep it elevated, and smiled. "Open a bottle of your finest elven wine, my friend, for we have something to celebrate."

"What is it? Tell me quickly. My thoughts have been filled with darkness," said Par-Salian.

34

"The good dragons have entered the war!"

Par-Salian stared at his friend for long moments; then he gave a great, shuddering sigh. "Praise be to Paladine! And to Gilean, of course," he added quickly with a glance at Justarius. "Tell me the details."

"Silver dragons arrived this morning to defend the city. The dragonarmies did not launch their anticipated attack. Laurana of the Qualinesti elves was named Golden General and made leader of the forces of Light, including the Knights of Solamnia."

"This calls for something special." Par-Salian poured wine for them both. "My last bottle of Silvanesti wine. Alas, there will be no more elven wine from that sad land for a long time, I fear."

He resumed his seat. "And so they have chosen the daughter of the elf king of Qualinesti to be Golden General. The choice is a wise one."

"A politic one," said Justarius wryly. "The Knights could not settle on a leader of their own. The defeat of the dragonarmies at the High Clerist's Tower was due in large part to Laurana's courage and valor and quick thinking. She has the power to inspire men with both words and deeds. The knights who fought at the Tower admire and trust her. In addition, she will bring the elves into the battle."

The two wizards lifted their glasses and drank to the success of the Golden General and to the good dragons, as they were popularly known. Justarius replaced the silver goblet on a nearby table and rubbed his eyes. His face was haggard. He settled back into his chair with a sigh.

"Are you well?" Par-Salian asked with concern.

"I have not slept in many nights," Justarius replied. "And I traveled the corridors of magic to come here. Such a journey is always wearing."

"Did the Lord of Palanthas ask for your help in defending the city?" Par-Salian was astonished.

"No, of course not," said Justarius with some bitterness. "I was prepared to do my part, however. I have my home, my family to protect, as well as my city, which I love."

He lifted his goblet again, but he did not drink. He stared morosely into the dark, plum-colored wine.

"Come, out with it," said Par-Salian grimly. "I hope your bad news does not offset the good."

Justarius gave a heavy sigh. "You and I have often wondered why the good dragons refused to heed our pleas for help. Why they did not enter the war when Takhisis sent her evil dragons to burn cities and slaughter innocents. Now I know the answer. And it is a terrible one."

He was silent again. Par-Salian took a drink of his wine, as though to brace himself.

"A silver dragon who calls herself Silvara made the horrible discovery," Justarius said. "It seems that years ago, sometime around 287 AC, Takhisis ordered the evil dragons to secretly creep into the lairs of the good dragons as they slept the Long Sleep and steal their eggs.

"Once their young were in her possession, Takhisis awakened the good dragons to tell them that she intended to launch a war upon the world. If the good dragons intervened, Takhisis threatened to destroy their eggs. Afraid for their young, the good dragons took an oath, promising that they would not fight her."

"And that oath is now broken," said Par-Salian.

"The good dragons discovered that Takhisis had broken *her* oath first," Justarius replied. "The wise have speculated as to the origin of the so-called lizardmen, the draconians . . ."

Par-Salian stared at his friend in horror. "You don't mean to tell me . . ." He clenched his fist. "That is not possible!"

"It is, I am afraid. Silvara and a friend, an elf warrior named Gilthanas, discovered the terrible truth. Through the use of dark and unholy magic, the eggs of the metallic dragons were perverted, changed from dragons into the creatures we know as draconians. Silvara and Gilthanas attest to this. They witnessed the ceremony. They barely escaped with their lives."

Par-Salian was stricken. "A terrible loss. A tragic loss. Beauty and wisdom and nobility transformed into hideous monstrosities."

He fell silent. Both men knew the question that must be asked next. Both knew the answer. Neither wanted to speak it aloud. Par-Salian was Master of the Conclave, however. The discovery of the truth, however unpleasant, was his responsibility.

"I notice you said that the eggs were perverted through the use of unholy magic and dark magic. Are you saying that one of our order performed this monstrous act?"

"I am afraid so," Justarius said quietly. "A Black Robe named Dracart in conjunction with a cleric of Takhisis and a red dragon devised the spells. You must take swift action, Par-Salian. That is why I came here in all haste tonight. You must dissolve the Conclave, denounce the Black Robes, cast them out of the Tower, and forbid them from ever coming here again."

Par-Salian said nothing. His right fist unclenched, clenched again. He stared into the fire.

"We are already suspect in the eyes of the world," Justarius said. "If people find out that a wizard was complicit in this heinous act, they would rise against us! This could well destroy us."

Still, Par-Salian was silent.

"Sir," said Justarius, his voice hardening, "the god Nuitari was involved in this. He had to be. He sided with his mother, Takhisis, years ago, which means that as head of the Black Robes, Ladonna must be involved, as well."

"You don't know that for certain," said Par-Salian sternly. "You have no proof."

He and Ladonna had been lovers, back in the past, back in their youth, back in the days when passion overthrows reason. Justarius was aware of their history and he was careful not mention it, but Par-Salian knew his friend was thinking it.

"None of us have seen Ladonna or her followers for over a year," Justarius continued. "Our gods, Solinari and Lunitari, have made no secret of the fact that they were dismayed and angered when Nuitari broke with them to serve his mother. We must face facts, sir. The Three Cousins are estranged. Our sacred brotherhood of wizards, the ties that bind us—white, black, and red—are severed. Already, Ladonna and her Black Robes may be poised to launch an assault against the Tower—"

"No!" Par-Salian said, slamming his fist on the arm of the chair, spilling the wine.

Par-Salian, with his long, white beard and quiet demeanor, was sometimes taken for a weak and benign old man, even by those who knew him best. The head of the Conclave had not attained his high position through lack of fire in his blood and belly, however. The heat of that fire could be astonishing.

"I will not dissolve the Conclave! I do not for one moment believe that Ladonna was involved in this crime. Nor do I blame Nuitari—"

Justarius frowned. "A Black Robe, Dracart, was seen in the act."

"What of it?" Par-Salian glowered at his friend. "He may have been a renegade—"

"He was," said a voice.

Justarius twisted around in his chair. When he saw who had spoken, he cast an accusing glance at Par-Salian.

"I did not know you had company," Justarius said coldly.

"I did not know myself," said Par-Salian. "You should have made yourself known, Ladonna. It is rude to eavesdrop, especially on friends."

"I had to make certain you still *were* my friends," she said.

A human woman in her middle-years, Ladonna scorned to try to conceal her age, as did some, using the artifices of nature and magic to bring plump youth to wrinkled cheeks. She wore her long, thick, gray hair as proudly as a queen wears a crown, coifing her hair in elaborate styles. Her black robes were generally made of the finest velvet, soft and sumptuous, and decorated with runes stitched in gold and silver thread.

But when she emerged from the shadowed corner where she had been secretly watching, the two men were shocked by the change in her appearance. Ladonna was haggard, pale, and seemed to have aged years. Her long, gray hair straggled out from two hastily plaited braids that hung down her back. Her elegant, black robes were dirty and bedraggled, tattered and frayed. She looked exhausted, almost to the point of collapsing.

Par-Salian hurriedly brought forth a chair and poured her a goblet of wine. She drank it gratefully. Her dark eyes went to Justarius.

"You are very quick to judge me, sir," she said acidly.

"The last time I saw you, madam," he returned in kind, "you were loudly proclaiming devotion to Queen

39

Takhisis. Are we to believe you did not commit this crime?"

Ladonna took a sip of wine, then said quietly, "If being a fool is a crime, then I am guilty as charged."

She raised her eyes, casting both men a flashing glance. "But I swear to you that I had nothing to do with the corruption of the dragon eggs! I did not know of this despicable act until only a short time ago. And when I found out, I did what I could to make amends. You can ask Silvara and Gilthanas. They would not be alive now if it were not for my help and the help of Nuitari."

Justarius remained very grim. Par-Salian regarded her with grave solemnity.

Ladonna rose to her feet and raised her hand to heaven. "I call upon Solinari, God of the Silver Moon. I call upon Lunitari, Goddess of the Red Moon. I call upon Nuitari, God of the Dark Moon. Witness my oath. I swear by the magic we hold sacred, I am speaking the truth. Withdraw your blessings from me, all the gods, if I am lying. Let the words of magic slip from my mind! Let my spell components turn to dust. Let my scrolls burn. Let my hand be stricken from my wrist."

She waited a moment then resumed her seat. "It is cold in here," she said, staring hard at Justarius. "Should I build up the fire?"

She pointed her hand at the fireplace, where the fire was dying, and spoke a word of magic. Flames danced on the iron grate. The fire grew so hot, the three had to draw back their chairs. Ladonna lifted her goblet and took a gulp.

"Nuitari has broken with Takhisis?" Par-Salian asked in astonishment.

"He was seduced by sweet words and lavish promises. As was I," Ladonna said bitterly. "The Queen's sweet words were lies. Her promises false."

"What did you expect?" Justarius asked with a sneer. "The Dark Queen has thwarted your ambition and hurt your pride. So now you come crawling back to us. I suppose you are in danger. You know the Queen's secrets. Has she set the hounds upon you? Is that why you've come to Wayreth? To hide behind our robes?"

"I *did* discover her secrets," Ladonna said softly. She sat for long moments, staring at her hands; her fingers were long and supple still, though the skin was reddened and drawn tightly over the fine bones. "And yes, I am in danger. We are all in danger. That is why I have come back. Risked my life to come back to warn you."

Par-Salian exchanged alarmed glances with Justarius. Both men had known Ladonna for many years. They had seen her in the magnificence of her power. They had seen her raging in anger. One of them had seen her soft and tender with love. Ladonna was a fighter. She had battled her way to the top of the ranks of the Black Robes by defeating and sometimes slaying in magical combat those who challenged her. She was courageous, a formidable foe. Neither man had ever seen the strong and powerful woman show weakness. Neither had ever seen her as they saw her at that moment: shaken . . . afraid.

"There is a building in Neraka called the Red Mansion. Ariakas sometimes lives there when he returns to Neraka. In this mansion is a shrine to Takhisis. The shrine is not as grand as the one in her temple; it is far more secret and private, open only to Ariakas and his favorites, such as Kitiara and my former pupil, and his mistress, the wizardess Iolanthe.

"To make a long story short, several of my colleagues were most horribly murdered. I feared I was next. I went to the shrine to talk to Queen Takhisis directly—"

Justarius muttered something.

"I know," said Ladonna. Her hand shook, spilling the wine. "I know. But I was alone, and I was desperate."

Par-Salian reached over and laid his hand on her hand. She smiled tremulously and clasped her fingers over his. He was startled and shocked to see tears glimmer in her eyes. He had never before seen her cry.

"I was about to enter the shrine when I realized that someone was already there. It was Highlord Kitiara, talking to Ariakas. I used my magic to make myself invisible and listened to their conversation. You have heard of the Dark Queen's search for a man called Berem? He is known as the Everman or the Green Gemstone man."

"The dragonarmies are all taxed with finding this man. We have been trying to discover why," said Par-Salian. "What makes him so important to Takhisis?"

"I can tell you," said Ladonna. "If Takhisis finds Berem, she will be victorious. She will enter the world in all her might and power. No one, not even the gods, will be able to withstand her."

She related the Everman's tragic story to her audience. The two men listened in astonishment and grief to the tale of Jasla and Berem, a tale of murder and forgiveness, hope and redemption.[2]

Par-Salian and Justarius were silent, each turning over what he heard in his mind. Ladonna slumped in her chair and closed her eyes. Par-Salian offered to pour her another glass of wine.

"Thank you, my dear friend, but if I drink any more, I will fall asleep where I sit. Well, what do you think?"

"I think we must act," said Par-Salian.

"I would like to do some investigating on my own," said Justarius crisply. "Madam Ladonna will forgive me

---

2 The story of Berem and Jasla can be found at the beginning of this book in the Prologue.

when I say that I do not entirely trust her."

"Investigate all you like," said Ladonna. "You will find that I have spoken the truth. I am too exhausted to lie. And now if you will excuse me—"

As she rose, she staggered with weariness and had to put her hand on the arm of the chair to steady herself. "I cannot travel this night. If I could have a blanket in the corner of some novice's cell—"

"Nonsense," said Par-Salian. "You will sleep in your chamber, as usual. Everything is as it was when you left. Nothing was moved or altered. You will even find a fire in the grate."

Ladonna lowered her proud head, then extended her hand to Par-Salian. "My old friend, thank you. I made a mistake. I admit it freely. If it is any consolation, I have paid dearly for it."

Justarius rose with some difficulty, leveraging himself up out of the chair. Sitting for any length of time caused his crippled leg to stiffen.

"Will you also spend the night with us, my friend?" Par-Salian asked.

Justarius shook his head. "I am needed back in Palanthas. I bring more news. If you could wait one moment, madam, this will be of interest to you. On the twenty-sixth day of Rannmont, Raistlin Majere was found, half dead, on the steps of the Great Library. One of my pupils happened to be passing and witnessed the incident. My pupil did not know who the man was, only that he was a wizard who wore the red robes of my order.

"That said, I do not think Raistlin will be of my order much longer," Justarius added. "Today one of the local cloth dyers brought me word that a young man came to his establishment with a request to dye red robes black. It seems your 'sword' has a flaw in it, my friend."

Par-Salian looked deeply troubled. "You are certain it was Raistlin Majere?"

"The young man gave a false name, but there cannot be many men in this world with golden-tinged skin and eyes with pupils like hourglasses. But to make sure, I spoke to Astinus. He assures me the young man is Raistlin. He is taking the Black Robes, and he is doing so without bothering to consult the Conclave, as is required."

"He's turning renegade." Ladonna shrugged. "You have lost him, Par-Salian. It seems I am not the only one to make mistakes."

"I never like to say I told you so," said Justarius grimly. "But I told you so."

Ladonna left for her chambers. Justarius returned to Palanthas via the corridors of magic. Par-Salian was alone again.

He resumed his seat in his chair by the dying fire, pondering all he had heard. He tried to concentrate on the dire news Ladonna had brought, but he found his thoughts straying to Raistlin Majere.

"Perhaps I did make a mistake when I chose him to be my sword to fight evil," Par-Salian mused. "But given what I have heard this night and what I know of Raistlin Majere, perhaps I did not."

Par-Salian drank the last of the elven wine; then tossing the lees onto the glowing embers, dousing them, he went to his bed.

3

Memories. An old friend.

3rd Day, Month of Mishamont, Year 352 AC

t wasn't the physical pain that clouded my mind. It was the old inner pain clawing at me, tearing at me with poisoned talons. *Caramon, strong and cheerful, good and kind, open and honest. Caramon, everyone's friend.*

Not like Raistlin—the runt, the Sly One.

"All I ever had was my magic," I said, speaking clearly, thinking clearly for the first time in my life. "And now you have that too."

Using the wall for support, I raised both my hands, put my thumbs together. I began speaking the words, the words that would summon the magic.

"Raist!" Caramon started to back away. "Raist, what are you doing? C'mon! You need me! I'll take care of you—just like always. Raist! I'm your brother!"

"I have no brother."

Beneath the layer of cold, hard rock, jealousy bubbled and seethed. Tremors split the rock. Jealousy, red and molten, coursed through my body and flared out of my hands. The fire *flared, billowed, and engulfed Caramon—*

A knocking on the door brought Raistlin back, abruptly, to reality.

He stirred in his chair and let go of the memory slowly and reluctantly, not because he enjoyed reliving that moment in time—far from it. The memory of his Test in the Tower of High Sorcery was horrible, for it brought back the bitter pangs of jealous fury, the sight of Caramon being burned to death, the sound of his twin's screams, the stench of charred flesh.

Then, after that, having to face Caramon, who had been witness to his own death at his brother's hands. To see the pain in his eyes, far worse in some ways than the pain of dying. For it had all been illusion, a part of the Test, to teach Raistlin to know himself. He would not have brought it all back to mind, would have kept the memory locked away, but he was trying to learn something from it, so he had to endure it.

The time was early morning, and he was in the small cell that he'd been given in the Great Library. The monks had carried him to the cell when they had thought he was dying. In the cell he had at last dared to look into the darkness of his own soul and dared meet the eyes that stared back at him. He had remembered the Test, remembered the bargain he'd made with Fistandilus in order to pass it.

"I said I was not to be bothered," Raistlin called out, annoyed.

"Bothered! I'll bother him," a deep voice grumbled. "I'll give him a good smack up the side of his head!"

"You have a visitor, Master Majere," called out Bertrem in apologetic tones. "He says he is an old friend of yours. He is concerned about your health."

"Of course he is," Raistlin said sourly.

He'd been expecting the visit. Ever since he'd watched Flint start to cross the street to the library, only to change his mind. Flint would have spent the night brooding, but he would finally come. Not with Tas. He would come alone.

Tell him to go away. Tell him you are busy. You have a great deal of work to do to prepare for your journey to Neraka. But even as Raistlin was thinking these things, he was removing the magical spell that kept the door locked.

"He may enter," Raistlin said.

Bertrem, his bald head glistening with sweat, cautiously shoved open the door and peered inside. At the sight of Raistlin sitting in the chair, wearing gray robes, Bertrem's eyes widened.

"But those are . . . you are . . . those are . . ."

Raistlin glared at him. "Say what you came to say and be gone."

"A . . . visitor . . ." Bertrem repeated faintly then hastened off, his sandals flapping on the stone floor.

Flint thumped inside. The old dwarf stood glowering at Raistlin from beneath his shaggy, gray eyebrows. He crossed his arms over his chest beneath his long, flowing beard. He was wearing the studded leather armor the dwarf preferred over steel. The armor was new and was embossed with a rose, the symbol of the Solamnic Knights.

Flint wore the same helm as always. He'd found the helm during one of their early adventures; Raistlin could not remember where. The helm was decorated with a tail made of horsehair. Flint always held that it was the mane of a griffon, and nothing would disabuse him of that notion, not even the fact that griffons did not have manes.

Only a few months had passed since they had last seen each other, but Raistlin was shocked at the change in the dwarf. Flint had lost weight. His skin had a chalky tinge to it. His breathing was labored, and his face was marred by new lines of sorrow and loss, weariness and worry. The old dwarf's eyes, glaring at Raistlin, flared with the same gruff spirit.

Neither spoke. Flint harrumphed, clearing his throat, as he cast sharp, swift glances around the cell, taking in the spellbooks lying on the desk, the Staff of Magius standing in the corner, the empty cup that had held his tea. All Raistlin's possessions, nothing of Caramon.

Flint frowned and scratched his nose, glancing from beneath lowered brows at Raistlin and shifting uncomfortably.

How much more uncomfortable he would be if he knew the truth, Raistlin thought. That I left Caramon and Tanis and the others to die. He wished Flint had not come.

"The kender said he saw you," Flint said, breaking the silence at last. "He said you were dying."

"As you see, I am very much alive," Raistlin said.

"Yes, well." Flint stroked his beard. "You're wearing gray robes. What is that supposed to mean?"

"That I sent my red ones to be washed," Raistlin said, adding caustically, "I am not so wealthy that I can afford an extensive wardrobe." He made an impatient gesture. "Did you come here to stare at me and comment on my clothes, or did you have some purpose?"

"I came because I was worried about you," Flint said, frowning.

Raistlin gave a sardonic smile. "You did not come because you were worried about *me*. You came because you are worried about Tanis and Caramon."

"Well, and I have a right to be, don't I? What has become of them?" Flint demanded, his face flushing, bringing some color into his gray cheeks.

Raistlin did not immediately respond. He could tell the truth. There was no reason he shouldn't. After all, he didn't give a damn what Flint thought of him, what any of them thought of him. He could tell the truth, that he had left them to die in the Maelstrom.But Flint would be outraged. He might even attack Raistlin in his fury. The old dwarf was no threat, but Raistlin would be forced to defend himself. Flint could get hurt, and there would be a scene. The Aesthetics would be in an uproar. They would throw him out, and he was not ready to leave.

"Laurana and Tas and I know you and the others escaped Tarsis," Flint said. "We shared the dream." He looked extremely uncomfortable at admitting that.

Raistlin was intrigued. "The dream in the nightmare land of Silvanesti? King Lorac's dream? Did you? How very interesting." He thought back, considering how that might be possible. "I knew that the rest of us shared it, but that was because we were *in* the dream. I wonder how the rest of you came to experience it?"

"Gilthanas said it was the starjewel, the one Alhana gave Sturm in Tarsis."

"Alhana said something about that. Yes, it could be a starjewel. They are powerful magical artifacts. Does Sturm still have it?"

"It was buried with him," said Flint gruffly. "Sturm's dead. He was killed at the Battle of the High Clerist's Tower."

"I am sorry to hear that," Raistlin said, and he was surprised to realize he truly was.

"Sturm died a hero," said Flint. "He fought a blue dragon alone."

"Then he died a fool," Raistlin remarked.

Flint's face flushed. "What about Caramon? Why isn't he here? He would never leave you! He'd die first!"

"He may be dead now," said Raistlin. "Perhaps they all are. I do not know."

"Did you kill him?" Flint asked, his flush deepening.

Yes, I killed him, Raistlin thought. He was engulfed in flames . . .

Instead he said, "The door is behind you. Please shut it on your way out."

Flint tried to speak, but he could only sputter with rage. Finally he managed to blurt out, "I don't know why I came! I said 'good riddance' when I heard *you* were dying. And I say 'good riddance' now!"

He turned on his heel and stomped angrily across the floor. He had reached the door and flung it open and was about to walk out when Raistlin spoke.

"You're having problems with your heart," Raistlin said, talking to Flint's back. "You are not well. You are experiencing pain, dizziness, shortness of breath. You tire easily. Am I right?"

Flint stopped where he stood in the doorway to the small cell, his hand on the handle.

"If you do not take it easy," Raistlin continued, "your heart will burst."

Flint glanced around, over his shoulder. "How long do I have?"

"Death could come at any moment," Raistlin said. "You must rest—"

"Rest! There's a war on!" Flint said loudly. Then he coughed and wheezed and pressed his hand to chest. Seeing Raistlin watching him, he muttered, "We can't all die heroes," and stumped off, forgetting, as he left, to shut the door.

Raistlin, sighing, rose to his feet and shut it for him.

Caramon screamed, tried to beat out the flames, but there was no escaping the magic. His body withered, dwindled in the fire, became the body of a wizened, old man—an old man wearing black robes, whose hair and beard were trailing wisps of fire.

Fistandantilus, his hand outstretched, walked toward me.

"If your armor is dross," said the old man softly, "I will find the crack."

I could not move, could not defend myself. The magic had sapped the last of my strength.

Fistandantilus stood before me. The old man's black robes were tattered shreds of night; his flesh was rotting and decayed; the bones were visible through the skin. His nails were long and pointed, as long as those of a corpse; his eyes gleamed with the radiant heat that had been in my soul, the warmth that had brought the dead to life. A bloodstone hung from a pendant around the fleshless neck.

The old man's hand touched my breast, caressed my flesh, teasing and tormenting. Fistandantilus plunged his hand into my chest and seized hold of my heart.

As the dying soldier clasps his hands around the haft of the spear that has torn through his body, I seized hold of the old man's wrist, clamped my fingers in a grip that death would not have relaxed.

Caught, trapped, Fistandantilus fought to break my grip, but he could not free himself and retain his hold on my heart.

The white light of Solinari; the red light of Lunitari; and the black, empty light of Nuitari—light that I could see—merged in my fainting vision, stared down at me, an unwinking eye.

"You may take my life," I said, keeping fast hold of the old man's wrist, as Fistandantilus kept hold of my heart. "But you will serve me in return."

The eye winked and blinked out.

Raistlin removed a soft leather pouch from the belt he wore around his waist. He reached his hand into the pouch and drew out what appeared to be a small ball made of colored glass, very like a child's marble. He rolled the glass ball around in the palm of his hand, watching the colors writhe and swirl inside.

"You grow to be a nuisance, old man," Raistlin said softly, and he didn't give a damn if Fistandantilus heard him or not.

He had a plan and there was nothing the undead wizard could do to stop him.

4

The cursed tower. The dragon orb. Silence.

4th Day, Month of Mishamont, Year 352 AC

The new black robes were still slightly damp around the seams and they smelled faintly of almond. The scent came from the indigo, the dyer told him. Raistlin was also convinced he could detect the odor of urine, which was used to set the dye, despite the dyer's assurance that the robes had been rinsed a great many times and that the smell was all in his imagination. The dyer offered to keep the robes and rinse them again, but Raistlin could not afford to take the time.

His biggest fear was that the Dark Queen would win her war before he had a chance to join her, impress her with his skill, and acquire her help in furthering his career. He pictured in his mind becoming a leader among the Black Robes of the Tower of High Sorcery in Neraka, her capital city. He pictured the Tower itself; it must be magnificent. He supposed the wizard Ladonna lived there, if she were still head of the Order of Black. He grimaced at the thought of having to abase himself before the old crone, treat her as his superior. He'd have to explain why he had taken the black robes without seeking her permission.

Ah, well. His servitude would not last long. With the support of the Dark Queen, Raistlin would be able to rise above them all. He would have no more need of them. His ambitious dreams would be fulfilled.

"Your dreams?" Fistandantilus snarled, his voice pounding like blood in Raistlin's ears. "Your dreams are *my* dreams! I spent a lifetime—many lifetimes—working toward my goal, becoming the Master of Past and Present. No sniveling, hacking upstart will steal it!"

Raistlin kept his own thoughts in check, refusing to be drawn into battle before he was ready. He walked rapidly, unerringly through the night toward his destination, toward his destiny. The Staff of Magius lit his way, the orb held in the dragon's claw shining softly, illuminating the dark streets that, in this part of the city, were very dark and very empty. No lights shone in the windows, most of which were broken. No laughter rang from within the tumble-down buildings. The streets were deserted. No one, not even the fearless kender, dared venture into the shadow of the Tower of High Sorcery—not by day and especially not by night.

The Tower of High Sorcery in Palanthas had once been the most beautiful of all the Towers of High Sorcery. Named the Lorespire, the Tower was to be dedicated to the search of wisdom and knowledge. The Tower graced Palanthas, its wizards assisting the knights to fight Queen Takhisis in the Third Dragon War. The wizards of all three orders came together to create the fabled dragon orbs and used them to lure the evil dragons into a trap. Takhisis was driven into the Abyss and the white Tower of the wizards and the High Clerist's Tower of the Knights were both proud guardians of Solamnia.

Then came the rise of the Kingpriests, who dictated that sorcery was evil. The Knights were strong supporters of the Kingpriests, and they came to view the wizards with distrust and finally demanded that the wizards abandon the Tower. Two Towers of High Sorcery had already been attacked, and the wizards had destroyed them, with devastating results to the populaces of those cities. The wizards of Palanthas decided to surrender their Tower. The Lord of Palanthas had intended to take over the Tower for his own use, as the Kingpriest had taken over the Tower of Istar, but before the lord could turn the key in the lock, a black robe wizard named Andras Rannoch cast a curse upon it.

The crowd who had gathered to rejoice in the eviction of the wizards watched in horror as Rannoch cried out, "The gates will remain closed and the halls empty until the day comes when the Master of Past and Present returns with power." Then he had leaped from the Tower and was impaled upon the barbs of the fence. As his blood flowed over the iron, he spoke a curse with his dying breath.

The beautiful tower was transformed into a thing of evil, horrible to look upon. Almost four hundred years had passed, and no one had dared come too near it. Many had tried, but few could summon up the courage to come within sight of the dread Shoikan Grove, a forest of oak trees that stood guard around the Tower. No one knew what went on in the grove. No one who entered the grove ever returned to tell.

Raistlin was here in this part of Palanthas because he had magic to perform, and it was vital that he be left alone. Any interruption—such as Bertrem knocking on his door—might well be fatal.

The Tower's twisted remains came into view, blotting out the stars, blotting out the light of the two moons, Solinari and Lunitari. Nuitari, the dark moon, was still visible, though only to the eyes of those who had been initiated into the dark god's secrets. Raistlin kept his eyes upon the dark moon and drew courage from it.

He pressed steadily on, even though he could feel the terror that flowed in a bone-chilling river from the Tower. Fear lapped at his feet. He shivered and drew his robes closer around him and went on. Fear grew deeper. He began to sweat. His hands trembled, his breath came fast, and he was afraid he would have a coughing fit. He gripped the Staff of Magius tightly, and though the shadow of the Tower snuffed out every other light in the world, the staff's light did not fail him.

The river of terror grew so deep that he could barely find the courage to put one foot in front of the other. Death awaited him. The next step would be his doom. Still he took that next step. Gritting his teeth, he took another.

"Turn back!" Fistandantilus urged him, his voice hammering inside Raistlin's brain. "You are mad to think of trying to destroy me. You need me."

You need me, Raist! Caramon's voice said, pleading. *I can protect you.*

"Shut up!" Raistlin said. "Both of you."

He came within sight of the Shoikan Grove, and he shuddered and closed his eyes. He could not go on, not without risking dying of the terror. He was far from the populated part of the city. It would do. He searched around for a suitable place to cast his spell. Nearby was an empty building with three gables and leaded pane windows. According to the sign that dangled at a crazy angle from a hook, the building had once been a tavern known as the Wizard's Hat, a name suitable for a tavern located near the Tower of High Sorcery of Palanthas.

The painted sign was extremely faded, but by the light of the staff, Raistlin could see a laughing wizard quaffing ale from a pointed hat. Raistlin was reminded of the senile old wizard, Fizban, who had worn (and continually mislaid) a hat that looked very much like the one portrayed on the sign.

The memory of Fizban made Raistlin uncomfortable, and he quickly banished it. He walked over to the door and shoved on it. The door creaked on rusty hinges and swung slowly open. Raistlin was about to enter when he had the feeling he was being watched. He told himself that was nonsense; no one in his right mind came to this part of the city. Just to reassure himself, he cast a glance around the street. He saw no one, and he was about to enter the tavern when he happened to look up at the sign. The painted eyes of the wizard were fixed on him. As he stared, one eye winked.

Raistlin shivered. The thought came to him that if he failed, he would die there and no one would ever know what had happened to him. His body would not be found. He would die and be forgotten, a pebble washed away in the River of Time.

"Don't be an idiot," Raistlin chided himself. He stared hard at the sign. "It was a trick of the light."

He walked swiftly into the abandoned tavern and shut the door behind himself. All that time, Fistandantilus was berating him.

"I cast the Curse of Rannoch! I am the Master of Past and Present. You are nothing, a nobody. Without me, you would have failed your Test in the Tower."

"Without me," Raistlin returned, "you would be lost and adrift in the vastness of the universe, a voice without a mouth, a scream no one can hear."

"You have used *my* knowledge," Fistandantilus said. "*I have fed you my power!*"

"*I* spoke the words that mastered the dragon orb," said Raistlin.

"I tell you the words to speak!" Fistandantilus retorted.

"You do," Raistlin agreed, "and all the while you mean to destroy me. You will wait until my life-force gives you strength, and then you will use it to kill me. You plan to become me. I won't let that happen."

Fistandantilus laughed. "My hand holds your heart! We are bound together. If you kill me, you will die."

"I am not convinced of that. Still, I will not take a chance," said Raistlin. "I do not intend to kill you."

He sat down upon a dust-covered bench. The tavern's interior was much as it had been centuries before, when the tavern had been a popular place for the wizards and their pupils to congregate. There was no bar, but there were tables surrounded by comfortable chairs. Raistlin would have expected the room to be filled with cobwebs and overrun by rats, but apparently even spiders and rodents were loath to live within the shadow of the Tower, for the dust lay thick and smooth and undisturbed. A mural on the wall portrayed the three gods of magic toasting each with mugs of foaming ale.

Raistlin looked around the empty tables and chairs, and he imagined wizards sitting there, laughing, telling tales, discussing their work. Raistlin saw himself seated there, discoursing, studying, arguing with his fellows. He would have been accepted for what he was, not reviled. He would have been loved, admired, respected.

Instead he was alone in the darkness with the specter of evil.

Raistlin leaned the Staff of Magius against the table, propping it with a chair so it would shed its pure, white light on the table. A cloud of dust rose as he sat down, and he sneezed and coughed. When the coughing fit ended, he took the orb from its pouch and placed it on the table.

Fistandantilus had gone quiet. Raistlin could no longer mask his thoughts from the old man, for he had to concentrate his entire being on taking control of the dragon orb. Fistandantilus saw the danger he was in, and he was trying to find a way to save himself.

Raistlin placed the dragon orb on the table, steadying the small globe so it did not roll off onto the floor. He took from another pouch a crudely carved wooden stand he had constructed during those days when he and Caramon and the others had traveled by wagon across Ansalon.

Raistlin had been happy then, happier than he had been in a long time. He and his brother had rediscovered some of their old camaraderie, remembering what it was like in their mercenary days, when it had been just the two of them relying on steel and magic for their survival.

He brushed dust from the table off the dragon orb and brushed the dust of Caramon from his mind. He placed the orb in the center of the wooden stand. The orb was cold to the touch. He could see, in the staff's light, the varied shades of green swirling around slowly inside. He knew what to expect, having used the orb before, and he waited, counseling patience, battling fear.

He thought back to the writings of an elf wizard named Feal-Thas, who had once possessed a dragon orb. Raistlin recalled one line.

Every time you try to gain control of a dragon orb, the dragon inside is trying to gain control of you.

The dragon orb began to grow to its original size, about the span of his hand measured with his fingers spread wide, from the tip of his thumb to the tip of his little finger.

He reached out to the orb.

"You will regret this," Fistandantilus said.

"I will add it to my list," Raistlin said, and he placed his hands upon the cold crystal of the dragon orb.

"Ast bilak moiparalan. Suh tantangusar."

He spoke the words he had learned from Fistandantilus. He spoke them once; then spoke them a second time.

The green color swirling around in the orb was subsumed by a myriad of colors, all whirling so rapidly that if he looked at them, they would make him dizzy. He shut his eyes. The crystal was cold, painful to the touch. He kept firm hold of it. The pain would ease, only to be replaced by far worse.

He said the words a third time and opened his eyes.

A light glowed in the orb. A strange light, formed of all the colors of the spectrum. He likened it to a dark rainbow. Two hands appeared in the orb. The hands reached out for his hands. Raistlin drew in a deep breath and took hold of the hands, clasped them tightly. He was confident, felt no fear. In the past, the hands had supported him, soothed him as a mother soothes a child, and he was startled, alarmed, to feel the hands close over his in a crushing grip.

The table, the chair, the staff, the tavern, the street, the Tower, Palanthas—everything disappeared. Darkness—not the living darkness of night, but the horrible darkness of everlasting nothingness—surrounded him.

The hands pulled on his hands, trying to drag him into the void. He exerted all his will, all his energy. All was not enough. The hands were stronger. They were going to drag him down.

He looked at the hands and saw, to his horror, that they were not the hands of the orb. The flesh of the hands had rotted and fallen off. The nails were long and bone yellow, like those of a corpse. The bloodstone pendant, its green surface spattered with the blood of so many young mages whose lives the old man had stolen, dangled from the scrawny neck.

The battle sapped Raistlin's fragile strength. He coughed, spitting blood, and since he dared not let go of the hands, he was forced to wipe his mouth on the sleeve of his new black robes. He spoke to the dragon, Viper, whose essence was trapped inside the orb.

"Viper, you acknowledged me as your master!" he said to the dragon. "You have served me in the past. Why do you abandon me now?"

The dragon answered.

Because you are prideful and weak. Like the elf king Lorac, you fell into my trap.

Lorac was the wretched king who had been arrogant enough to think he could control the dragon orb. The orb had seized control of Lorac and duped him into destroying Silvanesti, the ancient elven homeland.

"He destroyed what he loved most. I destroyed Caramon," Raistlin said feverishly, not even thinking about what he was saying. "The dragon has duped me . . ."

The hands tightened their grip and pulled him inexorably into the endless emptiness. Raistlin fought against it with a strength born of desperation. He had no idea what was going on, why the orb had turned on him. His arms trembled from the strain. He was sweating in the black robes. He was growing weaker.

"You float on the surface of Time's river." Raistlin gasped, struggling for breath against the choking sensation in his throat. "The future, the past, the present flow around you. You touch all planes of existence."

That is true.

"I have an enemy on one of those planes."

I know.

Raistlin looked into the orb, looked beyond the hands. He could see, on the other side of the River of Time, the face of Fistandantilus. Raistlin had seen rats on battlefields swarming over the corpses of the dead. He'd watched them devour flesh, strip it from the bones. The ruins the rats left behind were all that was left of the old man.

His eyes remained, burning with resolve and ruthless determination. His skeletal hands held Raistlin fast, one hand on his hand, one hand on his heart. Fistandantilus was fighting Raistlin for control of the dragon orb. And he was using Raistlin's own life-force to do it.

"I see the irony does not escape you," said Fistandantilus. His voice softened, grew almost gentle. "Stop fighting me, young magus. No need to continue to endure the struggle, the pain, the fear that is your wretched life. You stand before me naked and vulnerable and alone. All those who ever cared for you now loathe and despise you. You do not even have the magic. Your skills, your talent, your power come from me. And deep inside, you know it."

He speaks the truth, Raistlin thought in despair. I have no skill of my own. He told me the words to the spells. His knowledge gave me power. He watched over me, protected me as Caramon watched over me. And now Caramon is gone, and I have no one and nothing.

He is wrong. You have the magic.

The voice that spoke was his voice, and it came from his soul and drowned out the seductive voice of Fistandantilus.

"I have the magic," said Raistlin aloud, and he knew that pronouncement to be the truth. For him, it was the only truth. He grew stronger as he spoke. "The words may have been your words, but the voice was mine. My

62

eyes read the runes. My hand scattered the rose petals of sleep and flared with magical fire of death. I hold the key. I know myself. I know my weaknesses, and I know my worth. I know the darkness and the light. It was *my* strength, *my* power, *my* wisdom that mastered this dragon orb."

Raistlin drew in a deep breath, and life filled his lungs. His heartbeat was strong and vital. For a moment, the curse that had been laid on his hourglass eyes was lifted. He no longer saw all things withering with age. He saw himself.

"I have been afraid all my life. I fell victim to you because of my fear."

He saw his foe as a shadow of himself, cast across space and time. Raistlin gripped the hands firmly, confidently.

"I am afraid no longer. Our bargain is broken. I sever the tie."

"Only death severs our tie!" said Fistandantilus.

"Seize him," Raistlin commanded.

The blue and red, black and green, and white lights inside the orb swirled violently, dazzling Raistlin's eyes and bursting inside his head. The colors coalesced, with green predominant. The dragon, Viper, began to form inside the orb, various parts of the beast visible to Raistlin as it thrashed about: a fiery eye, a green wing, a lashing tail, a horned snout and snarling mouth, dripping fangs, ripping claws. The eye glared at Raistlin, and then shifted its glare to Fistandantilus.

Viper lifted his wings and, still inside the orb, he soared through time and space.

Fistandantilus saw his danger. He looked frantically around, seeking some means of escape. His refuge had become his prison. He could not flee the plane of his tenuous existence.

"To use your magic against the dragon, you must have your hands free," Raistlin said. "Let go of me, and I'll let go of you."

Fistandantilus swore and his grip on Raistlin tightened. Raistlin's shoulder and arm muscles burned, and his hands trembled with the strain. He could see, in the mists of the dragon orb, the dragon, Viper, swooping down on the wizard.

Fistandantilus shouted words of magic. They came out as so much meaningless drivel. With one hand caught in Raistlin's grip and the other clutching his heart, Fistandantilus could not use the gestures needed to unleash the power of his spell. He could not trace the runes in the air, could not cast balls of flame or send spiked lightning jabbing from his fingers.

The dragon opened his fanged mouth and extended his talons.

Raistlin was almost finished. Yet he would not let go. If the strain killed him, death would only tighten his grip, not break it.

Fistandantilus set him free. Raistlin sank onto the table, gasping for breath. Though his hands were weak and shaking, he managed to keep his hold on the dragon orb.

"Let go of me!" Fistandantilus raved. "Release me! That was our bargain."

"I do not have hold of you," said Raistlin.

He heard a shriek of rage and saw a rush of green; the dragon was returning to the dragon orb. Raistlin stared inside the orb, into the swirling mists.

He saw the face of an old man, a ravaged face, gnawed by time. Fleshless hands beat against the crystal walls of his prison. His yammering mouth shrieked threats.

Raistlin waited tensely to hear the voice in his head.

The mouth gibbered and gabbled, and Raistlin smiled.

He heard nothing. All was silence.

He ran his hand over the smooth, cold surface of the dragon orb, and it began to shrink in size. When it was no larger than a marble, he picked it up and dropped it into the pouch. He dismantled the crude stand and slid the pieces into a pocket of his black robes.

He paused a moment before he left the tavern to look around at the empty tables and chairs. He could see the wizards sitting there, drinking elven wine and dwarven ale.

"One day I will come here," Raistlin told them. "I will sit with you and drink with you. We will toast the magic. One day, when I am the Master of Past and Present, I will travel through time. I will come back. And when I come back, I will succeed where he failed."

Raistlin drew the cowl of his black robes over his head and left the Wizard's Hat.

* * *

5th Day, Month of Mishamont, Year 352 AC

Raistlin woke that morning after a sound night's sleep, a sleep uninterrupted by coughing fits. He drew in a deep breath of the morning air and felt it fill his lungs. He breathed freely. His heart beat strong and vibrantly. He was hungry and ate the bread soaked in milk, which was the monks' breakfast, with relish.

He was well. He was whole. Tears of joy stung his eyes. He brushed them away and packed up his few belongings, his spell components, his spellbooks, and the Staff of Magius. He was ready to depart, but first he had an errand to run. He needed to repay his debt to Astinus, who had given him, albeit inadvertently, the key: self-knowledge.

And he owed a debt to the Aesthetics, who had cared for him, fed him, and clothed him.

Raistlin sought out Bertrem, who was generally to be found hovering near Astinus's chamber, guarding his privacy or ready to dash forth at his command.

Bertrem's eyes widened at the sight of Raistlin's black robes. The Aesthetic swallowed several times. His hands fluttered nervously, but he blocked the way to Astinus's chamber.

"I don't care what you do to me. You will not harm the master!" said Bertrem bravely.

"I came only to take my leave of Astinus," Raistlin said.

Bertrem cast a fearful glance at the door. "The master is not to be disturbed."

"I think he will want to see me," said Raistlin quietly, and he advanced a step.

Bertrem stumbled back a step and bumped up against the door. "I am quite certain he would not—"

The door flew open, causing Bertrem to fall inside, nearly trampling Astinus. Bertrem ducked out of the way and flattened himself against the wall, trying in vain to become one with the marble.

"What is this banging and shouting outside my door?" Astinus demanded in acerbic tones. "I cannot work with all this commotion!"

"I am leaving Palanthus, sir," Raistlin said. "I wanted to thank you—"

"I have nothing to say to you, Raistlin Majere," said Astinus, preparing to shut the door. "Bertrem, since you are a failure at providing me with the peace and quiet I desire, you will escort this gentleman out."

Bertrem's face flushed with shame. He sidled out the door and, greatly daring, plucked at Raistlin's black sleeve. "This way—"

"Wait, sir!" Raistlin said, and he thrust his staff into the doorway to prevent Astinus from closing the door. "I ask you the question you asked me the day I arrived: What do you see when you look at me?"

"I see Raistlin Majere," Astinus replied, glowering.

"You do not see your 'old friend'?" Raistlin said.

"I don't know what you are talking about," Astinus said, and again he tried to shut the door.

Bertrem tugged harder at Raistlin's black sleeve. "You must not disturb the master—"

Raistlin ignored him and spoke to Astinus. "When I lay dying, you said to me, 'So this ends your journey, my old friend.' Your old friend, Fistandantilus, the wizard who crafted the Sphere of Time for you. Look into my eyes, sir. Look into the hourglass pupils that are my constant torment. Do you see your 'old friend'?"

"I do not," said Astinus after a moment. Then he added with a shrug, "So you won."

"I won," said Raistlin proudly. "I came to pay my debt—"

Astinus made a gesture as though brushing away gnats. "You owe me nothing."

"I always pay my debts," Raistlin said sharply. He reached into a pocket of the black velvet robes and drew out a scroll wrapped in black ribbon. "I thought perhaps you would like this. It is an account of the battle between us. For your records."

He held out the scroll. Astinus hesitated a moment; then he took the scroll. Raistlin removed the staff, and Astinus slammed shut the door.

"I know the way out," Raistlin told Bertrem.

"The master said I was to escort you," said Bertrem, and he not only walked with Raistlin to the door, but accompanied him down the marble stairs and out into the street.

"I washed the gray robes and left them folded on the bed," Raistlin said. "Thank you for the use of them."

"Of course," said Bertrem, babbling with relief at finally being rid of his strange visitor. "Any time."

He flushed, suddenly, and stammered, "That is . . . I don't mean 'any time.'"

Raistlin smiled at the Aesthetic's discomfiture. He reached into his pouch and clasped his hand around the dragon orb and made ready to cast his spell. It would be the first powerful spell he had cast without hearing that whispering voice in his head. He had bragged that the power was his. He would finally know whether or not he had spoken the truth.

Gripping the Staff of Magius in one hand and the dragon orb in the other, Raistlin spoke the words of magic.

"Berjalan cepat dalam berlua tanah."

A portal opened in the midst of space and time. He looked through it and saw the black, twisted spires of a temple. Raistlin had never been to Neraka, but he had spent time in the Great Library reading descriptions of the city. He recognized the Temple of Takhisis.

Raistlin entered the portal.

He looked out of it to see poor Bertrem, his eyes bulging, frantically pawing the empty air with his hands.

"Sir! Where have you gone? Sir?"

Unable to find his vanished guest, Bertrem gulped and turned and fled up the stairs to the library, running as fast as his sandaled feet would carry him.

The portal closed behind Raistlin and opened on his new life.

BOOK II

I

The Court of the Nightlord.

5th Day, Month of Mishamont, Year 352 AC

Iolanthe's formal title was "Wizardess to the Emperor." She was known informally as Ariakas's Witch or by other names even less flattering, though those were spoken only behind her back. No one dared say them to her face, for the "witch" was powerful.

The guards at the Red Gate saluted as she approached them. The Temple of Takhisis had six gates. The main gate was in the front. That gate, the Queen's Gate, was manned by eight dark pilgrims whose duty was to escort visitors through the temple. Five other gates were placed at various points around the temple's perimeter. Each of those gates opened into the camp of one of the five dragonarmies, which were fighting the Dark Queen's war of conquest.

Iolanthe avoided the main gate, for although she was the Emperor's mistress and under his protection, she was a wielder of magic, a worshiper of the gods of magic, and though one of those gods was the Dark Queen's son, the dark pilgrims viewed any wizard with deep suspicion and mistrust.

The dark pilgrims would have allowed her to enter the temple (not even the Nightlord, who was the head of the Holy Order of Takhisis, dared incur the wrath of the Emperor), but the clerics would have made her visit as unpleasant as possible, insulting her, demanding to know her business, and finally insisting upon sending one of the loathsome pilgrims as an escort.

By contrast, the draconians of the Red Dragonarmy, who were charged with guarding the Red Gate, fell over their clawed feet to be accommodating to the beautiful wizardess. A languishing glance from her lavender eyes, which glittered like amethysts beneath her long, black eyelashes; a gentle brush of her slender fingers on the sivak's scaly arm; a charming smile from carnelian lips; and the sivak commander was only too happy to permit Iolanthe to enter the temple.

"You are here late, Mistress Iolanthe," said the sivak. "It is well after Dark Watch. Not a good time to walk the halls of the temple alone. Would you like me to accompany you?"

"Thank you, Commander. I would appreciate the company," Iolanthe replied, and she fell into step beside him. He was new and she tried to recall his name. "Commander Slith, isn't it?"

"Yes, madam," said the sivak with a grin and a gallant flick of his wings.

Iolanthe found the Temple of Takhisis to be an unnerving place even during the daylight hours. Not that much daylight ever managed to beat its way inside, but at least the knowledge that the sun was shining somewhere made her feel better. Iolanthe had sometimes been forced to walk the halls of the temple after dark, and she had not liked it. The dark pilgrims, those clerics who were dedicated to the worship of the Dark Queen, performed their unhallowed rites in the hours of darkness. Iolanthe's own hands were far from clean, but at least she washed the blood of victims from her fingers; she did not drink it.

Iolanthe had another reason for wanting an armed escort. The Nightlord hated her, and he would have rejoiced to see her buried in sand up to her neck with buzzards pecking out her eyes and ants devouring her flesh. She was safe, at least for the moment. Ariakas held his strong hand over her.

At least for the moment.

Iolanthe knew quite well that he would eventually tire of her. Then his strong hand would either be clenched to a fist or, worse, wave dismissively. She did not think the time had yet come for him to want to get rid of her. Even if he did, Ariakas would not hand her over to the dark clerics. He disliked and distrusted the Nightlord as much as the Nightlord disliked and distrusted him. Ariakas was the type to simply strangle her.

"What brings you to the temple at this hour, madam?" Slith asked. "Not here for the Dark Watch service, are you?"

"Gods, no!" said Iolanthe with a shiver. "The Nightlord sent someone to fetch me."

She was wakened in the middle of the night by one of the dark pilgrims shouting outside the window of her dwelling, which was located above a mageware shop. The cleric would not risk contaminating himself by actually knocking on a wizard's door, and so he yelled from the street, waking the neighbors, who opened their windows, prepared to fling the contents of their chamber pots on whoever was making that ungodly racket. Seeing the black robes of a cleric of Takhisis and hearing him invoke the name of the Nightlord, the neighbors slammed shut their windows and probably went to hide under their beds.

The dark pilgrim did not wait to escort her. His task done, he hastened off before Iolanthe could dress and find out what was going on. She had never before been summoned to the Temple of Takhisis by the Nightlord, and she didn't like it. She had been forced to traverse the dangerous streets of Neraka after dark by herself. She had conjured a ball of bright, glowing light and held it, crackling, in the palm of her hand. It was not a difficult spell, but it was showy and would mark her as a user of magic. The outlaws who roamed the streets would know immediately that she was not an easy mark, and they would steer clear of her.

The streets had been sparsely populated; most of the troops were off fighting the Dark Queen's war. Unfortunately those soldiers who remained in Neraka were in a surly mood. Rumor had it that Takhisis's war, which had been as good as won, was not going so well after all.

A group of five human soldiers wearing the insignia of the Red Army had eyed her as she walked past the alley in which they were sharing a jug of dwarven spirits. They had called to her to come join them. When she had haughtily ignored them, two of the soldiers were inclined to take their chances and accost her. One, less drunk than the others, had recognized her as Ariakas's Witch, and after some heated discussion, they had let her alone.

The very fact that they had insulted Ariakas's mistress boded ill. In the early, glory days of the war, those soldiers would have never dared speak of Ariakas by name, much less make crude remarks about his prowess or offer to show her "what a real man" was like in bed. Iolanthe had not been in any danger from them. The soldiers would have been five greasy piles of ash in the street if they had attacked her. But she found it instructive to note the volatile mood of the troops. Dragon Highlord Kitiara would be interested to hear what she had to report. Iolanthe wondered if Kit had returned yet from Flotsam.

As Iolanthe and her draconian escort proceeded to enter the temple, Iolanthe told Commander Slith she had no idea where the Nightlord was to be found. The sivak said he would ask. Iolanthe liked the sivak. Oddly enough, she liked the draconian soldiers, whom most humans reviled as "lizardmen," due to the fact that they had been created from the eggs of the good dragons. The draconians were far more disciplined than their human counterparts. They were far more intelligent than goblins and ogres and hobgoblins. They were excellent fighters. Some of them were skilled magic-users and would have made good commanders, but most humans looked down on them and refused to serve under them.

Slith was a sivak draconian. Born from the murdered young of a silver dragon, Slith had scales that were shining silver with black tips. He had silver-gray wings, which would carry him short distances, and he was a talented magic-user. He offered to remove the magical traps that Iolanthe herself had laid upon the hall; traps that emulated the various breath weapons of each of the five dragons to which each gate was dedicated. The trap she had placed on the Red Gate filled the hall with blazing fire that would immediately incinerate any being caught trespassing.

Iolanthe accepted. She could have removed the magic herself, but dispersing the spell required effort, and she wanted to reserve her strength to deal with whatever lay behind the mysterious summons.

Accompanied by the draconian, Iolanthe swept through the halls of the Dark Queen's temple, her black cloak trimmed with black bear fur sweeping majestically behind her. She was wearing sumptuous, black velvet robes—a gift for passing her Test in the Tower from her mentor and teacher, Ladonna. The robes looked plain, but if one looked closely in certain lights (and knew what to look for), one could see runes traced in the fabric's nap. The runes overlapped like chain mail with much the same effect; they would protect her from harm, either spell-based or an assassin's dagger. The clerics of Takhisis were forbidden to use bladed weapons, but they were not forbidden from hiring those who could.

A dark pilgrim told the sivak that the Nightlord was in the Court of the Inquisitor, located in the dungeon level of the temple. Iolanthe had been in the dungeons, and they were not high on her list of places in Krynn to visit. The temple itself was horrid enough.

Built partially on the physical plane and partly within the Dark Queen's realm of the Abyss, the temple was here and not there, there but not here. Unreality was real. Existence was nonexistent. One hesitated to sit in a chair for fear it wasn't a chair or that it would move to the other side of the room or simply vanish. Halls that appeared to be short went on forever. Long corridors ended way too soon. Rooms seemed to move so nothing was where it had been previously.

Ariakas maintained chambers there, as did all the Dragon Highlords. None of them liked residing in the temple and rarely set foot in their apartments. Ariakas had once said he always heard Takhisis's voice, hissing in his ear, *Don't grow too comfortable. You may be powerful, but don't ever forget that I am your Queen.*

It was no surprise that the Highlords preferred to sleep in the crude tents of their military camps or in a small room in the city's inns, rather than the luxurious bedrooms in the Dark Queen's temple. Ariakas had actually acquired his own mansion, the Red Mansion, in order to avoid having to entertain high-ranking guests in the temple.

Iolanthe wondered, not for the first time, how the clerics of Takhisis who resided there did not succumb to madness. Perhaps it was because they were all lunatics to begin with.

She was glad she had brought Commander Slith along, for she soon became hopelessly lost. The temple was busy at night. Iolanthe tried to shut her ears to the horrible sounds. The commander, being new to the temple himself, had to ask a dark pilgrim to escort them to the dungeon level. The pilgrim inclined her head. She did not speak and was silent and sepulchral as a wraith.

"I have been summoned by the Nightlord," Iolanthe explained.

The dark pilgrim looked Iolanthe up and down. The pilgrim pursed her lips in disapproval but at last decided to deign to escort her.

"I heard there was trouble," the woman said grimly.

She was tall and gaunt. All the dark pilgrims seemed to be either tall and gaunt or short and gaunt. Perhaps serving in the temple took away one's appetite. Iolanthe knew it certainly did hers.

"What kind of trouble?" Iolanthe asked, startled. If there was trouble in the temple, why should the Nightlord summon her? Judging from the agonized screams of the tortured, he was quite capable of dealing with trouble on his own. "Why should it involve me?"

The pilgrim appeared to feel that she had said too much already. She clamped her lips shut.

"Creepy bastards, these pilgrims. Make my scales crawl," said Slith.

"You should keep your voice down, Commander," Iolanthe said quietly. "The walls have ears."

"The walls have feet too. Have you noticed the spooky way they jump around?" said Slith. "I'll be glad to get out of this place."

Iolanthe heartily agreed.

The pilgrim led them to the Court of the Inquisitor. The pilgrim would not permit Slith to enter. He offered to wait outside for Iolanthe, but the pilgrim shook her head at even that, and he was forced to depart.

Iolanthe hated this place. She hated the dreadful sounds and awful sights and noxious smells that always filled her with a nameless terror. The dark pilgrim eyed her with a smug expression, hoping and expecting to see her give way to her fear. Iolanthe gathered up the skirt of her robes and swept past the woman and entered the Court of the Inquisitor.

The room was large and dark save for a shaft of harsh light that beamed down from some unknown source, forming a pool of light in the center. At the far end, the Nightlord sat on a raised, judicial-looking bench. The executioner, known as the Adjudicator, stood off to one side. Responsible for inflicting torture and performing executions, the Adjudicator was short and stocky and powerfully built. He had no neck to speak of and bulging arm muscles, which he was enormously proud of and liked to show off. Though he wore long, black robes, the same as the other clerics, he had removed the sleeves, the better to exhibit his biceps. Dark pilgrims, acting as guards, ranged around the room, keeping in the shadows.

Iolanthe entered cautiously, unable to see her way clearly, for the bright pool of light made the surrounding darkness that much darker.

The Nightlord could have prayed to his Queen and been given the power to fill the room with unholy light if he had chosen. He preferred to hold his court in the shadows. By placing the victim in the harsh light and leaving the rest of the room in darkness, he made his victim feel isolated, alone, exposed.

Iolanthe remained standing near the door more by instinct than because she would have any hope of escape if something went wrong. She bowed to the Nightlord. He was an elderly human, somewhere in his seventies; of medium height, thin and wiry. With his long, gray hair, which was always neatly combed, and his kindly and benevolent face, the Nightlord had the appearance of a benign, old gentleman.

Until you looked into his eyes.

The Nightlord saw the darkest depths of evil to which the soul of man can sink, and he reveled in the sight. He took joy in the pain and suffering of others. The Adjudicator inflicted the torture as the Nightlord watched, reacting to the screams and torment in perverse ways that caused even those who served him to regard him with fear and loathing. The Nightlord's eyes were as dispassionate as those of a shark, as empty as those of a snake. The only time anyone ever saw his eyes gleam was when he was in the throes of his horrid pleasures.

He made Iolanthe's gorge rise, and she was not one to give way easily to fear. She was, after all, the mistress to Ariakas, the second most dangerous man in Ansalon. Even the Emperor grudgingly acknowledged that the Nightlord was the first.

With those horrid eyes fixed on her, Iolanthe would not give the man the satisfaction of seeing her cower. She made him a slight bow; then, as if bored by the sight of him, she shifted her gaze to his prisoner. She saw, to her vast astonishment, that the prisoner was a mage, that he was young, and that he was wearing the black robes. Her heart sank. No wonder the Nightlord had summoned her.

"You are in a great deal of trouble, Mistress Iolanthe," said the Nightlord in his mild voice. "As you see, we have captured your spy."

The Adjudicator smiled, and flexed his biceps.

"My spy?" Iolanthe repeated, astounded. "I never saw this man before in my life!"

The Nightlord regarded her intently. He had the goddess-given ability to tell when people were lying to him, though he did not often use it. Generally he did not care whether people were lying or not; he tortured them anyway.

"And yet," he said, "you two are birds of feather, so to speak."

"We both wear the black robes, if that's what you mean," Iolanthe replied disdainfully. "There are a great many of us who do. I don't suppose your lordship knows every servant of Takhisis in the world."

"You'd be surprised," the Nightlord returned dryly. "But if you two really do not know each other, allow me to introduce you. Iolanthe, meet Raistlin Majere."

Raistlin Majere, Iolanthe repeated to herself. I've heard that name before. . . .

Then she remembered.

By Nuitari! Iolanthe stared at the young man.

Raistlin Majere was Kitiara's brother!

2

The Mage. The Witch. And the Maniac.

5th Day, Month of Mishamont, Year 352 AC

he harsh light glared down on Raistlin, on him alone, making him seem the only person in the room. Iolanthe drew nearer to see him better.

He was leaning for support on a staff made of wood topped by a dragon's claw holding a crystal globe. Iolanthe recognized at once that the staff was magical and guessed that it was extremely powerful. The young man's other hand fiddled nervously with a leather pouch he wore attached to his belt. The pouch was nondescript, the sort any wizard might use to hold components necessary to the casting of spells. She noted that the mage wore several pouches, all of them undoubtedly containing various components. He kept his hand near only one.

And though she wondered immediately why that pouch was singled out for special treatment, she did not give the matter much thought. She was far more interested in the hand than the pouch. The skin of it glistened with a golden sheen, as though the mage had been dipped in the precious metal. The odd color was the result of some magical spell, no doubt, but what and why?

She shifted her gaze from the mage's hand to his face. He had removed his black cowl, leaving his face exposed, and Iolanthe searched for a resemblance to his sister. She did not find it in his features. His face was handsome, or would have been if it had not been thin and drawn and pale with exhaustion. The skin of his face was the same golden hue as that of his hands.

His eyes were astonishing. They were large and intense, the black pupils the shape of hourglasses. He turned to look at her with his strange eyes, and Iolanthe saw no admiration in them, no desire, as she saw in the eyes of almost every other man who looked at her. Then she knew the reason.

The eyes were cursed; it was known as the "curse of Realanna," for the fabled sorceress who had developed the spell. Every living being Raistlin looked upon would appear to age and wither and die. He saw her as she would look years in the future, perhaps an ugly, toothless, old hag.

Iolanthe shivered.

The resemblance to his sister appeared to be more in spirit than in body. Iolanthe saw Kitiara's ruthless ambition in her brother's firm, strong jaw; her fierce determination in the young man's fixed expression; and her pride and self-confidence in his thrust-back shoulders. By contrast, there were qualities Kitiara lacked. Iolanthe saw sensitivity in the long, slender fingers of Raistlin's hands and a shadowed look in his eyes. He had suffered in life. He had known pain, both physical and spiritual, and he had overcome both by the sheer force of his indomitable will.

She also noticed, as a point of interest, that there was no mark on him. He had not been beaten. His golden skin had not been flayed and fed to the dogs. His bones had not been broken on the rack, nor had the Adjudicator gouged out those interesting eyes. Somehow Raistlin had managed to thwart the Nightlord. Iolanthe found that fascinating.

She looked back at the Nightlord and saw that he was, in fact, annoyed and frustrated.

"I have never seen this person before," Iolanthe reiterated. "I do not know who he is or where he came from."

That was a lie. Kitiara had told Iolanthe all about her "baby" brother and their childhood in Solace. Raistlin had a twin brother, she recalled, a big, hulking, simple-minded fellow named Caringman or something odd like that. Supposedly the two were never apart. Iolanthe wondered what had become of Raistlin's twin.

The Nightlord regarded her grimly. "I fail to believe you, madam."

"I fail to understand any of this, your lordship," said Iolanthe in exasperation. "If you are so worried that this young mage is a spy, why did you permit him to enter the temple?"

"We didn't," said the Nightlord coldly.

"Well, then, the draconian guards at one of the gates must have cleared him—"

"They didn't," said the Nightlord.

Iolanthe's lashes fluttered in confusion. "Then how—?"

The Nightlord leaped upon the word. *"How!* That is the question I want answered! *How* did this mage come to be here? He did not enter by the front gate. The dark pilgrims would not have permitted it."

Iolanthe knew that to be true. They never allowed her to pass without harassment, and she carried the Emperor's authorization.

"He did not enter by any of the five dragonarmy gates. I have questioned the draconian commanders, and they all swear to me by the five heads of Takhisis that they did not allow him to pass. What is more"—the Nightlord gestured at the young man—"he himself admits that he did not come through any of the entrances. He appeared out of nowhere. And he will not say how he managed to evade all our warding spells."

Iolanthe shrugged. "Far be it from me to give you advice, but I have heard that your lordship has methods of persuading people to tell you whatever you want to know."

The Nightlord's eyes narrowed. "I tried. Some force protects him. When the Adjudicator attempted to 'question' him, Majere attempted to cast a Circle of Protection spell—the efforts of an amateur. I was able to dismantle it, of course. The Adjudicator then tried to seize hold of him. But he could not."

Iolanthe was puzzled. "I beg your pardon, lord, but what do you mean 'he could not'? What did this young man do to stop him?"

"Nothing!" said the Nightlord. "He did nothing. I tried to dispel whatever magic he was using, but there was nothing to dispel. Yet whenever the Adjudicator drew near him, the executioner's hands shook as with a palsy. One of the guards then tried to throw a rope around Majere. The rope slithered to the floor. We attempted to seize his staff, but it nearly burned the hand off the cleric who tried to take it."

Raistlin spoke up. His voice was well modulated, with a soft, husky quality about it. "I told your lordship I am under the protection of no magical spell. It is Queen Takhisis who watches over me."

Iolanthe regarded Raistlin with admiration. She had already resolved to do what she could to rescue Kitiara's brother from the Nightlord's clutches. The Blue Lady would be grateful, for she had expressed a fondness for her half-brothers, and Iolanthe was working hard to gain the trust and regard of the powerful Highlord. Iolanthe was starting to like the young man for himself, however.

She had to play it carefully, though, feel her way in the darkness.

"And so, lord, why did you summon me in the middle of the night? You have yet to tell me."

"I brought you here so that you can prove your loyalty to her Dark Majesty by removing his staff," said the Nightlord. "I am certain it is the staff that protects him. Once he is no longer protected by any magical force, the Adjudicator will deal with him. He will pay for his refusal to answer our questions, of that I can assure you."

Iolanthe had never before been asked to "prove her loyalty," and she wondered uneasily what to do. She did not want to hand Raistlin over to the Adjudicator, who was skilled in the art of torment. He hacked off limbs. He stripped skin off living victims. He bound iron bands studded with spikes around their heads and slowly tightened the screws. He thrust burning pokers into various orifices of the body. He would always stop just short of death, using spells to bring the prisoner back to life to endure more torment.

Iolanthe decided to play for time. "Did you ask him *why* he came, lord?"

"We know the answer to that, mistress," the Nightlord replied, fixing her with a withering gaze. "As do you."

Danger tugged at the hem of Iolanthe's skirt and laid clammy fingers on the back of her neck. Ariakas was away from Neraka. He had traveled to his headquarters in Sanction, a long distance from. And with rumors swirling that the Emperor was starting to let victory slip through his fingers, the Nightlord might be growing more bold. He had long felt that he should be the one to wear the Crown of Power. Perhaps Takhisis was starting to agree with him.

Iolanthe needed to find out what sort of monster was lurking in the shadows, waiting to pounce on her.

"I do *not* know what you mean," she said coldly before turning to the young wizard. "Why did you come to the Temple of Takhisis?"

"I have told his lordship repeatedly. I came to pay my tribute to Her Dark Majesty," said Raistlin.

He is telling the truth! Iolanthe realized in amazement. She could hear the respect in his voice when he named the Queen of Darkness, respect that was not perfunctory, not feigned, slavish, or groveling. It was respect that came from the heart, not from the threat of a beating. What marvelous irony! Raistlin Majere was probably the only person left in Neraka who still felt such respect for Queen Takhisis. And for that her loyal servants were going to put him to death.

As if to put an exclamation point to her thoughts, the Nightlord snorted. "He is lying. He is a spy."

"A spy?" Iolanthe repeated, startled. "For whom?"

"The Conclave of Wizards." The Nightlord spoke the last word with a hiss and a sneer.

Iolanthe stiffened. "I assure you, lord, that the Order of Black Robes is dedicated to the service of Queen Takhisis."

The Nightlord smiled. He rarely smiled and, when he did, his smile boded ill for someone. The Adjudicator smiled too.

"Apparently you have not been informed. It seems that the head of your order, a wizard named Ladonna, has betrayed us by assisting the enemies of our glorious Queen. In this, she was helped by your god, Nuitari. Ladonna was caught and executed, of course. Nuitari has begged forgiveness for his error in judgment and has returned to the side of his goddess mother. All is well, but it was an inconvenience."

Iolanthe felt danger's hands clutch her by the throat. She had firsthand knowledge that the Nightlord was lying, but she had to feign ignorance.

"I did not know any of this," she said, striving to appear calm. "I can assure you of my loyalty, Nightlord. If the Conclave has broken with the Dark Queen, then I will break with the Conclave."

The Nightlord snorted. He obviously did not believe her. Then why summon her? He was fishing for information, which meant he did not know all that he claimed to know.

Iolanthe launched into a voluble account of her dedication to Takhisis. All the while, as she was talking, she was thinking. I would have heard if Ladonna had been caught and executed. The entire Conclave—Black, Red, and White—would be in an uproar. The wizard's credo, born of long years of persecution, was: "Touch one and you touch all."

So what does this mean for me? Does the Nightlord suspect that I was involved in Ladonna's escape? Undoubtedly he does, if for no other reason than he believes spies and conspirators are lurking around every corner. He'd arrest his own shadow for following him if he could.

She was mulling that over and trying to decide how to get herself out of the tangle when the young wizard took matters into his own hands.

"As proof of my loyalty to Takhisis, I will hand over my staff," Raistlin said quietly. "The staff is an artifact I value as I value my life, but I will give it to you of my own free will. And I will tell your lordship how I came here. I entered through the corridors of magic. In my defense, I did not know that entering the temple was a crime. I am newly arrived in Neraka. I came to serve Queen Takhisis, to work to confound her enemies. May Her Dark Majesty strike me dead on the spot if I am lying."

Dark clerics, such as the Nightlord, repeatedly assured their followers that their Queen had the power to strike down traitors. Raistlin had proclaimed his loyalty to the Queen, and he'd done so by invoking her name. No lightning bolt streaked down from the sky. Raistlin did not go up in flames. His flesh did not melt from his bones. The young wizard stood calmly in the midst of the court, alive and well and unharmed. With a faint smile, Iolanthe waited for the Nightlord's reaction.

He glared at Raistlin in frustration. The Nightlord might well suspect that Raistlin was making a mockery of the proceedings, but he could not call into question his Queen's judgment, especially in front of witnesses. Takhisis had deemed that Raistlin should live. The Nightlord could not, therefore, execute him, but he could make his life miserable.

"You have our Queen to thank for saving you," the Nightlord said bitingly. "You can remain in the city of Neraka, but you are henceforth forbidden from entering the temple."

Raistlin bowed in acquiescence.

"Your staff will be confiscated," the Nightlord continued, "and held in storage until such time as you leave the city. You will, here and now, reveal the contents of your pouches."

The Nightlord might be perverted, sadistic, and insane, but he wasn't stupid. He had noticed, as had Iolanthe, the young mage's hand hovering protectively near the pouch he wore on his belt.

Raistlin looked uncertain. Iolanthe drew near to him and said softly, "Don't be a fool. Do as he says."

Raistlin cast her a glance, then placed his staff on the floor. Iolanthe wondered that he wasn't more concerned over its loss, for certainly he must know that any valuable object the Nightlord put "in storage" was gone for good.

"You will remain as a witness, madam," said the Nightlord, frowning at Iolanthe.

She sighed and joined Raistlin, who was opening first one pouch then another, emptying out the contents on the desk. There was the usual variety of spell components: cobweb, bat guano, rose petals, the skin of a black snake, black oil, coffin nails, cowry shells, and so forth. The Nightlord regarded those items with distaste and was careful not to touch any of them.

All the pouches except one lay on the Nightlord's desk. Iolanthe could see one pouch still attached to Raistlin's belt, though he had deftly maneuvered that pouch around to the side and covered it with the flowing sleeve of his black robe.

"Those are all my spell components, lord," said Raistlin, adding humbly, "I would appreciate it if you would return them to me, lord. I am not a wealthy man, and they cost me dearly."

"These items are contraband," said the Nightlord, "and will be destroyed."

He summoned one of the dark pilgrims, who reluctantly and gingerly picked up the various components, deposited them in a sack, and took them away. At his command, another dark pilgrim dropped a blanket over the staff, picked it up, and carried it from the room.

Raistlin made no argument, though; judging by the faint, sardonic smile that touched the young wizard's lips, he knew the Nightlord was being arbitrary to punish him.

Rose petals were not going to bring about the downfall of Her Dark Majesty. Every item in his pouches could be purchased at any mageware shop in the city.

"I abide by your decision, lord," Raistlin said, bowing. "Am I free to go?"

"If your lordship pleases, I will conduct him to the proper exit," said Iolanthe.

She rested her fingers on the young man's arm and was surprised to feel an unnatural warmth radiating through the black folds of his robe. He seemed to burn with fever, yet he showed no symptoms of illness, only a very natural fatigue. Iolanthe was more and more intrigued by Kitiara's brother. The two of them were bowing and starting to edge away when the Nightlord spoke.

"Show me the contents of that remaining pouch."

A flush suffused Raistlin's golden-toned skin. "I assure your lordship that it has nothing to do with magic." He did not appear afraid so much as embarrassed.

"I will be the judge of that," said the Nightlord smugly. He rapped on the table. "Put it here."

Raistlin slowly drew out the pouch, but he did not open it.

"You have no choice," Iolanthe whispered. "Whatever it is you are hiding, is it worth being disemboweled?"

Raistlin shrugged and dropped the pouch on the desk in front of the Nightlord. The pouch was lumpy and heavy and landed with a thud and a muffled *thunk*.

The Nightlord regarded the pouch with a suspicious frown. He did not touch it, instead turning to Iolanthe. "You, witch. Open it."

Iolanthe would have liked to have opened the man's scrawny throat, but she contained her anger. She was as curious as the Nightlord to see the contents the young mage was so carefully guarding.

She studied the pouch before she picked it up, noting that it was made of leather, well worn, and closed by a leather drawstring that ran through the top. No runes had been written on it. No spells of warding had been laid on it. She could have used a simple cantrip to find out if it was magically protected in some other way, but she did not want to give the Nightlord the impression that she mistrusted a fellow mage. She glanced at Raistlin from beneath her long lashes, hoping he would give her some sort of sign that she could proceed safely. His eyelids flickered beneath the hood. He slightly smiled.

Iolanthe drew in a deep breath and pulled open the strings to the pouch with a jerk. She looked inside and was at first startled, then she had to choke back her laughter. She upended the bag. The contents spilled out and went rolling off in all directions.

"What is this?" the Nightlord demanded, glaring.

The Adjudicator bent down to examine them closely. Unlike the Nightlord, the Adjudicator was both perverse and stupid.

"They would be marbles, my lord," the Adjudicator said solemnly.

Iolanthe controlled her twitching lips. Somewhere in the darkness someone did laugh. The Nightlord glared around, and the laughter was immediately stifled.

"Marbles." The Nightlord fixed Raistlin with a withering stare.

Raistlin's flush deepened. He appeared overcome by shame. "I know it is a child's game, my lord, but I am quite fond of it. I find that playing marbles relaxes me. I might recommend it to your lordship if you are occasionally bilious—"

"You have wasted enough of my time. Get out!" ordered the Nightlord. "And do not come back. Queen

Takhisis can do quite well without 'respects' from scum like you."

"Yes, my lord," said Raistlin, and he began to hastily scoop up the marbles that were still rolling on the desk.

Iolanthe bent to pick up one marble that had fallen on the floor and lay near the hem of the young mage's robes. The marble was green and shone with an eerie luster. She remembered from her own childhood that such a marble was called a cat's eye.

"Please, madam, do not trouble yourself," Raistlin said in his soft voice. He deftly intercepted her, plucking the marble out from under her fingers. As his hand brushed hers, she felt again the strange heat of his skin.

Another prisoner was being hauled into the court. He was bound in chains and manacles. He was covered in blood and looked more dead than alive. Raistlin glanced at him as he and Iolanthe hastened past.

"That could have been you," she said in a low voice.

"Yes," he said, adding, "I am grateful for your help, madam."

"No need to be so formal. My name is Iolanthe," she said, hustling him out of the courtroom. She had no idea where she was or how to escape the maze of tunnels, but she kept going. Her one thought was to put as much distance between herself and the Nightlord as possible.

"You are Raistlin Majere. I believe that is your name?"

"Correct, madam. I mean . . . Iolanthe," said Raistlin.

She was tempted to tell him she knew his sister, Kitiara, but decided against revealing too much too soon. Knowledge is power, and she had yet to determine how to make use of it or if she should even bother. A wizard who played at marbles . . .

She found a dark pilgrim, who was more than happy to escort them from the temple. She saw, as they walked the winding, twisting halls, that Raistlin missed nothing. His strange eyes were constantly roving, making mental notes of each turn, each staircase they passed, the banks of cells and pools of acid, the guard rooms. Iolanthe could have told him that if he were trying to map the place, he was wasting his time. The dungeons had been deliberately designed to be as confusing as possible. On the off chance that a prisoner would escape, he would quickly lose himself in the labyrinth and fall easy victim to the guards or tumble into an acid pool.

Iolanthe was eager to question the young mage, but she was mindful of the proximity of the dark cleric walking alongside them, whose ears were undoubtedly flapping beneath his hood. At last they came to a steep, winding, staircase that proved too narrow for them all to mount together. Their guide was forced to walk ahead of them.

They climbed the stairs slowly, for Raistlin almost immediately ran out of breath and had to lean on the iron railing.

"Are you all right?" Iolanthe asked.

"I was afflicted with an illness for many years," he said. "I am cured of it now, but it took its toll."

As they continued up the stairs, Iolanthe said something polite. He did not respond, and she realized he had not even heard her. He was abstracted, absorbed in his own thoughts. By the time they reached the top of the stairs, the dark pilgrim, believing that his charges were close behind him, had rounded a corner and was out of sight.

"Our guide seems to have lost us," Iolanthe said. "We should wait here for him. I never know where I am in this horrid place."

Raistlin was looking around at his surroundings.

"You were concentrating on something very deeply back there on the stairs. I spoke, but you didn't hear me."

"I am sorry," said Raistlin. "I was counting."

"Counting?" Iolanthe repeated, astonished. "Counting what?"

"The stairs."

"Whatever for?"

"I have a habit of observation. Twenty stairs led down to the guardroom from the abbey where I found myself. My sudden appearance out of thin air caused quite a stir," he added with a sudden flash of humor in the strange eyes.

"I can imagine," she said.

"Leaving the courtroom, we climbed forty-five stairs on the last staircase."

"All very interesting, I suppose," said Iolanthe, "but I fail to see any practical use for such knowledge. Especially in this weird place."

"You refer, of course, to the interplanal shifting between the physical world and the Abyss," said Raistlin.

"How did you know about that?" she asked, again astonished.

"I had read about the phenomenon prior to coming to Neraka. I was curious to see what it was like, which is one reason I made it a point to visit the temple. In truth, the corridors do not shift. They only appear to do so because the eye is fooled by the distortion between one plane and another. Rather like looking through a prism," he explained. "The building is not really jumping about or changing shape. I noted, however, that the visual distortion effects are mitigated when it comes to the stairs. That is only logical, otherwise the dark clerics would be forever tumbling down the staircases and breaking their necks. But I am stating the obvious.

You are a frequent visitor here. You must have noticed this yourself."

Once she thought of it, Iolanthe realized that she never did have any problem going up and down the stairs, though she had not considered such information important.

"The distortion makes walking about the temple very disorienting, which is precisely the reason for it," Raistlin continued. "The casual visitor is immediately lost, which makes him feel afraid and vulnerable, and thus his mind is opened to the power and influence of the Dark Queen. Did you never wonder how the dark clerics come to find their way about?"

As if on cue, their guide appeared at the end of the hall, an annoyed expression on his face. Spying them, he came marching grimly down the corridor.

"Not really," said Iolanthe. "I avoid the place when I can. What does the number of stairs have to do with anything?"

"The fact that the stairs are not subject to such distortions makes them useful tools for keeping track of one's whereabouts," said Raistlin. "I noted that the dark cleric who escorted me to the dungeon level was keeping count of the stairs. I saw him strike the numbers off with the fingers of his hand. I presume, though I do not know for certain, that every staircase has a different number of stairs and that is how they find their way around."

"I begin to understand," said Iolanthe, enlightened. "If I want to get to the Nightlord's courtroom, I look for the staircase with forty-five stairs."

Raistlin nodded and Iolanthe regarded him in wonder. She considered Kitiara a remarkable woman, and she now felt the same about her brother. Brains must run in the family.

The dark pilgrim took them once more in tow, with a stern admonition to keep up with him. He stalked down the hall ahead of them, moving at a rapid pace toward the nearest exit, obviously eager to be rid of them.

Iolanthe gave a relieved sigh when they passed through the main gate. She was always happy to escape the temple. She slipped her arm companionably inside Raistlin's.

She was startled to feel him flinch and stiffen. He drew back from her.

"I beg your pardon," she said coldly, dropping her hand.

"No, please," he said in confusion. "I am the one who should beg pardon. It's just . . . I don't like being touched."

"Not even by a pretty woman?" she asked with an arch smile.

"That is not something to which I'm accustomed," he said wryly.

"No time like the present," she said, and she twined her arm through his. "The streets are not safe," she added more somberly. "It will be better if we stick close together."

The streets were deserted for the most part. They passed one man lying in the gutter. He was either dead drunk or just plain dead; Iolanthe never looked too closely. She steered Raistlin to the other side of the street.

"Do you have a place to stay in Neraka?" she asked.

Raistlin shook his head. "I am newly arrived in this city. I came to the temple first. I was hoping to find rooms at the Tower. I trust there are some available? A small cell, such as they might give a novice, would suit me. The only possessions I own I carry with me. Or rather, I used to carry them."

"I am sorry about the loss of your staff," said Iolanthe. "I fear you will never see it again. The Nightlord knows magic, and he was quick to recognize its value—"

"There was no help for it," said Raistlin with a shrug of his thin shoulders.

"You do not appear to be overly concerned about its loss," Iolanthe said, giving him a sharp look.

"I can buy another staff at any mageware shop," Raistlin said with a rueful smile. "I cannot buy another life."

"I suppose that is true," Iolanthe conceded. "Still, the loss must be devastating."

Raistlin shrugged again.

He is taking it far too well, Iolanthe thought. Something else is going on here. What a marvelous mystery this young man is proving! She was growing quite fascinated by him.

"You can stay with me tonight," she said. "Though you will have to sleep on the floor. Tomorrow we will find you a room."

"I am an old campaigner. I can sleep anywhere," said Raistlin. He seemed disappointed. "You appear to be telling me there is no room for me in the Tower."

"You keep mentioning this tower? What tower are you talking about?" Iolanthe asked.

"The Tower of High Sorcery, of course," said Raistlin.

Iolanthe regarded him with amusement. "Ah, *that* Tower. I will take you there on the morrow. The hour is late—or early, depending on how you look at it."

Raistlin glanced up and down the street. No one was around, but he lowered his voice anyway. "What the Nightlord said about Ladonna and Nuitari. Is that true?"

"I was hoping *you* would know," said Iolanthe.

He started to reply, but she shook her head. "Such dangerous matters should be discussed behind closed doors."

Raistlin nodded in understanding.

"We will talk about it when we reach my home," Iolanthe said, adding demurely, "over a game of marbles."

3
A cup of tea. Memories.
A dangerous woman.

6th Day, Month of Mishamont, Year 352 AC

t was well after Dark Watch. Raistlin hoped they did not have far to go, for his strength was almost gone. They turned into a street outside the temple walls known as Wizard's Row, and he was relieved to hear Iolanthe say that this was the street on which she lived. The street was narrow and out of the way, little more than a glorified alley. The name came from the various shops that sold goods related to magic. Most of the shops, Raistlin noted, appeared to be empty. Several had *To Let* signs posted in broken windows.

Iolanthe's small apartment was located above one of the few mageware shops still in business. They climbed a long, narrow staircase, and he waited while she removed the wizard lock on her door. Once inside, she provided her guest with a pillow and a blanket and rearranged the furniture in the small room she termed her "library," so he could make up his bed on the floor. She bade him good night and went to her room, telling him as she left that she was a late riser and did not take kindly to being awakened before noon.

Exhausted from his experiences in the dungeon, Raistlin lay down on the floor, covered himself with the blanket, and fell immediately asleep. He dreamed of the dungeons, of hanging naked from chains, of a man holding a burning hot rod of iron coming toward him . . .

Raistlin woke with a gasp. Sunlight flooded the room. He did not at first remember where he was, and he stared around in confusion until memory brought the events of last night back to him. He sighed and closed his eyes. He reached out his hand, as he normally did of a morning, and felt the staff lying by his side; its smooth wood warm and reassuring.

Raistlin smiled to think of the discomfiture the Nightlord would feel when he went to gloat over the valuable artifact he had lately acquired, only to discover it had disappeared during the night. One of the staff's magical powers was that it always returned to its owner. Raistlin had known, when he handed it over, that the staff would come back to him.

Stiff from sleeping on the hard floor, he sat up, rubbing his back and neck to try to ease the kinks in his muscles. The small apartment was quiet. His hostess was not yet awake. Raistlin was glad for a chance to be alone, to sort out his thoughts.

He performed his ablutions then boiled water to prepare the herbal tea that eased his cough. The Nightlord had taken his herbs away from him, but they were common enough, and a rummage through Iolanthe's kitchen produced all he needed. It was only when he was pouring the water into the kettle that he remembered that he didn't need to drink his tea; his cough was gone. He was well again. Fistandantilus was no longer leeching away half his life.

Raistlin was accustomed to drinking the tea, and he continued to brew it. Unfortunately, the task brought back memories of his brother. Caramon had always fixed Raistlin's tea for him, making of it a daily ritual. Their friends, Tanis and the others, had watched Caramon do the menial work for his twin in disapproval.

"Your legs aren't broke," Flint had once said to Raistlin. "Fix your own damn tea!"

Raistlin could have brewed his own tea, of course, but it wouldn't have been the same. He allowed his brother to prepare his tea not, as his friends thought, to exhibit his ascendancy over Caramon or demean him. The homely act brought back fond memories to both of them, memories of the years they had walked strange and dangerous roads, each watching the other's back, each dependent on the other for companionship and protection.

Raistlin sat before the kitchen fire, listening to the water bubble in the teakettle, and he thought of those days alone on the road, their small cooking fire blazing beneath the greater, more glorious fire of the sun. Caramon would sit on a log or a boulder or whatever happened to be handy, holding the clay mug in one big hand that almost engulfed it, sprinkling the herbs from the bag into the water, measuring out the leaves with care and intense concentration.

Raistlin, sitting nearby, would watch with impatience, telling Caramon that he did not need to be so careful; he could just dump the leaves in the cup.

Caramon would always say no, it was important to have the proper mixture. Did he or did he not know how to make an excellent cup of tea? Raistlin would always admit that his brother did make wonderful tea; that was true. No matter how hard Raistlin tried, he had never been able to duplicate Caramon's recipe. No matter how hard he tried, Raistlin's tea did not taste the same. His scientific mind scoffed at the fact that love and care could make a difference to a cup of tea, but he had to admit he could find no other explanation.

He poured the boiling water into the mug and shook out the herbs, which floated on the top before sinking. The smell was always slightly unpleasant; the taste was not that bad. He'd grown to like it. He sipped at the tea, a stranger in a strange city, the heart of the forces of darkness, and he thought of himself and Caramon, sitting together in the sunshine, laughing over some silly jest, recalling incidents from their childhood, recounting some of their adventures and the wonders they had seen.

Raistlin felt a burning in his eyes and a choking sensation in his throat that did not come from his former malady. The choking came from a heart swelling with emotion, from loss and loneliness, guilt and grief and remorse. Raistlin took an unusually large gulp of the tea and burned the roof of his mouth. He swore angrily beneath his breath, and flung the contents of the mug into the fire.

"Serves me right for being maudlin," he muttered. He banished all thought of Caramon from his mind and, finding some bread in the pantry, toasted it over the fire and chewed on it as he thought over his situation.

His arrival in Neraka had not turned out as planned. He had deliberately chosen to appear in the temple by traveling the corridors of magic. His idea had been that he would materialize inside the temple to the awe and astonishment of all who witnessed him. The clerics would be so impressed by his exhibition of magical power, they would escort him straightway to

Emperor Ariakas, who would beg Raistlin to join him in conquering the world.

Things had not turned out as planned. Raistlin had achieved one of his goals; the dark pilgrims had certainly been astonished to see him burst out of thin air inside the abbey, just as they were starting services. One elderly pilgrim had nearly suffered apoplexy, and another had fainted dead away.

Far from being impressed, the dark pilgrims had been outraged. They had tried to seize him, but he had fended them off with the Staff of Magius, which administered a strong jolt to anyone it touched. As they crowded around him, shouting and threatening, Raistlin had urged everyone to remain calm. He was not here to cause trouble, he explained. He would go with them willingly. He wanted only to pay his respects to his Queen. He had found himself instead paying his respects to the loathsome Nightlord.

Raistlin had almost immediately seen the man for what he was: a demented man who took physical pleasure and gratification in the suffering of others. Raistlin had realized at once that he was in deadly peril, though he was confused as to why.

"We are all on the same side," the mage had tried to tell the Nightlord. "All of us want to see Queen Takhisis victorious. Why, then, do you view me with such enmity? Why threaten me with unspeakable horrors unless I reveal myself to be a spy for the Conclave? Why would the Conclave want to spy on the Dark Queen's clerics? It makes no sense."

Or rather, it had made no sense until he had heard the Nightlord say that Nuitari had turned against his mother.

The questioning had gone on hour after weary hour. All the while Raistlin could hear the shrieks and howls and screams of other prisoners, the turning of the rack, the snaps of the lash. He could smell the burning flesh.

The Nightlord had grown frustrated with Raistlin's denials.

"You will tell me all you know and more," the Nightlord had said. "Send for the Adjudicator."

Raistlin had tried to use the Staff of Magius, but the guards had rushed him and, at the cost of a few jolts, had knocked the staff out of his hand onto the floor. He had then cast a Circle of Protection around himself. The Nightlord was expert at dealing with uncooperative wizards, however. He had spoken a few words and pointed his bloodstained fingernails at Raistlin, and the protection spell had shattered like a crystal goblet dropped on a marble floor.

Raistlin had known fear unlike any he'd ever experienced, worse even than the time he'd been lying helpless beneath the claws of a black dragon in Xak Tsaroth. The guards began closing in on him, and he had no way to fight them. Then something strange had happened. He had yet to find an explanation. The guards had not been able to lay their hands on him.

He had not done anything to defend himself. He had no energy left to cast any more magic. The trip through the corridors of magic, the subsequent fight, the casting of the Circle of Protection spell, had all weakened him. Yet the simple fact was, every time the guards had tried to seize him, they had started to shake so severely, they could not make their fingers work.

Raistlin sat cross-legged on the floor. He opened the pouch containing the marbles and shook them out. The dragon orb rolled around, indistinguishable from the other marbles except to his eyes. One of the facts he had learned about the dragon orb was that it had an instinct for self-preservation as great or greater than his own.

He picked up the dragon orb and held it in his palm and gazed at it, pondering, wondering. He had taken a risk bringing the orb to Neraka, to the heart of the Dark Queen's empire. Made of the essence of evil dragons, the orb might feel emboldened, here among its own kind, so close to its evil Queen. It might turn on him, find a master more important, more powerful.

Instead, it seemed, the orb had chosen to protect him. Not out of love for him, Raistlin was sure. Raistlin shook his head, bemused at the thought. The orb was interested only in protecting itself. And that was an unsettling thought. The orb sensed danger. The orb believed it was in peril, and that meant he was in peril.

But from what? From whom? This city, of all places, should be a safe haven for those who walked the paths of darkness.

"By Nuitari, you really *do* play with marbles," exclaimed Iolanthe. She wrinkled her nose and coughed. "What is that ghastly smell?"

Raistlin had been so lost in his thoughts that he had not heard her stirring. Hastily, he scooped up the marbles along with the dragon orb and dropped them into the pouch.

"I fixed myself a cup of tea," he said blandly. "I have been ill, and I find it helps."

Iolanthe opened a casement to let in air, though the smell outside was almost as bad as that within. The air was gray with smoke that billowed from the forge fires and reeked from the stench of the garbage-filled alleys and the foul water that ran ankle deep in the gutters.

"This illness," said Iolanthe, waving her hand to dissipate the smell. "Was it a result of the Test?"

"An aftereffect," Raistlin replied, surprised that she would immediately jump to that conclusion.

"And was that how you came to have gold skin and hourglass eyes?"

Raistlin nodded.

"The sacrifices we make for the magic," Iolanthe said with a sigh. She shut the window and locked it. "I did not come out unscathed. No one does. I bear my scars on the inside."

Iolanthe rumpled her dark hair and sighed again. She was dressed in a silken gown known as a caftan by those who lived in the eastern land of Khur. The silk was sumptuous and vividly colored; red and blue birds amid purple and orange flowers, green leaves and twining vines.

Raistlin found himself disconcerted by the woman. Her frank manner of speaking, her charm, her wit, her humor and vivacity and her beauty—especially her beauty—made him uncomfortable.

For even with his accursed vision, he could see that Iolanthe was beautiful. Her blue-black hair and violet eyes and olive skin were different from the other women he'd known in his life. Women such as Laurana, the elf maiden, who was blonde, fair, ethereal; or Tika, with her fiery red curls and her generous smile; voluptuous, laughing, wholesome, and loving.

By contrast, Iolanthe was mystery, danger, intrigue. She made Raistlin nervous. Even her clothing, with its myriad colors, made him uneasy. He disapproved. Those who took the black robes and walked shadowy places should not bring beauty and color with them.

She was smiling at him, and he realized he'd been staring at her. His skin burned, much to his irritation. He had conquered a dragon orb, imprisoned Fistandantilus inside it, and faced down the Nightlord, but he felt himself blushing like a pimply teenager just because a lovely woman smiled at him.

"I see the Nightlord returned your staff," Iolanthe said. "How very kind of him. He is not usually so considerate."

Raistlin was startled by her remark; then he saw the glint of laughter in her violet eyes. He realized he should have had devised some explanation for the staff's reappearance, but he had been too absorbed in wondering about the workings of the dragon orb. He tried to think of something plausible to say, but he was tongue-tied. The woman confused him, turned his brain to gruel. The sooner he was away from her, the better.

Iolanthe knelt on the floor, her silken caftan floating around her, filling the air with the scent of gardenia perfume. She studied the staff, not touching it, but looking intently at the smooth wood and the dragon's claw clutching a crystal ball that adorned the top.

"So this is the famed Staff of Magius," she said.

Once again, she caught Raistlin off guard. He stared at her, dumbfounded.

"I took the opportunity of doing a little research last night after you were asleep," she told him. "There are not that many magical staffs in the world. I found the description in an old book. How did you come by it, if I might ask?"

Raistlin was going to tell her it was none of her business. Instead, he found himself saying, "Par-Salian gave it to me after I passed the Test."

"Par-Salian?" Iolanthe sank bank languidly on the floor, propping herself up on her elbow. "The Head of the Order of *White* Robes? He gave you this valuable gift?"

"I was a White Robe when I took the Test," said Raistlin. "Due to the kind interest Lunitari took in me, I afterward wore the red robes. I have only recently taken the black."

"All three," Iolanthe murmured. Her violet eyes gazed at him. The black pupils dilated, seeming to widen in order to absorb him. "How very unusual."

She rose gracefully to her feet, her caftan swirling around her bare feet. "It is said that the Master of Past and Present will be one who wore all three robes."

Raistlin stared at her.

"And now, if you will excuse me," she continued coolly, "I will go change into my *black* robes for our trip to the Tower of High Sorcery. I would wear my caftan, for I like bright colors, but the old buzzards who live there would have a collective stroke."

She wafted out of the room; her perfume lingering. The smell tickled Raistlin's nose and made him sneeze. She returned wearing robes of black silk similar to the caftan in cut and design, leaving her forearms bare. He heard a faint jingling of bells as she walked and saw that she wore a circlet of tiny, golden bells around her ankle. The sound was jarring and set his teeth on edge.

"I usually wear golden bracelets to match," Iolanthe remarked as though she read his thoughts. She nibbled on some of the dry toast Raistlin had left uneaten and, picking up the mug, sniffed at the remnants of his tea and made a face. "But I dare not wear my jewels around Neraka anymore. The soldiers have not been paid, you see. The Emperor was counting upon steel flowing into his coffers from the wealth he would seize in Palanthas. Unfortunately for him, we hear that silver dragons have come to guard that fair city."

"That is true," said Raistlin. "I saw them before I left."

"So you came from Palanthas," said Iolanthe. "How interesting."

Raistlin cursed himself for having revealed such information. The woman *was* a witch!

"Anyhow," Iolanthe continued, "Ariakas lost all that revenue. What was worse, having been confident he would gain the steel, he had already spent it. Now he is deep in debt, though only a few people know that."

"And why now am I one of them?" Raistlin asked, annoyed. "Why are you telling me this? I don't want to hear it. Spreading such rumors is . . . is . . ."

"An act of treason?" Iolanthe shrugged. "Yes, I suppose so. But they are not rumors, Raistlin Majere. They are facts. I should know. I am Ariakas's mistress."

Raistlin felt the hair rise on his arms and prick the back of his neck. His life hung by a silken thread.

"I am also," she added smoothly, "a friend to your half-sister, Dragon Highlord Kitiara uth Matar."

Raistlin's jaw dropped. "You know . . . my sister?"

"Oh, yes," Iolanthe said. She was quiet a moment, then launched suddenly into a tirade. *"Her* troops, the soldiers of the Blue Dragonarmy, are being paid . . . well paid. Although she failed to take Palanthas, she controls much of Solamnia. She demands and receives tribute from the wealthy cities which she had sense enough *not* to burn to the ground. And she sees to it that the payment goes to her soldiers. Kit's blue dragons are loyal and well disciplined unlike the reds, who are brainless and conceited and continually fight among themselves. Ariakas stupidly allowed his reds and his soldiers to pillage and loot and set fire the cities he took, and now he grumbles that he has no money."

Raistlin remembered Solace, the burned-out Inn of the Last Home where he had spent so many happy hours. He remembered the terrifying siege of Tarsis. He kept silent, but inwardly he allowed himself a grim smile of satisfaction at Ariakas's self-inflicted predicament.

The smile vanished when Iolanthe impulsively clasped his hand. "It's so good to have someone to talk to. Someone who understands. A friend!"

Raistlin withdrew his hand from hers. "I am not a friend," he said, and thinking that might sound rude, he added abruptly, "We just met. You hardly know me."

"I feel like I know you well," said Iolanthe, not the least offended. "Kitiara talks about you a great deal. She is very proud of you and your brother. Where is he, by the way?"

Raistlin decided it was time to change the subject. "What the Nightlord said last night about Nuitari—"

"True," said Iolanthe. "Every word, except for the part about Ladonna being executed. I would have heard. But Nuitari has broken with his mother, Takhisis, and now the Conclave of Wizards will unite against the Dark Queen."

Raistlin was quiet, noncommittal. He was not part of the Conclave. He had not sought their permission to take the black robes. He had done so without consulting them, in fact, and that made him a renegade. The Conclave considered renegade wizards outlaws.

Iolanthe drew nearer to him. Her perfume filled his nostrils and made his head throb.

"I know what you are thinking," she said softly, "because I am thinking the same: What does this mean for me?" She gave him a playful pat on the shoulder. "We should go to 'the Tower' and find out."

Casting him a glance over her shoulder, she added, "My people have a saying: 'A man should use his breath to cool his tea.' That's good advice anywhere in Neraka, but it especially applies to our fellow wizards."

"I understand," Raistlin said. He felt a flutter of excitement. At last he was to see the wondrous Tower of High

Sorcery, meet the wizards who would help shape his destiny.

"Shall we leave? Are you ready?" Iolanthe saw his eye go to his staff, and she shook her head. "You should not carry that in public. The Nightlord will be searching for it. The staff should be safe enough here. I always cast warding spells upon my door."

"The staff will keep itself safe," Raistlin said. He didn't like leaving it; he had come to depend on it. But he understood the wisdom of her advice.

Iolanthe shut and locked the door and traced a rune upon it with her fingertip; then she spoke a few words of magic. The rune began to glow a faint bluish color.

Iolanthe caught Raistlin's eye and flushed. "Amateurish, I know. A spell such as one casts in mage school. But weak minds find the glowing rune impressive. And believe me," she added, "we deal with a lot of weak minds around Neraka."

Iolanthe took hold of Raistlin's arm, telling him to act as her escort, whether he wanted to or not. "The streets are dangerous these days," she said. "It pays to have someone watching your back."

Raistlin didn't like it, but he could not very well repulse Iolanthe. She had already made it clear that she could help him or harm him and that the choice was his. The staircase was narrow, and she pressed against him, insisting on walking close by his side.

"How many stairs?" she asked teasingly.

"Thirty-one," he replied. "Counting the landing."

Iolanthe shook her head and laughed at him.

Raistlin could not see what she thought was so funny.

4

INN OF THE BROKEN SHIELD. THE TOWER OF HIGH SORCERY.

6th Day, Month of Mishamont, Year 352 AC

Iolanthe decided to first introduce Raistlin to her neighbor and landlord, the owner of the mageware shop. The proprietor was an elderly gentleman with the unlikely name of Snaggle. He was some sort of half-breed, so stooped and dried up and wrinkled that it was impossible to tell if he was half-dwarf or half-goblin or half-mongrel dog. He greeted Raistlin with a toothless grin and offered him a discount on his first purchase.

"Snaggle is an excellent man to know," Iolanthe explained as they walked down the broad, paved street that ran in front of the temple. "He never asks questions. He gives fair value for the steel. And because he is favored by the Emperor, who regularly shops there, Snaggle often carries items that would be difficult for others to acquire. He won't sell to just anyone, mind you, but he knows now that you are my friend, so you will find him accommodating."

Raistlin was not her friend, though he did not say so. He had never had friends. Tanis and Flint and the others called themselves his friends, but he knew that beneath their smiles they did not love him, did not trust him. He was not like his brother, jovial, warm-hearted Caramon—everyone's boon companion.

Raistlin studied his surroundings with his usual care as they continued on their way. "Where are we going?" he asked.

"To the White District," Iolanthe replied. "The city of Neraka is like Queen Takhisis in a way: A dragon with a single heart and five heads. The heart is the temple in the center; the heads are the armies that guard it. Since you materialized inside the temple, I take it you did not get a good look at the outside."

The temple was surrounded by high, stone walls and was difficult to see from their angle. Iolanthe led Raistlin to the front gate, which was standing wide open, for a better view. The mage gazed at the temple and thought he had never seen anything so hideous. Takhisis had a sense of humor, apparently, albeit a twisted one. Once long in the past there had been, in the city of Istar, a radiant and holy and beautiful temple dedicated to Paladine, God of Light. The Temple of Takhisis was a distorted, perverted mockery of that ancient temple, which lay fathoms deep beneath the Blood Sea. A thing of darkness, Takhisis's temple cast a pall over the entire city, like the unnatural darkness of an eclipse, when the moon blots out the sun, except that an eclipse ends. The temple's darkness in the midst of daylight was constant.

"Ugly as sin, isn't it?" Iolanthe said, regarding the temple with distaste. "Evil should be beautiful. It does so much more damage that way. Don't you agree?" Her violent eyes glittered, and she gave him a sly smile.

They continued along the main street, which ran outside the temple, known as Queen's Way.

"We are now in what they call the Inner City," Iolanthe said. "The temple is surrounded by a wall, and Neraka is surrounded by its own wall. Outside that wall, the five dragonarmies have their camps. Inside the wall, each dragonarmy has its own district."

Raistlin already knew that from his studies of Neraka in the Great Library. Due to distrust and intrigues and competition for advancement among the five Dragon Highlords—qualities Ariakas fostered—every district was self-sufficient. Each had its own smithies, shops, dwellings, barracks, and so on. No Highlord wanted to have to rely on another for anything. Needless to say, rivalries among the soldiers were also encouraged.

"We are going outside the walls. Bloody hell!" Iolanthe stopped. She looked annoyed. "I forgot. You don't have a black pass."

"A black pass? What is that?" Raistlin asked.

Iolanthe reached into one of the silken pouches she wore on her belt and took out a bit of paper. The ink was faded, but still possible to read. The seal of the Church—a five-headed dragon stamped in black wax—was affixed at the bottom.

"It's called a black pass because of the black wax seal. All citizens must have this letter from the Church giving us permission to live and work in the city. Once you are outside the walls, you won't be able to get back inside without this. And after last night, I doubt very much if the Nightlord will grant you one."

Iolanthe pondered the problem a moment, frowning and tapping her foot. Then her face cleared. "Ah, I have the answer. I don't know why I didn't think of this before. Come along."

She latched hold of him again and hauled him off, heading for the wall and the gate that led through it.

"Are you feverish?" Iolanthe asked suddenly, reaching up to feel his forehead.

"My body temperature is unnaturally high," Raistlin said, flinching away from her touch.

She seemed to find his reaction amusing. He wondered irritably if she enjoyed making him feel uncomfortable.

"Nervous energy?" she suggested.

Again, Raistlin was forced to turn the subject from himself. "You mentioned that Emperor Ariakas frequented your friend's shop. I had heard the Emperor is a wizard, something I find hard to believe since I also hear he is a warrior who wears armor and wields a sword. Others say he is a cleric, devoted to Takhisis. Which is the truth?"

"Both, in a way," said Iolanthe, her expression darkening. "The Emperor goes into battle wearing full plate and chain mail and carrying a two-handed greatsword. He is not one to lead from the rear. He is no coward. He loves nothing better than to be in the thick of the fray. And while he is lopping off heads with one hand, he is casting fiery darts of magic with the other."

"That is not possible," Raistlin said flatly.

As he was constantly having to remind Caramon, who was always wanting him to learn to wield a sword, the art of magic required constant, daily study. Those who dedicate themselves to the magic do not have the time to pursue other interests, including martial skills. In addition, armor impeded the mage from making the complex hand motions often required for spellcasting. And many mages, such as Raistlin, believed that magic was a far more powerful weapon than a sword.

"Lord Ariakas is something of a cleric," Iolanthe was saying. "He acquires his magic directly from Queen Takhisis herself."

They passed through the White Gate, under the control of the Green Dragonarmy, commanded by Highlord Salah-Kahn. The White Dragonarmy, formerly under the late Dragon Highlord Feal-Thas, had been considerably reduced since the Highlord's death, most of its troops reassigned. The soldiers of the Green Dragonarmy were from Iolanthe's homeland of Khur. She was well known among them and well liked, for she took care to cultivate their good opinion.

His hood pulled low to conceal his face, Raistlin watched in silence, as she flirted and laughed and teased her way through the gate. No one asked to see his pass.

"They will want to see it on the way back in, however," Iolanthe said. "But don't worry. All will be well."

Leaving the Inner City was like stepping from dark and quiet night into loud and blaring day. The sun blazed hotly, as though glad to escape the Dark Queen's shadow. The dirt streets were jammed with wagons, carts, and all manner of people, every one of them yelling at the top of his or her lungs.

Raistlin was trying to cross the street without being run down by a cart, when he bumped into a soldier, who swore at him viciously and pulled his knife. Iolanthe lifted her hand; flames crackled ominously from her fingers, and the soldier glared and went on. She dragged Raistlin off, both of them walking carefully to avoid tumbling into the deep ruts worn by the wagon wheels.

The streets were clogged with soldiers of all races—humans, ogres, goblins, minotaurs, and draconians. The draconians were disciplined, orderly, their weapons shining, leather polished. Human soldiers, by contrast, were slovenly, raucous, sullen, and surly. Ogres kept to themselves, looking brooding and put-upon. Two minotaurs walked proudly past, their horned heads held high, regarding all other puny beings with magnificent disdain. Goblins and hobgoblins, whom everyone despised, slogged through the mud, ducking their hairy heads to avoid blows.

Quarrels between the troops often broke out, resulting in heated exchanges and drawn swords. At the first shout, the elite draconian temple guards would appear, as if from nowhere. The combatants would eye them, then snarl and retreat, like curs when the master brandishes the whip.

The noise and confusion of rumbling carts, swearing men, barking dogs, and shrill-voiced whores gave Raistlin a throbbing headache. The air was thick with smoke from the forge fires and the cook fires of the various army camps, whose tents were visible in the distance. A most foul odor came from a nearby tannery and mingled with livestock smells from the stockyard and fresh blood from the butcher's.

Iolanthe covered her mouth with a perfumed handkerchief.

"Thank goodness we're almost there," said Iolanthe as she gestured to a large and sprawling collection of buildings across the street from where they were standing. "The Inn of the Broken Shield. You should seek lodging there."

Raistlin shook his head. "I have read of it. I can't afford it."

"Oh, yes, you can," said Iolanthe, and she winked at him. "I have an idea."

She glanced both ways, then plunged out into the street. Raistlin followed, both of them running and stumbling over the ruts, dodging horses and marching soldiers.

Raistlin had read a description of the inn in his studies of Neraka. An Aesthetic with the unlikely name of Cameroon Bunks had risked his life to venture into the city of the Dark Queen in order to explore it and return to report on what he had seen.

He wrote: *The Inn of the Broken Shield began when proprietor Talent Orren, a former sellsword from Lemish, used his winnings at gambling to purchase a one-room shack in the White District of Neraka. The story goes that Orren had no steel for a sign, so he nailed his own cracked shield over the door and called the shack the "Broken Shield." Orren served food that was plain, but good. He did not water the ale nor gouge his customers. With the influx of soldiers and dark pilgrims into Neraka, he soon had more business than he could handle. Later, Orren added a room to the shack and called it the "Broken Shield Tavern." Later still, he added several blocks of rooms to the tavern and changed the name to the "Inn of the Broken Shield."*

There were so many buildings, each with several entrances, that Raistlin had no idea which door was the main one. Iolanthe chose a door seemingly at random, as far as Raistlin could tell, until he glanced up to see a shield—cracked down the middle—hanging above it.

A weather-beaten placard nailed to the door bore the words, scrawled in Common, *Humans Only!* Ogres, goblins, draconians, and minotaurs did their drinking in the Hair of the Troll, popularly known as the Hairy Troll.

Iolanthe was starting to push on the swinging, double doors when they suddenly flew open. A man in a white shirt and leather doublet appeared, carrying a kender by the scruff of her neck and the seat of her britches. The man gave a heave-ho and flung the kender into the street, where she landed belly-first in the mud.

"And don't come back!" the man yelled, shaking his fist.

"Ah, you know you'd miss me, Talent!" the kender returned, cheerfully picking herself up. She wandered off down the street, wiping muck from her eyes and wringing mud from her straggling braids.

"Vermin!" the man muttered as he turned to smile at Iolanthe. He made a graceful bow. "Welcome, Madam Iolanthe. It is a pleasure to see you, as always. Who is your friend?"

Iolanthe performed introductions. "Raistlin Majere, meet Talent Orren, owner of the Inn of the Broken Shield."

Orren bowed again. Raistlin inclined his hooded head, and both men studied each other. Orren was of medium height, with a slender, almost delicate build. He was good looking, with brown eyes that were keen and penetrating. He had shoulder-length dark hair, carefully combed, and a thin mustache on his upper lip. He wore a white shirt with long, flowing sleeves, the neck open, and tight leather pants. A long sword hung from his side. He held the door open and politely ushered Iolanthe into the inn. Raistlin started to follow, only to find himself blocked by Orren's muscular arm.

"Humans only," Orren said, "as the sign says."

Raistlin flushed in anger and embarrassment.

"Oh, for mercy's sake, he *is* human, Orren!" said Iolanthe.

"I have never seen a human with such funny-colored skin," Orren said, unconvinced. His voice was cultivated. Raistlin thought he detected a faint Solamnic accent.

Iolanthe grabbed hold of Raistlin's wrist. "Humans come in all different colors, Orren. My friend happens to be a little peculiar; that's all."

She whispered into Orren's ear, and he regarded Raistlin with more interest. "Is this the truth? Are you Kitiara's brother?"

Raistlin opened his mouth to reply, but Iolanthe answered for him.

"Of course he is," she said briskly. "You can see the family resemblance." She lowered her voice. "And I wouldn't go shouting Kitiara's name in the streets. Not these days."

Talent smiled. "You have a point, Iolanthe, my sweet. You do resemble your sister, sir, and that is a compliment, for she is a lovely woman."

Raistlin did not comment. He did not think he and Kitiara looked alike; they were, after all, only half brother and sister. Kitiara had black curls and brown eyes. She took after her father, who had been darkly handsome. Raistlin's hair had been like Caramon's, a russet color, before the Test had turned his hair prematurely white.

What Raistlin did not realize was that both he and Kit had the same fire in their eyes, the same determination to gain what they wanted no matter what the cost—even to themselves.

Orren allowed Raistlin to enter, graciously holding the door for him. The inn was crowded and noisy; they were serving the midday dinner crowd. Iolanthe told Talent she needed to talk business. He stated that he had no time at the present, but he would talk to her when the rush was over.

She and Raistlin walked past several tables occupied by dark pilgrims, who regarded them with frowns and disapproving glares. Raistlin heard the muttered word "witch," and he glanced at his companion. Iolanthe had heard as well, to judge by the color that had mounted to her cheeks. She pretended she had not, however, and swept past them.

Several soldiers regarded her with more favor, speaking to her respectfully as "Mistress Iolanthe" and asking if she would join them. Iolanthe always declined, but with some clever remark that left the soldiers laughing. She guided Raistlin to a small table in a shadowed corner underneath the broad staircase that led to the upper rooms.

A soldier was already seated there, but he immediately rose when he saw her coming. Picking up his food and drink, he relinquished the table to her with a grin.

Raistlin sank gratefully into the chair. His health might be improved, but he still found that he tired easily. The serving girl came hurrying to take their order, pausing frequently on her way to knock aside a pawing hand, slap a face, or expertly jam her elbow into a rib cage. She did not appear angry or even overly annoyed.

"I can handle myself," she said, seeming to guess what Raistlin was thinking. "And the boys watch out for me."

She gave a nod to several very large men, who were standing with their backs against the walls, keeping watchful eyes on the patrons. At that moment, one of the men left his post and went charging into the crowd to break up a fight. Both combatants were speedily ejected.

"Strange to see peace reign in a tavern that caters to soldiers," Raistlin remarked.

"Talent learned early in his career that barroom brawls are bad for business, particularly with the religious types," Iolanthe said. "These dark pilgrims will watch a ritual blood sacrifice to their Queen without turning a hair, but let a man bloody another man's nose during the supper hour, and the pilgrims would keel over in shock."

The serving girl brought the food, which was, as the Aesthetic had written, plain but good. Iolanthe ate a shepherd's pie with a healthy appetite. Raistlin nibbled at some boiled chicken. What he could not finish, Iolanthe ate for him.

"You should eat more," she said to him. "Keep up your strength. You will need it this afternoon."

"What do you mean?" Raistlin asked, alarmed at her ominous tone.

"You will find the Tower of High Sorcery in Neraka a surprise," she said quietly.

Raistlin was going to press her for more information, but Talent Orren joined them at that moment. Hauling over a chair from another table, he turned it around and straddled it, resting his arms on the back.

"What can I do for you, my adorable witch?" he said with a playful smile for Iolanthe. "You know that I live to serve you."

"I know that you live to charm the ladies," returned Iolanthe, grinning.

Raistlin started to draw out his purse. Iolanthe shook her head.

"My lord Ariakas will have the pleasure of paying for lunch. Put our meals on the Emperor's tab, will you, Talent? And add something for the girl and for yourself."

"Your wish is my command," said Talent. "Anything else I can do for you?"

"I want a room in your boarding house for my friend," Iolanthe continued. "Just a small room, nothing fancy. His needs are simple."

"I am generally full, but as it happens, I have a room available," said Orren. "It opened up this morning." He added matter-of-factly, "Occupant died in his sleep."

He named a price. Raistlin did some rapid calculations and shook his head. "I am afraid I cannot afford—"

Iolanthe stopped him, closing her hand over his. "Kitiara will pay for him. He is, after all, her brother."

Talent slapped the back of the chair. "Then it is all settled. You can move in any time, Majere. I fear you will notice a strong odor of paint, but we had to use several coats to cover up the blood spatters. Collect the key on the way out. Number thirty-nine. Third floor, turn to your right, then make a left at the end of the corridor. Anything else?"

Iolanthe said something in a low voice. Talent listened intently, glanced at Raistlin, raised an eyebrow, then smiled.

"Of course. Wait here."

"You can put that on Ariakas's tab as well," Iolanthe called to him.

Talent laughed as he headed back to the bar.

"Don't worry," said Iolanthe when Raistlin began to protest. "I will speak to Kit. She will be thrilled to hear you are in Neraka. As for paying for your room, she can easily afford it."

"Nevertheless," said Raistlin firmly, "I will not be beholden to anyone, not even my sister. I will pay her back the moment I am able."

"How very noble," said Iolanthe, amused by his scruples. "And now, if you are feeling better, we will visit the Tower, and I will introduce you to your esteemed colleagues."

Iolanthe was in the act of reaching for her purse when the serving girl came by. Iolanthe stood up and the two collided, causing Iolanthe to drop her purse and spill the contents. Iolanthe angrily scolded the serving girl, who apologized most profusely and picked up the scattered coins and trinkets, some of which Raistlin recognized as spell components.

When Raistlin rose from the table, Iolanthe took hold of his hand and slipped a rolled-up bit of paper into his palm. He concealed the paper in the long, full sleeves of his robes and deftly slipped it into one of his pouches. The black wax of the "official seal" was still warm to the touch.

Raistlin collected the key to number thirty-nine from one of the bartenders, who instructed him that after he had moved in he was to drop the key off whenever he left the premises and pick it up on his return. Iolanthe bid good-bye to Talent Orren, who was seated at a table with two dark pilgrims, one male and one female. Talent kissed Iolanthe's hand, much to the disapproval of the pilgrims, then went back to their conversation.

"I can get what you want," Talent was saying, "but it will cost you."

The dark pilgrims glanced at each other, and the woman smiled and nodded. The man drew out a heavy purse.

"What was that all about?" Raistlin asked as they left the inn.

"Oh, Talent is probably selling them something on the black market," Iolanthe said with a shrug. "Those two are Spiritors, high in the clerical hierarchy. Like many of Her Dark Majesty's followers, they have developed a taste for the finer things in life, such as thoroughbred horses from Khur, wine and silk from Qualinesti, and jewelry from the dwarf artisans of Thorbardin. Once these things were sold in the shops, but with the supply lines getting cut and losses mounting, such luxuries are becoming scarce."

"Interesting that Talent can lay his hands on them," Raistlin said.

"He has a way with people," Iolanthe said, smiling.

She took Raistlin's arm again, much to his discomfiture. He had expected that they would head back into the heart of the city. The Tower of High Sorcery would not be as grand or imposing as the Temple of the Dark Queen, of course. That would not be politic. But it ought to be located somewhere near Takhisis's temple.

He had thought it curious that he had not found a description of the Tower of High Sorcery in the Aesthetic's writings on Neraka. There could be many reasons for that. Every Tower of High Sorcery was guarded by a protective grove. The Tower of Palanthas had the dread Shoikan Grove. The Tower of Wayreth was surrounded by an enchanted forest. Perhaps the grove around the Nerakan Tower rendered it invisible.

Iolanthe did not turn toward the Temple of the Dark Queen, however. She walked in the opposite direction, taking a street that led into what appeared to be a warehouse district. The streets were less crowded here, for soldiers did not frequent the area. Raistlin could see workmen inside the warehouses rolling barrels into place, shifting crates, and unloading sacks of grain from the ubiquitous wagons.

"I thought we were going to the Tower," Raistlin said.

"We are," said Iolanthe.

Rounding a corner, drawing him with her, she stopped in front of a three-story building made of bricks, huddling in between a cooper's business on one side and a blacksmith's on the other. The building was black, not by design, but because the bricks were covered with dirt and soot. There were few windows, and most of those were cracked or broken.

"Where is the Tower?" asked Raistlin.

"You're looking at it," said Iolanthe.

5

Boiled cabbage. The new librarian.

6th Day, Month of Mishamont, Year 352 AC

T here must . . . there must be some mistake," said Raistlin, appalled.

"There is no mistake," said Iolanthe. "You look upon the repository of magic in the Dark Queen's realm."

She turned to face him. "*Now* do you understand? *Now* do you see why Nuitari broke with his mother? This"—she made a scathing gesture to the shabby, dirty, and decrepit building—"is the regard in which magic is held by the Queen of Darkness."

Raistlin had never known such bitter disappointment. He thought of the pain he had endured, the sacrifices he had made to get to this place, and tears of anger and frustration burned his eyes and blurred his vision.

Iolanthe gave his arm a sympathetic pat. "I am sorry to say it only gets worse from here. You have yet to meet your fellow Black Robes."

Her violet eyes, gazing at him, were piercing in their intensity. "You must decide, Raistlin Majere," she said softly. "Which side will you choose? Mother or son?"

"What about you?" he hedged.

Iolanthe laughed. "Oh, that is easy. I am always on my own side."

And her side appears to include serving my sister, Kitiara, Raistlin thought. That might work well for me, or it might not. I did not come to serve. I came to rule..

Sighing, Raistlin picked up the ruins of his shattered ambition and packed away the pieces. The path he had been walking had carried him not to glory but to a pig sty. He had to watch every step, look closely where he put his feet.

The door to the Tower of High Lunacy, as Iolanthe mockingly termed it, was guarded by a rune burned in the wood. The magical spell was rudimentary. A child could have removed it.

"Aren't you worried that people will break in?" Raistlin asked.

Iolanthe gave a delicate snort. "It will give you some idea of how little the people of Neraka care about us when I tell you that thus far no one has *ever* attempted to break into our Tower. People are quite right not to waste their time. There's nothing in here of value."

"But there must be a library," said Raistlin, his dismay growing. "Spellbooks, scrolls, artifacts . . ."

"Everything of value was sold off long ago to pay the rent on the building," said Iolanthe.

Pay the rent! Raistlin burned with shame. He thought of the grand and glorious and tragic histories of the Towers of High Sorcery down through the ages. Magnificent structures designed to inspire fear and awe in all who gazed upon them. He watched a rat run into a hole at the base of the brick wall and felt sick to his stomach.

Iolanthe dispelled the rune and shoved open the door leading to a small and filthy entryway. To their right, a corridor extended into dusty darkness. A rickety-looking staircase led up to the second floor.

"There are rooms here, but you see why I suggested you live somewhere else," said Iolanthe.

She called out, pitching her voice to carry to the second level. "It's me! Iolanthe! I'm coming upstairs. Don't cast any fireballs." She added in a disparaging undertone, "Not that the old farts could. What spells they ever knew, they long ago forgot."

"What is down that corridor?" Raistlin asked as they climbed the stairs that creaked ominously underfoot.

"Classrooms," said Iolanthe. "At least that's what they were meant to be. There were never any students."

Silence had greeted their arrival, but once Iolanthe had announced herself, voices broke out, high-pitched and querulous, pecking and clucking.

The second level was the common living and working space. The bedchambers were on the third floor. Iolanthe pointed out the laboratory, which consisted of a long worktable, set with cracked and dirty crockery, and a cauldron bubbling over a fire. The escaping steam told of boiled cabbage.

Next to the laboratory was the library. Raistlin looked through the door. The floor was covered with stacks and piles of books, parchments, and scrolls. Someone appeared to have started to sort through them, for a few books had been placed neatly on a shelf. After that, nothing had been done, apparently, except to create a bigger mess.

The largest room on that level, located across from the staircase, was the central living area. Iolanthe entered with Raistlin trailing behind her, keeping his hood over his head, his face in shadow. The room was furnished with a couple of broken-down couches, several wobbly-legged chairs, and a few small tables and storage chests. Three Black Robes—human males, well into their middle years—descended upon Iolanthe, all talking at once.

"Gentlemen," she said, raising her hands for silence. "I will deal with your concerns in a moment. First, I want to introduce Raistlin Majere, a new addition to our ranks."

The three Black Robes differed only in that one man had long gray hair and one had sparse gray hair and one had no hair at all. They were alike in that they loathed and distrusted each other, and all believed that magic was nothing but a tool to satisfy their own needs. Whatever souls they might have once possessed had been gnawed away by ignorance and greed. They were in Neraka because they had nowhere else to go.

Iolanthe named the three swiftly. The names passed in and out of Raistlin's head. He did not consider it worth taking the time to learn them, and as it turned out, he had no need to know. The Black Robes were not the least interested in him. Their only interest was themselves, and they bombarded Iolanthe with questions, demanding answers, then refusing to listen when she tried to give them.

They crowded around her in a suffocating circle. Raistlin remained on the outside, listening and observing.

"One of you—*one* of you," Iolanthe repeated sternly when they all seemed about to talk, "tell me the reason for this uproar."

The reason was given to her by the eldest mage, a seedy-looking old specimen with a crooked nose who had, Raistlin was to learn, eked out a living selling vile charms and dubious potions to peasants until forced to flee for his life after poisoning several of his patrons.

According to Hook Nose, as Raistlin nicknamed him, they had all heard the rumor that Nuitari had broken with Queen Takhisis, that Ladonna had been killed, and that they were all doomed.

"The Nightlord's guards will be breaking down our door at any moment!" Hook Nose said in panicked tones. "They suspect us of working for Hidden Light. We'll all end up in the Nightlord's dungeons!"

Iolanthe listened patiently and gave a light and airy laugh. "You may rest easy, gentlemen," she said. "I, too, heard these rumors. I was myself uneasy, and so I sought out the truth. All of you know that the eminent wizardess Ladonna was my mentor and sponsor."

The old men apparently knew that and were not impressed, for they said loudly that anything involving Ladonna would only add to their problems. Raistlin, who had not known it, wondered what it might mean. Was Iolanthe loyal to Ladonna?

"I spoke to her only last night. The rumor is completely false. Ladonna remains subject to Takhisis, as does her son, Nuitari. You have nothing to worry about. We may continue with business as normal."

Seeing the old men glower, Raistlin guessed that "business as normal" was not all that great. In confirmation, Iolanthe drew out her silken purse and removed several steel coins stamped with the five heads of the Dark Queen. She rested the coins on a table.

"There you are. Payment for the services performed by the Black Robes of Neraka."

She reeled off a list that included such tasks as rodent removal for a tailor's shop and mixing potions as ordered by Snaggle. Raistlin thought privately he would rather use a potion mixed by gully dwarves than anything those three old coots had concocted. He would later learn from

Iolanthe that she poured the potions into the Neraka sewer system. She funded the Tower herself.

"Otherwise," she told Raistlin privately, "these buzzards would go seeking work on their own, and Nuitari knows what sort of trouble they would bring down on me."

The old men were reassured by the sight of the coins far more than by Iolanthe's words. Hook Nose latched onto the coins, as the other two watched him jealously, and they began a lively discussion on how the steel was to be divided, each claiming that he deserved the largest share.

"I hate to interrupt," Iolanthe said loudly, "but I have a bit more business to conduct. I have introduced you to Raistlin Majere. He is a—"

"—a mere student of magic, sirs," said Raistlin in his soft voice. Keeping his head humbly bowed and his hands in his sleeves, he kept to the shadows. "I am still learning, and I look to you, my esteemed elders, for teaching and advice."

Hook Nose grunted. "He's not planning to live here, is he? Because there's no room."

"I have taken other lodging," Raistlin assured him. "I would be glad to work here, however—"

"Can you cook?" asked one. His double chin and large belly showed clearly where his interests lay. Raistlin named him Paunchy.

"I was thinking I might be of more use to you if I cataloged the books and scrolls in the library," Raistlin suggested.

"We need a cook," countered Paunchy testily. "I'm sick to death of boiled cabbage."

"Young Master Majere has an excellent idea," Iolanthe said, taking Raistlin's cue. "Since the rest of you are busy with far more important work, we can assign the library to our novice wizard. Who knows? He may discover something of value."

Hook Nose's eyes gleamed at that and he agreed, though Paunchy still grumbled about needing a cook, not a librarian. Raistlin was a fairly good cook, having prepared meals for himself and his brother when they were left orphaned as teenagers, and he promised to assist in that capacity too. Having satisfied everyone, he and Iolanthe departed.

"My robes stink of cabbage!" Iolanthe said, after the two of them left the three old men arguing how to spend the steel. "That horrid smell permeates everything. I will have to go home to change. Will you join me for supper? No cabbage, I promise!"

"I need to move my things into the inn—" Raistlin began.

Iolanthe interrupted him. "It's growing late. The streets of Neraka are not safe to walk after dark, especially in the Outer City. You should spend another night with me, move into the inn tomorrow. After all," she added in her mocking tone, "we have yet to play our game of marbles."

"Thank you, but I have imposed on your hospitality enough," said Raistlin, ignoring the remark about the marbles. "It will be safer for me to transport my things after darkness, don't you agree? Especially the staff. And I do not fear walking the streets after nightfall."

Iolanthe eyed him. "I suppose you are right. I have no doubt that you can take care of yourself. Which makes me wonder what you were up to back there. You—a mere student of magic! You can cast circles of fire around those old bastards. I think only one actually took the Test. The others are low-level, just about capable of boiling water."

"If I proclaimed my true skill, they would view me as a threat and would constantly be watching me, on their guard against me," explained Raistlin. "As it is, they will take me for granted. Which brings me to a question of my own: Why did you lie to them, tell them the rumors were not true?"

"They are terrified of the Nightlord. I know for a fact that one or all of them are informing on me," Iolanthe replied calmly. "If I had told them the rumors were true, they would have knocked me down to be first out the door with the news."

"Which is why you pay them," said Raistlin in sudden understanding.

"And why I tell them what I want the Nightlord to hear," said Iolanthe. "You must understand," she added somberly. "When Ladonna and the other Black Robes first came to Neraka, we had grand schemes and plans. We traveled here to make our fortunes. We were going to build a magnificent Tower of High Sorcery, the Tower of your dreams," she said, glancing at Raistlin with a rueful smile and a sigh.

"It soon became apparent to Ladonna and the others that wizards were not welcome in Neraka, not wanted. At first there were clashes with the Church; then the persecutions began. Three wizards—those who had been loud in arguing our cause—were assassinated in the night. The Church denied all knowledge, of course."

Raistlin frowned. "How is that possible? If these were high-level spellcasters, they could have easily defended themselves—"

Iolanthe shook her head. "The Nightlord has powerful forces at his command. The murders followed the same pattern. The bodies were desiccated. They had been drained of blood, sucked dry. They looked mummified, like those ancient kings of Ergoth. Their skin stuck like horrid parchment to their bones. The sight was ghastly. I still have nightmares about it."

He felt her shiver, and she pressed closer to him, glad to feel warmth and living flesh and bone.

"There was no evidence that the wizards had fought their attacker," she continued. "They had all died in their sleep, or so it appeared. And these were men and women with powerful magicks at their command, who had placed protective spells on their doors and persons. Ladonna called the assassin the 'Black Ghost.' We had no doubt that the Nightlord had summoned up some foul fiend from beyond the grave and commanded it to slay our comrades.

"Ladonna complained to the Emperor that the Church was killing her wizards. Ariakas told her curtly that he was far too busy pursing the war to become involved in a feud between 'Skirts'—his disparaging term for all who wear robes. Fearing for their lives, some of the high-level wizards either quietly returned to their homes or, like Dracart and Ladonna, agreed to work on 'secret projects' for the Dark Queen, though Ladonna apparently couldn't stomach that for long."

"And you?" Raistlin asked. "You do not fear this Black Ghost?"

Iolanthe shrugged. "I am Ariakas's mistress and under his protection. The Nightlord has no love for the Emperor, but Queen Takhisis does, though how long that will last, with the forces of Light starting to turn the tide, is open to question. For the time being, however, the Nightlord dares not cross the Emperor."

"You are also my sister Kitiara's friend," said Raistlin.

"One needs all the friends one can get these days," Iolanthe said lightly, and just as lightly she changed the subject. "On thinking about it, I'm glad you're going to

135

be working in the Tower. I fear the old men may be right. The Church will undoubtedly take a renewed interest in us. More's the pity. By cataloging the books and cleaning up the library, you can find out what books are in their possession. And you can keep an ear open, hear what they say."

Iolanthe cast him a sidelong glance and gave a sly smile. "If you are thinking you will find anything of value in that rat's nest, you are sadly mistaken. I have a pretty good idea of what's there."

Iolanthe would have kept an eye open for anything of value and already removed it. Still, it would not hurt to look, Raistlin thought.

"It's not as if I have anything better to do for the moment," he muttered to himself.

Their conversation carried them to the White Gate. The sun was setting; the sky was smeared with red. They could hear laughter and noise emanating from the Broken Shield, which was across the road. Soldiers coming off duty and workers ending their shifts thronged to the tavern for food and drink. The gate guards were busy checking those leaving the Inner City, and dealing with those who wanted to enter Neraka. A few were clerics in their black robes, but most Raistlin recognized as mercenaries, coming to seek employment in the dragonarmies.

He and Iolanthe took their places in line behind two humans—a male and a female—who were chatting together.

"I've heard there's going to be a spring offensive," said the woman. "The Emperor pays well. That's why I'm here."

"Let's say the Emperor *promises* to pay well," said the man dourly. "I've yet to see the steel I'm owed, and I've been here two months. If you'll take my advice, you'll head north. Work for the Blue Lady. She pays good steel, and she pays on time. That's where I'm headed now. I'm just going back into town to pick up my things."

"I'm open to suggestion. Maybe you'd like a traveling companion?" said the woman.

"Maybe I would," said the man.

Raistlin recalled that conversation and what it portended only later. As he waited in line, all he could think of was the forged document, and his trepidation grew. He wondered nervously if the gate guards would accept it. He began to doubt that they would. He pictured himself being arrested, hauled off, perhaps thrown again into the Nightlord's dungeons.

He glanced at Iolanthe, who stood by his side, her hand on his arm. She was calm, chatting about something to which Raistlin was paying no attention. She had assured him repeatedly that he need not worry; the guard would not look twice at the forgery. Raistlin had compared his forged document with her real one, and he had to admit he could not tell any difference.

He had faith in her—or at least as much faith as he ever put in anyone. He was dubious about Talent Orren, however. Orren was a hard man to figure out. He appeared to be the usual sort of shallow, charming rogue who was out to make steel by any means, fair or foul. Raistlin had the feeling there was more to the man than that. He thought back to Orren's intense and penetrating gaze, the intelligence and shrewdness in the brown eyes. He remembered the faint hint of Solamnia in his voice. Like Sturm, perhaps, Orren was the son of a noble family who had lost everything and was forced to sell his sword. Unlike Sturm, Orren had chosen the side of Darkness over the side of Light.

At least, Raistlin thought, Talent Orren had shown better business sense.

The gate guard motioned them to come forward. Raistlin's heart beat fast, the blood rushing in his ears as he held his forged permit out to the guard. Iolanthe greeted the guard by name and asked if she would see him later in the Broken Shield. She told him laughingly he could buy her a drink. The guard had eyes for only her. He barely glanced at Raistlin's permit and did not look at Raistlin at all. The guard motioned the two through the gate and turned to the next in line.

"There, wasn't that easy?" Iolanthe said.

"Next time I won't have you with me," Raistlin said wryly.

"Bah, it's nothing. These men are not with the Highlord's army, though the Highlords ostensibly are in charge of the gates. These soldiers are members of the Neraka city guard. Their main job is to make sure that no one gets inside who might offend the Church. They aren't paid well enough to go to any trouble or take any risks. I saw a soldier stabbed in the street right in front of two of them one time. The Nerakan guards simply stepped over the body and kept on talking. Now if it had been a dark pilgrim who was murdered or robbed, that would have been a different story. The guards would have fallen all over themselves to catch the perpetrator."

After that, the two walked in silence. Raistlin was too tired and dispirited to keep up a conversation, and the talkative Iolanthe appeared to have been finally talked-out. By her expression, her thoughts were as dark as the shadows falling around them. Raistlin could not guess what she was thinking. For his own part, he was pondering his future and admitting to himself it looked very bleak.

They returned to Wizard's Row, and Raistlin understood why almost all the shops were boarded up and shuttered. He marveled that Snaggle managed to stay in business. Then again, being the only mageware shop in Neraka must have its advantages.

Raistlin resisted Iolanthe's pleas to stay for the evening meal. He was worn out, his exhaustion coming as much from discouragement and unhappiness as from any physical cause. He wanted to be alone, to think through all that had happened and decide what to do. And he had another reason for not wanting to remain around her. He did not like Iolanthe's continued teasing references to marbles. He did not consider it likely that she had figured out the truth about the dragon orb, but he did not dare take the risk.

Raistlin was polite, but firm in his refusal to stay. Unfortunately, when Iolanthe saw that he meant to have his way, she said she had nothing better to do. She would accompany him to the Broken Shield. They would dine together there.

He tried to think of some way of discouraging Iolanthe without hurting her feelings. Her friendship had already been of benefit to him, and he foresaw how she could be useful to him in the future. She could also be a formidable enemy.

He wondered why she was so insistent on dogging him, and, as he listened to her idle chatter as she moved around the apartment, tidying up the room, the realization struck him. She was lonely. She was hungry to talk to another wizard, someone like herself, who understood her goals and aspirations. His thoughts were confirmed when she turned to him to say, "I have the feeling we are very much alike, you and I."

Raistlin smiled. He almost laughed. What could he, a frail young man with strange-colored skin and stranger eyes, have in common with such a beautiful, exotic, intelligent, powerful, and self-possessed young woman? He wasn't attracted to her. He didn't trust her or even much like her. Every time she brought up marbles in her mocking tone, he could feel his skin crawl. Yet what she said was true. He did feel a kinship to her.

"It is the love of the magic that binds us," she said, answering his unspoken thought as clearly as if she had heard it. "And the love of the power the magic can bring us. Both of us have sacrificed comfort, safety and security for the magic. And we are both prepared to sacrifice still more. Am I right?"

Raistlin did not answer. She took his silence for his response and went into her bedchamber to change her clothes. He was resigning himself to being forced to spend the evening with her, which meant the strain of keeping a guard on everything he said and did, when he heard footfalls on the stairs leading to her apartment.

The feet were heavy, and there was a scraping sound, as of claws on wood. When Iolanthe came out of her room, she grimaced, as though she knew what the sounds meant.

"Oh, damn," she said softly and flung open the door.

A large bozak draconian, his wings brushing the ceiling, stood on the landing.

"Is this the lodging of Mistress Iolanthe?" asked the bozak.

"Yes," said Iolanthe with a sigh. "And I am Iolanthe. What do you want?"

"The Emperor Ariakas has returned to grace Neraka with his august presence. He requests your attendance upon him, madam," said the bozak. "I am to escort you."

The draconian's gaze shifted from her to Raistlin and back to Iolanthe. Seeing the reptilian eyes flicker dangerously, Raistlin rose to his feet, bringing the words of a deadly spell to his mind.

"I see you have company, madam," continued the bozak in a dire tone. "Have I interrupted something?"

"Only my dinner plans," said Iolanthe lightly. "I was going to dine at the Broken Shield along with this young man, a novice wizard, newly arrived in Neraka. The Emperor will be interested to meet him, I think. This is Raistlin Majere, brother to Dragon Highlord Kitiara."

The bozak's suspicious attitude disappeared. He regarded Raistlin with interest and respect. "I hold your sister in high esteem, sir," he said. "As does the Emperor."

"He only tried to have her executed," Iolanthe whispered to Raistlin as she handed him linens and a blanket, which she had told him he would need for his new lodging.

Raistlin stared at her, shocked at that news. What did she mean? What had happened? Were Ariakas and Kit enemies? More to the point, how would it affect him? Raistlin was desperate to know details, but Iolanthe only grinned at him and winked, well knowing she had just ensured the fact that he would be certain to seek out her company.

"You remember how to find your way to the Broken Shield, Master Majere?" she asked.

"Yes, madam. Thank you," said Raistlin humbly, playing his part.

Iolanthe held out her hand to him. "It may be some time before I see you again. Good-bye and good luck to you."

Under the watchful eyes of the bozak, Raistlin stuffed the bed linens into a sack and gathered up his possessions.

He did not take the Staff of Magius. He did not even glance at it as he left it standing in a corner. Iolanthe caught his eye and gave a slight nod in reassurance.

Raistlin made a deep bow to Iolanthe and another to the bozak. He slung the sack with the bed linens and his spellbooks and few belongings over his shoulder. Feeling like a peddler, he hurried down the staircase. Iolanthe held a lantern at the top to light his way.

"I will stop by the Tower tomorrow to see how you are coming along with your work," she called when he reached the bottom of the stairs.

She shut her door before he could answer. The bozak remained waiting for her on the landing.

Raistlin walked into the street, which was empty that time of night. He missed his staff, missed its shining light, the support it lent his weary steps. The sack was heavy, made his arms ache.

"Here, Caramon, you carry this—"

Raistlin stopped. He could not believe he had said that. He could not believe he had *thought* that. Caramon was dead. Furious with himself, Raistlin walked rapidly down the street, his way lit by the red rays of Lunitari and the silver rays of Solinari.

The Dark Queen's temple came into view. The moons' feeble light seemed incapable of reaching the Temple. The twisted towers and bulbous minarets caused the moons to shrink, the stars to vanish. Its shadow fell upon him, and he was crushed beneath it.

If she wins the war, her shadow will fall on every person in the world.

I did not come to serve. I came to rule.

Raistlin began to laugh. He laughed until the laughter caught in his throat and he choked on it.

6

Forces of the Dark Queen.
The search. The find.

8th Day, Month of Mishamont, Year 352 AC

Being a Treatise on the Subject of the Advisability of the Using of Parrots as Familiars, with Particular Emphasis on Teaching Said Birds the Words to Magical Spells, and Remarks on the Unfortunate Consequences Resulting Therefrom.

Raistlin gave a deep sigh. Tossing the manuscript into a large crate he had labeled "Ineffable Twaddle," he gazed in gloomy despair at the pile of manuscripts, books, scrolls, and various other types of documents that surrounded him. He'd been working for hours, all day the previous day and most of this day, sitting on a footstool, sorting through crap. The crate was almost full. He was half suffocated from the dust, and he could not tell that he had made any progress.

Iolanthe had been right. There was nothing of value in what could only be laughingly termed a "library." The high-level Black Robes must have taken their spellbooks and scrolls with them when they departed. Either that or, as Iolanthe had said, the books had been sold.

He resumed his task and was rewarded by unearthing a spellbook, nicely bound in red leather. He thought he'd stumbled across a treasure until he opened it to find it was a child's primer, a book meant to teach aspiring young wizards the art of spellcasting. He was flipping through it, thinking back to his own school days—the torment he endured, his inept teacher—when he heard a commotion outside the front door of the Tower. Someone began pounding on the door.

"Open in the name of Her Majesty the Queen!"

Down the hall from him, the three old men broke into panicked shrieks at the clamor. Raistlin rose to his feet.

"It's the Temple guards!" cried Hook Nose, peering out a filthy window. "The elite Temple guards! What do we do?"

"Let them in," said Paunchy.

"No, don't," said the third, whom Raistlin had dubbed Scrawny.

Raistlin made his way through the piles of junk to the door, which was standing wide open. Slowly and silently, he shut the door, leaving it open only a crack, and peered out.

The pounding on the door and the shouting continued, as did the arguing among the Black Robes. Eventually Hook Nose decided they should open the door; his reason being that if they did not, the guards would break it down, and the Black Robes would have to pay the landlord for the damage.

Raistlin kept his eye to the door. A contingent of draconians entered and climbed the stairs, their claws leaving scratch marks on the wood.

"I am Commander Slith," barked one. "I have orders to search the premises."

"Search? For what? This is an outrage," said Hook Nose, his voice trembling.

"It has come to the attention of Queen Takhisis that a powerful and potentially dangerous magical artifact has entered the city of Neraka," Commander Slith said in sonorous tones. "As you know, by law, all magical artifacts must be brought to the temple for evaluation and registration. Those artifacts which are deemed a threat to the good people of Neraka will be confiscated in the interests of public safety."

Raistlin thought immediately of the Staff of Magius, and he was thankful it was safely hidden in his room in the Broken Shield, tucked under the mattress. Security appeared to be somewhat lax around the Broken Shield, and he had been worried about thieves. He was puzzled however. The Staff of Magius was powerful, and it could be dangerous, but Raistlin did not think it was powerful enough to attract the attention of the Dark Queen.

"We know the law," Hook Nose was saying in angry tones. "And we have always obeyed it. We have no artifacts of any sort here."

"What about Mistress Iolanthe?" asked Paunchy eagerly. "She has dangerous artifacts. She doesn't keep them here, though."

"You should search her," prompted Scrawny.

"We have spoken to Mistress Iolanthe," said Commander Slith. "We met with her in the private chambers of Emperor Ariakas. Mistress Iolanthe assures us that she has no knowledge of this artifact. She gave us permission to search her apartment. We didn't find it."

"Why do you think we would have it?" Hook Nose demanded.

"We believe that some of you are members of Hidden Light," said Commander Slith.

Raistlin saw the sivak wink at one of the other soldiers.

"Hidden Light! No, no, no!" Hook Nose was babbling in terror. "We are all of us loyal subjects of our glorious Queen, I assure you!"

"Good. Then you won't mind if we search the building," said the commander coolly.

"Please do. We have nothing to hide. What is this artifact?" Hook Nose asked with pathetic eagerness. "We will be glad to hand it over to you if we find it."

"A dragon orb," said Commander Slith, and he ordered his detail to separate, sending some to the lower levels, some to the upper, and some to search the ground floor.

"Dragon orb?" Hook Nose glanced at his fellows.

"Never heard of it," said Paunchy, and Scrawny shook his head.

Commander Slith rattled off the description. "A crystal ball the size of a man's head. It can either be nondescript in appearance or it may swirl with color." He yelled at his men, "If you find anything that fits this description, don't touch it. Summon me at once."

Raistlin left the door, stumbling over books as he made his way back to his stool, hardly seeing where he was going. He pulled his cowl low, picked up a sheaf of parchment pages, and pretended to be absorbed in studying the contents. The words swam before his eyes. His hand crept to the leather pouch he wore on his belt, the pouch that was filled with marbles. None were as large as a man's head, but one of them indeed swirled with color.

He could hear wood splintering—the draconians on the lower level were kicking in the doors. His first panicked impulse was to shove the pouch underneath a stack of books or hide it behind a row of shelving. He swiftly regained command of himself and thought through the problem. Hiding the pouch would be the worst thing he could do. If the draconians discovered it, they would guess at once that it contained something valuable. Draconians were smart and they were users of magic. They would soon figure out that a large crystal globe known to possess magical properties might be able to reduce itself to a small size.

Far better to keep the pouch on his person, hidden in plain sight. He could hear the draconians chanting spells. He could not distinguish the words, but he knew the type of spell he would cast if he were searching for a hidden magical artifact. He would use a spell that would detect magic, cause the artifact to reveal itself, perhaps glow with light or make a humming sound.

Raistlin reached into the pouch. His sensitive fingers could distinguish the dragon orb from the other marbles by feel alone. The marbles were cool to the touch. The orb was slightly warm and its surface was far smoother, its shape more perfectly round.

Other draconians were searching the kitchen, flinging pots and pans to the floor, banging the door of the pantry, breaking crockery. They would reach the library next.

Raistlin took hold of the orb and clasped it in his hand, closing his fist over it. What if the orb gave itself away? What if the orb wanted to be found by Queen Takhisis? What if the orb had told Takhisis where to find it?

The orb grew warm in his hand. Viper's voice whispered to him. *Takhisis fears the orbs. She seeks to destroy the orbs. She knows the danger we pose. Keep me safe and I will keep you safe.*

The door to the library flew open, and two bozak draconians entered. They stopped dead in the doorway to stare.

Raistlin thrust the orb back into the pouch and rose respectfully, smoothing his robes with his hands and keeping his head bowed as though too frightened to lift his eyes.

"Commander, you better come see this," called the bozak.

Commander Slith strode into the room. He glanced around at the stacks and bundles and piles and snorted with disgust.

"Looks like gully dwarves have been living here," he said. The sivak eyed Raistlin. "Who in the Abyss are you?"

Hook Nose came bustling importantly through the door. "He's nobody, Commander. A novice. He does odd jobs for us. Look at the mess you've created, Majere! Get this cleaned up at once!"

"Yes, Master," said Raistlin. "I am sorry, Master."

"Are we going to search through all this junk, sir?" the bozak asked as Hook Nose hurried off to complain loudly about the fact that the draconians had scattered flour all over the kitchen floor. "It will take weeks!"

"Cast your spell and be done with it," replied Commander Slith. "Mistress Iolanthe warned us that coming here would be a waste of time, and she was right."

"Do you trust the witch, sir?" the bozak asked doubtfully. "What makes you think she hasn't got the orb herself?"

Commander Slith chuckled. "The witch has a strong sense of self-preservation. She knows that her life wouldn't be worth spit if Takhisis caught her with a dragon orb."

"What is a dragon orb, anyway?" The bozak kicked at a stack of books and sent them tumbling. "What does it do?"

"Beats me. All I know is that the orb was responsible for the Blue Lady losing the Battle of the High Clerist's Tower, or so I heard." Commander Slith rubbed his clawed hands. "I'd love to get my hands on it. Several people I know will pay a good price for it."

"Pay for it?" The bozak was shocked. "If we find it, we're under orders to give it to the Nightlord immediately."

Commander Slith shook his head sadly and draped his arm around the bozak's shoulders. "Glug, my boy, I keep trying to educate you. You never 'give' anything to anyone."

"But our orders—"

"Orders, shmorders!" Slith sniffed in disdain. "Who gives us orders? Humans. And who's losing this war? Humans. We dracos have got to start looking out for ourselves."

The bozak glanced nervously out the door. "I don't think you should be talking like that, sir."

Raistlin was sweating beneath his robes. He could do nothing except stand in the middle of the library, keeping his head down. He was afraid to move, afraid to draw attention to himself.

"This dragon orb must be powerful," Slith said longingly, "and worth a bundle. We've never been ordered to institute a citywide search for any kind of magical artifact before."

"Just that Green Gemstone Man, that Berem fellow," said Glug.

"I'd like to find him and earn that bounty." Slith smacked his lips. "I could buy a small city with the reward the Queen is offering!"

"A city, sir?" said Glug with interest. "What would you do with a city?"

Raistlin thought he would go mad if they stayed here much longer. His hands clenched beneath his robes.

"I'd build a wall around it," Commander Slith was saying. "Make it a city for dracos only. No humans, dwarves, elves, or any of the rest of that scum allowed inside. Well, maybe I'd let in a few dwarves," he conceded. "Keep my friends and me in dwarf spirits. I'd name it—"

He was interrupted by shouting.

"All finished downstairs, Commander! No sign of anything."

"Finished upstairs, sir!" called out another. "Nothing of interest."

"Cast your spell, Glug, and let's get out of here," said Commander Slith. "That foul stench coming from the kitchen is turning my stomach."

The bozak spoke a few words and waved a clawed hand. Under other circumstances, Raistlin would have been interested to study the bozak's spellcasting techniques. He was far too tense to pay any attention at the moment, however.

He held his breath, keeping his head lowered, his hands in his sleeves, his sleeves hiding the pouch. He saw in terror a telltale glow emanating from his left arm.

Raistlin's heart pulsed in his throat. His mouth went dry. His body shook. He prayed to all the gods of magic, prayed to every god he could think of, that the draconians would not notice. For a moment, he thought his prayers had been answered, for the bozak turned away. The sivak was about to follow when he glanced back over his shoulder. The sivak stopped.

"Go on ahead, Glug," Commander Slith ordered. "Assemble the troops. I'll be down in a moment."

Glug departed. The commander waded through the stacks and piles, shoving them aside, and came to stand in front of Raistlin.

"You going to hand over the bit of magic you're carrying, boy, or shall I take it?" Commander Slith asked.

Before Raistlin had a chance to answer, the sivak seized hold of Raistlin's left arm and shoved up the sleeve of his black robes. A dagger, attached to his wrist by a leather thong, gleamed with a bright silver light.

"Now ain't that something!" said Commander Slith in admiring tones. "How does this work?"

Raistlin was having trouble keeping his arm from trembling. He gave his wrist a flick, releasing the dagger from the thong. The dagger slid down into his hand.

Commander Slith eyed Raistlin shrewdly. "My guess is you're something more than a novice. Got them all fooled, don't you?"

"I assure you, sir—" Raistlin began.

Commander Slith grinned. His tongue flicked out from his teeth. "Don't worry. It's none of my business. But I do think I better confiscate this magical weapon. Could get you in trouble."

Commander Slith deftly removed the dagger and the leather thong.

"Please don't take it, sir," Raistlin said, thinking it would look suspicious if he did not protest. "As you can see, it is only a small dagger. It is worth little, but it means everything to me—"

"Sentimental value, eh?" Commander Slith cast an expert eye over the dagger. "I can get two steel for this, easy. I'll tell you what I'll do, boy, and this is only because I think you're the sort of human I could get to like. You know old Snaggle over in Wizard's Row? I'll sell it to him, then you can go round and buy it back."

Commander Slith slipped the dagger, which had lost its magical glow, into his harness. He made certain it was well concealed, then winked a reptilian eye at Raistlin and sauntered out, tromping over the books on the floor.

Weak with relief, Raistlin sank down onto the stool. He was sorry to lose the dagger, which did mean a great deal to him, but the sacrifice was worth it. The brighter glow emanating from the dagger had kept the sivak from noticing the very faint green glow shining from the pouch.

Outside the library, the three old men were bewailing the damage and threatening to complain to the Nightlord. None of them cared to volunteer for the job, however, and in the end they decided they would delegate Iolanthe to make their complaint. After that, they agreed to have a drink to calm their nerves. Hook Nose, passing the library on his way from the keg where they kept the ale, wanted to know why Raistlin was just sitting there. He should start cleaning up the mess in the kitchen.

Raistlin ignored him. He sat on his stool, surrounded by children's spellbooks and spell scrolls with half the words spelled wrong and trivial treatises on parrots and felt overwhelmed by the knowledge that the Queen of Darkness, the most dangerous and powerful goddess in the pantheon, was searching for him and the dragon orb. It would be only a matter of time before she found them both.

He could flee the city, but he had almost no steel. His departure, so soon after arriving, would look extremely suspicious. And he had nowhere to go. The members of the Conclave would have declared him a renegade wizard by that time. Every White Robe would be pledged to try to redeem him. Every Black Robe would be pledged to kill him on sight. He would be an outcast from society, with no way to earn his living except by resorting to the unsavory, the demeaning. He could see his future. He would become like those old men, consumed by greed, living on boiled cabbage.

"Unless Takhisis finds me first, in which case I won't have to worry about my future because I won't have one,"

Raistlin muttered. "I might as well be at the bottom of the Blood Sea with my fool brother."

He hunched forward on his stool, let his head sink into his hands, and gave way to despair.

In the living room, the Black Robes had quickly drowned their fear in ale and were getting belligerent.

"I'll tell you who has this dragon gourd," said Hook Nose.

"Orb, you bonehead," Paunchy said surlily. "Dragon orb."

"What does it matter?" Hook Nose snarled. "Hidden Light. You heard that draco say so!"

Raistlin raised his head. That was the third time he'd heard the name Hidden Light mentioned. Hook Nose had brought it up the previous day with Iolanthe, saying that he feared they would be suspected of being part of Hidden Light. The sivak had spoken of Hidden Light as well.

Raistlin had meant to ask Iolanthe about it, but with all his other worries, he'd forgotten. He left the library and walked across the hall to where the Black Robes were gathered in the living room, drinking warm ale and trying to figure out who else they could blame for their troubles.

"What are you doing here, Majere?" Hook Nose demanded angrily, spotting Raistlin. "You're supposed to be cleaning up the kitchen."

"I'll get right to it, sir," said Raistlin. "But I couldn't help wondering, what is this 'Hidden Light' you were talking about?"

"A band of traitors, assassins, and thieves," said Hook Nose, "who are working to bring about the destruction of our glorious Queen."

A resistance movement, Raistlin realized with amazement. Operating in Neraka, under Takhisis's very nose.

He asked for more details, but none of the old men were inclined to discuss the movement, except to be loud in their denunciation. Since they were all eyeing each other suspiciously, he guessed that each feared the others were informants and would hand him over to the Nightlord at the first opportunity.

They might well do that to me, Raistlin considered as he went to the kitchen to start cleaning up. He was glad to have physical labor to free his mind. Ideas and plans were forming so fast, he could barely keep track of them. One thought was predominant.

If Takhisis wins this war, I will be her slave, forced to beg for whatever scraps of power she might choose to toss to me. Whereas if Takhisis loses . . .

Raistlin wondered, as he swept up the flour and broken plates, how someone dedicated to the cause of Darkness could sign up to fight for the forces of Light.

7

WRONG PLACE. WRONG TIME.

8th Day, Month of Mishamont, Year 352 AC

aistlin worked all day in the Tower, cleaning the kitchen, then going room to room, righting overturned furniture and picking up splintered pieces of wood left behind after the draconians had kicked in the doors. The Black Robes drank ale and bickered and ate the meal he fixed for them and bickered some more, and went to their beds.

Night had fallen by the time he shut the door with its single rune that could have been opened by a magical talking parrot. He was physically tired, for the day had been long and wearing, but he knew he would never be able to fall asleep, for his mind was still in turmoil. He hated nothing more than lying awake, staring into the darkness.

The thought came to him that he could pay Snaggle a visit and try to recover his dagger. The sivak commander did not appear to be someone to let grass grow under his claws, especially when it came to steel.

Raistlin considered calling on Iolanthe while he was in the neighborhood. He was intensely interested in the organization known as Hidden Light, and she seemed to know everyone in the city of Neraka. She had her fingers on the pulse of its dark heartbeat. But he rejected the idea. Speaking to her would be too risky. She had an uncanny way of knowing what he was thinking, and he feared she would guess what he was considering. The woman was a mystery. He had no idea where her loyalties lay. Was she working to further the goals of Takhisis? Ariakas? Kitiara, perhaps? Iolanthe had not said much about Kit, but Raistlin had detected a warm tone of admiration in her voice whenever she mentioned his sister.

Given that Iolanthe is much like me, Raistlin reminded himself, her loyalties undoubtedly lie with Iolanthe, which means that she cannot be trusted.

He entered Neraka through the White Gate. The line was short at such a late hour, though Raistlin had to wait some time while the guards flirted with a barmaid from the Broken Shield, who had brought them a jug of cold ale, compliments of Talent Orren. Raistlin considered it clever of Orren to keep the Nerakan guards happy. Ale cost Orren little and gained him enormous goodwill.

Raistlin had gone back and forth through the White Gate several times, and no one had so much as glanced at his forged document. He no longer worried about it. As Iolanthe had assured him, the guards kept very lax watch. The only people Raistlin ever saw being turned away were kender, and that was only when the guards were sober enough to catch the little nuisances.

Having finally made his way through the gate, Raistlin walked swiftly to his destination, keeping his eyes open and his wits about him. He held rose petals in his hand, the words to a sleep spell running constantly through his mind. No one accosted him, and he made it safely to Wizard's Row.

The only lights in the street came from the window of Snaggle's mageware shop. Iolanthe's window was dark. Raistlin entered the shop, which was neat and well lit by several strategically arranged lanterns. Snaggle sat behind the counter, perched on a stool, drinking tarbean tea.

Raistlin had already met the proprietor and observed how Iolanthe dealt with him.

"You won't see any staves standing against the walls. No potion jars in bins. Nothing is out in the open, for obvious reasons in this city," she had cautioned him. "Snaggle stores all his wares in labeled bins and boxes stacked on shelves that stretch from floor to ceiling behind a long counter. No customer is ever allowed behind the counter. The last guy who tried they had to mop up with a sponge. Tell Snaggle what you need, and he'll fetch it for you."

Snaggle gave a toothless smile. "Master Majere. In the market for cobweb? I have some lovely web, sir. Just came in today. Spun by spiders raised by the dark dwarves of Thorbardin. Very content, these spiders. Nothing like a contented spider for weaving fine-quality web."

"No, thank you, sir," said Raistlin. "I've come about a dagger. It might have been sold to you today by a draconian guard. A sivak commander of the temple guard—"

"Commander Slith," said Snaggle, nodding sagely. "I know him well, sir. One of my best customers. New in town, but he's already made his mark. He was here today, yes. Brought me a dagger. Fine quality. Once belonged to Magius. Comes with a leather thong so you can wrap it around your wrist—"

"I know," said Raistlin dryly. "The dagger used to be mine."

"Ah, that Slith!" Snaggle chuckled. "He'll go far. You'd be liking your property back, sir, I suppose. Just to be on the sure side, could you describe it for me? Any distinguishing features?"

Raistlin patiently described the dagger and mentioned that it had a small nick in the blade.

"Happen during a daring escapade, sir?" Snaggle asked with interest. "Fighting a troll? Battling goblins?"

"No," Raistlin said, recalling the incident with a smile. "My brother and I were playing mumblety-peg—"

He stopped. He hadn't meant to talk about—or even think about—Caramon. Raistlin went on to describe the leather thong, which was of his own design.

Snaggle rose from his stool and went to one of the boxes, pulled it out from its place, and brought it back to the counter. He opened the lid, revealing several daggers. Raistlin saw his and was about to pick it up, when Snaggle deftly intercepted him.

"That's your dagger, is it, sir? Five steel and I'll be glad to return it to you."

"Five steel!" Raistlin gasped.

"It belonged to Magius, I was told, sir," said Snaggle solemnly.

"And so did five thousand other daggers floating around Ansalon," Raistlin said.

Snaggle merely grinned at him and replaced the dagger in the box and closed the lid.

"I will make you an offer," Raistlin said. "I have no money, but I understand you are in the market for potions. I have been concocting potions for a very long time, and I have some skill at it."

"Bring around a sample of your work, sir. If the potion's as good as you claim, we'll have a deal."

Raistlin nodded his thanks and took his leave, planning

to return to the Broken Shield. The exercise had done him good. He was weary; he could sleep.

As he was walking down one of the sidewalks along Queen's Way, heading toward the White Gate, he noted three men clad in the long, black robes of dark pilgrims coming toward him. The three walked abreast, arm-in-arm, and they were engaged in animated conversation. They had perhaps been to the Broken Shield themselves, for they were slurring their words and bawling at each other, their voices unnaturally loud in the otherwise quiet night.

Two of the men carried lanterns, and by the light Raistlin recognized the bulldog face and bulging arms of the Adjudicator. The executioner was doing most of the talking, drunkenly relating in gruesome detail the death throes of one of his victims. The other two were listening avidly, fawning all over him and laughing heartily at every twist of the screw or lash of the whip. The three were walking directly toward Raistlin on a collision path.

Raistlin knew quite well he ought to avoid an encounter. The Adjudicator, even drunk, was a dangerous man. Raistlin should turn down an alley or meekly cross to the other side of the street. As he watched the Adjudicator, however, Raistlin remembered the screams of those poor wretches in the torture chamber, and anger burned inside him. He had always hated bullies, probably because he had so often been their target, and *bully* was a kindly term when it came to the Adjudicator.

Raistlin halted in the middle of the sidewalk. The Adjudicator and his two friends, their arms linked, walked right toward him. Either they were too drunk to notice him or they assumed he would move.

Raistlin stayed where he was. The three would have to stop or run him down.

At last the Adjudicator saw him. He and his companions staggered to a halt.

"Move aside, scum, and let your betters pass," said the Adjudicator with a snarl.

Raistlin inclined his hooded head. "If you three would be so kind as to step to one side, Revered Sirs, I could pass—"

"You dare ask *us* to step aside!" cried one of the lantern-carrying clerics. "Don't you know who this is?"

"I neither know nor care," said Raistlin evenly.

"I recognize that voice. I've met this dung-eater before," said the Adjudicator. "Hold the light so that I can see him—"

The Adjudicator's body suddenly stiffened. His back arched, his eyes bulged. He gave a gasp that bubbled into a cry of agony, then he made a gargling sound and lurched forward, his hands outstretched. He fell on his belly onto the sidewalk. Blood trickled from the Adjudicator's mouth. The light of the two lanterns glinted on the handle of a butcher's knife protruding from the Adjudicator's back. Raistlin caught a fleeting glimpse of a black-clad figure disappearing around the corner.

The two dark pilgrims stared down at the dead man in ale-soaked bewilderment. Raistlin was as stunned as either of the dark pilgrims. He was the first to recover from the shock, and he knelt beside the dead man, feeling for a life beat in the bull-like neck, though it was obvious to him the man was dead. One of the dark pilgrims gave a sudden screech.

"You!" he cried, pointing a finger at Raistlin. "He's dead because of you!"

He swung his lantern, aiming a wild blow at Raistlin's head that came nowhere close to hitting its mark.

The other dark pilgrim began shouting for the guards. "Murder! Help! Assassins! Murder!"

Raistlin understood his danger. The dark pilgrims thought he had deliberately stopped the Adjudicator and held him in conversation so the assassin could slip up and stab him. Raistlin could proclaim his innocence all he wanted, but appearances were against him. No one would believe him.

Raistlin scrambled to his feet. He had been fingering the rose petals. The words of the sleep spell were in his mind, and in a split second the words were on his tongue.

"Ast tasarak sinuralan krynawi!"

He flung the rose petals into the faces of the two dark pilgrims, and they slumped to the pavement, one rolling into the gutter, the other landing at Raistlin's feet. One of the lanterns fell to the ground and broke. Its light went out. Unfortunately, the other lantern continued to shine. Raistlin would have liked to have taken time to douse the light, but he didn't dare. He could hear whistles and shouts, and he recalled what Iolanthe had told him about how seriously Nerakan guards took the murder of any dark pilgrim. At the murder of the Adjudicator, they would turn out the entire garrison.

Raistlin hesitated a moment, thinking what to do. He could whisk himself into the corridors of magic and travel safely back to his rooms. He glanced into the heavens and seemed to see Lunitari's red eye wink at him. The goddess had always taken a liking to him. This might be the break he had been seeking. Though he was putting himself at risk, he could not spurn the opportunity.

Raistlin recalled the black-clad figure running down the street, and he took the same route. Solinari's silver gleam mingled with Lunitari's red glow, and Raistlin saw immediately that the assassin had made a mistake. In his haste, he had rushed into a cul-de-sac. The end of the alley was blocked by a high, stone wall. The assassin must still be here. Unless he had wings, he could not have escaped.

Raistlin slowed his pace, moving cautiously, peering into the shadows, listening for the slightest sound. The assassin might be carrying more than one knife, and Raistlin did not want to feel the blade between his ribs. Hearing a scraping noise, he saw the assassin, dressed all in black, attempting to scale the stone wall. The wall was too high; the stones were smooth and offered no foot or handhold. The assassin slid back down to the ground with a thud and crouched there, swearing.

Half seen in the moonlight and shadows, the assassin was short and slender, and Raistlin thought at first that the killer was a child. He moved nearer and, by Lunitari's light, Raistlin was astounded to recognize the female kender Talent Orren had thrown out of the Broken Shield. She was no longer wearing a kender's usual bright clothing, but was dressed all in black: black blouse, black trousers. She had stuffed her yellow braids into a black cap.

Steel glinted in her hand. Her eyes gleamed. Her face bore a most unkender-like expression: grim, determined, cold, and resolved.

"Yell for the guards, and I'll slit your throat for you," she told him. "I can do it too. I'm fast with a knife. Maybe you saw just *how* fast."

"I'm not going to yell," said Raistlin. "I can help you get over that wall."

"A weakling like you?" The kender sneered. "You couldn't heft a kitten."

Behind them, the guards were shouting and blowing their whistles. The kender did not look at all nervous or frightened—in that, she was acting like any normal kender.

"I can use my magic," said Raistlin. "Though it will cost you."

"How much?" asked the kender, scowling.

"You're hardly in a position to bargain," he said coldly, and he held out his hand to her. "Take it or leave it."

The kender hesitated, eyeing him suspiciously. The sound of more whistles and feet pounding on the pavement helped her make up her mind. She took hold of his hand. He spoke the words to the spell and the two of them rose up and floated over the wall. They landed on the street on the other side, dropping down lightly as feathers.

Tasslehoff would have oohed and ahhed and wanted to discuss the magic and insist that Raistlin float him off again. This kender kept her mouth shut. The moment they hit the ground, she was off like an arrow sped from a bow.

Or rather, she tried to take off. Raistlin had a firm hold of her hand and, familiar with a kender's tricks, he managed to retain his grip, even when she twisted her arm, nearly breaking her wrist and almost dislocating her shoulder.

Judging by the sounds rising up from behind them, more guards were gathering at the crime scene and starting to expand the search for the killer.

"You owe me," he said, maintaining a firm grip on the kender.

"I don't have any steel," said the kender.

"Not steel. Information."

"I don't have any of that either," the kender said, and she tried again to break free of him.

"What's your name?" he asked.

"None of your business."

"My name is Raistlin Majere," he told her. "There, you know mine. Tell me yours. That can't hurt, can it?"

The kender thought it over. "I guess not. I'm Marigold Featherwinkle."

Raistlin thought that in all the long history of Krynn, there had probably never been a more improbable name for a cold-blooded killer.

"They call me Mari," the kender added. "Do they call you Raist?"

"No," said Raistlin. Only one person had ever called him that. "You are a member of Hidden Light, aren't you, Mari," he went on, making it a statement, not a question.

"Hidden Light? Never heard of it," said Mari.

"I don't believe you. I know something of kender, and I know you did not conceive of this daring plan all by yourself."

"I did so too!" Mari cried indignantly.

Raistlin shrugged. "I can always magic you back over the wall."

They could both hear the guards swarming into the alley.

Mari pouted and stubbornly said nothing.

"I can help," said Raistlin. "As you've seen just now."

"You're wearing the Black Robes," she said.

"And you're a merry-hearted kender," said Raistlin, "with blood on your face."

"Do I?" Mari lifted a handkerchief and scrubbed her cheeks.

"I believe that is mine," said Raistlin, eyeing the handkerchief, which he recognized.

"I guess you must have dropped it." Mari looked at him with wide eyes. "Do you want it back?"

Raistlin smiled. At least some things in the world never changed. He felt strangely comforted. "Tell me how to contact Hidden Light, Mari, and I will let you go."

Mari studied him, seemed to be trying to make up her mind about him. On the other side of the wall, the guards could be heard poking around in trash heaps and knocking on back doors.

"We don't have much time," Raistlin said. "Someone will eventually think to search this street. And I'm not going to let go until you tell me what I want to know."

"All right, I may have heard of this Hidden Light bunch," said Mari grudgingly. "From what I recollect, you should go to a tavern called Hair of the Troll and order a drink and say, 'I escaped the Maelstrom,' and then wait."

"Escaped the Maelstrom!" Raistlin repeated, shocked and alarmed. He gripped her more tightly. "How did you know about that?"

"About what? Stop that! You're hurting me," said Mari. Raistlin relaxed his grip. He was being foolish. There was no way she could have known about the Maelstrom, the ship sinking, the Blood Sea. Maelstrom was a code word, nothing more. He released his hold on the kender and was about to add his thanks, but Mari was already running down the street. She vanished into the darkness.

Raistlin sagged back against the wall. Once the excitement and danger were over, he felt drained, exhausted. And he had a long walk back to the Broken Shield. In the buildings around him, lights were flaring as people heard the shouts of the guards and woke up and leaned out their windows, demanding to know what was going on. Adding to the confusion, the guards were issuing orders that the city gates should be closed, no one allowed in or out.

Raistlin had strength enough for one last spell. He clasped his hand over the dragon orb, spoke the words, and entered the corridors of magic. He stepped out into his room in the Broken Shield. He removed his pouches and placed them under his pillow, then stripped off his robes and collapsed upon the bed and was soon asleep.

He dreamed, as usual, about Caramon. Only Caramon was in company with a kender who kept poking Raistlin in the ribs with a butcher knife.

8

The morning after. The alibi.

9th Day, Month of Mishamont, Year 352 AC

aistlin was awakened by knocking on his door. Jolted out of a deep sleep, he sat bolt upright in bed, his heart pounding. He glanced out the window. Night still shrouded the city. He had been asleep only a short time.

"Open the damn door!" Iolanthe hissed through the keyhole.

One of his neighbors yelled for quiet. Raistlin took one more moment to consider his situation; then, grasping the Staff of Magius, he spoke the word, "*Shirak*," and the crystal on top of the staff began to glow with a soft light.

"Let me get dressed," he called out.

"I'm sure you don't have anything I haven't seen on a man before," Iolanthe said impatiently. "Except maybe it's gold."

Raistlin was not amused. He dressed himself hurriedly, then opened the door.

Iolanthe, enveloped in a voluminous, night-blue cloak, hurried past him into his room.

"Shut the door," she said, "and lock it."

Raistlin did so and stood blinking at her sleepily.

"I brought you a cup of tarbean tea." She handed him a steaming mug. "I need you to be alert."

"What time is it?" he asked.

"Near morning."

He took hold of the mug without thinking and burned his hand. He set the mug down on the floor. Iolanthe took the room's only chair, forcing Raistlin to sit on the edge of his bed. He rubbed the sleep from his eyes.

Iolanthe clasped her hands on her lap and leaned forward. "Have they been here yet?" she asked tensely.

"Has who been here?"

"The temple guards. So they haven't. They don't know where you live. That's good. That gives us time." She eyed him. "Where have you been tonight?"

Raistlin blinked at her groggily. "In bed? Why?"

"You weren't in bed *all* night. Just answer my question," she said, her tone sharp.

Raistlin ran his hand through his hair. "I was kept late at the Tower cleaning up after the draconians, who came to search for some artifact—"

"I know all about that," Iolanthe snapped. "Where did you go after you left the Tower?"

Raistlin stood up. "I'm tired. I think you should leave."

"And I think you should answer me!" said Iolanthe, her violet eyes flaring. "Unless you want the Black Ghost after *you*."

Raistlin regarded her intently, then sat back down.

"I paid a visit to your friend, Snaggle. One of the lizardmen had confiscated my dagger—"

"Commander Slith. I know about that too. Did you see Snaggle?"

"Yes, we made a deal. I'm going to trade him potions—"

"To the Abyss with your potions! What happened then?"

"I was tired. I came home and went to bed," said Raistlin.

"You didn't hear the uproar, see the commotion in the streets?"

"I wasn't *on* the streets," said Raistlin. "When I left the mageware shop, I was so exhausted, I did not feel up to walking. I traveled the corridors of magic."

Iolanthe stared at him. He met her eyes and held them.

"Well, well," she said, relaxing, giving him a slight smile. "That is good to hear. I was afraid you might have been involved."

"Involved in what?" Raistlin asked impatiently. "Why all the mystery?"

Iolanthe left the chair and came to sit beside him on the bed. She lowered her voice, speaking barely above a whisper. "The Adjudicator was assassinated during the night. He was walking down the sidewalk near the temple, not far from Wizard's Row, when he was accosted by a wizard wearing black robes. As this Black Robe held the Adjudicator in conversation, the assassin sneaked up behind him and stabbed him in the back. Both the assassin and the wizard fled."

"The Adjudicator . . ." said Raistlin, frowning as if trying to remember.

"That lump of muscle who does the Nightlord's dirty work," said Iolanthe. "The Nightlord was furious. He is turning the city upside down looking for black-robed wizards."

Iolanthe stood up and began to pace the room, restlessly beating a clenched hand into an open palm.

"This could not have happened at a worse time! Wizards were already suspect and now this! The guards came seeking me first. Fortunately I had an alibi. I was in Ariakas's bed."

"So you believe they will come after me," said Raistlin, trying to sound nonchalant and all the while thinking that he was in serious trouble. He had forgotten how few Black Robes there were in the city.

Iolanthe halted in her pacing and turned to face him. "I told them who they sought."

"You did?" Raistlin asked, rising in alarm.

"Yes. The guilty are now all dead," said Iolanthe with equanimity. "I've just returned from the Tower. I saw the bodies."

"Dead?" Raistlin repeated, bewildered. "Bodies? Who—"

"The Black Robes in the Tower," said Iolanthe. She sighed and added, "Who knew those old men could be so dangerous? Here they were, working for Hidden Light, right under my nose. I must have been blind not to see it."

Raistlin stared at her; then he asked slowly, "How did they die?"

"The Nightlord sent the Black Ghost." She shuddered. "It was a horrible sight. All three of the old men lying in their beds, their bodies sucked dry—"

Raistlin shook his head. "That seems unlikely to me. Why didn't the Nightlord arrest them? Torture them? Ask them about their accomplices?"

"Do I look like the Nightlord to you?" Iolanthe snapped. She began pacing again. "It is only a matter of time before they find out where you live. The Nightlord's guards will be here to question you, perhaps even arrest you. I must place you somewhere safe, out of his reach."

She kept walking, kept beating her hand into her palm. Suddenly she turned to him. "You said you traveled here using the corridors of magic. Your door was locked. You never picked up your key, did you?"

"No, I came directly into my room."

"Good! You're coming with me."

"Where?" asked Raistlin.

"The Red Mansion. You never used your key. Talent Orren can testify to that. No one saw you enter the inn. You can say you spent the night working late. I will vouch for you, and so will Ariakas."

"Why should he do that?" Raistlin asked, frowning.

"To tweak the Nightlord's nose, if for no other reason. The Emperor is not in a good mood, and whenever something goes wrong, he blames the clerics. Luckily for you, your sister, Kitiara, is back in favor. He had a meeting with her that went well apparently. He'll be glad to assist her little brother. You had best bring the Staff of Magius. They'll search your room, of course."

As she spoke, she was making up his bed so that it would look as if he had not slept in it.

"Where is this mansion?" he asked.

"Near the camp of the Red Dragonarmy. Outside the city walls, which is another good point. The Nerakan Guard sealed the gates after the murder. No one is allowed in or out. Therefore, if you were out, you were not in. And if you were in, you could not have gotten out."

Raistlin considered her plan and decided it was a good one. Besides, he had been wanting a chance to meet with Ariakas. Perhaps the Emperor would make him an offer. Raistlin was still open to all possibilities. He tied his pouches containing his spell components to his belt.

"Got all your 'marbles'?" Iolanthe asked with a sly smile. "The draconians didn't confiscate any of them, did they? I heard they cast spells to search for magical artifacts."

"No, they did not take them," Raistlin replied. "They are, after all, only marbles."

Iolanthe grinned at him. "If you say so."

She reached into one of her pouches and brought forth what appeared to be a glob of black clay. Clasping the clay in her hands, she rolled it between her palms until it was soft, all the while muttering words of magic beneath her breath. Raistlin tried his best to hear them, but she was careful to keep her voice low. When she had finished her chanting, she flung the clay onto the wall. The clay stuck to the surface, then began to grow, looking very much like fast-rising bread dough. The black clay expanded, flowing over the wall until it covered a surface as large as Iolanthe was tall.

She spoke a single word of magic, and the clay dissolved, as did the wall. A corridor leading through time and space opened before them.

"The goo cost me a fortune," said Iolanthe. She clasped hold of Raistlin's wrist. He tried instinctively to pull away, but she tightened her grip.

"You really don't like to be touched, do you?" she said softly. "You don't like letting people get too close."

"I've just heard what happens to those who get too close to you, madam," said Raistlin coldly. "You know as well as I do, those old men were not involved in the murder."

"Listen to me, Raistlin Majere," said Iolanthe, drawing so near him, he could feel her breath on his cheek. "There were five black-robed wizards in this city last night. Only five. No more. I know where I was. I know where those three fools in the Tower were. That leaves one unaccounted for. You, my friend. What I did, I did to save your golden hide."

"It could have been someone masquerading as a Black Robe," Raistlin said. "Or some Black Robe who found himself in the wrong place at the wrong time and is perfectly innocent."

"It could have." Iolanthe squeezed his hand. "But we both know it wasn't. Don't worry. You have risen in my regard. If there was ever a man who needed a knife in his ribs, it was the Adjudicator. I ask only one thing in return for my silence."

"What is that?" Raistlin asked.

"Tell Kitiara what I am doing for you," said Iolanthe.

She entered the magical corridor, drawing Raistlin with her. Once inside, she let go of him and reached out to grab hold of the clay and pull it off the wall, which had not, in fact, disappeared as much as become invisible. The entrance to the corridor closed behind them. A door opened in front of them. Raistlin found himself in a well-appointed and luxurious bedroom, which smelled strongly of gardenia.

"This is my room," said Iolanthe. "You can't stay here. It would be as much as our lives are worth if he caught me with another man."

She steered Raistlin toward the door. Opening it a crack, she peered into the hall. "Good. No one is about. Make haste and douse that light on your staff! There is a spare room, third door on your left."

She shoved him into the dark hallway and shut and locked her door behind him.

9

The Red Mansion. The Dark Queen.

18th Day, Month of Mishamont, Year 352 AC

aistlin spent more than a week in the Red Mansion, fretting and fuming with impatience, bored out of his mind, alone and apparently forgotten. The Red Mansion, despite its name, was black in both color and mood. The building was called the Red Mansion because it was located on a cliff overlooking the camp of the Red Dragonarmy. Raistlin could stand on the portico located in the back of the mansion and look down upon row after row of tents that housed the soldiers. In the distance was the city wall and the Red Gate. Beyond that reared the ugly, twisted spires of the temple.

The mansion had been built at great expense by a high-ranking cleric of Takhisis. The Spiritor had become embroiled in a conspiracy to overthrow the Nightlord. Some said that Ariakas had been involved in that attempt and that it had failed because he had switched sides at the last moment, and betrayed his comrades.

No one knew if that tale was true or not. All anyone knew was that one night the Spiritor had disappeared from his fine mansion and the next day Ariakas had moved in. The mansion was constructed of black marble and was very grand and very dark and very cold. Raistlin spent his time either in the library, studying the many spellbooks he found there, or roaming the halls, waiting for an audience with the Emperor.

Iolanthe assured Raistlin that she had spoken to Ariakas on Raistlin's behalf. She said Ariakas was eager to meet the brother of his dear friend Kitiara and would most certainly find a place for him.

Apparently, Ariakas was able to contain his eagerness. He spent very little time in the mansion, preferring to work in his command post located in the camp of the Red Dragonarmy. Raistlin encountered him only in passing. The Emperor did not even glance at him.

After seeing the man and hearing people talk about him, Raistlin wasn't sure he wanted to be introduced, much less serve him. Ariakas was a large man of powerful build, proud of his brute strength and accustomed to using his size to intimidate. He was highly skilled with sword and spear and had the ability to lead and inspire his soldiers. He was an effective military commander and, as such, had proved himself useful to his Queen.

Ariakas should have been content with commanding the fighting of her war, but his ambition had prompted him to leave the relative safety of the battlefield and enter the far more dangerous and deadly arena of politics. He had demanded the Crown of Power, and Takhisis had granted his wish. That had been a mistake.

The moment Ariakas put on the Crown of Power, he became a target. He was convinced that his fellow Highlords were plotting against him, and he was right.

Since he had done all he could to foment their rivalries and jealousies, thinking it would ensure strong leaders, he had no one to blame but himself when they turned their knives on him.

In many ways, Ariakas reminded Raistlin of a dark-souled, arrogant version of Caramon. Ariakas was, at heart, a bluff and simple soldier, who was floundering about in the muck and mire of intrigue and politics. Weighted down by his heavy armor, he was starting to sink, and he would take all those who were hanging on to him down with him.

After three days, Raistlin told Iolanthe that he was leaving. She urged him to be patient.

"Ariakas is caught up in his war," Iolanthe said. "He has no interest in anything else and that includes ambitious, young wizards. You must put yourself forward. Draw his notice."

"And how do I do that?" Raistlin asked scathingly. "Trip him as he walks by?"

"Pray to Queen Takhisis. Urge her to intercede for you."

"Why should she?" Raistlin shrugged. "You said yourself she has turned against all wizards since Nuitari abandoned her."

"Ah, but the Dark Queen seems to favor you. She saved you from the Nightlord, remember?" said Iolanthe with a mischievous smile. "It *was* the Dark Queen who saved you, wasn't it?"

Raistlin muttered something and walked off.

Iolanthe's questions and insinuations were starting to grate on his nerves. He did not know where he stood with the woman. True, she had saved him from being arrested. The temple guards had arrived to question Raistlin shortly after the two of them had fled the Broken Shield.

But Raistlin had the feeling that Iolanthe had saved him for the same reason a dragon spares her victims: she was keeping him alive to be devoured later.

Raistlin had no intention of talking to Takhisis. The Dark Queen was still seeking the dragon orb. And although he was confident that he was strong enough to hide it from her, he did not want to take any chances. That was another reason he was leaving. Takhisis had a shrine in the Red Mansion, and he could sense her presence there. Thus far, he had managed to avoid going anywhere near the shrine.

He spent the morning of the day he was planning to depart in the mansion's library. Since Ariakas was a magic-user, Raistlin had hoped to find his spellbooks. Ariakas cared little about magic, apparently, for he kept no spellbooks and was, it seemed, not given to reading books of any sort. The only books in the library were those left behind by the Spiritor, and they were devoted to the glories of Takhisis. Raistlin yawned his way through a few of those, then gave up the search.

He came across only one volume of interest, a slender book that Ariakas had actually read, for Raistlin found the man's crude notes scrawled in the margins: *The Crown of Power: A History.* The volume had been written by some scribe in the service of the last Kingpriest, Beldinas, and gave an account of the crown's creation, which the Kingpriest believed dated back to the Age of Dreams.

The crown had been crafted by the ruler of the ogres and had been lost and purportedly found and lost again many times down through the ages. Judging by the book's account, the crown had been in the possession of Beldinas prior to the fall of Istar. A note added at the end by Ariakas indicated that the crown had been rediscovered shortly after Takhisis unearthed the Foundation

Stone. He had also included a list of some of the crown's magical powers, though, to Raistlin's disappointment, Ariakas had not provided details. Ariakas did not seem much interested in the crown's powers, save for one—the crown had the ability to protect the wearer from physical attack. Ariakas had underlined that.

Raistlin shelved the volume and left the library. He walked the halls of the mansion, his head bowed in thought. Arriving at what he thought was his room, he opened the door. A strong smell of incense caught him by the throat and made him cough. He looked around in alarm to find that he was not in his room. He was in the last place on Krynn he wanted to be. He had somehow blundered into the shrine of Takhisis.

The shrine was small and oddly shaped, resembling an egg. The ceiling was domed and adorned with the five heads of the dragon, all looking down on Raistlin. The dragons' eyes had been painted in such a way that they seemed to follow him, so no matter where he walked, he could not escape their gaze. An altar to Takhisis stood in the center of the room. Incense burned perpetually, smoke rising from an unknown source. The smell was cloying, filling the nostrils and lungs. Raistlin felt himself start to grow dizzy and, fearing it was poisonous, he covered his nose and mouth with his sleeve and tried to breathe as little as possible.

Raistlin turned to leave, only to find that the door had shut and locked behind him. His alarm grew. He searched for another way out. A door stood open at the end of the nave. To reach it, Raistlin would have to walk past the altar, which was wreathed in the smoke that was definitely having some sort of strange effect on him. The room was shrinking and expanding, the floor rolling in waves beneath his feet. Gripping the Staff of Magius in one hand, using it to support his faltering steps, he staggered among the pews, where the worshipers were meant to sit and reflect on their worthlessness.

He was arrested by a woman's voice.

You will kneel before me.

Raistlin froze, the blood congealing in his veins. He leaned on the Staff of Magius to steady himself. The voice did not speak again, and he doubted, after long moments of silence, if he had heard it or imagined it.

He took another step.

Kneel before me! Give yourself to me, the voice said, adding in sultry tones, *I offer rich reward to those who do.*

Raistlin could no longer doubt. He looked up at the ceiling. A dark light, like the light of the dark moon, shone in the eyes of the five dragons. He went down on his knees and bowed his head.

"Your Majesty," Raistlin said. "How may I serve you?"

Place the dragon orb on the altar.

Raistlin's hands shook. His heart constricted. The poisonous fumes clouded his mind, made thinking an effort. He reached into the pouch and clasped his hand possessively over the dragon orb. He seemed to hear the voice of Fistandantilus, desperately and furiously chanting the words of magic, hoping in vain to destroy the dragon and free himself from his prison.

"I will serve you in everything except that, my Queen," said Raistlin.

A crushing weight fell on him, trying to beat him down. The weight was the weight of the world, and he was collapsing under it. Takhisis was going to smash him, pulverize him. He gritted his teeth and kept fast hold of the dragon orb and did not move.

Then suddenly, the weight lifted, eased.

I will hold you to your promise.

Raistlin crouched on the floor, trembling. The voice did not speak again. He slowly and shakily rose to his feet. The dark light shone in the dragons' eyes. He could still feel the Queen's malice, a cold breath hissing through sharp teeth.

Raistlin was relieved, though confused, to find he was still in one piece. Takhisis could have crushed him like an eggshell. He wondered why she hadn't.

The reason came to Raistlin, and a thrill of excitement made him shiver. He had felt the weight of the world, but not the weight of Takhisis.

"She cannot touch me," he breathed.

With the return of her evil dragons, the wise had assumed that Takhisis had also returned. But now Raistlin was not so certain. Takhisis could touch mortals with a spiritual hand, but not with a physical one. She was not able to exert the full force of her power and her might, which meant that she had not yet fully entered the world. Something was stopping her, blocking her way.

Pondering that question, Raistlin almost ran toward the exit. He felt her cruel eyes and their dark enmity boring into his back. The double doors seemed to be as far away as time's ending, but he finally reached them. He pushed on them, and they swung open at his touch. He walked out of the shrine and heard the doors sigh shut behind him. He breathed fresh air gratefully. The dizzy feeling passed.

He found himself in a large hall whose ornate ceiling was supported by thick, black, marble columns. He had never been in this part of the mansion, and he was wondering how to find the way out when he heard someone coming and looked up to see Ariakas. And for the first time, Ariakas saw him.

This is no coincidence, Raistlin thought, and he tensed.

Ariakas asked him about his quarters, if he found them to his liking. Raistlin replied that he did, not mentioning that he meant to leave those quarters the moment he had the chance. Ariakas mentioned that Raistlin had Kit to thank for his "post" which, since Raistlin didn't have a post yet, meant he had Kit to thank for nothing. Raistlin said merely that he owed his sister a good deal.

Ariakas apparently did not like his tone, for he frowned and said something to the effect that most men cringed and cowered before him. Having just refused to cringe and cower before the Queen, Raistlin was unlikely to cower before the servant. He was not above a little flattery, however, and he said something to the effect that being impressed did not make him fearful, adding that he knew Ariakas had no use for fearful men.

"I would have you admire me," Raistlin countered.

Ariakas began to laugh and said something about not admiring him yet, but maybe some day when he had proven himself. Ariakas walked off.

That day Raistlin left the Red Mansion. He traveled the corridors of magic to avoid having to pass through one of the city gates. He had to walk the streets, however, and his pulse quickened when he saw two draconians wearing the insignia of the temple guard.

Fortunately for him, the furor over the death of the Adjudicator had died down. The Nightlord believed the Black Robes in the Tower had been complicit in the murder, and since they had were all dead, he was no longer actively seeking out wizards. He had made numerous arrests of their "accomplices", tortured the victims until they confessed, put them to death, and announced that the case was closed.

Raistlin had been worried that the small fish, Mari, might have been caught in the Nightlord's huge net. He asked around and found out that the suspects had been human, which put his mind at ease. He told himself his concern for the kender was merely the fact that he'd been foolish enough to give her his real name.

Certain that he would not hear from Ariakas about a job, Raistlin had to earn a living, buy back his dagger, and pay for his room and board. The best and fastest way to earn steel, he decided, was to sell his potions to Snaggle.

Raistlin returned to the Broken Shield. He picked up his key and opened the door to his room to find the mattress ripped apart, the furniture broken, and a hole punched in the wall.

Raistlin also found a bill tacked to the bedpost from Talent Orren demanding two steel to pay for the damages. Raistlin sighed deeply and set to work.

10

Hair of the Troll.
A Maelstrom special.

14th Day, Month of Mishamont, Year 352 AC

aistlin spent the next two days working on his potions in the empty confines of the Tower. He had arrived on the morning of the thirteenth to find draconians finally removing the bodies of the murdered Black Robes. Raistlin asked to view the last corpse before it was hauled off. He could not have recognized the man from the desiccated remains that were left. He knew it was Paunchy only because the bones with their parchmentlike casing of skin were lying in Paunchy's bed.

The body had been drained of fluid. Death must have been slow and prolonged and agonizing. The corpse's mouth was wide open, jaws locked in a scream. The skeletal fingers gripped the bedsheets. The legs had twisted in their death throes. The eyes rattled around in the sockets like shriveled grapes.

The draconians fidgeted in the room while Raistlin carefully examined the corpse, constantly peering over their shoulders and fingering their weapons. When Raistlin said he was finished, they hurriedly wrapped the body in the bed linens, carried it out and dumped it in a cart with the others.

Raistlin went to work cleaning up the kitchen. As he scrubbed the kettle, he went over the evidence in his mind and came to the conclusion that he knew the identity of the Black Ghost.

"But it makes no sense . . ."

An idea struck him. Raistlin paused in the act of throwing out rotting cabbages, thought it over, and said to himself, with a shrug, "Kitiara. Of course."

Raistlin had not forgotten his interest in the resistance movement, Hidden Light. For two days, he thought of little else as he worked. The decision he was considering would be life-altering, maybe even life-ending, and he would not rush it. He finally made up his mind to at least do some investigating, see what he could learn. After he finished his work for the day, he went in search of the Hair of the Troll.

The tavern was located on the outskirts of the Green District. Raistlin had no trouble finding it, for the tavern was the only building of any size in that part of the city. Unlike the White District, which was home to warehouses and smithies, tanneries and artisans of various kinds necessary to support the military, the Green District was home to nothing much except vermin—two-legged as well as four-legged.

The Dark Queen could have not pursued her war without the loyalty and sacrifice of those races who worshiped her: goblins, hobgoblins, ogres, minotaurs, and the newly created race of draconians. But it was humans who, with few exceptions, were running Takhisis's war, and the human commanders made no secret of the fact that they despised the "scum" who were doing much of the fighting and most of the dying.

Goblins and hobgoblins, ogres and minotaurs were accustomed to such persecution, though that didn't mean they liked it. The draconians were not, however. They considered themselves far superior to humans in strength, intelligence, and skill. Having been taught to fight from the time they were hatched, draconians were starting to rebel against their human commanders and generating unrest among the goblins and hobgoblins, who were also sick and tired of spilling their blood and getting nothing except whippings and bad food in return.

As a consequence, morale among the dragonarmies was dangerously low. The bodies of human commanders were discovered on the battlefield with arrows in their backs; shot from behind by their own forces. Several divisions of hobgoblins had thrown down their arms, refusing to fight until they were paid. Due to the segregation of the forces by race, the "hobs and gobs, dracos and cows," as they were disparagingly known, congregated in the Green District, the only district where they were welcome.

They thronged the streets, most of them in various stages of inebriation; ale being a cheap morale booster. The soldiers were always spoiling for a fight, eager to avenge their wrongs, and humans were their favorite targets. Those humans who were forced to enter the Green Gate and walk through the Green District had learned to bring along friends to watch their backs.

Raistlin had assumed he would have to pass some sort of test to prove himself, but it had not occurred to him that the first test would be to actually reach the Hair of the Troll alive. The moment he set foot on the streets, he was surrounded by a jeering mob. The fact that he was wearing the black robes of a wizard meant little to draconians. Raistlin removed his cowl, allowing the late afternoon sun to shine on his golden skin and his long white hair. His strange appearance caused the crowd to back off and allow him to pass, though they continued to jeer and make threats.

He forced himself to walk at an even pace. He kept his gaze fixed on his destination and did not react when a dirt clod struck him between the shoulder blades. He had no intention of being goaded into a fight. He had about another block to go, though he was beginning to doubt he would make it.

Another dirt clod struck him, this time on the head. The blow was not hard or even particularly painful, but he could see that the situation was rapidly deteriorating. A group of slavering goblins, armed with knives, not dirt, closed in on him. Raistlin was starting to think he would have to fight. He took a bit of fur from his pouch and was about to speak the words to a spell that would shoot a bolt of lightning from his hands to one goblin after another when he felt a tug on his sleeve. He looked down to see Mari.

"Hullo, there, Raist," she said cheerfully.

She was no longer dressed in black, but in the bright colors kender favored. She appeared to have "borrowed" most of her outfit, for nothing fit her. Her blouse was too long; the sleeves were constantly falling over her hands. Her breeches were too short, permitting a good view of her mismatched and ragged stockings. She had tied her yellow braids in a knot on top of her head, leaving the ends to dangle down around her face, giving her the look of a lop-eared rabbit.

She added something that Raistlin couldn't hear over the noise. Mari shook her head. Turning to the goblins, she yelled shrilly, "Shut up, you buggers!"

The goblins subsided to a dull roar.

"What brings you to this part of town?" Mari shouted the question.

Raistlin wondered what in the name of the Abyss she was talking about, then he remembered the correct reply. Keeping one eye on the goblins, he replied, "I have just escaped the Maelstrom," he said, adding coldly, "And my name is *not* Raist."

Mari grinned at him. "Right now I'd say your name was Dead Duck. You look like you could use some help."

Before he could answer, Mari raised her voice. "Free ale at the Hairy Troll! Our friend Raist here is buying!"

The jeers changed to cheers in an instant. The goblins broke into a run, pushing and shoving each other to be first to reach the tavern.

Raistlin watched them dash off. He returned the fur to his pouch. "How much is that going to cost me?" he asked with a rueful smile.

"We'll put it on your tab," said Mari.

She took hold of his hand and tugged him along toward the tavern. Raistlin was somewhat dubious about entering the ramshackle wooden structure, which looked extremely unstable; a healthy sneeze would knock it into a heap. The tavern was two stories tall, but Mari gleefully informed him that a goblin who had ventured onto the second floor had ended up crashing through the rotting floor boards and got stuck in the hole, much to the delight of the crowd in the bar below. Patrons would still proudly point out the hole in the ceiling and relate how the unfortunate goblin's legs could be seen kicking wildly until someone had pushed him through and he had crashed onto the tables below.

There had once been a fireplace, but the chimney had fallen in, and no one had bothered to repair it. The outside of the building was painted with lewd drawings and scrawls. A large signboard featuring a very hairy troll had once hung in front, but it had fallen down, and now either the sign leaned against the building or the building leaned against the sign; Raistlin wasn't sure which. The locals maintained that the sign was the only thing keeping the building standing.

A door had apparently once guarded the entrance, but all that was left of it were rusting hinges. No door was needed anyway, according to Mari, because the Hairy Troll never closed. It was always crowded, day or night.

The stench of stale ale, vomit, and sweaty goblin almost stunned Raistlin as he walked through the door. The smell was bad, but the din was mind-numbing. The bar was jammed with soldiers. Empty casks of ale passed for tables. The patrons either stood around them or sat on wobbly benches. There was no bar. The tavern's owner, a half-ogre named Slouch, sat beside a keg of ale, filling mugs and taking steel, which he dumped in an iron box at his side. Slouch never spoke and rarely moved from his place by the iron box. He paid no heed to anything going on in the bar. Fights might rage around him, but Slouch would never so much as glance up. He kept his attention firmly focused on the ale flowing into the glasses and the steel coins flowing into his coffer.

The rule was that a patron paid for his drink in advance (Slouch did not trust his customers, with good reason) then took a seat. The ale was delivered by gully dwarf servers, who scuttled around underfoot, dodging kicks and ducking punches. Mari escorted Raistlin to a three-legged table and told him to sit down. He closed his eyes to the filth and took a seat.

"What would you like to drink?" she asked.

Raistlin looked at the dirty glasses being shoved into the hands of the patrons by dirtier gully dwarves and said he wasn't thirsty.

"Hey, Maelstrom!" Mari hollered, her shrill voice carrying over the howls and grunts and laughter. "Tell Slouch that my friend Raist here wants one of your specials!"

Her shout was directed at the only other human in the room, one of the largest, ugliest men Raistlin had ever seen. Maelstrom was as tall as a minotaur and as broad through the chest and shoulders as one of those monsters. He was swarthy, his black eyes barely seen beneath overhanging beetling black brows and long, black, greasy hair that he wore in a braid down his back. He wore a leather vest and leather pants and tall leather boots. He was never known to wear anything else; no shirt, no cloak, and he went bare chested even during the coldest days of winter.

Maelstrom's black eyes had been fixed on Raistlin from the moment he'd entered, and at Mari's shout, he gave a slow nod and said something to Slouch, who shifted his bulk and thrust two mugs beneath the spout of another, smaller cask. Maelstrom deigned to deliver the mugs himself, moving with ease through the crowd, shouldering aside draconians, knocking aside goblins, and leaving overturned gully dwarves in his wake. He never once took his eyes from Raistlin.

Maelstrom lowered himself onto the long bench that groaned with the enormous man's weight, causing the other end to tilt, nearly lifting Raistlin off the floor. Maelstrom plunked one mug down in front of Raistlin and kept the other mug for himself.

"This is my friend Raist," said Mari. "The one I was telling you about. Raist, this is Maelstrom."

"Raist," said Maelstrom with a slow nod.

"My name is Raistlin."

"Raist," Maelstrom repeated, frowning, "drink up."

Raistlin recognized the pungent, earthy smell of dwarf spirits and was reminded forcibly of his brother, who was overly fond of the potent liquor. Raistlin pushed the mug away.

"Thank you, no," he said.

Maelstrom drank his mug of spirits in one long, smooth gulp, tilting back his head and seeming to pour it directly down his throat. All the while, even with his head tilted, he kept his gaze fixed on Raistlin. Maelstrom brought his mug down with a thud.

"I said, 'drink up,' Raist." Maelstrom's thick brows came together. Leering, he thrust his jaw into Raistlin's face. "Or maybe, seein' as how you're a high-falutin' muckety-muck wizard, you think you're too good to drink with the likes of me and my friend?"

"Naw, Raist doesn't think that," said Mari, who was leaning her elbows on the cask that served as a table. "Do you, Raist?" She pushed the mug of dwarf spirits toward him.

Raistlin took the mug and lifted it to his lips, sniffed, and swallowed. The fiery liquid burned his throat, stole his breath, brought tears to his eyes, and set him to coughing. Mari thoughtfully supplied him with his own handkerchief, which she pulled out from the top of her stocking. He hacked and choked, aware of Maelstrom's eyes on him, as Mari helpfully pounded him on the back.

Maelstrom kicked at a gully dwarf in passing and ordered two more mugs. "Drink up, Raist. There's another one coming."

Raistlin lifted his mug, but his fingers didn't seem to work properly, and it slipped from his hand and landed with a crash on the floor at his feet. Two gully dwarves cleaned it up, immediately dropping to their knees and lapping up the spill.

Raistlin slumped over the cask. His eyes closed. His body went limp.

Maelstrom grunted. "Weak and spindly," was his comment. "I say we toss him back."

"Aw, Raist's all right. He's just not used to the good stuff," said Mari.

Maelstrom grabbed hold of Raistlin's head by his hair and yanked it up. He peered into Raistlin's eyes.

"Is he playin' possum?"

"I don't think so," said Mari. She gave Raistlin's arm a hard pinch. He did not move. His eyelids did not flicker. "He's out cold."

Maelstrom grabbed hold of Raistlin and plucked him off the bench and slung him over his shoulder with as much ease as if he'd been one of the gully dwarves.

"You be careful of him, Mal," said Mari. "I found him. He's mine."

"You kender are always 'findin' ' things," Maelstrom muttered. "Most of which is best left in the gutter."

He yanked Raistlin's cowl down firmly over his head, wrapped one arm securely around Raistlin's legs, and hauled him out of the Hair of the Troll to raucous laughter and rude remarks about humans who couldn't hold their liquor.

II
Lute's Loot. A job offer.

14th Day, Month of Mishamont, Year 352 AC

he night was fine, at least as fine as any night could be in the city of Neraka, which seemed to be always sullenly lurking under a perpetual cloud of haze and smoke and dust. Talent Orren was in a good mood, and he whistled a merry dance tune as he sauntered through the Red Gate. The guards on duty greeted him with enthusiasm, thirstily eyeing the wineskin he had brought with him, which they immediately "confiscated." Talent handed over the wine with a grin and said he hoped they enjoyed it.

No moons being visible that night, Talent carried a lantern to light his way. He made a left turn at the first street, then headed for a T-shaped building that stood at the very end. He was not alone. Human and draconian soldiers patrolled the streets of the Red District, going about their business with an air of orderly efficiency—a marked contrast to the foul mood of the hobs and gobs in the Green District. The relative calm might have something to do with the fact that the Red Dragonarmy commander, Ariakas, was currently in residence.

The draconians ignored Talent as they tended to disdainfully ignore most humans. Most of the human soldiers knew and liked him, though, and they called out good-natured insults. Orren gave back as good as he got. He would see them all later in his tavern, where he would be happy to relieve them of their pay.

Talent's destination was a pawn shop known as Lute's Loot. On his arrival, Talent opened the door and walked inside. He paused a moment to allow his eyes to adjust to the bright light, which was indicative of the shop's success. Seven crystal lamps of remarkable beauty hung from beams in the ceiling. Lute claimed to have purchased them from an elf lord desperate to escape Qualinesti before the dragonarmy's attack. Lute had paid the Emperor's witch, Iolanthe, a tidy sum to cast a magical light spell on the lamps. The light was soft white and though some of the customers considered it harsh and claimed it burned their eyes, Talent found it calming, even soothing.

When his eyes were no longer dazzled and he was in no danger of breaking his neck amid the clutter, he bid a good evening to Lute's guardians, two enormous mastiffs. Named Shinare and Hiddukel, the mastiffs greeted Talent with wagging tails and large quantities of dog slobber. One of them, standing on his hind legs, placed his front paws on Talent's chest to lick his cheek. The dog topped the man by several inches.

Talent played with the dogs and waited to speak to Lute, who, seated on a tall stool against the back wall, was occupied with business, making some sort of deal with a soldier of the Red Dragonarmy. Catching sight of Talent, Lute paused in his bargaining to grumble at his friend.

"Hey, Talent, what was that swill you sent over for my dinner?"

Lute was a short, squat individual with a large head, a rotund belly, and a surly disposition who boasted proudly that he was the laziest person in Ansalon. Every morning he moved from his bed, which was located in a room directly behind the counter, to his stool, where he sat all day, leaving it only to use the chamber pot. When time came to close up shop late at night, Lute slid off the stool and waddled the few steps to his bed. A mop of curly, black hair fell over his eyes, meeting his full, curly, black beard somewhere in the vicinity of his nose, so it was difficult to tell where the beard began and his hair left off. Small, keen eyes glinted out from the thatch.

"Rabbit stew," Talent said.

"Flummery! Boiled gully dwarf is more like it!" Lute said irately.

"You should have sent it back," Talent said.

"A fellow has to eat something," Lute snarled and returned to his haggling.

Talent grinned. His rabbit stew was good; none better in this part of the world. Lute was not happy unless he was complaining about something.

If Lute had a surname, no one knew it. He claimed to be human, but Talent knew better. One night early in their long relationship, Lute, having imbibed a bit too much in the way of dwarf spirits, had told Talent that his father had been a dwarf from the kingdom of Thorbardin. When Talent had mentioned that the next morning, Lute had flown into a rage and denied that he'd ever said any such thing. He had gone for a week without speaking to his friend, and Talent had never brought it up again.

Talent lounged among the heaps and piles of junk that covered the floor of the warehouse. Lute's Loot was a repository for goods from all of Ansalon. Talent often said he could trace the progress of the war in the variety of the store's wares. The contents of the room included furniture, paintings, and tapestries from Qualinesti; a set of chairs said to have come from the famous Inn of the Last Home in Solace; a few objects from the dwarven kingdom, though not many, for Thorbardin had fought off the dragonarmies. There was nothing from the elven kingdom of Silvanesti, for the land was said to be cursed and no one went near it. There were large quantities of items from the eastern part of Solamnia, which had fallen to the might of the Blue Lady, though as far as Talent could hear, Palanthas was still holding out.

He waited patiently for the soldier to finish his dealing. The man finally agreed to a price, which he claimed was way beneath the value of whatever it was he was trying to sell. The soldier left in foul mood, clutching his coins in his hand. Talent recognized him as a regular, and he guessed that those coins would soon find their way into his strong box.

When the soldier had banged his way irritably out of the door, Lute lifted his black cane and waved it in the air, a signal that Talent should shut the door and lock up for the night. If Talent had not been around to perform that task, Lute had trained Shinare to shut the door; then her mate, Hiddukel, would hit an iron bar with his nose so that it dropped down into place to keep the door from being forced open. Thus Lute was spared the fatigue of walking from the counter to the door and back again.

The mastiffs' main duty was to deter thieves. They would greet patrons at the door and escort them through the shop, growling if anyone dared touch anything without first obtaining permission from Lute. And in case anyone might decide to try to snatch an object and flee, Lute would simply pick up the small, handheld crossbow that rested on the counter beside his cup of thick, honey-laced tarbean tea. Should anyone doubt Lute's ability to use the crossbow, he would point to a goblin's skull with a bolt through its eye that he had nailed to the wall.

Talent had just shut the door and was preparing to lower the bar when he heard a knock. Talent peered out. At first he didn't see anything.

"Down here, doofus," said Mari.

Talent lowered his gaze to the kender.

"The delivery's been made," she said.

"Well done, thanks," said Talent.

Mari waved at him and ran off into the night. Talent shut the door and locked it.

"Was that the kender?" Lute said, scowling. "You didn't let the little thief inside, did you?"

Talent smiled. "No, you're safe. She came to report that the goods have been delivered."

"Fine. You deal with it. I'm going to bed."

Lute began the task of maneuvering his bulk off his high stool. Talent, accompanied by the two mastiffs, navigated the convoluted trails that led through the maze of junk and arrived at last at the counter.

"Any word on the Berem fellow?" he asked.

"Nothing so far," said Lute. "Two men, both name of Berem, entered the city this week. Our boys were waiting at the gates and managed to get hold of them before the Nerakan guards did. Maelstrom took them to the Hairy Troll and questioned them."

"Neither had a green gemstone embedded in his chest, I take it," said Talent, "or 'an old-looking face with young eyes.' "

"One had an old face with a shifty eye, and the other a young face with a young eye. Though that wouldn't have stopped the Nightlord from torturing them, just to make sure. Remember the Berem guy they caught last fall? The Nightlord sliced open his chest and cracked his breastbone just to make sure he wasn't hiding an emerald in his craw."

"What happened to the two latest Berems?"

"One was a pickpocket. Maelstrom warned him that if he was planning on staying in Neraka, he should stay out of the Hairy Troll and he might want to change his name. The other Berem was a fourteen-year-old kid—some farmer's son who had run away from home and came here to make his fortune. No need to warn the kid. After what he'd seen of our fair city, the poor kid was half dead with fright. Maelstrom gave him a steel piece and sent him home to his mama."

"I wonder what is so special about this Berem," Talent mused, not for the first time.

Lute grunted. "Other than the fact that he sports a green gemstone among his chest hairs?"

"Only a goblin would be gullible enough to believe such a ridiculous tale. More likely he wears a green gemstone necklace or some such thing. A jewel embedded in his chest, my ass!"

"I dunno," said Lute quietly. "You and I've seen stranger things, my friend. What are you going to do with the newly arrived goods?"

"Have a talk with him. Maybe give him a job if I like his looks."

Lute frowned, causing what little could be seen of his face to vanish between his hair and his beard. "What the deuce do you want to give him a job for? To start with, he's a wizard, and they're all scum—"

"Except the lovely Iolanthe," said Talent slyly.

Lute may have blushed. It was hard to tell underneath all the hair. At any rate, he pointedly ignored Talent's insinuation. "Ten-to-one he's an agent of the Nightlord."

"Then why would he save Mari's life?"

"What better way to be accepted into our ranks? Discover our secrets?"

Talent shook his head. "The Nightlord's agents generally aren't that smart. But if he is, I'll soon find out. He'll turn down the job I'm offering him because it will mean he will have to leave Neraka, and he won't want to do that if he's been sent to spy on us for the Nightlord. If he takes it, he may be the real deal."

"What job is that?"

"You know, the one we were discussing the other night. He's *her* brother."

"And you trust him?" Lute glowered. "You're cracked in the head, Orren. I've often said so."

"I don't trust him as far as I can see his black robes on a moonless night," said Talent. "Mari likes him, though, and kender have good instincts about people. She likes you, after all."

Lute gave an explosive snort that nearly toppled him. Recovering his balance, he leaned on his cane and, taking his tea and his crossbow with him, started off to bed. Halfway there, he turned around. "What happens if your wizard turns down the job?"

Talent ran a finger over his mustache. "Have you fed the mastiffs tonight?"

"No," said Lute.

"Then don't," said Talent.

Lute nodded and went to his bedroom and shut the door.

Talent whistled to the two dogs, who came trotting obediently after him. He headed toward the back of the shop, dodging around and sometimes forced to climb over boxes and crates and barrels, piles of rags, bundles of clothes, tools of all sorts, a broken-down plow, and a large variety of wooden wagon wheels.

Lute had constructed a kennel of sorts for the dogs in the back corner. The dogs, thinking it was time for bed, went obediently into two large crates, where they curled up on blankets and began chewing on bones.

"Not so fast, friends," said Talent. "We still have work to do tonight."

He whistled and the dogs left their crates and their bones and came bounding to his side. Talent went over to Hiddukel's crate. The dog trotted after him, keeping a jealous eye on his treat.

"Easy, friend. I've had my dinner," said Talent, petting the dog's head.

Hiddukel apparently didn't believe him, for he ducked past Talent and snatched up the bone. Clamping his teeth over it, Hiddukel growled a warning at Shinare to keep her distance.

Talent shoved the crate to one side. Beneath the crate was a trapdoor. Talent pulled open the trapdoor, grinning to think what the mastiff would do to a stranger who dared encroach upon the dog's "lair." Crudely built stairs led down into semidarkness. Somewhere in the distance, a dim lamp burned, giving a faint yellow light.

Talent pulled the trapdoor shut and descended the stairs. The mastiffs came along behind him, sniffing the air, noses twitching and ears pricked. Hiddukel dropped his bone, and both dogs barked, their tails wagging. They had spotted a friend.

Maelstrom was standing guard over "the goods," a man slumped in a chair. Talent could not get a look at him, for the man's head was bowed. His arms were bound behind his back, his feet tied to the chair. He wore black robes and carried several pouches on his belt.

"Hello, Maelstrom," said Talent, walking over to greet his friend.

The man's large hand engulfed Talent's, giving it an affectionate squeeze that caused Talent to wince.

"Ah, careful there. I might need my fingers some day," said Talent. He looked down with frowning interest at the man in the chair. "So this is Mari's wizard. He's a tenant of mine, you know. I was surprised when she said it was him."

"He's a sickly lot," Maelstrom sniffed. "Almost puked at the smell of good dwarf spirits. Still, he's talented at what he does, seemingly. Old Snaggle says his potions are the best he's ever used."

"So where's he been keeping himself? He hasn't slept in his room for several nights."

"He's been at the Red Mansion," said Maelstrom.

Talent frowned. "With Ariakas?"

"More likely with the witch. Iolanthe seems to have made this fellow her pet. She's trying to get Ariakas to hire him. The Emperor has other things on his mind these days, however, and Raist here didn't get the job. He left in a huff. Since then, he's been working in the Tower, making up glop and bartering it to old Snaggle."

"So he tried selling himself to Ariakas, and when that didn't work, he thought he'd hire on with us."

"Either that or he *did* sell himself to Ariakas," Maelstrom growled, "and he's here to spy on us."

Talent regarded Raistlin in thoughtful silence. The dogs lay down at the wizard's feet. Maelstrom stood over him, arms folded across his chest.

"Wake him up," said Talent abruptly.

Maelstrom grabbed hold of Raistlin by the hair, jerked his head back, and smacked him a couple of times.

Raistlin gasped. His eyelids flared opened. He grimaced at the pain and blinked in the flickering light. Then his gaze focused on Talent, and a look of astonishment crossed his face. He raised an eyebrow and gave a slight nod, as if thinking it all made sense.

"You still owe me for the damage to your room, Majere," said Talent.

Drawing over a chair, he spun it around and seated himself on it, resting his arms on the chair's back.

"I'm sorry, sir," said Raistlin. "If that's what this is about, I have the steel . . ."

"Forget it," said Talent. "You saved Mari's life. We'll call it even. I hear you might be interested in working for Hidden Light."

"Hidden Light?" Raistlin shook his head. "I never heard of it."

"Then why did you go to the Hair of the Troll tonight?"

"I went for a drink—"

Talent laughed. "No one goes to the Hair of a Troll for a drink unless you're unusually fond of horse piss." He frowned. "Cut the crap, Majere. Mari gave you the code word. For some reason she's taken a fancy to you."

"No accounting for taste," said Maelstrom, and he gave Raistlin a cuff on the head that knocked him sideways. "Answer the boss's questions. He don't take kindly to prevaricators."

Talent waited for Raistlin's ears to quit ringing from the blow; then he said, "Want to try again? Why did you go to the Hair of the Troll?"

"I admit, I *am* interested in working for Hidden Light," said Raistlin, licking blood from a split lip.

"A wizard who wears the black robes wants to help in the fight against Takhisis. Why should we trust you?"

"Because I wear the black robes," said Raistlin.

Talent regarded him thoughtfully. "You might want to explain yourself."

"If Takhisis wins this war and frees herself from the Abyss, she will be the master and I will be her slave. I will not be a slave. I much prefer to be the master."

"At least you are honest," said Talent.

"I see no reason to lie," Raistlin said, shrugging as well as his bound arms would permit. "I am not ashamed of wearing the black robes. Nor am I ashamed of my ambition. You and I fight the battle against Takhisis for different reasons, sir, or at least so I presume. You fight for the good of mankind. I fight for the good of myself. The point is: we both fight."

Talent shook his head in wonderment. "I've met all manner of men and women, Majere, but never anyone quite like you. I'm not certain whether I should embrace you or slit your throat."

"I know what I'd do," muttered Maelstrom, fingering a large knife he wore on his belt.

"I'm sure you will understand if we ask you to prove yourself," said Talent, briskly getting down to business. "I have a job for you, one for which you are uniquely qualified. I hear that Kitiara uth Matar, known as the Blue Lady, is your sister."

"She is my *half* sister," said Raistlin. "Why?"

"Because the Blue Lady is plotting something, and I need to know what," said Talent.

"It has been years since I have seen Kitiara, but from what I hear, she is commander of the Blue Dragonarmy, an army that is currently ravaging Solamnia, making hash of the Solamnic Knights. What she is plotting is undoubtedly the demise of the Knighthood."

"You might want to speak of the Solamnic Knights with more respect," Talent said.

Raistlin gave a half smile. "I thought I detected a faint Solamnic accent. Don't tell me, sir. I can guess your story. You were an impoverished knight, reduced to selling his sword. You sold it to the wrong people, briefly walked the side of Darkness, had a change of heart, and now you're on the side of Light. Am I right?"

"I didn't have a change of heart," said Talent quietly. "I had a good friend who changed it for me. He saved me from myself. But we're not talking about me. We're talking about a job. As it happens, Kitiara is *not* busy pursuing the war in Solamnia. She has left the war to her commanders. No one has seen her on the battlefield in weeks."

"Perhaps she was wounded," Raistlin suggested. "Perhaps she is dead."

"We would have heard. What we do hear is that she is working on some secret project. We want to know what this project is and, if possible, prevent its completion."

"And since I am her brother, you expect her to tell me everything. Unfortunately, I do not know where Kit is."

"Most fortunately, we do," said Talent. "You've heard of the death knight Lord Soth?"

"Yes," said Raistlin warily.

"Soth is alive—so to speak. The death knight resides in an accursed castle known as Dargaard Keep. And your sister, Kitiara, is with him."

Raistlin stared, incredulous. "You can't be serious."

"I have never been more so. The entry of the dragons of Light into the war caught Takhisis unprepared. She now fears she might lose. Kitiara is in Dargaard Keep with Lord Soth, and we believe they are plotting something to crush out this spark of hope. I want to know what they are plotting. I want you to find out and come back to tell me."

"And if I refuse?"

"I don't recall giving you a choice," said Talent, smoothing his mustache. "You came to *me*, Majere. And now you know too much about us. Either you agree to travel to Dargaard Keep, or your bones will be Hiddukel's dinner this night. Hiddukel the dog," Talent added by way of clarification, petting the mastiff's head, "not the god."

Raistlin looked at the mastiff. He glanced back over his shoulder at Maelstrom. Then he gave a slight shrug. "I will need a day or two to put my affairs in order and devise some excuse for my absence. There are those who would find my sudden disappearance suspicious."

"I'm sure you'll think of something," said Talent. He stood up from the chair. The dogs, who had been lying at his side, jumped to their feet. "Maelstrom will see to it you get home safely. You won't mind being blindfolded, I hope."

"It will be better than being drugged," said Raistlin wryly.

Maelstrom drew his knife and cut the ropes that bound Raistlin's hands and feet.

"One thing I meant to ask," said Talent. "The gate guards have been told to watch for a man named Berem who has a green gemstone embedded in his chest. Sounds like the kind of man a wizard might know. You don't happen to, do you? Or know anything about him?"

"I'm afraid not," said Raistlin, his face a blank mask.

He stood up stiffly, rubbing his wrists. His lip was starting to swell, a bruise was turning the golden skin of his face an unsightly green color.

Maelstrom brought out a strip of black cloth. Talent held up his hand, indicating he should wait.

"Then there's this magical artifact the guards are searching for. A dragon globe or some such thing."

"Dragon orb," said Raistlin.

"You have heard of it?" Talent affected surprise.

"I would be a poor excuse for a student of magic if I had not," said Raistlin.

"You don't know where it is, do you?"

The young wizard's strange eyes glinted. "Believe me, sir, when I tell you that you would not want me to find it." He wiped blood from his lip.

Talent eyed him, then shrugged. "Let Mari know when you're leaving for Dargaard Keep," he said. Whistling to the dogs, he turned to go.

"One moment," said Raistlin. "I have a question for you. How did you corrupt the kender?"

"Corrupt?" Talent repeated angrily. "What do you mean? I didn't corrupt Mari."

"You made her a cold-blooded killer. What do you call that if not corruption?"

"I did not corrupt her," Talent reiterated. "I don't know Mari's story. She never talks about it. And just to be clear, I never sent her to murder the Adjudicator. She undertook to kill him herself. I didn't know anything about the murder until she'd done it, and then I was appalled."

Raistlin frowned, dubious.

"I swear by Kiri-Jolith," said Talent earnestly, "that if I had known what Mari meant to do, I would have chained her up in the cellar. She put all of us in danger." He paused, then added, "Thank you for helping her, by the way, Majere. Mari means a lot to us. The evil in the world has destroyed much that was beautiful, innocent. Take you, for example. I must assume that before you turned to evil, you were once a happy, carefree child—"

"You would assume wrong," sharply interjected Raistlin. "Am I free to go?"

Talent nodded. Maelstrom tied the blindfold around the wizard's eyes, then pulled his cowl over his face and guided him out of the subterranean chamber.

After they'd gone, one of the dogs gave a sudden shudder, causing her skin to twitch. She shook herself all over.

"I know, girl," said Talent, placing his hand soothingly on the mastiff's head. "He gives me the creeps too."

12

A Meeting with Ariakas. Another Job Offer.

15th Day, Month of Mishamont, Year 352 AC

he morning after his meeting with Talent, Raistlin was working in the laboratory in the Tower, mixing up the last of the potions for Snaggle. He had already purchased his dagger. He needed only enough more steel to pay for his room at the inn. He would not go to Kitiara beholden to her. More importantly, he would not spy on her and then take her charity.

"You would be proud of me, Sturm," Raistlin remarked as he spooned a concoction meant to help ease sore throats into a jar. "It seems I do have some smattering of honor."

From downstairs came the sound of the front door opening and closing and light footsteps ascending the stairs at a run. Raistlin did not halt in his work. Even without the faint scent of gardenia, he would have known his visitor was Iolanthe. No one else came near the Tower, rumor having gone around the city that it was haunted by the ghosts of the dead Black Robes.

"Raistlin?" Iolanthe shouted.

"In here," he called.

Iolanthe entered the room. She was breathing hard from her exertions. Her hair was disheveled, her eyes bright and eager.

"Drop what you are doing," she said. "Ariakas wants to meet with you."

"Meet with *me?*" Raistlin asked, his eyes on his task.

"Yes, you! Who else would I be talking about? He wants to talk to you *now!* Put that down," Iolanthe said, snatching the spoon from his hand. "He does not like to be kept waiting."

Raistlin's first alarmed thought was that Ariakas had somehow discovered his involvement with Hidden Light. But, he reasoned, if that were the case, Ariakas would have sent draconians after him, not his mistress.

"What does he want with me?"

"Ask him yourself," said Iolanthe.

Raistlin placed the stopper in the jar.

"I will go, but I cannot leave this yet." He bent over a small kettle he had placed upon the cooktop. "It must come to a rolling boil."

Iolanthe peered into the kettle and wrinkled her nose. "Ugh. What is it?"

"An experiment," said Raistlin.

Mindful of the adage that a watched pot never boils, he turned to another task, carefully packing the jar of sore throat medicine in a crate along with several other potions and ointments he had readied to sell. Iolanthe watched him, tapping her foot and drumming her fingers on her arms, fuming with impatience.

"Your pot is boiling," she said.

Raistlin took hold of the handle with a cloth and removed the pot from the fire. Setting it down on the counter, he took off the apron he had worn to protect his robes.

"Is that all? What happens now?" Iolanthe asked, regarding the concoction with distaste.

"It must ferment," said Raistlin, folding the apron neatly. "On the Night of the Eye, I will—"

"Night of the Eye! Oh, yes!" Iolanthe said, slapping her forehead. "What a ninny I am. That's coming up, isn't it? Are you traveling to the celebration at the Tower in Wayreth?"

"No, I plan to remain here and work on my experiments," said Raistlin. "What about you?"

"We'll talk about it on the way to the Emperor." She grabbed his hand and hustled him down the stairs and out the door.

"Why aren't you going to Wayreth?" she asked.

He glanced at her sharply. "Why aren't you?"

Iolanthe laughed. "Because I will have a better time in Neraka. I know, it's hard to believe. But Talent always throws a huge party in the Broken Shield on the Night of the Eye and there's another party at the Hairy Troll. The ale is free. Everyone gets drunk . . . or rather they get drunker. People light bonfires in the streets and everyone dresses up like wizards and pretends to cast magic spells. It's the only fun anyone ever has in this city."

"I wouldn't think the Nightlord would approve," said Raistlin.

"Oh, he doesn't. And that's half the fun. Every year, the Nightlord issues an edict against the celebration and threatens to send out soldiers to shut the taverns down. But since all the soldiers will be attending the party, his threats never amount to anything."

She smiled coyly at him. "You didn't answer my question. Why aren't *you* going to the Tower?"

"I would not be welcome. I did not ask the Conclave for permission to change my allegiance from Red to Black."

"Well, that was stupid," said Iolanthe bluntly. "You seem to go out of your way to make enemies. All you would have had to do was go before the Conclave and explain your reasons and ask for their blessing. It is a mere formality. Why forgo it?"

"Because I do not like asking anyone for anything," said Raistlin.

"And so you throw away all the advantages you could enjoy by keeping in good graces with your fellow wizards, not to mention putting your life at risk. What for? What do you gain?"

"My freedom," said Raistlin.

Iolanthe rolled her eyes. "Freedom to end up dead. I swear by the three moons, I do not understand you, Raistlin Majere."

Raistlin wasn't sure he understood himself. Even as he shrugged off the thought of going to the Tower of Wayreth for the Night of the Eye celebration, he felt a pang of regret that he would not be there. He had never attended one of the celebrations; after taking his Test, he didn't have the means of traveling to the Tower. But he knew what happened, and he had often longed to participate.

The Night of the Eye: A night when all three moons of magic came into alignment to form an "eye" in the sky. The silver moon was the white of the eye, the red was the iris, the black the pupil. On that night, wizardly powers were at their height. Mages from all over Ansalon traveled to the Tower in Wayreth to make use of the magical power that would sparkle in the air like moonbeams. They would use the power to craft magical artifacts or imbue them with magic, record spells, concoct potions, summon demons from the nether planes. Wondrous magicks would be performed that night, and he would miss it.

He shrugged it off. He'd made his decision, and he did not regret it. He'd stay here and watch over his own wondrous magicks.

That was, if Ariakas didn't have other plans for him.

Iolanthe did not take Raistlin to the Red Mansion, as he had expected. Ariakas was in his headquarters in the camp of the Red Dragonarmy, a spare, squat building where he could nail his maps to the wall, engage in swordplay with his soldiers if he felt like it, and speak his mind without fear that his words were going to be carried straight to the Nightlord.

Two enormous, armor-clad ogres, the largest ogres Raistlin had ever seen, stood guard at the door to Ariakas's office. Raistlin was not one to be impressed, but the thought came to him that their armor alone probably weighed twice as much as he did. The ogres knew and obviously admired Iolanthe, for their hairy faces split into smiles when they saw her. They were still professional in their treatment of her, asking her to remove any pouches she was wearing.

Iolanthe stated that she wasn't wearing any pouches, as they well knew. She then raised her arms, inviting them to search her body for weapons.

"Which of you won the coin toss today?" she asked teasingly.

One of the ogres grinned, then ran his hands over her. The ogre was obviously enjoying his task, but Raistlin noted that the ogre was nevertheless professional and thorough. The bodyguard was well aware of the terrible fate that would befall him if someone pulled a knife on his commander.

The ogre cleared Iolanthe and turned to Raistlin. Iolanthe had warned him in advance that no wizard was allowed to bring any sort of spell component or magical staff into the room, and he had left his pouches and staff back in the Tower. The pouch containing the marbles and the dragon orb had long before been safely secreted in a bag of weevil-infested flour.

The ogres searched him and, finding nothing, told him he could enter.

Iolanthe ushered him through the door, but she did not go in herself. "Don't worry," she said, "I'll be in the next room, eavesdropping."

He had the feeling she wasn't kidding.

Raistlin entered a small, sparsely furnished room. Maps adorned the wall. A window looked out onto a courtyard, where draconian troops were practicing maneuvers.

Ariakas was much less formally dressed than when Raistlin had encountered him in the palace. The day was warm with a hint of spring in the air that made it almost breathable. Ariakas had taken off his cape and tossed it on a chair. He wore a leather vest of fine quality. He smelled of leather and sweat, and Raistlin was again reminded unpleasantly of Caramon.

The Emperor was engaged in reading dispatches, and he gave no sign that he was even aware Raistlin was in the room. He did not offer him a chair. Raistlin stood, waiting, his hands folded in the sleeves of his robes, until the great man should deign to notice him.

At last, Ariakas put down the dispatch. "Sit." He indicated a chair near his desk.

Raistlin obeyed. He said nothing, but waited in silence to hear why he had been summoned. He was certain it would be for some insignificant, boring assignment, and he was already preparing to turn it down.

Ariakas stared at him rudely a moment then said, "Damn, but you're ugly. Iolanthe tells me your skin disease is the result of your Test."

Raistlin stiffened in anger. He made no response beyond a cold nod, or so he thought. Apparently he'd been wrong, for Ariakas grinned.

"Ah, now I see your sister in you. That glint in your eyes. I've seen it in hers, and I know what it means: you'd just as soon stick a knife in my gut as not. Or in your case, you'd roast me with a fireball."

Raistlin kept silent.

"Speaking of your sister and knives," Ariakas said amiably, continuing his thought. "I want you to do a job for me. Kitiara is up to something, along with that death knight of hers, and I want to know what."

Raistlin was startled. Talent Orren had used almost those very same words in regard to Kit. He had not put much stock in Orren's claim that Kit was working on some secret assignment. After Ariakas mentioned it, he began to think that perhaps there was something to it and wondered what his sister was plotting.

Raistlin did not like the way Ariakas was staring at him. It might be what it appeared to be on the face of it—a request to spy on his sister. Or it might be an attempt to find out if Raistlin was involved. He was in dangerous waters, and he had to tread carefully.

"As I told Your Imperial Majesty," Raistlin said, "I have not seen my half sister, Kitiara, in some time, nor have I had any contact with her—"

"Tell it to someone who gives a rat's ass," said Ariakas, cutting him off impatiently. "You are *going* to contact her. You are going to go pay her a brotherly visit. You're going to find out what she and the accursed death knight are doing, and you're going to report back to me. Understood?"

"Yes, my lord," said Raistlin evenly.

"That's all," said Ariakas, gesturing in dismissal. "Iolanthe will take you to Dargaard Keep. She has some sort of magical spell that she uses to transport herself. She will assist you."

Raistlin felt demeaned. "I do not require her assistance, lord. I am quite capable of traveling using my own magic."

Ariakas picked up a dispatch and affected to be reading it. "You wouldn't happen to be using a dragon orb to do that, would you?" he asked offhandedly.

He had set the trap so neatly, asked the question so smoothly, that Raistlin very nearly fell into it. He caught himself at the last moment and managed to speak calmly and, he trusted, with conviction.

"I am sorry, lord, but I have no idea what you are talking about."

Ariakas raised his eyes and gave him a piercing look; then he glanced back at the dispatch and summoned his guards.

The ogres opened the door and waited for Raistlin. He was sweating, shaking from the encounter. Yet he'd be damned if he was going to be dismissed like just one more sycophant.

"I beg your pardon, your lordship," said Raistlin, his heart beating fast, the blood rushing in his ears. "But we have yet to discuss what I am to be paid for my services."

"How about I don't slit your damn impertinent throat," said Ariakas.

Raistlin smiled faintly. "The job is dangerous, lord. We both know Kitiara. We both know what she would do to me if she found out I was sent there to spy on her. My pay should be commensurate with the risk I am running."

"Son of a bitch!" Ariakas glowered at Raistlin. "I give you the chance to serve your Queen, and you haggle with me like some damn fishwife. I should strike you dead where you stand!"

Raistlin realized he'd gone too far, and he cursed himself for being a bloody fool. He had no spell components, but one of his commanders, back when he'd been a mercenary, had taught him to cast spells without the use of components. A wizard had to be desperate to try it. Raistlin considered that desperate was the word for what he was feeling. He brought a spell to mind—

"One hundred steel," said Ariakas.

Raistlin blinked and opened his mouth.

"If you dare demand more," Ariakas added, his dark eyes glinting, "I will melt that golden skin of yours into coins and pay you with that. Now get out!"

Raistlin left with alacrity. He glanced around for Iolanthe and, not seeing her, did not think it would be wise to wait around for the wizardess. He was halfway down the street when she caught up with him, and he nearly jumped out of his robes when he felt her touch.

"You must have a death wish!" Iolanthe again clasped his arm, much to his annoyance. "What were you thinking? You nearly got us both killed. He is furious at me now, blames *me* for your 'damned cheek.' He could have killed you. He's killed men for less. I hope that was worth one hundred steel."

"I didn't do it for the steel," Raistlin said. "Ariakas can throw his steel in the Blood Sea for all I care."

"Then why risk it?"

Why, indeed? Raistlin pondered the question.

"I'll tell you why," Iolanthe answered for him. "You're always having to prove yourself. No one can be taller than you. If they are, you cut them off at the knees. Someday someone's going to cut *you* off."

Iolanthe shook her head. "People tend to think that because Ariakas is strong he is slow-witted. When they find out they're wrong, it's too late."

Raistlin was forced to admit that he had underestimated Ariakas and he had very nearly paid for it. He didn't like to be reminded and wished irritably that she would go away and let him think. He tried to slide his arm from her hold, but she clung to him more tightly.

"Are you going to Dargaard Keep?"

"I'm being paid one hundred steel to do so," he said.

"You will need my help to get there—dragon orb or no dragon orb."

Raistlin glanced at her sharply, wondering if she was teasing. With her, he could never tell. "Thank you," he said, "but I am perfectly capable of going on my own."

"Are you? Lord Soth is a death knight," she said. "Do you know what that is?

"Of course," said Raistlin, not wanting to talk or even think about it.

She told him anyway. "A fearsome and powerful undead who can freeze you with his touch or kill you with a single word. He does not like visitors. Do you know his story?"

Raistlin said he had read about Soth's downfall and tried to change the subject, but Iolanthe appeared obsessively intent on relating the dark and hellish tale. Forced to listen, Raistlin tried to think of Kitiara living in the same dread castle with the murderous fiend. A fiend he might soon be forced to encounter. He thought bitterly that Ariakas could have found easier ways of having him killed.

"Before the Cataclysm, Soth was a Solamnic Knight, respected and revered. He was a man of strong and violent passion, and he had the misfortune to fall in love with an elf woman—some say at the elves' connivance, for they were loyal to the Kingpriest of Istar and Soth was opposed to his dictatorial rule.

"Soth was married, but he broke his vows and seduced the elf maid and she became pregnant with his child. His wife happened to conveniently disappear at about this time, freeing Soth to marry his elf mistress. When she came to Dargaard Keep, the elf maid discovered his terrible secret, that he'd murdered his first wife. Horrified, she confronted him with his crime. His better nature came to the fore, and he begged her forgiveness and asked the gods to grant him the chance to redeem himself. The gods heard his prayer, and they gave Soth the power to stop the Cataclysm, though it would be at the cost of his own life.

"Soth was on his way to Istar when he was waylaid by a group of elf women. They told him that his wife had been unfaithful; the child she carried was not his. His passions overcame him. Soth flew into a rage. Abandoning his quest, he rode back to his keep. He denounced his wife just as the Cataclysm struck. The ceiling collapsed, or maybe it was a chandelier fell down; I can't recall. Soth could have saved his wife and child, but he was too angry, too proud. He watched them both die in the flames that swept through his castle.

"His wife's last words were a curse upon him, that he should live forever with the knowledge of his guilt. His knights were transformed into skeletal warriors. The elf women who were the cause of his downfall were cursed and became banshees, who sing to him of his crimes every night."

He felt Iolanthe shudder. "I have met Lord Soth. I have looked into his eyes. I wish to the gods I had not."

A shiver ran up Raistlin's spine. "How does Kitiara live in the same castle with him?"

"Your sister is a remarkable woman," said Iolanthe. "She fears nothing this side of the grave or beyond."

"You have been to Dargaard Keep. You have visited my sister there. Do you know what she is doing? Why Ariakas mistrusts her? You told me only a few days ago that they had met and all was well between them."

Iolanthe shook her head. "I thought it was."

"Ariakas knows you've been to see Kit. He said you were to take me. Why didn't he send you on this mission?"

"He doesn't trust me," said Iolanthe. "He suspects me of being too friendly to Kit. He views her as a rival."

"Yet he sends me, and Kitiara is kin to me. Why does he think I would betray my sister?"

"Perhaps because he knows you betrayed your brother," said Iolanthe.

Raistlin stopped to stare at her. He knew he should deny it, but the words wouldn't come out. He couldn't make himself say them.

"I tell you that as a warning, Raistlin," said Iolanthe. "Do not underestimate Lord Ariakas. He knows every secret you have. I think sometimes the wind itself acts as his spy. I have been ordered to escort you to Dargaard Keep. When do you want to leave?"

"I must deliver my potions and make certain preparations," said Raistlin, adding dourly, "But why am I telling you this? Undoubtedly you and Ariakas know what I'm going to be doing before I do it."

"You can be angry all you want, my friend, but what else did you expect when you chose to serve the Dark Queen? That she would give you rich reward and ask nothing in return? Far from it, my dear," Iolanthe said, her voice a purr. "Takhisis demands you serve her with body and soul."

Iolanthe knows I have the dragon orb, Raistlin thought. Ariakas knows and so does Takhisis.

"She bides her time," said Iolanthe, speaking to his thoughts, as though she could see them flickering in his eyes. "She waits for her opportunity to strike. One stumble, one mistake . . ."

Iolanthe removed her hand from his arm.

"I will meet you back in the Tower early tomorrow morning. Bring the Staff of Magius, for you will need its light in Dargaard Keep."

She paused a moment, then added somberly, "Though no light, magical or otherwise, can banish that awful endless night."

One stumble. One mistake. They are sending me to Dargaard Keep to confront a death knight. I am a fool, Raistlin thought. A bloody fool . . .

13
Changing the Darkness.

15th Day, Month of Mishamont, Year 352 AC

hat evening, as the sun was setting, Raistlin wrapped his potion jars carefully in cotton wool to prevent them from breaking, then packed them in a crate to carry them to Snaggle's. He was glad for the chance to walk, to think as he walked, trying to decide what to do. Life had seemed so simple back in Palanthas. The path that led to the fulfillment of his ambitions had been smooth and straight. Except that somewhere along the way he'd veered off it, taken a wrong turn, and found himself floundering in a deadly swamp of lies and intrigue. The slightest misstep would plunge him to his death. He would sink beneath the foul water as . . .

As I sank beneath the Blood Sea, said a voice.

"Caramon?" Raistlin stopped, startled. He looked around. That had been Caramon's voice. He was certain of it.

"I know you are here, Caramon," Raistlin called. "Come out of hiding. I am in no mood for your silly games."

225

He was in Wizard's Row and the place, as usual, was empty. The wind blew down the street, rustling autumn's dead leaves, picking up trash, moving it along, and dropping it back down. No one was around. Raistlin broke into a chill sweat. His hands shook so he nearly dropped the crate, and he was forced to set it down.

"Caramon is dead," he said aloud, needing to hear himself say the words.

"Who is Caramon?"

Raistlin turned, a spell on his lips, to see Mari sitting on a front stoop. Raistlin let go of the spell with a sigh. At least that voice had been real, not in his head . . . or his heart.

"Never mind," he said. "What do you want?"

"What's in the crate?" Mari asked, reaching out her hand to touch one of the jars.

Raistlin picked up the crate, holding it just out of her reach. He continued on his way to Snaggle's shop.

"Want me to help carry that for you?" Mari offered, trotting along at his side.

"No, thank you," Raistlin said.

Mari shoved her hands in her pockets. "I guess you know why I'm here."

"Talent wants my answer," said Raistlin.

"Well, that too. First he wants to know why you went to see Ariakas."

Raistlin shook his head. "Is everyone in this city a spy?"

"Pretty much," said Mari, shrugging. "A mouse doesn't eat a crumb in Neraka without Talent knowing about it."

Raistlin noticed that she was busy pulling off the stopper from one of his jars and was about to stick a dirty finger into the pristine potion. Raistlin set down the crate, took away the jar, and put the stopper back on it.

"Is it supposed to smell like that?" asked Mari.

"Yes," said Raistlin. He wondered what to do.

He could betray Hidden Light to Ariakas. Raistlin had known the dwarf spirits he'd been given were drugged; he had smelled the opiate when he brought the glass to his lips. He had pretended to drink and feigned unconsciousness. He could lead the Emperor's guards to Lute's Loot and the tunnels beneath. He would be handsomely rewarded.

Or he could betray Ariakas, join in Hidden Light's battle to bring down the Emperor and the Dark Queen. From what Raistlin had heard and seen of the enemies arrayed against him, he considered that was the most dangerous choice with the highest odds against succeeding.

Both sides wanted him to spy on his sister. He wondered, suddenly, which side Kit was on.

She's like me, he guessed. Kit's on the side that favors Kit.

"Ariakas summoned me to ask if I knew anything about this man everyone is hunting for," Raistlin said. "The one with the green gemstone."

"You mean Berem? Say, do you know why everyone is looking for him?" Mari asked eagerly. "I mean, sure it's not every day you come across a guy who has an emerald stuck in his chest, but what's so special about him? Apart from the emerald, I mean. I wonder how it got stuck there. Do you know? And what would happen if someone tried to pull it out. Would he bleed to death? Do you know what I think? I think—"

"I don't know anything about Berem," said Raistlin, finally managing to get a word in. "All I know is that is why Ariakas wanted to see me."

"That's all?" said Mari, and she gave a whistle of relief. "Good. Now I won't have to kill you."

"That's not funny," said Raistlin.

"It wasn't meant to be. So are you going to take the job for Talent? Can I come with you? We make a great team, you and me."

"Talent didn't tell you where he's sending me, did he?" Raistlin asked in alarm. If a kender knew, so would half of Neraka.

"Naw, Talent never tells me anything, which is probably smart," Mari said. "I'm not much good at keeping secrets. But, hey, wherever it is, you'll need my help."

He'd heard those words before, spoken by another kender. Raistlin recalled how many times Tasslehoff had been extremely *un*helpful, rummaging through his spell components, spoiling half of them and stealing the other half, sneaking tastes of the potions (with sometimes disastrous results), walking off with various household items from spoons to soup kettles, and forever landing him and his friends in trouble.

Only the previous autumn, Tasslehoff had grabbed what he'd thought was a plain, ordinary staff, only to have it turn into blue crystal and perform a miracle . . .

Was that really only last autumn? Raistlin asked himself. It seems a lifetime.

"Hey, Raist, wherever you are, come back," said Mari, twitching his sleeve and waving her hand at him. "Are you going to see old Snaggle? 'Cause if you are, we're here."

Raistlin halted. He set down his crate on the doorstep and sat down beside it.

"You cannot come with me, Mari. In fact, you should leave Neraka," he said to her. "Quit working for Talent. It is too dangerous."

"Oh, Talent's always telling me that," said Mari. "And see, nothing's happened to me yet!"

"Yes, it has," said Raistlin gently. "Kenders belong to the Light, not the Darkness, Mari. If you stay here, the Darkness will destroy you. It is already starting to change you."

"It is?" Mari's eyes opened wide.

"You murdered a man. You have blood on your hands."

"I have some of today's lunch on my hands and a little glob of that yucky potion and some goblin slime from the tavern, but no blood. Look, you can see for yourself." Mari held up her hands, palms out for his inspection.

Raistlin shook his head and sighed.

Mari patted him on the shoulder. "I know what you mean. I was only teasing. You mean I have the blood of the Adjudicator on my hands. But I don't. I washed it off."

Raistlin rose to his feet. He picked up his crate. "You had better run along, Mari. I have serious business here."

"We all have serious business here," said Mari.

"I doubt you know the meaning of the word."

"Oh, but I do," Mari said. "We kender don't *want* to be serious, but we can if we have to. My people are fighting the Dark Queen all the world over. In Kendermore and Kenderhome and Flotsam and Solace and Palanthas and lots of other places I've never even heard of, kender are fighting, and sometimes we're dying. And that's sad, but we need to keep fighting because we have to win, because horrible things will happen if we don't. Takhisis *hates* kender. She ranks us right up there with elves, which is awfully flattering to us kender, though maybe not to the elves. So you see, Raist, the Darkness isn't changing us. We're changing the Darkness."

Mari's eyes were bright. Her smile was cheerful. "What do I tell Talent?"

"Tell him I will take the job," Raistlin said. Smiling, he reached out and took yet another jar from her hand just as she was about to slip it into a pocket. "I wouldn't want you to have to kill me."

BOOK III

I

Brother and sister, and brother and sister.

23rd Day, Month of Mishamont, Year 352 AC

Early that morning Raistlin and Iolanthe traveled the corridors of magic to Dargaard Keep. The two emerged from the rainbow ethers into the only room in the ruined keep that was fit for habitation—Kitiara's bedchamber and sitting room. Even there, Raistlin noted black stains on the walls, evidence of the fire that had swept through the keep so long ago.

The glass in the lead-paned windows had been broken and never replaced. A chill wind hissed through what was left of the latticework, like breath through rotting teeth. Raistlin looked out that window onto a scene of desolation, destruction, and death. Ghostly warriors with visages of fire kept horrible vigil, walking the parapets that had been gloriously red for the color of the rose and were transformed to a hideous red with their own blood.

Dargaard Keep, so legend said, had once been one of the wonders of the world. The keep had been designed to resemble the symbol on the family crest, the rose. Petal-shaped stone walls had once glistened in the morning sun. Rose-red towers had proudly soared into the blue skies. But the rose had been afflicted by a canker, destroyed from within by the knight's dark passions. The rose walls were blackened, stained with fire, death, dishonor. Broken towers were shrouded in storm clouds. Some said that Soth wrapped himself and his keep in a perpetual tempest, deliberately banishing the sun, so he might shield his eyes from the light that had become hateful to him.

Raistlin gazed on the ruin of a noble man, led to his downfall by his inability to control his passions, and Raistlin thanked whatever gods had blessed him at his birth that he was not afflicted by such weakness.

He turned his eyes from the dread sight outside the window to his sister. Kitiara was seated at a desk, writing orders that could not wait. She had asked her visitors to be patient until she finished.

Raistlin took the chance to study her. He had seen Kit briefly in Flotsam, but that hardly counted, for she had been riding her blue dragon and wearing the armor and helm of a Dragon Highlord. Five years had passed since they were together, when they had vowed to meet again in the Inn of the Last Home, a vow Kit had broken. Raistlin, who had changed beyond all measure in five years, was surprised to see that his sister had not.

Tall and lithe, with a warrior's strength and hard-muscled body, Kitiara, who was in her mid-thirties, looked much the same as she had looked at twenty. Her crooked smile still charmed. Her short, black curls clustered around her head, luxurious and rampant as when she was young. Her face was smooth, unmarred by lines of sorrow or joy.

No emotion ever touched Kitiara deeply. She took life as it came, living each moment to the fullest, then forgetting the moment to leap to the next. She had no regrets. She rarely thought about past mistakes. Her mind was too busy plotting and scheming for the future. She had no conscience to sting her, no morals to get in her way. The one crack in her armor, her one weakness, was her obsession with Tanis Half-Elven, the man she had not wanted until he turned his back on her and walked away.

Iolanthe roamed nervously around the room, her arms clasped beneath her cloak. The room was chill, and she was shivering, though perhaps not so much from the cold as from dread. She had insisted they arrive early in the day, so they could be gone before nightfall. Raistlin continued to watch Kit, who was struggling with her missive.

Writing was laborious work for Kitiara. Fond of action and excitement, easily bored, she had always been a poor student. She had never had a chance to go to school. Their mother, Rosamund, had an affinity for magic that she would later pass onto her son. Sadly, Rosamund was not able to cope with the gift. For her, the gift became an affliction. After her twin sons were born, she drifted for years on a sea of strange dreams and fantasies, barely clinging to sanity. When her husband died, Rosamund's hand slipped from the last bit of reality that had been keeping her afloat and sank beneath the waves. Kit had taken over raising her younger brothers. She had remained with the boys until she determined that they were old enough to take care of themselves. Then she had gone off on her own, leaving her brothers to fend for themselves.

Kitiara had not forgotten her half brothers, however. She had returned to Solace some years later to see how they were getting along. It was then that she had met their friend Tanis Half-Elven. The two had begun a passionate affair. Raistlin had known at the time that the affair would end badly.

The last Raistlin had seen of Kitiara, she had been riding on the back of her blue dragon, Skie, and he had been on board a ship sailing to its doom in the Blood Sea. Caramon had wrung an admission from Tanis that he had been spending his time in Flotsam dallying with Kit, that he had betrayed his friends to the Dragon Highlord. Raistlin recalled Caramon's outraged anger, yelling accusations at Tanis as their ship was swept up into the storm.

"So that's where you've been these four days. With our sister, the Dragon Highlord! . . ."

"Yes, I loved her," Tanis had said. "I don't expect you to understand."

Raistlin doubted if Tanis understood himself. He was like a man who cannot overcome his thirst for dwarf spirits. Kitiara intoxicated him, and he could not get her out of his system. She had been the ruin of him.

Kitiara was dressed for combat. She wore her sword, boots, and blue dragonscale armor, with her blue cape thrown over her shoulders. She was wholly absorbed in her work, hunched over the desk like a child in the schoolroom, forced to complete some hateful assignment. Her head, with its mass of black curls, almost touched the paper. Her teeth were clamped on her lower lip; her brow furrowed in concentration. She wrote, muttering, then scratched out what she had written and started again.

At last Iolanthe, mindful of the passing time, gave a delicate cough.

Kitiara held up her hand. "I know you're waiting, my friend." Kit stopped to sneeze. She rubbed her nose and sneezed again. "It's that gods-awful perfume of yours! What do you do? Bathe in it? Give me a moment. I'm almost finished. Oh, damn it to the Abyss and back! Look what I've done!"

In her haste, Kit had passed the heel of her hand over the page, smearing the last sentence she had written. Swearing, she flung down the pen, spattering ink over the page and contributing to its final demise.

"Ever since that fool Garibaus got himself killed, I must write all my orders myself!"

"What about your draconians?" Iolanthe asked, glancing toward the closed door, through which they could hear the scraping of claws and subdued voices of Kit's bodyguards. The draconians were grumbling. Apparently even the lizardmen found Dargaard Keep a loathsome place. Raistlin wondered how Kit could stand living here. Perhaps it was because, like much else in her life, the tragedy and horror of Dargaard Keep skidded off her hard surface, like skaters on ice.

Kitiara shook her head. "Draconians are good warriors, but they make lousy scribes."

"Perhaps I might be of assistance, Sister," said Raistlin in his soft voice.

Kitiara turned to face him. "Ah, Baby brother. I am glad to see you alive. I thought you had perished in the Maelstrom."

No thanks to you, my sister, Raistlin wanted to say caustically, but he kept quiet.

"Your baby brother conned Ariakas out of one hundred steel to come here to spy on you," said Iolanthe.

"Did he?" Kitiara smiled her crooked smile. "Good for him."

The two women laughed conspiratorially. Raistlin smiled in the shadows of his cowl, which he had kept deliberately drawn low over his face, so he could observe without being observed. He was pleased to find his suspicions about Iolanthe confirmed. He decided to see what more he could discover.

"I do not understand," he said, glancing from one woman to the other. "I thought—"

"You thought Ariakas hired you to spy on me," said Kitiara.

"That is precisely what we wanted you to think," said Iolanthe.

Raistlin shook his head, as though deeply puzzled, though in truth he had already suspected as much.

"I will explain later," said Kit. "As I said, I was glad to hear from Iolanthe that you were still alive. I feared you and Caramon and the others would not escape the Maelstrom."

"I escaped," said Raistlin. "The others did not. They died in the Blood Sea."

"Then you don't know . . . ?" Kitiara began, then stopped.

"Know what?" Raistlin asked sharply.

"Your brother did *not* die. Caramon survived, as did Tanis and that red-haired barmaid whose name I can never recall, as well as that woman with the blue crystal staff and her barbarian hulk of a husband."

"That can't be possible!" said Raistlin.

"I assure you it is," Kit replied. "They were all in Kalaman yesterday. And there, according to my spies, they met up with Flint and Tas and that elf woman Laurana. You knew her too, I think."

Kit continued to talk about Laurana, but Raistlin wasn't listening. He was glad he had kept his hood covering his face, for his mind reeled and staggered around like a drunkard. He had been so certain that Caramon was dead. He had convinced himself of it, repeated it over and over, every morning, every night . . . He closed his eyes to keep the room from spinning and gripped the arms of the chair with his hands to try to regain control of himself.

What do I care whether Caramon is alive or dead? Raistlin asked himself, digging his fingers into the wood. It is all the same to me.

Except that it wasn't. Somewhere deep, deep inside, some weak and much-despised part of him, a part he had long tried to excise, could have wept.

Kitiara was watching him, waiting for him to reply to some question he had not heard.

"I did not know my brother was alive," Raistlin said, working to keep his emotions in check. "It's odd that he would be in Kalaman. That city is half a world away from Flotsam. How did our brother come to be there?"

"I did not ask. It was neither the time nor place for a family reunion," said Kitiara, laughing. "I was too busy telling the populace what they would have to do to ransom their so-called Golden General."

"Who is that?" asked Raistlin.

"Laurana, the elf maid."

"Oh, yes," said Raistlin. "I heard the Knights selected her when I was in Palanthas. It seems the choice was inspired. She has been winning."

"A fluke," said Kitiara angrily. "I have put an end to her victories. She is now my prisoner."

"And what do you intend to do with her?"

Kitiara paused, then said, "I intend to use her to gain the Crown of Power. I told the people of Kalaman that if they want her back, they must hand over Berem Everman."

Raistlin was starting to understand. He recalled the man at the wheel of the ship. The man who had steered the ship into the Blood Sea. An old man with young eyes. "Berem is with Tanis, isn't he?"

Kit stared at him, surprised. "How did you know?"

Raistlin shrugged. "A hunch, nothing more. You think Tanis will trade Berem for Laurana?"

"I know he will," said Kitiara. "And I will trade Laurana for the crown."

"So this is your secret plan. Where are Tanis and my brother now?" Raistlin asked.

"Trying to find some way to rescue the elf maid. My spies were on their trail, but they lost track of them, though they did come across someone who remembered a kender resembling Tasslehoff asking for directions to a place called Godshome."

"Godshome . . ." Raistlin repeated thoughtfully.

"Have you heard of it?"

Raistlin shook his head. "I am afraid not." Though of course he had heard of it. Godshome was a sacred, holy site dedicated to the gods. He wasn't going to impart such information to his sister. Knowledge is power. He wondered why Tanis and his brother and the others would be traveling there.

"It is said to be located somewhere near Neraka in the Khalkist mountains," Kit continued. "I have patrols out searching. They will soon find them, and Tanis will lead me to Berem."

"What is so important about this man?" Raistlin asked. "Why is half the army looking for him? What makes him worth the Crown of Power?"

"You don't need to know."

"If you want my help, I do."

"My baby brother is a self-serving bastard." Kitiara grinned at him. "But that's how I raised you. I will tell you a story."

She drew up a chair and sat down. Since there were only two chairs in the room, Iolanthe sat cross-legged on the bed.

"You'll find this story interesting," said Kitiara, her lips parting in a crooked smile. "It's about two siblings, one of whom kills the other."

If she expected Raistlin to react, she was disappointed. He sat still, unmoved, and waited.

"According to the tale," said Kit, "this man named Berem and his sister were out walking when they came across a broken column covered in rare and precious jewels. The two were poor, and the man, Berem, decided to steal an emerald. His sister opposed him and, to make a long story short, he bashed her head in."

"She fell and hit her head on the stone," said Iolanthe.

Kitiara waved her hand. "It doesn't matter. What does matter is that Berem ended up cursed by the gods with the emerald stuck in his chest. He's been wandering the world since, trying to escape his guilt. Meanwhile, his sister forgave him, and her good spirit entered the stone, and when Takhisis tried to get around her, she couldn't. She was blocked from coming into the world."

Raistlin would have been dubious of the remarkable story, except he had seen for himself the emerald embedded in Berem's chest.

I was right, he thought, Takhisis cannot enter the world in all her might. A good thing. Otherwise this war would have ended before it began.

"The broken column is the Foundation Stone from the Temple of Istar," Iolanthe explained. "Takhisis found it and brought it to Neraka and built her temple around it. She seeks Berem in order to destroy him, for if he joins his sister, the door to the Abyss will slam shut."

"And what am I to do?" Raistlin asked. "Why bring me into this? It seems you have thought of everything."

Kitiara cast a glance from beneath her lashes at Iolanthe, a glance the witch was not meant to see. The glance told Raistlin, *You and I will discuss this in private.* She changed the subject. "Are you in such a hurry to leave? I haven't seen you in years. Tell me, what do you think of this elf female?"

"Kitiara," said Iolanthe in warning tones. "The walls have ears. Even burnt walls."

Kit ignored her. "Everyone raves about her beauty. She's so pale and all one color, like bread dipped in milk. But then, I saw her at the High Clerist's Tower right after the battle. She was not looking her best."

"Kitiara, we have more important matters—" Iolanthe began, but Kit silenced her.

"What did you think of her?" Kit insisted.

What did Raistlin think of Laurana? That she was the only beauty left for him in the world. Even his accursed vision, which saw all things age and wither and die, had not been able to sabotage her. Elves were long-lived, and age touched the elf maiden gently. The years made her, if possible, more beautiful still.

Laurana had been a little in awe of him, a little afraid of him. She had trusted him, however. He had not known why, except that she had seemed to see something in him others could not, something even he could not see. He had appreciated her trust, been touched by it. He had loved her . . . no, not loved her, cherished her, as a man parched with thirst and lost in the desert cherishes a sip of cool water.

"She is everything you are, my sister, and all that you are not," Raistlin said softly.

His sister laughed, pleased. She took it as a compliment.

"Kitiara, I need to speak to you," Iolanthe said, exasperated. "In private."

"Perhaps I could finish writing that letter for you," Raistlin suggested.

Kitiara waved him toward the desk and walked over to the window, where she and Iolanthe put their heads together to talk in hushed tones.

Raistlin sat down. He placed the Staff of Magius at his side, keeping it near his hand. His thoughts busy, he began mechanically to copy the words of the blotted and misspelled original onto a new sheet of paper. He wrote smoothly, swiftly, and far more legibly than Kit.

As Raistlin worked, he gently pushed his cowl behind his ear to try to hear what the two were discussing. He caught only a few words, enough to give him a general impression of what they were discussing.

". . . Ariakas suspects you . . . That's why he sent your brother . . . We have to think of something to tell him . . ."

Raistlin continued the letter. Absorbed in listening, he had been paying little attention to the words he was writing until a name seemed to catch fire, blaze a hole in the page.

Laurana. The orders were about her.

Raistlin paid no more heed to Kit and Iolanthe. He gave all his attention to the letter, reading over what he had written. Kit was sending the missive to a subordinate, telling him that his orders had changed. He was no longer to bring the "captive" to Dargaard Keep. He was to take her directly to Neraka. The subordinate was to make certain Laurana was alive and unharmed—at least until the exchange for the Everman was complete. After that, when Kitiara had the crown, Laurana would be given in sacrifice to the Dark Queen.

Raistlin pondered. Kitiara was right. Tanis was certain to come to Neraka to try to save Laurana. Was there some way Raistlin could help? Kitiara wanted him here for some reason; he could not figure out why. She did not need him to capture Berem. That plot was well advanced, and there was nothing for him to do. Ariakas had sent him to betray Kit. Hidden Light had sent him to betray Kit and Ariakas. Iolanthe had some scheming plot of her own. Everyone had a knife drawn, ready to plunge it into someone else's back. He wondered if they would all end up stabbing each other.

His musings were interrupted by the sound of heavy footfalls ringing hollowly on the stone floor. Iolanthe went deathly pale.

"I must take my leave," she said hurriedly and flung her cloak around herself. "Raistlin, come see me when you return to Neraka. We have much to discuss."

Before he could say a word, Iolanthe threw her magical clay against the wall, squeezed inside the portal before it was halfway open, and shut it swiftly behind her.

The footfalls drew closer, moving slowly, resolutely, purposefully. A chill like death flowed into the room.

"You are about to meet the master of Dargaard Keep, Baby brother," said Kitiara, and she tried to smile the crooked smile, but Raistlin saw it slip.

2

Knight of the Black Rose.
The Hourglass of Stars.

23rd Day, Month of Mishamont, Year 352 AC

Death's chill flowed beneath the door, seeped through the cracks in the stone walls, sighed through the broken window panes. Raistlin shivered from the dreadful cold, and he laid down the quill pen and thrust his hands into the sleeves of his robes to try to warm them. He rose to his feet to be ready.

"Soth is very terrible," said Kitiara, her gaze fixed on the door. "But he will not harm you, so long as you are under my protection."

"I do not need your protection, my sister," said Raistlin, angered at her patronizing tone.

"Just be careful, will you, Raistlin?" said Kitiara sharply.

He was startled. She rarely, if ever, called him by name.

Kitiara added softly, "Soth could kill us both with a single word."

The door opened, and terror entered.

The death knight stood in the doorway, an imposing figure clad in the armor of a Solamnic Knight from the time of the rise of Istar. Beautifully crafted armor that had once shone silvery bright, but was now blackened and stained with blood that only the waters of redemption could remove, and Soth was far from seeking forgiveness. A black cape, bloody and tattered, hung from his shoulders.

His eyes shone red in the eye slits of his helm; red with the passion that had been his doom and that he could not control. He raged at his fate; raged at the gods; raged, sometimes, at himself. Only at night, when the banshees sang to him the mournful song of his own downfall, was the blazing fire reduced to smoldering embers of remorse and bitter regret. When the song ceased with the coming of day, Soth's rage blazed anew.

Raistlin had walked many dark places in his life, perhaps none darker than his own soul. He had taken the dread Test in the Tower. He had journeyed through Darken Wood. He had been trapped in the nightmare that was Silvanesti. He had been a prisoner in Takhisis's dungeons. In all those places, he had known fear. But when he looked into the hellish fire that blazed in the eyes of the death knight, Raistlin knew fear so awful, so debilitating that he thought he would die of it.

He could clasp the dragon orb and speak the magic and be gone as swiftly as Iolanthe. He was fumbling for the orb with his shaking hands when he saw Kitiara watching him.

Her lips curled. She was testing him, taunting him as she had when he was a child, and she was trying to force him to take a dare.

Anger acted on Raistlin like a potion, restoring his courage and his ability to think. He recognized then what he should have seen earlier but for his terror: the fear was magical, a spell Soth had cast on him.

Tit for tat, two could play at that game.

"Delu solisar!" Raistlin said swiftly. He let go of the orb and raised his hand to trace a rune in the air.

The rune caught fire and blazed brightly. The dueling magicks hung, quivering, in the air. Kitiara watched, one hand on her hip, the other clasping the hilt of her sword. She was enjoying their contest.

Soth's magic snapped. Raistlin ended his spell. The fiery rune vanished, leaving behind an afterimage of blue and wavering smoke.

Kitiara nodded in approval. "Lord Soth, Knight of the Rose, I have the honor to present Raistlin Majere." Kitiara added, half teasing and half proud, "My baby brother."

Raistlin bowed in acknowledgment of the introduction; then, raising his head and standing tall, he forced himself to look directly into the eye slits of the death knight's helm, to stare into the fires of a tortured soul's torment, though the sight made Raistlin's own soul shrivel in horror.

"You are powerful in magic for one so young," said Lord Soth. His voice was hollow and deep, burning with his constant rage, undying regret.

Raistlin bowed again. He did not yet trust himself to speak.

"You cast two shadows, Raistlin Majere," said the death knight suddenly. "Why is that?"

Raistlin had no idea what he was talking about. "I do not cast *one* shadow in this terrible place, my lord, let alone two."

The death knight's red eyes flickered.

"I do not speak of shadows cast by the sun," Lord Soth said. "I dwell on two planes, forced to dwell on the plane of the living and cursed to dwell in the plane of the dead who cannot die. And in both I see your shadow, darker than darkness."

Raistlin understood.

Kitiara had no idea what Soth meant. "Raistlin has a twin brother—" she began.

"No longer," Raistlin said, casting her an irate glance. She could be as stupid as Caramon sometimes.

Between the spellcasting, the terror, and the intrigue, Raistlin was suddenly worn out. "You brought me here because you required my help, my sister. I have pledged you and Takhisis my allegiance. If you wish me to serve you in some way, tell me how. If not, allow me to go home."

Kitiara glanced at Lord Soth. "What do you think?"

"He is dangerous," said Soth.

"Who? Raistlin?" Kitiara scoffed, startled and amused.

"He will be your doom." The death knight stared at Raistlin, his flame eyes flickering.

Kitiara hesitated, watching Raistlin, frowning, and fingering the hilt of her sword. "Are you saying I should kill him?"

"I am saying you could try," Raistlin said, his gaze going from one to the other. His fingers closed over a bit of amber.

Kitiara stared at him, and suddenly she began to laugh. "Come with me," she said, grabbing a blazing torch from the wall. "I have something to show you."

"What about him?" Raistlin asked, not moving from where he stood.

The death knight had walked over to the window and gazed down at the desolation.

"Evening is coming," said Kitiara. "Soth has somewhere else to go. Make haste," she added, shivering. "You don't want to be anywhere close."

The wail was distant, yet the eerie and awful sound pierced Raistlin, smote his heart. He slowed his pace and looked over his shoulder, stared back down the corridor. The song was ghastly, yet he seemed compelled to listen to it.

Kitiara caught hold of his wrist. "Stop up your ears!" she said warningly.

"What is it?" he asked. He could feel the hair prickling on his neck, rising on his arms.

"Banshees. The elf women who share his curse. They are compelled to sing to him every night, recite the story of his crimes. He sits in the chamber where his wife and child perished and stares at the bloodstain on the floor and listens."

They both hastened down the corridor, increasing their pace. Still the evil song pursued them. The wailing seemed to beat on Raistlin with black wings and tear at him with sharp claws. He tried to muffle his ears with his hands, but the song throbbed in his blood. He saw that Kitiara was very pale, and she was sweating.

"Every night it is the same. I never get used to it."

The corridor they walked came to a dead end. Raistlin guessed they had not walked all that way for nothing, and he waited patiently to see what happened. Kit handed the torch to Raistlin to hold. Raistlin could have offered to use the light from his staff, but he never liked to reveal its power to people unless there was some good reason to do so. He held the torch so she could see what she was doing.

Kitiara put her left hand on a certain stone in the wall, her right hand on another stone, and pressed a third stone on the floor with her foot. By force of habit, Raistlin made a mental note of the precise location of each stone with regard to its neighbors. He certainly hoped he would never have to return to Dargaard Keep, but one never knew. Grinding on its hinges, the wall that was actually a door swung slowly open. Kit sprang through the opening into the darkness beyond. Raistlin glanced around, then followed cautiously after her.

Kitiara placed her hand on a stone on the other side, and the door swung shut, muffling the banshees' wail. He and Kitiara both shared a sigh of relief.

She took the torch from him and went ahead of him, lighting the way. Stairs carved out of rock, enclosed by rough-hewn rock walls, spiraled downward. Kitiara descended rapidly, her boots ringing on the stone, drowning out all sound of the banshees. Raistlin followed. He noted that the stairway was not charred and that there was no smell of smoke or death.

"This stonework is new," he said, running his hand over the rock and collecting dust on his fingers. "Recently built."

"By the hand of our Queen," said Kitiara.

Raistlin stopped walking. "Where are you taking me? What is down here?"

Kitiara smiled slyly. "Perhaps you'd rather go back upstairs to listen to the choir?"

Raistlin resumed his descent. The staircase—he counted forty-five stairs—led to a door made of solid steel. Raistlin stared at it, impressed. The door alone was worth all the wealth in Neraka. He could not imagine what treasure lay behind it.

Kitiara placed her right hand, palm flat, on the center of the door, which was smooth, without a mark that Raistlin could see. Kit spoke a single word, "Takhisis," and light flared white beneath her palm. She invoked the name of the Dark Queen again, and a green light glowed. Kitiara said the name three more times, and three times the light changed colors, going from red to blue to black.

The outline of a five-headed dragon blazed, etched into the door, and the door rose, silently and smoothly, until it disappeared into the ceiling.

Kitiara motioned Raistlin to go inside. He remained outside the door, regarding her coldly.

"You first," he said.

Kitiara laughed and shook her head and walked ahead of him. She held the torch high, so he could inspect the vault. The light shone on walls carved out of solid rock. The vault was not large, perhaps twenty paces by twenty paces. The ceiling was low. Raistlin could have reached up his hand to touch it.

The vault contained only three objects—an hourglass, made of crystal encased in gold; the golden pedestal on which the hourglass stood; and a candle marked with red, numbered stripes placed at regular intervals, starting with one and ending at twenty-four. The candle kept count of the hours of the day. It had burned nearly to the bottom.

Raistlin still did not trust Kitiara, but curiosity overcame caution. He entered the room and walked over to inspect the hourglass. He had no need to cast a spell to tell that it was enchanted.

The top of the hourglass was filled with sand; the bottom held darkness, utter and eternal. Raistlin looked closely and saw that a single grain of sand was lodged in the narrow opening between the two halves. The grain had not fallen. It was blocking the rest of the sand, preventing it from dropping.

"It's clogged," said Raistlin.

"Wait!" Kitiara breathed.

"For what?"

"For Dark Watch," said Kitiara.

Raistlin watched the flame of the candle consume the wax, eating away at the white until it reached the red stripe that marked the end of a day. When the red began to melt, he looked at the hourglass and drew in a soft breath.

The single grain of sand that was lodged in the narrow opening between the two halves began to sparkle. The grain shone, bright as a star, and like a star, it streaked through the darkness, falling to the bottom. The grain flickered a moment in the darkness; then the light faded and went out. Another small grain dropped into the narrow opening and hung there.

Kitiara replaced the candle that marked the hours with a new candle, lighting the new one from the guttering flame of the old. The flame burned clear and unwavering in the still air of the vault.

"What is this?" Raistlin asked, his voice soft with awe.

"The Hourglass of Stars," said Kitiara. "It began keeping time on the first day of creation, and when the sand runs out, time will end."

Raistlin longed to touch the glistening sides of the crystal, but he kept his hands clasped together in the sleeves of his robes. One needed to be wary of artifacts.

"And what is it doing here? How did Takhisis come by it?"

"She forged it," said Kitiara.

"What does this have to do with Ariakas?" Raistlin asked.

"Nothing," said Kitiara.

He looked at her, startled.

"Oh, I know that's what I told Iolanthe. I had to tell her something for her to bring you here, otherwise she would have been suspicious. How do you think that wizardess

Ladonna escaped? Iolanthe helped her. The witch is not to be trusted, Baby brother."

Raistlin was not surprised. That fit with his suspicions.

"I do not trust her," said Raistlin. "I trust no one."

"Not even me?" Kitiara asked playfully.

She reached out her hand as if to smooth back his hair as she had done when he was a child burning up with fever.

Raistlin drew back, avoiding her touch. "Why am I here? What do you want from me?"

Kitiara lowered her hand and rested it on the golden top of the hourglass. "The Sly One. That's what they called you. Perhaps that's why you were always my favorite. It seems that Nuitari has betrayed his mother for the last time. Takhisis has decided to get rid of the god of magic and his two treacherous cousins. She is bringing in three new gods, Gods of the Gray. They will answer directly to their Queen, and she will give them the magic."

Raistlin staggered as though he'd been punched in the face. If he had not been holding on to his staff, he would have fallen. All thoughts of rescuing Laurana flew from his mind. He had himself to consider. He was in deadly peril. Kit was talking about destroying the gods of magic, destroying the magic that was his lifeblood.

He could feel the Dark Queen very near him. He could feel her breath upon the back of his neck. He heard her voice as he had heard it in her shrine in the Red Mansion.

Serve me! Bow down before me!

This was her punishment for his disobedience. He had to be careful here, very careful.

"An interesting notion," said Raistlin cooly. "Removing three gods cannot be easy, even for Takhisis. How does she plan to accomplish this?"

"With your assistance, Baby brother." Kitiara gazed into the flame of the candle. "Tomorrow night, the

Night of the Eye, the most powerful wizards in Ansalon will gather in one place—the Tower of High Sorcery in Wayreth. You are going to destroy that Tower and those within."

"And if I refuse?" Raistlin asked.

"Why should you? You owe these wizards nothing. They made you suffer," said Kitiara. "Takhisis will make you far more powerful than Par-Salian ever was, more powerful than all wizards in the world combined. You have only to ask her."

Raistlin watched the flame of the candle eat into the wax.

"What do you want of me?" he asked.

"Serve Takhisis and she will give you everything your heart desires," said Kitiara. She ran her hand over the top of the hourglass. "Betray her and she will devour you."

"That is not much of a choice," said Raistlin.

"You are lucky she is giving you a choice at all. I do not know what you did, but our Queen is not pleased with you. She gives you this chance to prove yourself. What is your answer?"

Raistlin shrugged. "I bow to my Queen."

Kitiara smiled that crooked smile. "I thought you might."

3

Broken door. A question of trust.

24th Day, Month of Mishamont, Year 352 AC

I t was long after Dark Watch. The new day had begun, the day that would change his life. Raistlin was back in his room in the Broken Shield without any memory of how he came to be there. He was appalled to realize he'd cast spells and traveled the corridors of magic, all without being consciously aware of what he was doing. He was glad to think that some part of his brain was working rationally when it seemed that the rest of his brain was running around, shrieking wildly, and flinging up its hands.

"Calm down!" he said to himself, pacing the length of the small room. "I have to be calm. I have to think this through."

Someone banged on the floor from the room underneath. "It's the godsdamned middle of the godsdamned night!" a voice shouted up through the floorboards. "Stop that godsdamned tromping around, or I'll come up there and godsdamned stop it for you!"

Raistlin briefly considered hurling a fireball at the floor, but that would only burn down the inn and accomplish nothing. He flung himself on his bed. He was exhausted. He needed sleep. He tried closing his eyes, but when he did, he saw the tiny grain of sand blazing to life and falling into darkness. He saw the candle burning away the hours.

Tonight, the Night of the Eye.

Tonight, I must destroy the magic.

Tonight, I must destroy myself.

For that's what it amounted to. The magic was his life. Without it, he was nothing, less than nothing. Oh yes, Takhisis had promised that he would receive his magic from her, as did Ariakas. Raistlin would have to pray to her, beg her. And she might choose to toss him a crumb or not.

And if he refused, if he went against her, where could he go in the wide world that the goddess could not find him?

Raistlin felt half suffocated. He rose from the bed and walked to the window and flung open the shutters to the cool night air. In the distance the dark outline of the temple dominated Neraka, seeming to obliterate the stars. The towers and spires writhed in his fevered vision, changed to a clawed hand that lunged at him, reaching for his throat . . .

Raistlin came to himself with a gasp. He had fallen asleep while standing on his feet. He staggered back to his bed and collapsed down on it. He closed his eyes, and sleep came, pouncing on him like a wild beast and dragging him down into dark depths.

But as he slept, the cold and logical part of his mind must have continued to work, for when he woke only a few hours later, he knew what he had to do.

Day was dawning, time for the changing of the watch. Soldiers coming off duty were in a good mood, heading for the taverns. Soldiers coming on duty grumbled and swore as they took up their posts. Gray mists like tentacles slid sullenly over the city. The clouds would blow away. The Night of the Eye would be clear. The Night of the Eye was always clear. The gods saw to that.

Raistlin walked swiftly, his hands in his sleeves, his head bowed, his cowl pulled low. He bumped into soldiers, who glared at him and shouted insults to which he paid no heed. The soldiers muttered, but went on their way, either late for duty or eager for pleasure.

Raistlin entered the Red District, passed through the gate, and stopped to get his bearings. He'd been here only once before, and that had been after dark and he'd been pretending to be unconscious.

He followed the route Maelstrom had taken and found what he thought was the entry point to the tunnels at the back of a large building. The entrance was well hidden, and Raistlin couldn't be sure. He walked around to the front, glanced up at the sign—a lute suspended from a rope above the door. The wind had a trick of vibrating the strings, making them hum.

Raistlin banged on the door. Dogs barked.

"We're not open yet!" a deep voice yelled from inside.

"You are now," said Raistlin. He drew a bit of dung out of a pouch and began rolling it between his fingers as he spoke the words to the spell. *"Daya laksana banteng!"*

Strength filled his body. Raistlin kicked the heavy wooden door and shattered it to splinters. The iron lock dropped off and fell to the floor. Raistlin knocked aside some of the wooden shards with the end of his staff and entered the shop.

He was immediately set upon by two mastiffs. The dogs did not attack. They stood in front of him, their heads lowered, ears flat. The female curled her lip, showing yellowed fangs.

"Call off your dogs," said Raistlin.

"Go to the Abyss!" howled a black-bearded man seated on a stool in the back of the cluttered room. "Look what you've done to my door!"

"Call off your dogs, Lute," Raistlin repeated. "And do not even think of touching that crossbow. If you do, the only thing left on that stool will be a greasy, hairy glob of burnt dwarf."

Lute slowly moved his hand from the crossbow.

"Shinare," he said sullenly. "Hiddukel. Come to me."

The dogs gave Raistlin a parting growl and slunk back to their master.

"Lock them in that room," Raistlin ordered, indicating the half-dwarf's bedroom.

Lute ordered the dogs into his room and, heaving himself, grumbling, off the stool, he locked the door on them. Raistlin made his way through the piles of junk to the back of the store.

"What do you want?" Lute asked, glaring at Raistlin.

"I need to speak to Talent."

"You've come to the wrong place. He's at the Broken Shield—"

Raistlin slammed his hand down on the counter. "I am in no mood for your lies. Tell Talent I must talk to him now!"

Lute sneered. "I'm not your bloody errand boy—"

Raistlin seized hold of Lute's thick, full beard and gave it a twist that brought tears to the half-dwarf's eyes.

Lute yelped and tried desperately to break Raistlin's grip. The half-dwarf might as well have tried to break one of the oak beams holding up his ceiling. Raistlin was still under the empowering effects of the spell. He gave Lute's beard a sharp yank, drawing blood, and making him moan with pain. Hearing their master's cry, the dogs barked furiously and flung themselves against the door.

"I'll tear your beard out by the roots," said Raistlin, hissing the words through his teeth, "unless you do as I ask. You will send for Talent now. You will tell him to meet me in the same place we met last time: the tunnels beneath this building."

Lute muttered a curse.

Raistlin yanked harder.

"I'll do what you say!" Lute shrieked, pawing at Raistlin's hand. "Let go of me! Let go!"

"You'll talk to Talent?" Raistlin asked, retaining his hold on the beard.

Lute gave a nod. Tears streamed down his cheeks.

Raistlin released his grip, flinging Lute backward.

The half-dwarf massaged his burning chin. "I'll have to send Mari. I can't go myself. You broke down my door. I'll be robbed blind."

"Where is Mari?"

"She generally comes around about this time."

As if conjured up by his words, the kender appeared at the entrance.

"Hey, Lute, what happened to your door?" she asked. "Oh, hullo, Raist. I didn't see you there."

"Never you mind about anything," Lute growled. "And don't you set foot in here. Run and fetch Talent. Tell him to go to the tunnels."

"Sure, Lute, I'll go. But what happened to the door—?"

"*Now*, you lame-brain!" Lute bellowed.

"You must hurry, Mari," said Raistlin. "It's urgent."

The kender looked from one to the other, then dashed off.

"And bring back a carpenter!" Lute shouted after her.

"How do I get to the tunnel?" Raistlin asked.

"You're so smart, you figure it out," Lute said. He was still rubbing his chin.

Raistlin cast a swift glance around the cluttered shop. "Ah, of course, the trapdoor is beneath the dog kennel. Not terribly original. Is it locked? Is there a key?"

Lute muttered something.

"I can always blast a hole in your floor," said Raistlin.

"No key," Lute said. "Just lift up the damn door and go down the damn stairs. Watch your step. The stairs are steep. It would be a pity if you fell and broke your neck."

Raistlin went over to the dog crate and shoved aside the bedding to find the trap door beneath. The spell he'd cast on himself was starting to wear off, but fortunately he had just strength enough to be able to pull open the heavy wooden door. It was at times such as this that he missed Caramon.

Raistlin peered down into the darkness that would be even darker once he shut the trap door.

"*Shirak*," he said, and the crystal on top of his staff began to glow.

He gathered up the hem of his robes and carefully navigated the stairs as the trapdoor fell shut behind him. The subterranean chamber was silent and smelled of loam. He could hear the drip of water in the distance. He flashed the light around and, after a few moments, found the chair to which he'd been chained and the chair Talent had straddled.

Raistlin took Talent's chair and sat down to wait.

Talent was not long in coming. Raistlin had not even had time to grow impatient before he heard the sound of booted feet thudding on the dirt floor and saw the light of a lantern shining in the darkness. Raistlin had his rose petals in his hand and the words to a sleep spell on his lips, just in case Talent had decided to send someone else to the meeting; someone such as Maelstrom.

But it was Talent himself who appeared in the circle of light cast by the staff.

"Sit down," said Raistlin, and he shoved out a chair with his foot.

Talent remained standing. He folded his arms over his chest.

"I'm here, but not because I want to be. You could have put us all in danger—"

"You are already in danger," said Raistlin. "I have been to Dargaard Keep. I have spoken to my sister. Please sit down. I don't like to have to crane my neck to look up at you."

Talent hesitated, then sat down. His sword hung from his side. The tip brushed the dirt floor.

"Well?" he said tersely. "What did the Blue Lady have to say?"

"A great many things, but most do not concern you. One does. You have been betrayed. Takhisis knows everything. She has ordered Ariakas to kill you and Mari and all the rest of your gang."

Talent frowned. "It's not that I don't believe you, Majere, but if Ariakas knows, why haven't I been arrested?"

"Because you are far more popular in Neraka than the Emperor," said Raistlin. "There would be rioting in the streets if you were arrested and the Broken Shield was closed down. The same with your hairy friend upstairs. His business is crucial to most of the people in this city, especially now that many of the troops aren't being paid. And then there are the clerics in the temple, half of whom are in your pocket. They'd have to give up all the black market luxuries they've come to enjoy."

Talent gave a sardonic smile. "I suppose that's all true enough. So Ariakas doesn't plan to have us arrested—"

"No. He's simply going to have you killed," said Raistlin.

"When is all this supposed to happen?"

"Tonight," said Raistlin.

"Tonight?" Talent stood up in alarm.

"The Night of the Eye. Iolanthe tells me that you and your friend at the Hairy Troll always throw a street party where you set bonfires. Tonight the bonfires will flare out of control. The flames will spread to both the Hairy Troll and the Broken Shield. As you fight the flames, there will be a terrible accident. You and Mari and Maelstrom and other members of Hidden Light will be trapped inside the blazing building. You will burn to death."

"What about Lute?" Talent asked harshly. "He won't be at these celebrations. He never leaves this shop."

"His body will be found in the morning. By a strange mischance, his own dogs will turn on him and rip him apart."

"I see," said Talent grimly. "Who is the traitor? Who betrayed us?"

Raistlin stood up. "I do not know. Nor do I care. I have my own troubles, and they are far greater than yours. Which brings me to my final request. There are two others who are marked for death this night. One is Iolanthe—"

"Iolanthe? Ariakas's Witch?" Talent said, amazed. "Why would he want to kill her?"

"He does not, but the Blue Lady does. The second is Snaggle, the owner of the mageware shop on Wizard's

Row. He will not want to leave his shop. He'll have to be 'persuaded'."

"What in the Abyss is going on?" Talent demanded, aghast.

"I can't tell you the entire plot. What I can tell you is that this night, Queen Takhisis will seize control of magic. By her command, the Blue Lady is sending out death squads to kill as many wizards as possible. Snaggle and Iolanthe are both on her list."

Talent stared at him, silent and appalled. Then he said, "Why tell me? Why not tell Iolanthe?"

"Because I cannot trust her," said Raistlin. "I am not certain even now whose side she is on."

Talent shook his head. "Iolanthe is a threat to you, and yet you want to protect her. I thought your type would be more likely to laugh as you watched her go up in flames. I don't understand you, Majere."

"I imagine there is a great deal in this world you do not understand," said Raistlin caustically. "Unfortunately, I don't have time to explain it to you. Suffice it to say I owe both Iolanthe and Snaggle a debt. And I always pay my debts."

He picked up his staff with the glowing light and started to leave.

"Hey!" said Talent. "Where are you going?"

"I am taking the back way out," said Raistlin. "Your friend Lute would not be pleased to see me again."

"You're probably right. I heard about the broken door," said Talent, falling into step beside Raistlin. "But you'll get lost. I'll have to show you."

"Do not bother. I remember the route from when I was here the last time."

"You remember it? But you couldn't. You were—" Talent stopped. He stared at the mage. "You only pretended to be drugged. But how did you know the drink was spiked—?"

"I have an excellent sense of smell," said Raistlin.

The two walked together. The only sounds were the gentle thump of the staff on the dirt floor, the slight swishing of the black robes, and the thudding of Talent's boots. Talent walked with his head down, his hands behind his back, lost in thought. Raistlin cast keen glances around him, noting the many tunnels branching off from the one they were using. He pictured a map of the city in his head and used it to try to calculate where each might lead.

"This system is quite extensive," Raistlin remarked. "I would guess, for example, that this tunnel"—he pointed with his staff—"leads to the Dark Queen's temple. And this." He pointed out another tunnel. "This one leads to the Broken Shield."

"And this," said Talent grimly, placing his hand on the hilt of his sword, "leads to the death of people who do too much damn guessing."

Raistlin smiled and inclined his head.

"Something I'm wondering," said Talent abruptly. "You don't trust Iolanthe, a fellow wizard. The gods know I don't trust you. Yet you trust me. You must since you told me all this. Why is that?"

"You remind me of someone," said Raistlin after a moment's pause. "Like you, he was a Solamnic. *Est Sularus uth Mithas.* He lived that motto. His honor *was* his life."

"Mine isn't," said Talent.

"Which is why you are still alive and Sturm is not. And why I trust you."

Talent escorted the mage out of the tunnels. Once they were on street level, Talent kept an eye on Raistlin, watching until the black robes had merged with the crowds in the street. Even after Raistlin had gone, Talent remained standing in the alleyway, going over the wizard's words in his mind.

It seemed too incredible to be believed. Takhisis trying to destroy the gods of magic! Well, so what? Who would miss a few wizards anyway? The world would be a better place without wizards, or so most people believed. Most people, including Talent Orren.

Take that young man, Talent thought. He makes my flesh crawl. Only pretending to be drugged! Maelstrom will have to be more careful next time. Only there may not be a next time. Not if what Majere says is true. Do I trust him? This might all be a trap.

Talent left the alley and made his way to Lute's shop. There he found that his friend, for the first time in memory, had actually summoned up the energy to walk from the counter to the front of the shop. Lute stood glaring at the wreckage of his front door, poking at the fragments with his cane and swearing. Mari sat on the stoop, her chin in her hands, listening to Lute's colorful language with evident enjoyment.

"Mari," said Talent, kneeling down beside the kender to look her in the eye. "What do you think of that wizard, Majere?"

"He's my friend," said Mari promptly. "We had a long talk, him and me. We're going to change the darkness."

Talent regarded her in silence a moment. Then he stood up. "We have a problem."

"Damn right we do!" Lute said angrily. "Look what that rutting bugger did to my door!"

"A bigger problem than that," said Talent Orren. "Come back inside, both of you. We have to talk."

4

God of White. God of Red. God of Black.

24th Day, Month of Mishamont, Year 352 AC

ambskin," said Raistlin. "The finest. And a quill pen."

"What type?" asked Snaggle, taking down a box. He placed it on the counter and opened it. "I have some lovely swan feathers, sir. Just come in. Black swans as well as white."

Raistlin studied the quills, then picked one up. He eyed the tip carefully, for it had to be perfect, and ran his fingers over the soft feather. His mind went back to that day in Master Theobald's class, the day that had changed his life. No, that was not right. That day his life had not been changed. His life had been affirmed.

"I will take the crow quill," said Raistlin.

Snaggle pursed his lips. "Crow? Are you certain, sir? You can afford better. Those potions of yours are marvels. I can't keep them in stock. I was planning on ordering more."

He shoved the swan feather temptingly forward. "I

have peacock, as well. Iolanthe uses only peacock feathers for her work."

"I am not surprised," said Raistlin. "Thank you, but this is the one I want."

He placed the lowly crow feather on the counter. He selected the strip of lambskin with great care. For that item, he did choose the best.

Snaggle added up the purchases and found that they equaled what he owed Raistlin for the potions. He gave Raistlin an order for more, an order that would never be filled. Raistlin would, he hoped, be able to save the old man, but he would not be able to save the shop, which would be burned to the ground. Raistlin looked at the neatly labeled boxes stacked on the shelves, boxes containing spell components and artifacts, scrolls and potions. He thought of Iolanthe's apartment above the shop, of her spellbooks and scrolls, clothes and jewels, and other valuables. All lost in the flames.

Pausing on his way out, Raistlin glanced back at Snaggle, who was seated on his stool, calmly drinking tarbean tea, unaware of the fury rolling toward him.

"How do you celebrate the Night of the Eye, sir?" Raistlin asked.

Snaggle shrugged. "Same as any other night for me. I drink my tea, lock up the shop, and go to my bed."

Raistlin had a momentary vision of flames engulfing the shop, engulfing the old man's bed. Secreting his precious purchases in the long, flowing sleeve of his robes, he returned to the street, heading to his next destination, the Tower of High Sorcery in Neraka.

Raistlin cast a spell of holding on the door, as powerful as he could make it. He did not think anyone was likely to come calling, but he could not take a chance on being disturbed. He walked up the stairs slowly. Time was slipping away. He could see the grain of sand lodged in the narrow part of the hourglass. Every moment that passed, the grain slipped a little closer to oblivion.

Raistlin was tired. He had been on the move since before dawn, unable to rest until he had spoken to Talent and made certain all was well there. He had taken care of the less important matters first. Arriving at the moment of decision, his steps slowed. Even by warning Talent, Raistlin had not yet committed himself to the battle against Takhisis. He could always back out, do what he was supposed to do, what he had assured Kitiara he would do.

Raistlin continued his climb.

He sat on the high stool in the shabby, little kitchen that still smelled of boiled cabbage. Unwrapping the package, he gently withdrew the lambskin and placed it on the table in front of him. He smoothed it with his hands as he had as a child. He lifted the crow quill pen and dipped it in the ink. He saw his hand, and it was the hand of the child. He heard a voice, and it was the voice of his master, Theobald, hated and despised.

You will write down on this lambskin the words, 'I, Magus.' If you have the gift, something will happen. If not, nothing.

The adult Raistlin wrote the words in sharply angled, bold, large letters.

I, Magus.

Nothing happened. Nothing had happened that first time either.

Raistlin turned inward, to the very core of his being, and he vowed, I will do this. Nothing in my life matters except this. No moment exists except this moment. I am born in this moment, and if I fail, I will die in this moment.

He remembered his prayer, the words forever seared on his heart.

Gods of magic, help me! I will dedicate my life to you. I will serve you always. I will bring glory to your names. Help me, please help me!

The prayer he prayed as an adult was different.

"Gods of magic," he said, "I promised I would dedicate my life to you. I promised to serve you always. This day, I keep my promise."

He stared down at the words he had written, at the simple words of a child's test, and he thought of the sacrifices he had made, the pain he had endured, and the pain he would continue to endure until the end of his life. He thought of the blessings he had been given and how that made the pain worthwhile. He thought of how the magic, the pain, the blessings might be swept away, leaving him like the child he had been: weak and sickly, alone and afraid.

He thought of Antimodes, his mentor, a mage of practical mind, a businessman; Par-Salian, wise and far seeing but perhaps not wise and far-seeing enough; Justarius, whose leg had been crippled in the Test, who wanted only to be left in peace to raise a family. He thought of Ladonna, who had believed the Dark Queen's promise and been betrayed and burned with fury.

They would all die this night unless he stopped Takhisis.

Raistlin raised his voice and looked to the heavens. "I know I have disappointed all of you. I know that you do not approve of what I am. I know that I have broken your laws. That does not mean I do not revere you or that I lack respect. This night I prove it. By coming to you, I risk my life."

"Not much of a risk," said Nuitari. "Without the magic, you have no life."

The god stood over Raistlin. His face was round as a moon, and his eyes were dark and empty, which made the anger in them all the more terrible. He was dressed in black robes, and he held in his hand a scourge of black tentacles.

"You did, as you say, break our laws," said Solinari, coming to stand beside his cousin. Dressed in white robes, the god held a scourge of ice. "The Conclave of Wizards was established for a purpose—to govern the magic and those who use it. You not only break the laws, you flout them, mock them."

"Yet I understand him," said Lunitari, beautiful and awful, her hair black streaked with white. Her robes were red, and she carried a scourge of fire. "I do not condone his actions, but I understand. What do you want of us, Raistlin Majere?"

"To save what will be lost this night. In Dargaard Keep, there is an underground chamber. Within this chamber is the Hourglass of Stars. Takhisis forged it. The sand she poured into it is the future she desires, a future in which she reigns supreme. Each grain that falls brings that future closer to coming to pass.

"This night, Takhisis will bring three gods—the Gods of the Gray, gods of 'new magic' to guard the Hourglass. She intends for these gods of no color to replace you. Her new gods will be loyal to her. All magic will flow through her. You three will no longer be needed."

The cousins stared at him in silence, too amazed to speak.

"This night," Raistlin continued, "you can ambush these three gods, and break the Hourglass. This night, you can save yourselves. You can save the magic."

"If what you say is true—" Solinari began.

"Look into my heart," said Raistlin tersely. "See if I speak the truth."

"He does," Lunitari said and her voice trembled with anger.

Solinari frowned. "To fight gods, we must exert all our power. We will have to withdraw our magic from the world. What will happen to our wizards? They will be left powerless."

"The majority of wizards will be in the Tower of High Sorcery. I will undertake to protect them."

"And we are supposed to trust you!"

Raistlin faintly smiled. "You have no choice."

"If you do this, Takhisis will know you betrayed her. She will be your enemy not only in this life, but in the life beyond," Lunitari warned.

"Join the Conclave of Wizards. Conform to the law," said Solinari. "We will protect you."

"Otherwise, you will be on your own," said Nuitari.

"I will consider your proposal," said Raistlin.

What else could he say, withering in the heat of the scourge of flame and burning in the cold of the scourge of ice and writhing with the sting of the black tentacles?

Solinari and Nuitari were not pleased, but they had work to do, and they did not stay to argue or cajole. The two departed, and only Lunitari remained.

"You have no intention of joining the Conclave, do you?"

Raistlin looked down at the words on the lambskin. Black ink on white. He traced over them with his finger.

"I, Magus," he said softly.

He was startled to see the words turn red, as though written in blood. He shivered and crumpled the lambskin in his hand.

When he looked up, Lunitari was gone.

Raistlin sighed deeply and closed his eyes and let his head sink into his hands. They were right. He was playing a dangerous game, a deadly game. He was risking not only his life, but his soul. Still, as Nuitari had said, it was not much of a risk.

Raistlin felt worn out, and there was still work to be done before the day turned into momentous night. He left the Tower of High Sorcery in Neraka, never to return.

Raistlin entered the city proper, using his forged pass to get through the gate. He had to wait in long lines, for the gate was crowded with soldiers. He remembered Kitiara saying something to the effect that Ariakas had summoned all the Highlords to Neraka. She was coming herself, once the matter of the gods of magic was settled.

Raistlin went straight to the temple. He entered through the front, humbly requesting one of the dark pilgrims to act as his guide.

The pilgrim took him to the Abbey. Raistlin prostrated himself on the floor before the altar, lying down on his belly, his forehead touching the floor, and prayed to Takhisis.

"My Queen, I have done as you asked. I beseech your blessing."

5

The prayer meeting.

24th Day, Month of Mishamont, Year 352 AC

The Night of the Eye was the time when the moons that were the representations of the gods of magic were in alignment, forming an unblinking eye in the heavens and granting power to their wizards throughout Ansalon.

But that night, the moons did not rise. The light of Solinari did not gild the lakes with silver. The red light of Lunitari did not set the skies aflame. The black light of Nuitari, visible only to those who had dedicated themselves to him, was invisible to all. The moons were gone. And so was the magic.

The Eye had closed.

Across the continent, the death squads of Queen Takhisis went forth to seek out the hapless, powerless wizards and destroy them. Squadrons of draconians, armed with swords and knives, dutifully set out from the temple in Neraka. One squad went to the ramshackle Tower of High Sorcery. Finding no one there, they set it ablaze. Another went to the mageware store of Snaggle on Wizard's Row. He was gone, much to their astonishment, for Snaggle had never before been known to leave his shop.

Angry and frustrated, the draconians ransacked the shop, removing the neatly labeled containers from the shelves and emptying their contents into the street, then setting them on fire. The draconians smashed bottles and broke jars and confiscated artifacts to be taken back to the temple. When the shop was empty, they set fire to the building. Other squads were dispatched to the Broken Shield and the Hairy Troll to arrange for the "accidental" fires that would burn down the taverns and, by sad mischance, kill the owners.

The squadron sent to the Broken Shield was led by Commander Slith, and he was not happy. Slith didn't give two clicks of his scales for wizards and would just as soon see them slit from gut to gullet as not. But he liked Talent Orren. Slith liked Talent and he especially liked the steel Talent paid him. Slith not only procured many of the goods Talent sold on his black market, the draconian was paid a commission on all customers he sent Talent's way.

Slith was reflecting gloomily that with his income about to be reduced to nothing except his army pay, which he had not received, he no longer had a reason to hang around Neraka. Slith did not belong here. He was a deserter who had left the army long before, only stopping in Neraka because he'd heard there was steel to be made. The sivak tramped down the dark street, racking his brain, trying to figure out some way to disobey orders without actually having to disobey orders. He became aware that one of his subordinates was trying to claim his attention.

"Yeah, what?" Slith snarled.

"Sir, there's something wrong," said Glug.

"If you mean Takhisis forgot to give you a brain, that's already common knowledge," Slith muttered.

"It's not that, sir," said Glug. "Look at the tavern. It's . . . well, it's quiet, sir. Too quiet. Where's the party?"

Slith came to a halt. That was a damn good question. Where *was* the party? There were supposed to be bonfires, crowds in the streets, crowds that had been paid well to set fire to the tavern. Slith saw lights in the Broken Shield, but there was no raucous laughter, rowdy merriment, or drunken revelry. The Broken Shield was quiet as a tomb.

That thought was not comforting. He looked up the street, and he looked down. He saw no one.

"What do we do, sir?" asked Glug.

"Follow me," Slith said.

He marched across the street, his squadron scraping along behind.

Slith approached the door to the Broken Shield. A large human, who went by the name of Maelstrom and who was one of Slith's particular pals, was acting as guard.

"No dracos," Maelstrom said, and he pointed to the sign, "Humans only."

"We're here in the name of the Dark Queen," said Slith.

"Oh, well, that's different," said Maelstrom, and he grinned and opened the door. "Go right in."

"You men wait," Slith ordered, leaving his squad in the street.

He walked inside the tavern and came to a dead stop, blinking in astonishment.

The tavern was packed. Every table was occupied, and those who hadn't been able to find a seat lined the walls. Most of the patrons were soldiers, but a large number of dark pilgrims were there as well, seated in places of honor near the front. Slith recognized some of Talent's best black market customers. As the sivak stood, gaping, one of the dark pilgrims rose and began to lead the crowd in prayer.

"Forgive us, Dark Majesty," the pilgrim cried out, raising her hands. "We ask you to restore to us the moons you have swept from the heavens! Hear our plea!"

As the soldiers and pilgrims began to chant the name of Takhisis, Talent Orren, spotting Slith, made his way through the crowd.

"What in the Abyss is going on here?" Slith asked, staring.

"You are welcome, Commander," said Talent solemnly. "You and your men. Come, join us in our supplications to the Dark Queen."

Slith gave a snort. His tongue flicked in and out of his fangs. "Cut the crap, Talent," he rasped.

"The Dark Queen has taken the moons out of the sky," Talent continued in loud and reverent tones. "We have come together to seek her forgiveness." His voice dropped. *"All* of us have come together, if you take my meaning."

Slith saw old man Snaggle looking extremely irate. Judging from the way he was squirming, he was tied to his chair. A female kender sat beside him, grinning widely. And there was Lute, his great bulk overlapping a stool, his two dogs lying at his feet.

"You were tipped off," Slith said in sudden realization.

"Join me in prayer!" Talent cried loudly.

He grabbed hold of Slith's shoulder and drew him close and whispered in his ear. "I think it only fair to warn you, my friend, that these pious men, who have come here tonight to pray, are armed to the teeth and outnumber you three to one. They will take it very badly if you interrupt their prayers, and they'll take it far worse if you burn down their tavern."

Slith saw that everyone in the crowd was watching him. He saw hands resting on knives and clubs, the hilts of swords, or sacred medallions.

"I suppose they're holding prayer services in the Hairy Troll tonight as well," said Slith.

"Indeed they are," said Talent.

Slith shook his head. "You won't get away with it, Talent. The Nightlord will be furious when he finds out. He'll come here himself to arrest you."

"He'll find the birds have flown the coop," said Talent. "Maelstrom and Mari and Snaggle and myself."

Talent's expression grew serious and, under the cover of some particularly loud exhortations, he said softly, "Have you seen Iolanthe?"

"The witch? No."

"I don't know where she is. She was supposed to meet me here."

Slith eyed his friend. The sivak was not particularly good at reading the emotions of humans, probably because he didn't really give a rat's ass, but Talent's affliction was so obvious, the draconian couldn't very well miss it. There being no female draconians, Slith had never experienced that particular emotion himself, and although sometime he regretted the loss, at times such as this, seeing the pain of worry and fear on Talent's face, Slith considered himself lucky.

"Iolanthe'll be all right," Slith said phlegmatically. "The witch can take care of herself. If it's any comfort, she wasn't at home when they burned down her house."

Since Talent didn't seem particularly cheered by the news, Slith changed the subject, "Where will you go?"

"Wherever the forces of Light are fighting the Dark Queen. The army will be hunting for us. We need a couple of hours start."

Talent pressed a large purse that jingled with the sound of steel coins into the draconian's hand. Slith weighed it and did some rapid calculations in his mind.

"I hear the Hairy Troll is serving free dwarf spirits," said Talent.

Slith grinned. His tongue flicked out of his mouth. "I suppose I should go investigate."

He stuffed the purse into his belt, then gave a sigh. "I guess this means our little business venture has come to an end."

"It's all coming to an end, Slith," said Talent quietly. "The long night is almost over."

Slith patted his purse. "I'm thinkin' all hell's going to break loose around here. I might just take this opportunity to retire from the military—again. Join up with some buddies of mine."

"Build that city you're always talking about," said Talent.

Slith nodded. "Good luck to you, Talent. It's been a pleasure doing business with you."

"Same here. Good luck to you."

The two shook hand and claw. Slith saluted Talent, then turned in brisk military fashion on his heel, and marched back out the door. He cast a glance and a grin at Maelstrom, who winked in return.

Slith's troops were disappointed when they heard they were not to burn down the Broken Shield, but cheered up immediately when he told them they were going to the Hairy Troll.

"Could be they're serving bad dwarf spirits," Slith said. "You'll need to taste them to find out."

"Where are you going, sir?" asked Glug.

"I'll be along," said Slith. "Take the boys and go on ahead. I'll meet you there. Don't drink all the dwarf spirits before I get there."

Glug saluted and ran off. The squadron pounded eagerly behind him.

Slith stood in the streets, gazing at the temple that writhed in the distance. He lifted his clawed hand in farewell and turned and walked in the opposite direction.

"Good luck, Your Majesty," he called out over his shoulder. "I have a feeling you're going to need it."

6

The Night of No Moons.

24th Day, Month of Mishamont, Year 352 AC

he Tower of Wayreth was the oldest Tower of High Sorcery in Ansalon, one of two Towers left standing, and the only Tower still in use.

Built after the end of the Second Dragon War, the Tower of Wayneth rose out of a disaster. In those days, magic was wild and raw. A spell cast by three powerful wizards, intended to end a war, slipped from their control and devastated much of the world. The gods of magic realized that something must be done to keep magic and those who wielded it under control. Nuitari, Lunitari, and Solinari taught the discipline of magic to three wizards and sent them forth to establish the three Orders of High Sorcery, which would be ruled by a governing body known as a Conclave.

The wizards needed a central location, a place where students of magic could come learn the skills of their art, where the newly designed Test of High Sorcery could be administered, where artifacts could be created and stored, spells tested, books written and archived. It would also need to be a fortress and refuge, for many in the world did not trust wizards and sought to do them harm.

The three wizards came together to construct the Tower of Wayreth. The Tower's two spires, built atop a dome and enclosed by a triangular wall, were conjured out of silver mist, which slowly, over time, coalesced into stone. During that period, the Tower came under attack from a tribe of barbarians, who wanted to make it their own. The Tower and the wizards inside were saved by a black robe wizard who cast a spell that created a magical forest surrounding the Tower. The wizard died, but the enchanted Forest of Wayreth sprang up and drove away the barbarians. From that day forward, the forest's magic hid the Tower and protected it from foes.

"You do not find the Tower of Wayreth," the saying goes. "The Tower finds you."

The Forest of Wayreth was kept busy finding a great many mages traveling to the Tower to celebrate the Night of the Eye. Generally, only wizards who had already taken the Test of High Sorcery or those coming to take the Test were permitted to enter the Tower. But a Night of the Eye was a rare and special occurrence, and on this occasion promising students, accompanied by their masters, were also admitted.

The Tower was filled with magic-users who had traveled from all parts of Ansalon. Every bed in every cell was occupied, with many more sleeping on blankets on the floor or setting up camp in the courtyard. The mood was celebratory. Old friends greeted each other with warm embraces and exchanged the latest news. Students wandered about in awe and excitement, losing themselves in the labyrinthine hallways and blundering by mistake into restricted areas. Familiars of all sorts roamed and flew, crept and crawled through the halls, always in danger of being trampled underfoot or flying into someone's hair.

Some wizards were in the laboratories, hard at work preparing the ingredients for potions and other concoctions, ready to mix them when the power of the moons was most potent. Other wizards were holed up in the libraries, studying the spells they meant to cast that night. Black Robes and Red Robes rubbed shoulders with White Robes, everyone putting aside differences to talk magic, though occasionally arguments did break out, particularly in those turbulent times.

There were a few White Robes, for example, who were still bitter over the fact that the Black Robes had defected to Queen Takhisis. Those White Robes did not believe the Black Robes should be forgiven and took the opportunity to state their views. The Black Robes took offense, and shouting matches were the result. Such rows were quickly quelled by the Monitors, red robe wizards who were assigned to patrol the Tower, keep tempers in check, and make certain no untoward incidents marred the important night. For the most part, wizards of all three robes were glad to be united once again in their love of magic, even if they were united in nothing else.

There would be no meeting of the Conclave on that Night of the Eye, a break from tradition. Word was given out that the heads of the orders had decided to dispense with the meeting, which took time away from important work. Since the meeting was notable only for Par-Salian's traditional Night-of-the-Eye speech, which was considered among the young wizards to be a snoozer, the news was greeted with applause.

Only a few, a very few, knew the true reason for the cancellation. The three heads of the orders were not going to be in the Tower of Wayreth this night. Ladonna, Par-Salian, and Justarius were planning to undertake a daring and dangerous mission to Neraka. Accompanying the three would be six bodyguards—strong, young wizards who had been spending the past several days equipping themselves with combat spells designed to repel almost any type of foe, living or undead, and spells of protection to cast upon themselves and their leaders.

As evening was falling, the other wizards were attending a sumptuous and lavish banquet, set up in the courtyard. Ladonna and Justarius and Par-Salian were locked in one of the Tower's upper chambers, discussing their plans. They sat in the shadows, their faces indistinct, their eyes shining in the light of the fire. Seeing that the fire was dying and feeling the chill of the night air, Par-Salian rose to add another log.

An hour-counting candle stood upon the mantelpiece, the unwavering flame slowly eating away the time until the three moons would move into alignment and the wizards could undertake the dangerous journey through time and space to the temple of the Dark Queen.

"Timing is critical," said Ladonna. She was wearing fur-trimmed robes, pendants around her neck, and rings on her fingers. None of the jewels were for vain show. All of them were either magical or could be used as spell components. "Jasla's spirit must be removed from the Foundation Stone with my necromancy spell first."

She added, with a stern glance at Par-Salian, "This is only logical, my friend," continuing an argument that had been ongoing between them for days. "If you raise your barriers to seal off the stone before I cast my spell, you will seal the girl's spirit inside it."

"My concern is what will become of Jasla's soul," said Par-Salian. "Her spirit is a good one, by your own account,

Ladonna. I want assurances that you will set her free, not keep her a prisoner."

"You must admit that finding out how the spirit managed to block Queen Takhisis would be extremely valuable information," Ladonna said coldly. "I want merely to ask her some questions. You are outvoted. Justarius agrees with me."

"It is a matter of the greater good," Justarius said. He carried several scrolls thrust into his belt, as well as pouches of spell components.

Par-Salian shook his head, unconvinced.

"You can be present during the interrogation," Ladonna conceded, though she did not sound pleased. "And you can see for yourself that I will set her free."

"There. Are you satisfied? This argument is wasting precious time," said Justarius.

"Very well," said Par-Salian. "So long as I can be present. Ladonna will cast her spell first, remove Jasla's spirit, and take it to a secure location. Justarius, you will then cast your spells to alter the nature of the Foundation Stone—"

"For all the good *that* will do," Ladonna muttered.

Justarius bristled. "We have gone over this a hundred times . . ."

"And we will go over it a hundred more, if need be," said Ladonna acerbically. "This is too important to undertake lightly."

"She is right," said Par-Salian. "Some who go to Neraka this night will not return. Each of us must be fully committed. State your reasoning."

"Again?" Justarius asked, exasperated.

"Again," said Par-Salian.

Justarius sighed. "The original stone, which was made of white marble, was blessed and sanctified by the gods.

Takhisis cast her own 'blessing' upon it, in an attempt to corrupt it. But Par-Salian and I both agree that the stone is still pure at its heart, which is why Jasla's spirit is able to find sanctuary there. If the corruption is removed and the stone can be returned to its original form and it is further protected with powerful spells of warding that Par-Salian will cast upon it, Takhisis will not be able to again pervert it."

"And since her temple rests upon the Foundation Stone, if it is transformed, the temple will fall, forever sealing the Dark Queen inside the Abyss," Par-Salian said.

Ladonna sat in silence. They were all silent, their expressions troubled. Each of them knew the arguments were desultory, meaningless, meant to avoid the subject that was uppermost in everyone's mind. At last Ladonna was driven to speak what she knew they were all thinking.

"I have sought Nuitari's blessing on this plan of ours. The god of the dark moon pays no heed to me. I do not believe I have offended him, but if I have—"

"It is not you, Ladonna. I have approached Solinari and with the same result," said Par-Salian. "No response. You, my friend?"

Justarius shook his head. "Lunitari will not speak to me. And this is all the more troubling because the goddess enjoys chattering about even trivial matters. This plan of ours is the most dangerous undertaking any wizards have performed since the Sacred Three ended the Second Dragon War, and my goddess will not speak a word. Something is wrong."

"Perhaps we should call this off," said Par-Salian.

"Don't be such an old woman!" Ladonna said scornfully.

"I am being practical. If the gods do not—"

"Hush!" Justarius said peremptorily, raising his hand. Shouts and cries could be heard coming from outside the door. "What is the cause of all this commotion?"

"A surfeit of elven wine," said Par-Salian.

"That is not merry-making," said Ladonna, alarmed. "It sounds more like a riot!"

The shouts grew louder, and the wizards could hear people running in panicked haste down the corridor. Someone started beating on their door, then others joined in, raining blows on the wood. The wizards began to call out for their leaders, some yelling for Par-Salian, others for Ladonna or Justarius.

Angry at such unseemly behavior, Par-Salian rose to his feet, stalked across the room and flung open the door. He was startled to find the hall was dark. The magical lights that generally illuminated all the passageways in the Tower had apparently failed. Seeing some in the crowd carrying candles or lanterns, Par-Salian felt a sense of foreboding.

"What is the meaning of this?" he demanded sternly, glowering at the crowd of wizards milling around in the hallway. "Cease this tumult at once!"

The wizards crowding the darkened hallway fell silent, but only for a moment.

"Tell him," said one.

"Yes, tell him!" urged another.

"Tell me what?"

Several began to speak at once. Par-Salian quieted them with an impatient gesture and searched around in the darkness for someone to be the spokesperson.

"Antimodes!" Par-Salian said, sighting his friend. "Tell me what is going on."

The crowd parted to allow Antimodes to make his way to the front. Antimodes was an older wizard, highly respected and well liked. He came from a well-to-do family and was wealthy in his own right. He was passionate about advancing the cause of magic in the world, and many young mages had benefited from his generosity. A businessman, Antimodes was known to be level-headed and practical, and at the sight of his face, which was pale, strained, Par-Salian felt his heart sink.

"Have you looked outside, my friend?" Antimodes asked. He spoke in a low voice, but the crowd was straining to hear. They immediately caught hold of his words and repeated them.

"Look outside! Yes, look outside!"

"Silence!" Par-Salian ordered, and again the crowd hushed, though not completely. Many grumbled and muttered in a low, rumbling undercurrent of fear.

"You should look outside," said Antimodes gravely. "See for yourselves. And witness this." He lifted his hand, pointed a finger and spoke words of magic. *"Sula vigis dolibix!"*

"Are you mad?" Par-Salian cried, alarmed, expecting to see fiery traces burst from his friend's hands. But nothing happened. The words to the spell fell to the floor like dead leaves.

Antimodes sighed. "The last time that spell failed me, my friend, I was sixteen years old and thinking about a girl, not my magic."

"Par-Salian!" Ladonna called in a shaking voice. "You must see this!"

She was leaning on the window ledge, perilously close to falling out, her back arched, her head craned to stare into the heavens. "The stars shine. The night is cloudless. But . . ."

She turned toward him, her face pale. "The moons are gone!"

"And so is The Forest of Wayreth," Justarius reported grimly, gazing out past Ladonna's shoulder.

"We have lost the magic!" a woman wailed from the hall. Her terrified cry threw everyone into a panic.

"Are you witless gully dwarves to behave so?" Par-Salian thundered. "Everyone, go to your rooms. We must keep calm, figure out what is going on. Monitors, I want the halls cleared at once."

The shouting ceased, but people continued to mill around aimlessly. Antimodes set the example by leaving for his chambers and taking friends and pupils with him. He glanced back at Par-Salian, who shook his head and sighed.

The Monitors in their red robes began moving through the crowd, urging people to do as the head of the Conclave decreed. Par-Salian waited in the doorway until he saw the hall starting to clear. Most would not go to their rooms. They would flock to the common areas to speculate and work themselves into a frenzy.

Par-Salian shut the door and turned to face his fellows, who were both standing at the window, gazing searchingly into the heavens in the desperate hope that they were mistaken. Perhaps an errant cloud had drifted across the moons, or they had miscalculated the time and the moons were late rising. But the evidence of the vanished forest was horrifying and could not be denied.

As Par-Salian gazed across the bleak and barren landscape of treeless, rolling hills, he tried to cast a spell, a simple cantrip. He knew the moment he spoke the words, which came out as gibberish, that the magic would fail.

"What do we do?" Ladonna asked in hollow tones.

"We must pray to the gods—"

"They will not answer you," said a voice from the darkness.

A wizard dressed in black robes stood in the center of the room.

"Who are you?" Par-Salian demanded.

The wizard drew back his hood. Golden skin glistened in the firelight. Eyes with pupils the shape of hourglasses regarded them dispassionately.

"Raistlin Majere," said Justarius, his tone harsh.

Raistlin inclined his head in acknowledgment.

"This is your doing!" Ladonna said angrily.

Raistlin gave a sardonic smile. "While I find it flattering that you think I have the power to make the moons disappear, madam, I must disabuse you of that notion. I did not cause the moons to vanish. Nor did I take away the magic. What you fear is true. Your magic is gone. The gods of the moons have been rendered impotent."

"Then how did you travel here, if not by magic?" Par-Salian said, glowering.

Raistlin bowed to him. "An astute observation, Master of the Conclave. I said *your* magic was gone. *My* magic is not."

"And where does *your* magic come from, then?"

"My god. My Queen," Raistlin said quietly, "Takhisis."

"Traitor!" Ladonna cried.

She took hold of one of the pendants she wore around her neck and tore a piece of fur from her collar. *"Ast kiranann kair Gardurm . . ."* She faltered, then began again. *"Ast kianann kair—"*

"Useless," Justarius said bitterly.

"I am not the traitor," said Raistlin. "I am not the one who betrayed your plot to enter the temple and seal the Foundation Stone to the Dark Queen. If it were not for me, you would all be dead now. The Nightlord and his pilgrims are there now, waiting for you."

"Who was it, then?" Ladonna demanded, glowering.

"The walls have ears," said Raistlin softly.

Ladonna crossed her arms over her chest and began to restlessly pace the room. Justarius remained by the window, staring out into the night.

"Did you come here to gloat over us?" Par-Salian asked abruptly.

Raistlin's eyes narrowed. "You chose me as your 'sword,' Master of the Conclave. And all know that a sword cuts both ways. If your sword has caused you to bleed, that is your own fault. But to answer your question, sir, no, I did not come here to gloat."

He jabbed a finger toward the window. "The Forest of Wayreth is gone. This moment, a death knight called Soth and his undead warriors are riding toward this Tower. Nothing stands in their way. And when they get here, nothing will stop them from tearing down these walls and slaughtering everyone inside."

"Solinari save us!" Par-Salian murmured.

"Solinari fights to save himself," said Raistlin. "Takhisis brought new gods to this world, Gods of the Gray, she calls them. She plans to depose our gods and seize control of the magic, which she will then dole out to her favorites. Such as myself."

"I don't believe you," said Justarius harshly.

"Believe your eyes, then," said Raistlin. "How are you going to fight Lord Soth? His magic is potent, and it does not come from the moons. It springs from the curse the gods cast upon him. He can blast holes in these walls with a gesture of his hand. He can summon corpses from their graves. He has only to speak a single word, and people will drop dead. The terror of his coming is so great that even the bravest will not be able to withstand it. You will cower behind these walls, waiting to die. Praying to die."

"Not all of us," said Justarius grimly.

"You might as well, sir," Raistlin scoffed. "Where are your swords and shields and axes? Where are your mighty warriors to defend you? Without your magic, you cannot defend yourselves. You have your little knives, that is true, but they will barely cut through butter!"

"You, obviously, have the answer," said Par-Salian. "Otherwise you would not have come."

"I do, Master of the Conclave. I can summon help."

"And if you work for Takhisis, why should you? And why should we trust you?" Ladonna asked.

"Because, madam, you have no choice," replied Raistlin. "I can save you . . . but it will cost you."

"Of course!" Justarius said bitterly. He turned to Par-Salian. "Whatever the price, it is too high. I would sooner take my chances with this death knight."

"If it were our lives alone, I would be inclined to agree with you," said Par-Salian ruefully. "But we have hundreds in our care, from our pupils to some of the best and most talented wizards in all of Ansalon. We cannot condemn them to death because of hurt pride." He turned to Raistlin. "What is your price?"

Raistlin was silent a moment; then he said quietly, "I have chosen to walk my own road, free of constraints. All I ask, Masters, is that you allow me to continue to walk it. The Conclave will take no action against me either now or in the future. You will not send wizards to try to kill me or trap me or lecture me. You will let me to go my way, and I will help you remain alive so that you may go yours."

Par-Salian's brows came together. "You imply by this that our magic will come back, that the gods of magic will return. How is that possible?"

"That is my concern," said Raistlin. "Are we agreed?"

"No. There is too much we do not know," said Ladonna.

"I agree with her," said Justarius.

Raistlin stood calmly, his hands folded in the sleeves of his black robes. "Look out the window. You will see an army of undead soldiers wearing charred and blackened armor marked with a rose. Flames devour their flesh as the warriors ride. Their faces wither in the holy fire that endlessly consumes them. They carry death, and Death leads them. Soth will shatter the walls of this Tower with a touch. His army will ride through the melted rock, and your pupils and your friends and colleagues will be helpless to withstand him. Blood will flow in rivers down the corridors—"

"Enough!" Par-Salian cried, shaken. He looked at the others. "I ask you both plainly: Can we fight this death knight without our magic?"

Ladonna had gone deathly pale. Her lips set in a tight, straight line, she sank down in a chair.

Justarius looked defiant at first; then, his face haggard, he gave an abrupt shake of his head. "I am from Palanthas," he said. "I have heard tales of Lord Soth, and if a tenth of them are true, it would be perilous to fight him even if we had our magic. Without . . . we do not stand a chance."

"Mark my words, if we make this bargain with Majere, we will live to regret it," Ladonna said.

"But at least you will live," murmured Raistlin.

He drew from his belt a small leather pouch and dumped the contents onto the floor. Marbles of all colors rolled out onto the soft carpeting. Ladonna, staring at them, gave an incredulous laugh.

"He is making fools of us," she said.

Par-Salian was not so sure. He watched Raistlin's long, slender fingers, delicate and sensitive, sort through the marbles until he found the one he sought. He lifted the marble and held it in the palm of his hand and began to chant.

The marble grew in size until it filled the palm of Raistlin's hand. Colors swirled and shimmered inside the crystal globe. Par-Salian, looking in, saw reptilian eyes, looking out.

"A dragon orb!" he said, amazed.

Par-Salian drew nearer, fascinated. He had read about the famed dragon orbs. Five orbs had been created during the Age of Dreams by mages of all three orders who had come together then, as they had come together in his day, to fight the Queen of Darkness. Two of the orbs had been kept at the ill-fated Towers of Losarcum and Daltigoth and had been destroyed in the explosions that had leveled those Towers.

One of the orbs had dropped out of knowledge, only to be discovered by Knights of Solamnia in the High Clerist's Tower. The Golden General, Laurana, had used the orb to hold the Tower against an assault by evil dragons. That orb had been lost in the battle.

Another orb had been given for safe-keeping to the wizard Feal-Thas, who had kept it locked up in Icewall for many centuries. The orb's strange and tragic journey had led to its destruction by a kender at the meeting of the Whitestone Council.

The orb Par-Salian looked at, the last one in existence, was controlled by Raistlin Majere. How was that possible? Par-Salian was a powerful wizard, perhaps one of the most powerful ever to have lived, and he wondered if he would have the courage to lay his hands on the orb that could seize hold of a wizard's mind and keep him enthralled, caught forever in a twisted, living nightmare, as it had done the wretched Lorac. The young mage,

Raistlin Majere, had dared to do so, and he had succeeded in bending the orb to his will.

As Par-Salian gazed into the orb, both fascinated and repelled, he had his answer. He could see the figure of a man, an old, old man, barely skin and bones, more dead than alive. The old man's fists were clenched in fury, he seemed to be shouting, screaming in rage, but his screams went unheard.

Par-Salian looked in amazement and awe at Raistlin, who gave a confirming nod.

"You are right, Master of the Conclave. The prisoner is Fistandantilus. I would tell you the story, but there is no time. You must all be quiet. Speak no word. Make no movement. Do not even breathe."

Raistlin placed his hands upon the dragon orb. He cried out in pain as hands reached out from the orb and grasped hold of him. He closed his eyes and gasped.

"I command you, Viper, summon Cyan Bloodbane," said Raistlin. His voice was a gasp. He shuddered, yet he kept his hands firmly on the orb.

"Bloodbane is a green dragon!" Ladonna said. "He lied! He means to kill us!"

"Hush!" Par-Salian ordered.

Raistlin was intent upon the orb, listening to an unheard voice, the voice of the orb, and apparently he did not like what it was saying.

"You cannot relax your guard!" he said angrily, speaking to the dragon within the orb. "You must not set him free!"

The hands of the orb tightened on Raistlin's, and he gasped in pain from either the strengthening grip or the agony of the decision he was being asked to make.

"So be it," Raistlin said at last. "Summon the dragon!"

Par-Salian, staring into the orb, saw the colors swirl wildly. The tiny figure of Fistandantilus disappeared.

Raistlin grimaced, but he kept his hands on the orb, concentrating his will on it, oblivious to what was happening around him.

"Ladonna, are you mad? Stop!" Justarius cried.

Ladonna paid no heed. Par-Salian saw a flash of steel and leaped at her. He managed to grab hold of her hand and tried to wrest away the knife. Ladonna turned on him, striking at him and slashing a bloody gash in his chest. Par-Salian staggered back, staring down at the red stain on his white robes.

Ladonna lunged at Raistlin. He paid no heed. The orb began to glow with a bright, green, gaseous radiance. Tendril-like mists swirled out from the orb and wrapped around Ladonna's body. She screamed and writhed. The smell was noxious. Par-Salian covered his mouth and nose with his sleeve. Justarius began to gasp for air and stumbled to the window.

"Do not harm them, Viper," Raistlin murmured.

The tendrils released their grip on Ladonna, who sagged back into a chair. Justarius was trying to catch his breath, staring out the window.

"Par-Salian," Justarius said and pointed.

Par-Salian looked out.

A dragon circled the Tower of High Sorcery, his massive body shining a sickly gray-green in the lambent light of a moonless sky.

7

Green Dragon. Dead Knight.

24th Day, Month of Mishamont, Year 352 AC

he ancient green dragon, Cyan Bloodbane, despised every being he had ever encountered in a life that spanned centuries. Mortal and immortal, dead and undead, gods and other dragons, he hated them all. Some, however, he hated more than others: elves, for one, and Solamnic Knights, for another. It had been a Solamnic Knight—one Huma Dragonsbane—who had ruined Cyan's fun when, as a young dragon, he had taken part in the Second Dragon War.

The detestable knight with his brain-searing, eye-burning dragonlance had driven Cyan's Queen, Takhisis, back into the Abyss, first wringing from her a promise that all her dragons would have to leave the world, hide themselves in their lairs, and fall into an endless sleep.

Cyan had tried hard to avoid that terrible fate, but he could not fight the gods, and he had succumbed like all the others to an enforced nap that had lasted for countless years. But first he had told his Queen what he thought of her.

Several centuries later, he woke, still mad. Takhisis had appeased him by promising him he could avenge himself on the wicked elves, who had once had the nerve to raid his lair during the Second Dragon War, inflicting wounds on him that he was convinced still troubled him.

The fool elf Lorac, King of Silvanesti, had stolen a dragon orb, and when he tried to use it to summon a dragon to save his beloved homeland from the armies of Dragon Highlord Salah-Kahn, Cyan had answered the call.

The green dragon had come to Silvanesti to find that the dragon orb had wrapped Lorac in its terrible coils. Cyan could have slain the wretched elf, but where was the fun in that? Cyan had inflicted wounds that would grievously hurt every elf ever born, from then until the end of time. He had seized their beloved land. He had taken the heart-aching beauty of Silvanesti and twisted it and stabbed it, slashed it and burned it.

He had tortured the trees and caused them to bleed and writhe in agony. He had blackened the lush meadows and transformed crystal lakes into foul and poisonous swamps. What was most enjoyable, he had whispered those nightmares into Lorac's ear, forcing the elf king to watch the horror unfold before his eyes and making him believe that it was his doing.

Tormenting Lorac had been fun for a while, but Cyan had soon grown bored. Silvanesti lay in tortured ruins. Lorac had gone mad. Cyan had perked up when a party of brigands and thieves led by Lorac's daughter, Alhana Starbreeze, arrived in Silvanesti. Cyan had enjoyed tormenting them, for a time. His fun had ended abruptly when a young wizard who still had eggshell on his head, as the saying went among dragons, had managed to break the orb's hold—and Cyan's—on Lorac.

Cyan had at first been thrilled to watch the young wizard foolishly attempt to take control of the dragon orb. Foreseeing yet another mortal to torture, Cyan had been cruelly disappointed. Not only had Raistlin taken control of the orb, he had ordered the orb to take control of Cyan.

The green had struggled and fought, but the dragon orb was strong, and even he could not resist its call. And that was why he was in western Ansalon, flying high above some gods-forsaken tower, there to do the bidding of his hateful master. Cyan had no idea why he was there, for his master had not yet deigned to tell him. The dragon circled the Tower aimlessly, thinking that he could always divert himself by breathing his poisonous gas on the hapless wizards who were milling around in the courtyard below.

Then Cyan heard the blare of trumpets. He knew that sound, and he hated it. He looked out across the hills and saw a Solamnic Knight riding toward him.

Cyan Bloodbane knew nothing about death knights. If someone had told Cyan that this knight was cursed and that he was evil and that he and Cyan were fighting for the same cause, the dragon would have snorted a gaseous snort. A foul Solamnic Knight, cursed or uncursed, dead or undead, was a foul Solamnic Knight and must be destroyed.

Cyan Bloodbane dived down out of the skies. He would use his dragonfear to terrify the knight, then his poisonous breath to kill him.

Lord Soth was intent upon leading his undead warriors in a charge on the Tower's walls. Concentrating on his attack, Soth paid no heed to what was happening in the skies above him. He did not so much as glance in the dragon's direction. The dragonfear washed harmlessly over him.

Cyan was disappointed. He had been counting on the dragonfear to send the knight into a screaming panic, so he would have the pleasure of a little sport, chasing the knight around the fields, before finally killing him.

Cyan began to dimly realize that this was no ordinary knight, and it was then he noticed that the blasted knight was already dead! Which was going to take much of the fun out of the killing of him. Cyan cast a few random spells at the knight, hurled a couple of magic missiles and tried to envelop him in a web, but nothing came of his effort. Cyan gnashed his teeth in frustration. He might not be able to slay the knight, but the dragon could certainly make his undead life unlivable.

Soth, seeing magic missiles explode around him and cobweb dropping from the skies, was at first puzzled as to who was using the magic. It could not be the wizards. Their moons were gone. He lifted his head in time to see a green dragon diving on him like a stooping hawk, claws extended. Astonished beyond measure, wondering where the dragon had come from and why the beast was attacking him, Soth did not have time to try to explain. He didn't have time to do much of anything except draw his sword. And that proved useless.

Cyan Bloodbane caught hold of Soth in his claws and dragged the knight off his horse. The dragon carried Soth, who was slashing at him with the sword, into the heavens, then flung him to the ground. Cyan then flew headlong into the ranks of the charging undead warriors. He smashed into them bodily, ripping with his claws and snapping with his fangs, rending and tearing and scattering their bones or crunching them in his powerful jaws.

By that time Soth had recovered and was back in the saddle. His sword flaring with unholy fire, he rode in pursuit of the dragon, who wheeled ponderously in the sky and flew again to the attack. The death knight struck the dragon a savage blow in the neck that caused Cyan to howl in rage and veer off. Sullenly circling, the dragon flew down for yet another strike.

Lord Soth, wheeling on his black horse, raised his sword.

"Thus does evil turn upon its own," said Raistlin.

Par-Salian turned from the window where he had been watching the strange battle. Raistlin had his eyes fixed upon the hour candle, which had only a small amount of wax left. He looked exhausted. Par-Salian could not imagine the strain on body and mind required to keep control of the orb.

"I must take my leave," Raistlin said. "It is nearly time."

"Time for what?" Par-Salian asked.

"The end." He shrugged. "Or the beginning."

He held the glowing dragon orb in his hand. The multicolored, swirling light shone on the golden skin and gleamed in the hourglass eyes. As Par-Salian stared at the dragon orb, he was struck by a sudden thought. He sucked in a breath, but before he could say anything, Raistlin was gone, disappearing as swiftly and quietly as he had come.

"The dragon orb!" exclaimed Par-Salian, and the other two left off watching the battle to stare at him. "Of all the magical artifacts ever created, Takhisis feared those orbs the most. If she knew Majere had one, she would never permit him to keep it."

"More to the point, she would never permit him to use the orb's magic," Justarius agreed, realization and hope dawning.

"So what does this mean, if anything?" Ladonna asked, looking from one to the other.

"It means our survival is in the hands of Raistlin Majere," said Par-Salian.

And it seemed he could hear, hissing through the darkness, the young mage's words.

"Remember our bargain, Master of the Conclave!"

8

Black Maelstrom.

24th Day, Month of Mishamont, Year 352 AC

he gods of magic, their moons gone from the skies, entered Dargaard Keep. Lord Soth was not there. He and his warriors were riding on the wings of fury to the Tower of Wayreth. The Forest of Wayreth was gone. The wizards who had gathered in the Tower for the Night of the Eye were bereft of their magic and would be vulnerable to the death knight's horrific attack. Their joyous celebration might well end in bloody death and the destruction of their Tower.

That could not be helped, however. Takhisis must be fooled into thinking that the moon gods had fallen victim to her plot, that they had battled the three new Gods of the Gray and been slain by them. Warned in advance by Raistlin Majere, the three had come to the Tower to meet those new gods and ambush them when they tried to enter the world.

"Our world," said Lunitari, and the other two echoed her.

The banshees hid away in terror at the coming of the gods. Kitiara was in the bedroom, asleep, dreaming of the Crown of Power.

The gods went at once to the chamber Raistlin had described to them, passing through stone and earth to reach it. They entered the vault and gathered around the sole object in the room, the Hourglass of Stars. They watched the sands of the future glitter and sparkle in the top half of the hourglass. The other was dark and empty.

Suddenly Nuitari pointed. "A face in the darkness!" he said. "One of the interlopers is coming!"

"I see one as well," said Solinari.

"And I see the third," said Lunitari.

The gods gathered the magic, drawing it from all parts of world, grasping the fire and the lightning bolt, the tempest and the hurricane, the blinding dark and the blinding light, and they entered the hourglass to challenge their foes.

But when they were inside the blackness into which the stars fell, the gods of magic saw no foe. They saw only each other and, in the distance, the stars glittering far above them. As they watched, the stars began to spin, slowly at first, then faster, whirling around a black vortex, spiraling away from them.

And all around them was darkness and silence, utter and eternal. They could no longer hear the song of the universe. They could no longer hear the voices of their fellow gods. They could no longer hear each other. Each could see the others falling away, being pulled into the emptiness. The three tried to reach out to each other, to grab hold, but they were falling much too fast. They desperately sought some way to escape, only to realize there was no escape.

They had fallen into a maelstrom—a maelstrom in time that would keep spinning and spinning, dragging down the stars, one by one, until the end of all things.

Their hands could not touch, but their thoughts could.

A mirror image, Solinari thought bitterly. *There are no other gods. We looked into the hourglass and saw ourselves.*

Trapped in time, Nuitari raved. *Trapped for eternity. Raistlin Majere duped us. He betrayed us to Takhisis!*

No, thought Lunitari in sorrow and despair, *Raistlin was duped as well.*

9

BROTHER AND SISTER.
THE HOURGLASS OF STARS.

24th Day, Month of Mishamont, Year 352 AC

Raistlin walked out of the corridors of magic and into Dargaard Keep. The glowing colors of the dragon orb in his hand were rapidly fading. The orb had shrunken to the size of a marble. He opened the pouch that hung at his side and dropped the orb into it.

The room was dark and, mercifully, silent. The banshees had no reason to sing their terrible song, for the master of the keep was away. Soth would be away for some time, Raistlin imagined. Cyan Bloodbane was not one to give up, especially when his foe had drawn blood.

The dragon would never be able to defeat the death knight. Soth would never be able to slay the dragon, for Cyan thought too well of himself to put himself in any true danger. So long as he could harass and torment his enemy, he would stay around to fight. Once the battle began to turn against him, the dragon would choose the better part of valor and leave the field to his foe.

Raistlin entered Kitiara's bed chamber. Kit lay in her bed. Her eyes were closed; her breathing was deep and even. Raistlin smelled the foul stench of dwarf spirits, and he guessed she had not fallen asleep as much as passed out, for his sister was still dressed. She wore a man's shirt, slit at the neck, with long, full sleeves, and tight-fitting leather trousers. She was even still wearing her boots.

She had good reason to celebrate. She would be leaving Dargaard Keep soon. A few days earlier, Queen Takhisis had summoned her Highlords to Neraka for a council of war.

"There is speculation that Takhisis will decide Ariakas has made one mistake too many in his handling of the war," Kitiara had told her brother. "She will choose another to take over the empire, someone in whom she has more confidence. Someone who has actually done something to advance our cause."

"Such as yourself," Raistlin had said.

Kitiara had smiled her crooked smile.

Raistlin drew near his sleeping sister. She lay sprawled on her back, her black curls in disarray, one arm flung over her forehead. He remembered watching her sleep when they had been children. He had watched her during the nights he was ill, the fever burning his frail body, the nights Caramon had entertained his ill brother with his silly hand shadows. Raistlin remembered Kit waking and coming to him to bathe his forehead or give him a drink. He remembered her telling him, irritably, that he really should work on getting well.

Kit had always been impatient with his weakness. She had never been sick a day in her life. To her way of thinking, if Raistlin had just put his mind to it, he could have willed himself healthy. Yet despite that, she had treated him with a rough sort of gentleness. She had been the one who had recognized his talent for magic. She had been the one to seek out a master to teach him. He owed her a great deal, possibly his life.

"And I am wasting time," he said to himself.

He reached into his pouch for the rose petals.

Kit's eyes moved beneath her closed eyelids. She was deep in a dream, for she was mouthing words and starting to twitch and shift restlessly. Suddenly she gave a terrible cry and sat up in bed. Raistlin cursed and drew back, thinking he had awakened her. Kit's eyes were wide with fear.

"Keep him away, Tanis!" Kitiara cried. She reached out her hands in pleading. "I have always loved you!"

Raistlin realized she was still asleep. He shook his head and gave a snort. "Love Tanis? Never!"

Kitiara moaned and slumped back down onto the pillow. Curling up into a ball, she pulled the rumpled blanket over her head, as though she could hide from whatever horror pursued her.

Raistlin stole near her and, opening his fingers, he let the rose petals drift down onto her face.

"Ast tasarak sinuralan krynawi," he said.

He noticed as he spoke that the words did not feel right to him. They seemed dry, lifeless. He put it down to his own weariness. He waited until he was certain she was under the enchantment, sleeping soundly, then he left.

He was gliding out the door when the voice stopped him, the voice he'd hoped and prayed never to hear again.

"The wise say two suns cannot travel in the same orbit. I am weak now, after my imprisonment, but when I have recovered, this matter between us will finally be resolved."

Raistlin did not respond to Fistandantilus. There was nothing to say. He was in complete agreement.

Raistlin had memorized the route Kitiara had taken to reach the secret vault below Dargaard Keep. He traveled the dark and silent corridors, following the map in his head. He carried with him the Staff of Magius, which he had left in Dargaard Keep to await his return.

"*Shirak*," he said, and though the word again sounded tinny and flat, the crystal ball atop the staff began to glow.

Raistlin was glad for the light. The keep was empty; its master and undead warriors were gone; the banshees were silent. But fear and dread and horror remained full-time occupants. Death's bony fingers plucked at his robes or brushed, cold and horrifying, against his cheek. The ground shook, the stones fell from the walls, and the walls began to collapse. He could hear the screams of the dying woman, begging Soth to save her child, and the piercing cries of a small child being burned alive.

The horror almost overwhelmed him. His hands started to shake; his vision blurred. He could not catch his breath, and he leaned against a wall and made himself breathe deeply, clear his head, reassert his own will.

After he had recovered, he continued down the stairs that spiraled into the stone. He doused the staff's light when he reached the steel door, for he wanted to see before he was seen. Fumbling in the impenetrable darkness, he placed his hand on the door and felt with his fingers for the graven image of the goddess. He invoked the name of Takhisis, and white light glowed. He spoke the name four more times, as Kitiara had done, and each time a different-colored light flared beneath his palm. The door clicked open.

Raistlin did not immediately enter the room. He remained in the darkness, quiet, unmoving, holding his breath so as not to make a sound. The room appeared to be empty except for the Hourglass of Stars standing upon its pedestal. As he watched, the small grain of sand dropped into the narrow opening between the top half and the bottom and hung there.

Raistlin breathed a sigh of relief. The night was almost over. The gods of magic must have won their battle. Odd, though, that they had not destroyed the hourglass . . .

His stomach tightened. Something was not right. He walked into the room, his black robes rustling around his ankles. He leaned the Staff of Magius against the wall and went to stare intently into the hourglass. Three moons, the silver and the red and the black, glimmered in the darkness at the bottom of the hourglass. Their light still shone, but it was dim and would not shine for long. What had happened?

Raistlin did not understand and reached out his hand for the hourglass.

A voice stopped him, nearly stopped his heart. "You are wrong, Baby brother," she said softly. "I do love Tanis."

Kitiara emerged from the darkness, her sword on her hip.

Raistlin lowered his hand and slipped it into the folds of his robes. He managed to keep his voice under careful control and said with a shrug, "You are incapable of loving anyone, my sister. In that, you and I are alike."

Kitiara gazed at him, her dark eyes shining in the starlight glimmering from the hourglass. "Perhaps you are right, Baby brother. It seems we are incapable of love. *Or* loyalty."

"By loyalty I assume you are referring to your betrayal of Iolanthe," said Raistlin.

"Actually I was speaking of *your* betrayal of our Queen," said Kitiara. "As for Iolanthe, I did feel a small twinge of conscience about handing her over to the death squads. She saved my life, you know. She rescued me from prison when Ariakas had sentenced me to death. But she couldn't be trusted. Just as you, Baby brother, cannot be trusted."

Kitiara drew nearer. She walked with a swagger, her hand resting casually on her sword's hilt.

Raistlin's hand, hidden in the folds of his robes, slipped into one of his pouches.

"I have no idea what you are talking about," he said. "I did what I promised I would do."

"Right now you are supposed to be in the Tower of Wayreth, betraying your wizard friends to Lord Soth."

Raistlin gave a grim smile. "And you are supposed to be asleep."

Kitiara began to laugh. "We're a pair, aren't we, Baby brother? Takhisis gave you the gift of her magic, and you used it to betray her. Ariakas gave me my command, and I plan to do the same to him."

She sighed and added, "You left poor Caramon to die. And now I must kill you."

She shifted her gaze to the hourglass. Raistlin saw the three waning moons reflected in her dark eyes, and he understood the truth. She was not asleep because the magic spell he had cast on her had not worked. And it had not worked because there was no magic. He had been duped. He watched the grain of sand slide down the narrow opening, falling a little closer to the darkness.

"There were never any Gods of the Gray, were there?" Raistlin said.

Kitiara shook her head. "Takhisis had to find some way to lure Nuitari and his cousins into her trap. She knew that the idea of new gods coming to supplant them would be too much for them to bear." She passed her hand over the smooth, clear crystal. "Think of this as a whirlpool in time. Your gods have fallen into the whirlpool, and they cannot escape."

Raistlin stared into the glass. "How did you know I would warn the gods? Bring them here?"

"If you didn't, Iolanthe would have. So it really didn't matter." Kitiara drew her sword from the scabbard. The blade made a ringing sound as it slid out. She held it expertly, wielding it with easy, practiced skill. She was implacable, remorseless. She might feel some regret, perhaps, for having to kill Raistlin. But she would go through with it, of that he had no doubt, because that was what he would have done.

Raistlin did not move. He did not try to flee. What was the point in that? He could picture himself racing in terror down the hall, his robes flapping around him, running until his legs faltered and his breath gave out, and he would stumble and his sister would stab from behind. . . .

"I remember the day you and Caramon were born," Kitiara said suddenly. "Caramon was strong and healthy. You were weak, barely alive. You would have died if it hadn't been for me. I gave you life. I guess that gives me the right to take it. But you *are* my little brother. Do not fight me, and I will make your death quick and clean. Over in an instant. All you have to do is give me the dragon orb."

Raistlin thrust his left hand into the pouch. His fingers grasped hold of the orb, closed over it. He kept his eyes fixed on Kit, holding her gaze, her attention.

"What good is the dragon orb?" he asked. "It is dead. The magic is gone, after all."

"Gone from *you*, perhaps," said Kitiara, "but not from the dragon orb. Iolanthe told me all about how the orb works. Once an object is enchanted, it will always remain enchanted."

315

"You mean, like this?" Raistlin spoke the word, "*Shirak*," and the Staff of Magius burst into flaring light.

Momentarily blinded, Kit tried to shield her eyes from the bright glare and raised her sword, jabbing wildly into the darkness. Raistlin dodged the attack easily and, bringing out a fistful of marbles, he tossed them on the floor under Kit's feet.

Unable to see clearly, Kitiara trod on the marbles and slipped, losing her footing. Her feet went out from under her. She fell heavily to the stone floor, striking her head.

Raistlin snatched up his staff and stood over his sister, ready to smash in her skull if her eyelids so much as twitched. She lay still, however, her eyes closed. He thought perhaps she was dead, and he knelt down to feel the lifebeat in her neck, still strong. She would wake with a terrible headache and blurry vision, but she would wake.

He probably should kill her, but as she had said, she had given him life. Raistlin turned away. One more debt repaid.

He turned his attention to the Hourglass of Stars. The three moons glimmered in the glass like fireflies trapped in a jar.

He heard Fistandantilus shout, "Smash it!"

Raistlin picked up the hourglass. Expecting it to be heavy, he found it was deceptively light, and he almost dropped it. He was about to smash it, as the old man urged. Then he paused. Why was Fistandantilus helping *him*?

Raistlin held the hourglass poised above the floor. His thought had been to smash the hourglass and free the gods. But what if that didn't happen? What if, by smashing it, he sealed them in the darkness forever?

Raistlin stared at the hourglass. The shining grain of sand quivered, about to fall. And then came the ghastly song of the banshees lifted in a terrible wail of welcome and revulsion.

Lord Soth had returned to Dargaard Keep.

Raistlin could hear, beneath the song, the death knight running down the stairs. Raistlin had some thought of trying to hide, and he was about to replace the hourglass on the pedestal when the shining grain of sand started to fall . . .

Raistlin watched it, and suddenly light flashed in his mind as the light had flared from his staff. Hoping he wasn't too late, he swiftly turned the Hourglass of Stars upside down.

The grain of sand reversed, fell back into the top half, which had become the bottom.

The three moons vanished.

Raistlin could not see the moons' blessed light. He did not know if his desperate act had succeeded or failed. He extended his hands, palms upward.

"Kair tangus miopiar!" he said, his voice shaking.

He felt nothing for a moment, and his heart stopped in fear; then the familiar, soothing, exciting, searing warmth burned in his blood and fire flared in his hands. He watched the flames leap from his palms, and he was weak with relief. The gods were free.

Raistlin hurled the Hourglass of Stars against the stone wall. The crystal shattered into a myriad of sharp shards. Spilled sand glittered in the light like tiny stars.

Raistlin picked up the dragon orb from among the marbles and held it fast. The door was opening, pushed by the death knight's hand. He had just strength enough left to speak the words of magic . . .

. . . Barely.

10

No rest for the wizard. Revenge.

25th Day, Month of Mishamont, Year 352 AC

aistlin emerged from the corridors of magic into his bedroom in the Broken Shield. He was exhausted, and he was looking forward to his bed, to falling into exhausted sleep.

He found, to his astonishment, that his bed was occupied.

"Welcome home," said Iolanthe.

She was seated on the bed. As she lifted her head, he saw her face was battered and bruised. Both eyes were blackened, one almost completely swollen shut. Her lip was split. Her fine clothes were torn. Purple bruises covered her neck.

"Thank you for saving my life this night, my dear," she said, mumbling through her bloody lips. "Too bad I can't return the favor."

She cast a sidelong glance at the man who was standing at the window, gazing out at the three moons, which had just come together to form one unblinking eye. Emperor Ariakas did not bother to turn around. He merely glanced over his broad shoulder. His face was dark, expressionless.

Raistlin felt nothing. He was going to die in the next few moments, and he was too worn, too drained to care. He supposed he should try to defend himself, cast some sort of deadly spell. The words of magic fluttered in his brain and flew off before he could catch them.

"If you're going to kill me, do so now," he said wearily. "At least that way I will get some rest."

Iolanthe tried to smile, but it hurt. She winced and pressed her fingers to her lip.

"My lord wants the dragon orb," she said.

Raistlin tore the pouch from his belt and tossed it onto the floor. The pouch opened. Marbles and the dragon orb rolled out onto the floor and lay there, gleaming in the moonlight. The three moons were starting to separate, drifting apart, yet never far apart.

The moonlight—silver and red—shone on the orb and, as if basking in the magic, the orb seemed to grow and expand. Its own colored lights swirled in response.

Ariakas gazed at the orb, entranced. He left the window and squatted down on his haunches to peer at it. The hands in the orb reached out to him. Ariakas's fingers twitched. He must be longing to touch it, to see if he could control it. He actually started to reach for it. With a dark smile, he drew back.

"Nice try, Majere," said Ariakas, standing up. "I'm not as stupid as King Lorac—"

"Oh, yes, you are, my dear," said Iolanthe.

A blast of frigid air, chill as the frozen wastes of Icewall, struck Ariakas from behind. The magical cold turned his flesh blue and stole his breath. His hair and beard and armor were rimed with hoarfrost. His limbs shuddered.

His blood congealed. A look of fury and astonishment froze on his face. Unable to move, he crashed to the floor with a thud like a block of ice.

"Never turn your back on a wizard," Iolanthe advised him. "Especially one you just beat up."

Raistlin watched, stupid with fatigue, as Iolanthe walked to Ariakas's side. She knelt down, put her hand to his neck, and began to swear.

"Damn it to the Abyss and back! The bastard is still alive! I thought I had killed him for certain. Takhisis must love him."

Iolanthe thrust a small crystal cone into her bosom and reached out her hand to Raistlin. "I know you're tired. I'll transport you. Hurry! We have to get out of here before his guards come to see what has happened to him."

Raistlin stared at her. He was too tired to think. He had to cajole his brain into working. He shook his head and, ignoring her outstretched hand, he picked up the glowing dragon orb. It shrank at his touch, and his hand closed over it tightly.

"You go," he said.

"You can't stay in Neraka! Ariakas isn't dead. He will send the Black Ghost after you—"

"He tried that tonight, didn't he?" said Raistlin, looking at Iolanthe intently.

A blush suffused her face. She was beautiful and alluring. Small wonder those unsuspecting Black Robes had opened their doors to her sultry whispers in the dead of night.

"How did you know?" she asked.

"I count stairs, remember. How long have you been working for Hidden Light?"

"Ever since—" Iolanthe stopped then shook her head. "It's a winter's tale, meant to be told around the fire. We don't have time for it now. My friends and I are leaving Neraka. Come with us."

Raistlin was gazing into the dragon orb, watching the colors. Black and green, red and white and blue twined and writhed and twisted.

"I have to change the darkness," he said.

She stared at him, not understanding. Then she squeezed his hand and kissed him gently on the cheek. "Thank you, Raistlin Majere. You saved the people who are most dear to me."

She flung her magical clay on the wall. The portal opened, expanded, and Iolanthe stepped into it.

"Go with the gods," she called to him.

The portal shut behind her.

"I plan to," said Raistlin.

He held the glowing dragon orb in his hands and looked out the window to the three moons.

"You owe me," he told them.

The hands in the dragon orb reached out to him, caught him up, and carried him away.

II
Godshome. Old Friends.

25th Day, Month of Mishamont, Year 352 AC

aistlin woke to find himself lying on hard rock, cold and polished, so it seemed he was resting on the surface of a glittering, black ice-bound lake. He was surrounded by a circle of twenty-one pillars of stone, shapeless and roughhewn. The pillars stood separate and apart, yet so close together that Raistlin could not see what lay beyond them.

He had no idea how long he had been asleep. He recalled periods of drowsy semiconsciousness, thinking that he should wake, that the sands in his hourglass were falling fast, the world was turning beneath him, events were happening, and he was not there to shape them. He tried several times to grasp hold of the rim of consciousness and pull himself out of sleep's deep well, only to find he lacked the strength.

Once he was awake, he was loath to move, as one is reluctant to rise from bed on a gray morning when raindrops pelt gently on the window pane. The air was still and pure, and it carried to him the scent of spring. But the scent was faint, the season far away, distant, as though there, in that vale, the passing of years did not matter.

Raistlin looked up into the sky and judged by the position of the stars that the time was early morning, though what the date might be, he had no idea. The sky was black as death above. Faint light, glimmering in the east, promised a rosy dawn. The stars shone bright, none brighter than the red star, the forging fire of Reorx. The constellations of the other gods were visible, all of them at once, which was not possible.

The previous autumn, Raistlin had looked into the sky and seen that two constellations were missing: that of Paladine and that of Takhisis. How long past that seemed! Autumn's leaves had gone up in flame and smoke. Winter had honored the dead with snow, white and pure. The snow was melting and new life, born of death and sacrifice, was stubbornly fighting to push its way through the frozen ground.

"Godshome," said Raistlin to himself softly.

He had slept on the hard rock without even a blanket, yet he was not stiff or sore. He rose to his feet and shook out his robes and checked to make certain that the Staff of Magius was at his side. He could see the constellations reflected in the shining, black surface.

Stars above and stars below, much like an hourglass.

The pillars that surrounded him were much like prison bars. He saw no way to pass between them.

For some, faith is a prison, he reflected. For others, faith brings freedom.

Raistlin walked steadily toward the pillars and found himself on the other side without knowing how he came to be there.

"Interesting," he murmured.

He was thirsty and hungry. He rarely ate much at the best of times, and he had undergone such tension and inner turmoil the previous day that he had forgotten to eat at all. As if thinking made it so, he found a stream of clear water, running down from the mountains. Raistlin drank his fill and, dipping a handkerchief in the water, he laved his face and body. The water had restorative powers, it seemed, for he felt strong and revived. And though there was nothing to eat, he was no longer hungry.

Raistlin had read something of Godshome, though not much, for not much had been written. The Aesthetic who had traveled to Neraka had tried to find Godshome, which was very near that dread city, but he had been unsuccessful. Godshome was the most holy site in the world. Who had created it and why were not known. The Aesthetic had offered various theories. Some said that when the gods had finished creating the world, they came together in this place to rejoice. Another theory held that Godshome was man made, a holy shrine to the gods erected by some lost and forgotten civilization. What *was* known was that only those chosen by the gods were permitted to enter.

Raistlin felt a sense of urgency, the gods breathing down his neck.

Everything happens for a reason. I need to make sure the reason is mine.

Raistlin settled himself on the rocky floor near the stream and drew the dragon orb from the pouch. He placed the dragon orb on the surface before him and, chanting the words, reached out to the hands that reached out to him. He had no idea if his plan would work, for he was still discovering the orb's capabilities. From what he had read, the wizards who created the orb had used it to look into the future. If the orb's eyes could see into the future, why not the present? It seemed a much easier task.

"I am looking for someone," he told the orb. "I want to know what this person is doing and hear what he is saying and see what he is seeing at this very moment. Is that possible, Viper?"

It is. Think of this person only. Concentrate on this person to the exclusion of all else. Speak the name three times.

"Caramon," said Raistlin, and he brought his twin to mind. Or rather, he no longer attempted to drive him away.

"Caramon," Raistlin said again, and he stared into the orb that was swirling with color.

"Caramon!" Raistlin said a third time, sharply, as when they were young and he was trying to waken him. Caramon had always been fond of sleeping in.

The orb's colors dissipated like morning mists. Raistlin saw pouring rain, the wet face of a rock wall. Standing around in a sodden group were his friends: Tanis Half-Elven; Tika Waylan; Tasslehoff Burrfoot; Flint Fireforge; and his twin brother, Caramon. With them was an old man in mouse-colored robes and a disreputable hat.

"Fizban," Raistlin said softly. "Of course."

Tanis and Caramon wore the black armor and the insignia of dragonarmy officers. Tanis had put on a helm that was too big for him, not so much for protection as to conceal the pointed ears that would have revealed his elven blood. Caramon was not wearing a helm. He had probably not been able to find one big enough. His breastplate was a tight fit; the straps that held it on were stretched to their limit over his broad chest.

As Raistlin watched, Tanis—his face distorted with anger—looked swiftly around at the small group. His gaze focused on Caramon.

"Where's Berem?" he asked in urgent tones.

Raistlin's ears pricked at the name.

His brother's face went red. "I—I dunno, Tanis. I—I thought he was next to me."

Tanis was furious. "He's our only way into Neraka, and he's the only reason they're keeping Laurana alive. If they catch him—"

"Don't worry, lad." That was Flint, always Tanis's comforting father. "We'll find him."

"I'm sorry, Tanis," Caramon was mumbling. "I was thinking—about Raist. I—I know I shouldn't—"

"How in the name of the Abyss does that blasted brother of yours work mischief when he's not even here?"

"How indeed?" Raistlin asked with a smile and a sigh.

So Tanis *had* captured Berem and was apparently planning to exchange him for Laurana. Only Caramon had lost him. Raistlin wondered if Tanis knew the reason the Dark Queen wanted Berem so desperately. If he knew, would he be so eager to hand him over? Raistlin did not hazard a guess. He did not know these people. They had changed; the war, their trials had changed them.

Caramon, good-natured, cheerful, outgoing, was lost and alone, seeking the part of himself that was missing. Tika Waylan stood beside him, trying to be supportive, but unable to understand.

Pert and pretty Tika, with the bouncing, red curls and hearty laughter. Her red curls might be wet and drooping, but their fire was still bright in the spring rain. She carried a sword, not mugs of ale, and wore pieces of mismatched armor. Raistlin had been annoyed by Tika's love for his brother. Or perhaps he had been jealous of that love. Not because Raistlin had been in love with Tika himself, but because Caramon had found someone else to love besides his twin.

"I did you a favor by leaving, my brother," Raistlin told Caramon. "It is time for you to let go."

His attention shifted to Tanis, the leader of the group. Once he had been calm and collected, but he was falling apart as Raistlin watched. The woman he loved had been taken from him, and he was desperate to save her, though it meant destroying the world in the process.

Fizban, the befuddled old wizard in the mouse-colored robes, standing apart, watching and waiting quietly, patiently.

Raistlin remembered a question Tanis had asked him once, long in the past, when the autumn winds blew cold.

"Do you believe we were chosen, Raistlin? . . . Why? We are not the stuff of heroes . . ."

Raistlin remembered his answer. "But who chose us? And for what purpose?"

He looked at Fizban, and he had his answer. At least that was part of the answer.

Tasslehoff Burrfoot, irrepressible, irresponsible, irritating. If Berem was the Everman, Tas was the Everchild. The child had grown up. Like Mari. More's the pity.

As Raistlin watched, Tanis angrily ordered the rest of the group to search for Berem. They wearily retraced their steps, backtracking along the trail to see if they could find where Berem had left it. It was Flint who discovered Berem's footprints in the mud and gave chase, leaving the others behind.

"Flint! Wait up!" Tanis yelled.

Raistlin lifted his head, startled. The shout had not come from the orb. It had come from the other side of the rock wall! Raistlin looked in the direction of Tanis's voice and saw a narrow, tunnel-like opening in the wall, an opening he could have sworn had not been there earlier.

He had no time for wonder and no more need for the dragon orb, apparently. Kitiara had been right. His friends had been searching for Godshome, and it seemed they had found it.

Raistlin returned the orb to its pouch. Picking up the staff, he hurriedly whispered the words to a spell, hoping as he did so that magic worked in that sacred place.

"Cermin shirak dari mayat, kulit mas ente bentuk."

Raistlin had cast a spell to make himself invisible. He looked into the stream. He could not see his own reflection, and if he could not see himself, his friends would not be able to see him. The magic had worked.

The one possible exception might be Fizban. Taking no chances, Raistlin glided between the pillars of stone and concealed himself behind them just as a man crawled through the opening in the rocks.

It was the man with the old face and young eyes, the man who had been onboard the ship in Flotsam, the man who had steered them into the whirlpool. As Berem rose to his feet, an emerald, embedded in his chest, flashed green in the morning sun.

Berem Everman. The Green Gemstone Man. Jasla's brother. The man who could set Queen Takhisis free or keep her forever imprisoned in the Abyss.

Berem looked fearfully behind him. He wore a hunted expression, a fox fleeing the hounds. He ran across the stone floor of the vale. Flint and the others would not be far behind, but for the moment, Berem and Raistlin were alone in Godshome.

A few magical words and Raistlin could spellbind Berem, make him a prisoner. He could use the dragon orb to transport them back to Neraka. He could present Takhisis with a gift of inestimable value. She would be grateful. She would give him whatever his heart desired.

He might even be able to bargain for Laurana's freedom. But he would always have to sleep with one eye open . . .

Raistlin watched Berem run past him. The Everman had sighted what appeared to be another opening in a far wall. And here came Flint, running after him. The dwarf's face was flushed with excitement and exertion. Berem had a lengthy head start. It seemed unlikely that Flint would win the race.

Hearing a shout behind him, Raistlin turned to see Tasslehoff crawling through the narrow tunnel. The kender emerged into the vale and was exclaiming loudly over the stone pillars and the stone floor and other wonders. Raistlin heard the voices of his friends on the other side of the tunnel. He could not make out what they were saying.

"Tanis, hurry!" Tas called.

"There's no other way?" Caramon's voice echoed dismally through the narrow hole.

Tasslehoff searched the vale, trying to find Flint, but the pillars stood between the dwarf and the kender, blocking his view. Running back to the opening, Tas bent down and peered inside.

He yelled something into the tunnel, and someone yelled back. By the sounds of it, they had tried to crawl through it. Caramon, it seemed, was stuck.

Flint was actually gaining on Berem. The morning sunlight sent shadows crawling over the rock walls, and Berem had seemingly lost sight of the opening. He was running back and forth, like a rabbit trapped at a fence line, searching for the way out. Then he found it and made a dive for it.

Berem was about to crawl through the hole. Raistlin was pondering what he should do, wondering if he should try to stop Berem, when suddenly Flint gave a terrible cry. The dwarf grabbed at his chest and, moaning in pain, sagged to his knees.

"His heart. I knew it," Raistlin said. "I warned him."

He started instinctively to go the dwarf's aid, then brought himself up short. He was no longer a part of their lives. They were no longer a part of his. Raistlin watched and waited. There was nothing he could do anyway.

Berem heard Flint cry out and turned fearfully around. Seeing the old dwarf drop to the ground, Berem hesitated. He looked at the opening in the wall, and he looked at Flint and then came running to help. Berem knelt beside the dwarf, whose face was ashen.

"What is wrong? What can I do?" Berem asked.

"It's nothing," Flint gasped for air. His hand pressed against his chest. "An upset stomach, that's all. Something I ate. Just . . . help me stand. I can't seem to catch my breath. If I walk around a little . . ."

Berem assisted the old dwarf to his feet.

From the opposite side of the vale, Tasslehoff had finally found them. But, of course, the kender got it wrong. He thought Berem was attacking Flint.

"It's Berem!" the kender shouted frantically. "And he's doing something to Flint! Hurry, Tanis!"

Flint took a step and staggered. His eyes rolled up in his head. His legs buckled. Berem caught the dwarf in his arms and laid him down gently on the rocks, then hovered over him, uncertain what to do.

Hearing the sounds of feet pounding toward him, Berem stood up. He seemed relieved. Help was coming.

"What have you done?" Tanis raved. "You've killed him!"

He drew his sword and plunged the blade into Berem's body.

Berem shuddered and cried out. He sagged forward, his body impaled on the sword, falling onto Tanis, his weight nearly carrying them both to the ground. Blood washed over Tanis's hands. He yanked his blade free and turned, ready to fight Caramon, who was trying to pull him away. Berem was moaning on the ground, blood pouring from the fatal wound. Tika was sobbing.

Flint had seen none of it. He was leaving the world, starting on his soul's next long journey. Tasslehoff took hold of the dwarf's hand and urged him to get up.

"Leave me be, you doorknob," Flint grumbled weakly. "Can't you see I'm dying?"

Tasslehoff gave a grief-stricken wail and fell to his knees. "You're not dying, Flint! Don't say that."

"I should know if I'm dying or not!" Flint said irately, glowering.

"You thought you were dying before, and you were just seasick," Tas said, wiping his nose. "Maybe you're . . . you're . . ." He glanced around at the stone floor of the vale. "Maybe you're ground-sick . . ."

"Ground-sick!" Flint snorted. Then, seeing the kender's misery, the dwarf's expression softened. "There, there, lad. Don't waste time blubbering like a gully dwarf. Run and fetch Tanis for me."

Tasslehoff gave a snuffle and did as he was told.

Berem's eyelids fluttered. He gave another moan and sat up. He put his hand to his chest. The emerald, soaked with blood, sparkled in the sunlight.

Hope lives. No matter the mistakes we make, no matter our blunders and misunderstandings, no matter the grief and sorrow and loss, no matter how deep the darkness, hope lives.

Raistlin left his place by the pillars and came, unseen, to stand over Flint, who lay with his eyes closed. For a moment, the dwarf was alone. Some distance away, Caramon was trying to restore Tanis to sanity. Tasslehoff was tugging on Fizban's sleeve, trying to make him understand. Fizban understood all too well.

Raistlin knelt beside the dwarf. Flint's face was ashen and contorted with pain. His hands clenched. Sweat covered his brow.

"You never liked me," said Raistlin. "You never trusted me. Yet you were good to me, Flint. I cannot save your life. But I can ease the pain of dying, give you time to say good-bye."

Raistlin reached into his pouch and drew out a small vial containing juice distilled from poppy seeds. He poured a few drops into the dwarf's mouth. The lines of pain eased. Flint's eyes opened.

As his friends gathered around Flint to say good-bye, Raistlin was there with them, though none of them ever knew it. He told himself more than once that he should leave, that he had work to do, that his ambitious plans for his future hung in the balance. But he remained with his friends and his brother.

Raistlin stayed until Flint sighed and closed his eyes and the last breath left the dwarf's body. Raistlin chanted the magic beneath his breath. The corridor opened before him.

He walked into it and did not look back.

12
Kitiara's Knife. Par-Salian's Sword.
25th Day, Month of Mishamont, Year 352 AC

itiara reached Neraka early on the morning of the twenty-fifth, fearing she was late for the council meeting, only to find that Ariakas himself had not yet arrived. The plans for the meeting were thrown into confusion, for none of the other Highlords or their armies could enter the city ahead of the Emperor. Ariakas did not trust his fellow Highlords. If they were allowed inside Neraka, they might shut its gates and fill its walls with warriors and try to keep him out.

Kitiara had been expecting to move into her luxurious quarters in the temple. Instead, she was forced to camp outside the city walls, living in a tent that was so small and cramped, she could not pace about, as she was wont to do when she needed to think.

Kitiara was in a foul mood. She was still suffering a headache from where she'd hit her head on the stone floor of the vault. She was glad for the excuse to leave Dargaard Keep. Though she felt like crap, she had summoned Skie and flown to join her army. The thought of challenging Ariakas for the Crown of Power had eased the pain in her head. But she had arrived here only to discover that no one knew where Ariakas was or when he would deign to grace them with his presence. And that left Kitiara nothing to do except fume and complain to her aide-de-camp, a bozak draconian named Gakhan.

"Ariakas is doing this deliberately to unsettle the rest of us," Kitiara muttered. She was sitting hunched over a small table, her head in her hands, massaging her throbbing temples. "He's trying to intimidate us, Gakhan, and I won't stand for it."

Gakhan made a noise, a kind of snort and sneer. The bozak grinned, his tongue flicked out of his mouth.

Kitiara raised her head and looked at him sharply. "You've heard something. What's going on?"

Gakhan had been with Kitiara since before the beginning of the war. Though officially known as her aide-de-camp, his unofficial title was Kitiara's Knife. Gakhan was loyal to Kitiara and to his Queen, in that order. Some said he was in love with the Blue Lady, though they were always careful to say that behind his back, never to his face. The bozak was smart, secretive, resourceful, and extremely dangerous. He had earned his nickname.

Gakhan glanced out the tent flap, then drew it shut and tied it securely. He leaned over Kitiara and spoke softly, "My lord Ariakas is late because he was wounded. He very nearly died."

Kitiara stared at the bozak. "What? How?"

"Keep your voice down, my lord," the draconian said solemnly. "News like this, should it leak out, might embolden the Emperor's enemies."

"Yes, of course, you are right," said Kit with equal solemnity. "Do you trust your source for this . . . um . . . disturbing information?"

"Completely," said Gakhan.

Kitiara smiled. "I need details. Ariakas has not been in battle lately, so I assume someone tried to assassinate him."

"And very nearly succeeded."

"Who was it?"

Gakhan paused to build the suspense, then said with a grin, "His witch!"

"Iolanthe?" Kitiara said loudly, forgetting in her astonishment that she was supposed to be circumspect.

Gakhan cast her a warning glance, and Kit lowered her voice. "When did this happen?"

"The Night of the Eye, my lord."

"But that's not possible. Iolanthe died that night." Kitiara gestured to some dispatches. "I have the reports—"

"Fabricated, my lord. It seems that Talent Orren—"

Kitiara glared at him. "Orren? What does he have to do with this? I want to know about Iolanthe."

Gakhan bowed. "If you will be patient, my lord. It seems that Orren found out about the plot to kill him and his fellow members of Hidden Light. He sent word around among the troops that the Church was going to try to 'clean up' the city of Neraka. Orders had been given to burn the Broken Shield and the Hairy Troll. Naturally, the soldiers were not pleased. When the death squads arrived to carry out their orders, they found armed soldiers guarding the taverns. Orren and his friends escaped."

"What has this to do with Iolanthe?" Kit demanded impatiently.

"She is a member of Hidden Light."

Kitiara stared. "That's impossible. She saved my life!"

"I believe she had some thought of serving you at the time, my lord. She grew disenchanted with you, however, after you wanted to take away the magic. She had been doing odd jobs for Orren. The two became lovers, and she threw in her lot with him."

"So how does Ariakas fit into this?" Kit asked, confused.

"The Emperor wanted the dragon orb your brother has in his possession. Ariakas saved Iolanthe from the death squads, though not from love. He told her that if she valued her own life, she would have to kill Raistlin. Ariakas went with her to make certain she did as she was told and to obtain the dragon orb."

"But Iolanthe, instead of attacking Raistlin, turned on Ariakas," said Kitiara.

"I am told that if it were not for the intervention of the Nightlord, at the behest of Her Dark Majesty, the Emperor would have died of frostbite."

Kitiara threw back her head and laughed.

Gakhan permitted himself a smile and a flick of his tail, but that was all.

"Has Ariakas thawed out?" asked Kitiara, still chuckling.

"The Emperor has been restored to health, my lord. He will arrive in Neraka tomorrow."

"What happened to Iolanthe?"

"She fled, my lord. She left Neraka with Orren and the rest of Hidden Light."

"It's a shame I underestimated her." Kitiara shook her head. "I could have used her. What about Raistlin?"

"He has vanished, my lord. It is assumed he also left Neraka, though no one knows where he went. Not that it matters," said Gakhan with a shrug. "He is a marked man.

The Emperor wants him dead. Queen Takhisis wants him dead. The Nightlord wants him dead. If Raistlin Majere is still in Neraka, he is a monumental fool."

"And whatever my brother is, he was never that. Thank you for the information, Gakhan. I must think about all of this," said Kitiara.

The bozak bowed and departed. One of the aides came in to light a lantern, for night had fallen, and ask her if she wanted supper. Kit ordered him to leave.

"Post a guard outside. No one is to disturb me this night."

Kitiara sat staring at the flickering flame of the candle, seeing Ariakas's brutish face. He believed she was conspiring against him.

Well, she was.

And he had no one to blame but himself. He had always encouraged rivalry among his Highlords. The knowledge that each Highlord was in danger of being replaced by a rival kept them all on their toes. The flaw in that was that some Highlord might decide to slit another Highlord's throat and that throat could be Ariakas's.

Ariakas distrusted all his Highlords, but he distrusted her most. Kitiara was popular among her forces, far more popular with her troops than Ariakas was with his. She saw to it that her soldiers were paid. Most important, Kitiara was looked upon with favor by the Dark Queen, who was not viewing Ariakas fondly those days. He had made too many mistakes.

He should have won the war with a few swift and brutal, crushing blows, ending it before the good dragons entered to fight on the side of Light. He should have taken the High Clerist's Tower before the knights could reinforce it. He should have relied on dragons, who could attack from the air, where they had the advantage, and far less on ground troops. And he should *not* have allowed Kitiara to ally herself with the powerful Lord Soth.

Takhisis was undoubtedly regretting having chosen Ariakas to lead her dragonarmies. Kitiara seemed to feel Her Dark Majesty's hand on her shoulder, pushing her toward the throne, urging her to take the Crown of Power.

Strange . . . Kitiara really did feel a hand on her shoulder.

"What the—"

Kitiara jumped to her feet and drew her sword all in the same swift movement. She was about to strike when she saw who it was.

"You!" she gasped.

"The monumental fool," said Raistlin.

Kitiara held her sword poised and regarded him through narrowed eyes. "Why are you here? Why have you come?"

"*Not* to kill you, my sister, if that's what you fear. You were going to kill me, that is true, but I am willing to put our quarrel down to sibling rivalry."

Kitiara smiled, though she did not sheathe her sword.

"I'll keep my weapon handy just in case *you* feel the stirrings of sibling rivalry. So why are you here, Baby brother? You are in danger. You've made powerful enemies. The Emperor wants you dead. A *goddess* wants you dead!" Kit shook her head. "If you're expecting me to protect you, there's nothing I can do."

"I expect nothing *from* you, my sister. I came with something *for* you."

Raistlin stood with his hands hidden in the sleeves of his robes, his cowl thrown back. The lantern light flickered in the strange hourglass eyes.

"You want the Crown of Power," he told her. "I can help you take it."

"You are mistaken," said Kitiara gravely. "Ariakas is my Emperor. I am his loyal subject."

"And I am the king of the elves," said Raistlin with a sneer.

Kitiara's lips twitched. "In truth, I am concerned for the Emperor's health."

She ran her index finger along the groove in the sword that allowed the blood to run down the blade and keep from fouling it. "Ariakas wears himself out with affairs of state. He should take a rest . . . a long, long rest. So what do you have in mind? How can you help me?"

"I have many arrows in my quiver," said Raistlin coolly. "Which I choose to use will depend on the circumstances in which I choose to use it."

"You blather like the king of the elves," said Kit irritably. "You won't tell me because you do not trust me."

"It's a good thing I don't, my sister, otherwise I would be dead by now," Raistlin said dryly.

Kitiara stared at him a moment; then she sheathed her sword and resumed her seat. "Let us say I accept your offer. You help make me Emperor. What do you expect in return?"

"The Tower of High Sorcery in Palanthas."

Kitiara was astonished. "That monstrosity? It's cursed! Why would you want that?"

Raistlin smiled. "This from the woman who lives in Dargaard Keep."

"Not for long," Kitiara said. "You can have your cursed Tower. I don't suppose anyone else would want it." She put her elbows on the table and regarded him expectantly. "What is your plan?"

"You must get me inside the Temple tomorrow when the council meets."

Kitiara stared at him. "You *are* a monumental fool! You might as well just walk into a dungeon cell and lock yourself up and be done with it. All your enemies will be there, including Queen Takhisis! If she or any of them discovered you, you would not survive long enough for death to rattle in your throat."

"I have the ability to conceal myself from my mortal enemies. As for the immortal, you must persuade Takhisis that I am of more use to her alive than dead."

Kit snorted. "You thwarted her plot to destroy the gods. You betrayed her trust on more than one occasion. What could I possibly say to convince Takhisis to let you live?"

"I know where to find Berem Everman."

Kitiara caught her breath. She gazed at him in disbelief, and then she leaped to her feet and seized hold of his arms. He was bone and skin, no muscle, and she was reminded of the sickly, little boy she had helped to raise. As if he were that little boy, she gave him an impatient shake.

"You know where Berem is? Tell me!"

"Do we have a bargain?" Raistlin countered.

"Yes, yes, we have a bargain, damn you! I'll find a way to get you inside the temple, and I'll talk to the Queen. Now—tell me, where is the Everman?"

"Our mother gave birth to only one fool, my sister, and that was Caramon. If I tell you now, what is to prevent you from killing me? To find Berem, you must keep me alive."

Kitiara gave him a shove that nearly knocked him down. "You're lying! You have no idea where Berem is! Our deal is off."

Raistlin shrugged and turned to go.

"Wait! Stop!" Kitiara gnawed her lip and glared at him. Finally she said, "Why should I go along with you?"

"Because you want the Crown of Power. And Ariakas wears it. I have read about this crown, and I know how the magic works. Anyone who wears the crown is invincible to—"

"I know all that!" Kitiara interrupted impatiently. "I don't need a damn book to tell me."

"I was about to say the crown is 'invincible to physical attacks and most types of ordinary, magical assaults,' " Raistlin finished coolly.

Kitiara frowned. "I don't get it."

"I have never been 'ordinary,'" said Raistlin.

Kitiara's eyes gleamed beneath her long, dark lashes. "We have a deal, Baby brother. Tomorrow will be a momentous day in the history of Krynn."

13

The Spiritor.
Temple of the Dark Queen.

26th Day, Month of Mishamont, Year 352 AC

he sun rose, bloodshot and bleary eyed and sullen after a night of drunken chaos. The gutters of the streets of Neraka ran red with blood in the predawn hours of that momentous day, and yet the enemy was nowhere in sight. The forces of the Dragon Highlords were fighting among themselves.

Since the Emperor had been late in arriving, the troops of the other Highlords had been forbidden to enter the city of Neraka, which meant they were forbidden to partake of Neraka's ale and dwarf spirits and other pleasures. The soldiers, many of whom had been forced-marched in order to reach Neraka in time, had made the march and endured the floggings, the putrid water, and the bad food because they were promised a holiday in Neraka. When they were told that they could not enter the city and they had to keep eating the same bad food and drink nothing but water, they mutinied.

Two Highlords, Lucien of Takar, half-ogre leader of the Black Dragonarmy, and Salah-Kahn, leader of the Green, had been waging their own private war for a month; each wanted to extend his holdings into the other's territory. The humans of Khur, under the leadership of Salah-Kahn, had always hated the ogres, who, for their part, had always hated the humans. The two races had become reluctant allies in the war, but with the war going badly, every Highlord was looking out for himself. When fights broke out among their troops, each blamed the other and neither did anything to stop the fighting.

The White Dragonarmy was in the worst state, for the army had no leader. The hobgoblin Toede, who held that position, had not shown up for the meeting, and rumor had it that he was dead. Draconian and human commanders began fighting among themselves for leadership, each hoping to ingratiate himself with the Emperor and no one doing anything to maintain discipline and order in the ranks.

Only one Highlord, the Blue Lady, Kitiara, managed to keep her forces under control. Her officers and troops were loyal to her and highly disciplined. They were proud of their Highlord and proud of themselves, and though some grumbled that they were missing out on the fun, they stayed in their camp.

Soldiers of the Red Dragonarmy were already in the city, and they had been given orders to keep the others out until the Emperor arrived. That proved a difficult task since draconians could simply fly over the walls, and they crowded into the Broken Shield and the Hairy Troll (both under new management).

When the Nerakan Guard, backed by the soldiers of the Red Dragonarmy, tried to expel the draconians during the night, fights broke out. The Nightlord, seeing that the

Nerakan Guard was unequal to the task of dealing with the unruly mobs and afraid that the fighting would spill over onto temple grounds, dispatched temple guards to assist. That left the temple undermanned at a critical time, right when the Nightlord was preparing for the war council.

The Nightlord was furious and laid all the blame on Ariakas, who, whispers said, had been so stupid as to nearly get himself done in by his own trollop. The Nightlord ordered every dark pilgrim in the city and surrounding environs to assemble at the temple to assist with security.

Raistlin was up before dawn. He had spent the night in the tunnels beneath Lute's shop. That morning, he took off his dyed black robes. He ran his hand over the cloth. The dyer had not lied; the black color had not faded, had not turned green. They had served him well. He folded them and laid them neatly on the chair.

He tied the pouches containing his spell components and the dragon orb onto a strip of leather and hung the pouches around his neck. He attached the thong with the silver knife onto the wrist of his hand and tested it to make certain the knife would fall into his palm at a flick of his wrist. Finally, he dressed himself in the black velvet robes and golden medallion of a Spiritor, a high-ranking cleric of the gods of Darkness. Kitiara had given Raistlin the disguise, telling him how she had encountered the Spiritor during her escape from Ariakas's prison.

The soft cloth slid down Raistlin's neck and shoulders. He arranged the bulky fabric so his pouches were underneath, concealed from sight. Clerics drew their holy magic from prayers to their gods, not from rose petals and bat guano.

That done, he set the dragon orb on the table and placed his hands upon it.

"Show me my brother," he commanded.

The colors of the orb shimmered and swirled. Hands appeared in the orb, but they were not the familiar hands. They were skeletal hands, fleshless with bony fingers and the long, hideous nails of a corpse . . .

Raistlin gasped, abruptly breaking the spell. He snatched his hands away. He heard the sound of laughter and the hated voice.

"If your armor is made of dross, I will find a crack in it."

"We both want the same thing," Raistlin said to Fistandantilus. "I have the means to achieve it. Interfere, and we both lose."

Raistlin waited tensely for the reply. When it did not come, he hesitated; then, not seeing any hands, he grabbed the orb and thrust it into the pouch. He did not use the orb again, but made his way through the tunnels that took him underneath the city wall and into Neraka.

A large crowd of dark clerics was gathered in front of the temple by the time Raistlin arrived. The line extended down the street and wrapped around the building.

Raistlin was about to take his place at the end when it occurred to him that a Spiritor such as he was pretending to be would not wait in line with lowly pilgrims. To do so might look suspicious. Raistlin rapped the shins of those in front of him with the end of the Staff of Magius, ordering them to get out of the way.

Several rounded on him angrily, only to shut their mouths and swallow their ire when they saw the sunlight flash on his medallion. Sullenly, the dark pilgrims drew aside to allow Raistlin to bully his way through to the front of the line.

Raistlin kept his hood pulled low over his head. He was wearing black leather gloves to conceal his golden skin as well as his knife. He feigned a limp, giving him a plausible reason for leaning on a staff. And though the Staff of Magius garnered some curious glances, the staff had a way of appearing nondescript as circumstances required.

Arriving at the temple entrance, Raistlin presented his pass, also provided by Kit, and waited with unconcealed impatience as the draconian guard studied it. The draconian finally waved a clawed hand.

"You have leave to enter, Spiritor."

Raistlin started to walk through the ornate double doors, which were adorned with the representation of Takhisis as the five-headed dragon, when another guard, a human, halted him.

"I want to see your face. Remove your hood."

"I wear my cowl for a reason," said Raistlin.

"And you'll take it off for a reason," said the guard, and he reached out his hand.

"Very well," said Raistlin. "But be warned. I am a follower of Morgion."

He drew back his hood.

The guard's face twisted in fear and revulsion. He wiped his hand on his uniform to remove any possible contamination. Several clerics waiting their turn in line behind Raistlin shoved each other aside in their haste to move away from him. Of all the gods in the dark pantheon, Morgion, god of disease and corruption, was the most loathsome.

"Would you like to see my hands?" Raistlin asked and started to pull off the black gloves.

The guard muttered something unintelligible and jerked his thumb toward the doors. Raistlin drew his hood over his head, and no one stopped him. As he entered the temple, he could hear, behind him, the shocked comments from the onlookers.

"Chunks of flesh falling off . . ."

". . . lips rotted away! You could see the tendons and the bone . . ."

". . . living skull . . ."

Raistlin was pleased. His illusion spell had worked. He considered maintaining the illusion, but keeping the spell going all day would be draining. He would simply keep his hood over his face.

Raistlin joined a black mass of clerics milling around in the entryway. He asked one how to find the council chamber.

"I have traveled from the east. This is my first time visiting Her Dark Majesty's temple," Raistlin said by way of explanation. "I do not know my way around."

The dark pilgrim was pleased to be singled out by a cleric of such high office, and she offered to personally escort the Spiritor. As she led him through the convoluted corridors to the council hall, she described the events planned for the war council, or the "High Conclave," as Ariakas termed it.

"The meeting of the Highlords will commence with the setting of the sun. An hour after"—the pilgrim's voice grew soft with awe—"our Dark Queen, Takhisis, will join her Highlords to declare victory in the war."

A trifle premature, Raistlin thought.

"What happens during the High Conclave?" he asked.

"First the Emperor's troops will take their places at the foot of his throne. Then the troops of the Highlords will enter and, after that, the Highlords themselves. Last to come will be the Emperor. When all are assembled, the Highlords will swear their loyalty to the Emperor and Her Dark Majesty. The Highlords will present the Emperor with gifts to the goddess as a mark of their devotion.

"We hear," the dark pilgrim added in a confidential tone, "that one of the gifts will be the elf woman known as the Golden General. She will be sacrificed to Takhisis in the Dark Watch rites. I hope you will be able to attend, Spiritor. We would be honored by your presence."

Raistlin said he looked forward to it.

"This is the council chamber," announced the pilgrim, bringing him to the main door. "We are not permitted to go in, but you can see inside. It is most impressive!"

As with all other chambers in the temple, the circular council hall existed half on the ethereal plane and half in the real world and was designed to unsettle all who looked upon it. Everything was as it appeared to be, and nothing was what it appeared. The black granite floor was solid and shifted underfoot. The walls were made of the same black granite, making the observer feel the dark rising all around him in a tidal wave meant to drown the world.

Raistlin, peering upward to the domed ceiling, was astonished and displeased to see several dragons perched among the eaves. He was staring at the dragons and wondering how they might affect his plans, when he suddenly had the horrible impression that the ceiling was falling on him. He ducked involuntarily, then heard the dark pilgrim give a dry chuckle. Raistlin stared at the ceiling until the sinking feeling in the pit of his stomach subsided.

"On those four platforms," said the guide, gesturing, "are the sacred thrones of the Dragon Highlords. The white is for Lord Toede, the green for Salah-Kahn, the black for Lucien of Takar, and the blue is for the Blue Lady, Kitiara uth Matar."

"The platforms are rather small," said Raistlin.

The guide bristled, taking offense. "They are most imposing."

"I beg your pardon," said Raistlin. "What I meant was that the platforms are not large enough to hold the Highlord and all his bodyguards. Don't you fear assassins?"

"Ah, I see what you mean," said the guide stiffly. "No one other than the Highlord is permitted on the platform. The bodyguards stand on the stairs that lead up to the platform, and they encircle the platform itself. No assassin could possibly get by."

"I assume the large, ornate throne with all the jewels at the front of the hall is for the Emperor?"

"Yes, that is where His Imperial Majesty will sit. And you see the dark alcove above his throne?"

Raistlin had found it difficult to look at anything else. His eyes were constantly drawn to that shadowy area, and he had known what the alcove housed before the guide told him.

"That is where our Queen will make her triumphant entrance into the world. You are fortunate, Spiritor. You will be there with her."

"I will?" Raistlin asked, startled.

"The Emperor has his throne beneath her. Our Nightlord stands close to Her Dark Majesty, and dignitaries such as yourself, Spiritor, will be standing alongside her."

The guide sighed with envy. "You are very lucky to be so close to Her Dark Majesty."

"Indeed," said Raistlin.

He and Kit had planned that he would join her on her own platform. He could work his magic from there. There were risks in that. He would be in full view of everyone in the council hall, including Ariakas. And though Raistlin was disguised as a cleric, the moment he started to cast his spell, everyone in the hall would know he was a wizard. The longer he thought about it, the more he realized that the Nightlord's platform would serve him far better.

I will be standing above Ariakas, he reflected. The Emperor will have his back to me. True, I will be close to Takhisis, but she will not be paying attention to me. Her attention will be focused on her Highlords.

"We should be going," the guide said abruptly. "It is almost time for midday rituals. You can accompany me."

"I do not want to be a burden," said Raistlin, who had been wondering how to get rid of the woman so he could go exploring on his own. "I will find my own way around."

"Attendance is mandatory," said the guide sternly.

Raistlin swore beneath his breath, but there was no help for it. His guide steered him away from the hall and into the maze that was the temple, where they immediately got caught up in a confused mass of dark clerics and soldiers, all attempting to enter the council hall. The heat from the hundreds of bodies was intense. Raistlin was sweating in his velvet robes. His palms in the black, leather gloves were itchy and wet. He disliked the feeling, and he longed to rip the gloves off. He dared not do so. His golden skin would have caused comment; he feared he would be recognized from the time when he'd been imprisoned here.

Just as the crowd seemed about to thin out, a large baaz draconian appeared out of nowhere and barged into them.

"Make way!" the draconian was yelling. "Dangerous prisoners. Make way! Make way!"

People fell back as ordered. The prisoners came into view. One of them was Tika, walking directly behind the guard. Her red curls were limp and bedraggled, and she had long, bloody scratches on her arms. Whenever she slowed down, a baaz draconian gave her a shove from behind.

Caramon came next, carrying Tasslehoff, slung over his shoulder.Caramon was protesting loudly that they had no reason to arrest him, he was a commander in the dragonarmy, they'd made a big mistake. So what if he didn't have the right papers? He demanded to see whoever was in charge.

Tas's face was bloody and bruised, and he must have been unconscious because he was quiet. And Tasslehoff Burrfoot, in such an interesting situation, would have never been quiet.

Where is Tanis? Raistlin wondered. Caramon— insecure and self-doubting—would never abandon his leader. Perhaps Tanis was dead. The fact that Tasslehoff was injured suggested a fight had taken place.Kender never did know when to keep their mouths shut.

There was one other person in the group, a tall man with a long, white beard. Raistlin didn't recognize him at first, not until Tika stumbled. The baaz draconian shoved her, and she fell against the bearded man. His false beard slipped and Raistlin knew him—Berem.

Tika put her hand to Berem's face, pretending to be concerned about him, but in reality to repair the damage, swiftly sticking the beard back into place.

The group passed so close by Raistlin that he could have reached out his hand and touched Caramon's arm, the strong arm that had so often supported him, held him, comforted him, defended him. Raistlin turned his attention to the man with the false beard.

Raistlin had promised to deliver Berem Everman to Takhisis, and there was the Everman, not an arm's length away.

Raistlin drew in a soft breath. The idea burst like an exploding star inside his head, dazzling him. His heart leaped with excitement; his hands shook. He had thought only to see his sister, Kitiara, wear the crown. That had been the extent of his ambition, his desire. He had never dreamed he would be handed the ability to bring down Queen Takhisis. He quickly squelched the thought, mindful of the voice in his head. Fistandantilus was out there, watching, waiting, biding his time.

Two suns cannot travel in the same orbit.

Raistlin dragged his hood over his face and shrank back against a wall. Clerics and soldiers shoved past him, shielding him from sight. The draconians continued on, bullying their way through the crowd, until Raistlin lost sight of them.

"Where are they taking the prisoners?" he asked his guide.

"To the dungeons below the temple," she replied. Her lip curled in disapproval. "I don't know why the stupid guards brought that filth into the main level. The dracos should have entered through the proper gate. But what can you expect of those lizard-brains? I always said creating them was a mistake."

True, thought Raistlin, but not for the reason the guide imagined. The Dark Queen's draconians, born into the world to help her conquer it, were taking the one man in the world who could cause her to lose it to the one place in the world where he needed to be:

The Foundation Stone.

14

A reunion of sorts. The spell trap.

26th Day, Month of Mishamont, Year 352 AC

Midday services were held at various locations throughout the temple. Raistlin's guide led him up twenty-six stairs to a place known simply as the Abbey.

"A place of worship and meditation," according to his guide, "where no sight or sound intrudes on the senses that might distract one from adoring our Queen."

Apparently that included light. They entered a winding passageway that was utterly, impenetrably dark. Raistlin had to feel his way along, keeping one hand on the stone wall and shuffling his feet over the floor so as not to trip over something. His guide considered the darkness deeply symbolic.

"We mortals are blind and must rely upon our Queen to guide us. We are deaf and hear only her voice," the pilgrim told him before they entered the sacred place. "No light is permitted in the Abbey. No one is allowed to speak. Holy spells maintain the darkness and the silence."

Raistlin thought it all highly annoying.

He knew the passage ended only when he bumped into a wall and bruised his forehead. He could not see anything; he could not hear anything. He could smell and he could feel, however, and both those senses told him that the room was filled with people. Raistlin's guide pressed her hand on his shoulder, indicating he was to kneel. Raistlin pretended to do so, and the moment she let loose of him, he slipped away from her. Not wanting to become lost, he kept near the door, and remained standing by the entrance, leaning on the Staff of Magius.

At least, he reflected, he had time to think, examine his plan, go over it in his mind. He was settling down to enjoy the silence when he was startled and unnerved to hear voices rising in a chant. A shiver crept over his flesh. The room was silent, yet the voices were loud and dinned in his ears.

"Everything happens for a reason—because Takhisis wants it to happen," the clerics intoned.

"Everything I do is done by Her Dark Majesty's grace. Everything I do is at Her Dark Majesty's behest. Freedom is an illusion."

As Raistlin listened, the terrible thought came to him. What if they are right? What if everything I am doing is because Takhisis is telling me to do it? What if she is the one who brought me to Neraka? What if she is the one who has protected me, saved me, guided me? She is leading me to my destruction . . .

He was standing by the door, and he had only to turn and leave. He turned and found himself pressed against a wall. He slid along the wall, hoping he was going the right way, only to find his path blocked by the bodies of devout clerics. He tried another direction, and by that time he was turned around in the blinding, suffocating night. He could not find the way out.

He was sweating. The gold medallion around his neck was like a stone, seeming to weigh him down. He shuffled along the floor, tripping over people. A hand reached out and clutched at his ankle, and his heart nearly stopped beating.

This will be my future if I give in to her, Raistlin realized suddenly. I will be lost in the darkness, disembodied, like Fistandantilus. I will be alone and afraid, always afraid.

"Everything I do is done by Her Dark Majesty's grace. Everything I do is at Her Dark Majesty's will."

Lies . . . all lies, he thought. Fear, that is her will.

Raistlin came to a halt. He stared fixedly into the darkness. And it seemed to him that the darkness blinked.

When the hour of prayer and meditation finally ended, the dark pilgrims rose stiffly from where they had been kneeling on the floor and began to wend their way out. The darkness spell remained, and they moved slowly, feeling their way. Raistlin found the exit easily. He had been standing right next to it all the time.

He breathed an inward sigh of relief when he once more returned to the main part of the temple. Although the light here was dim, it was light.

"I must attend to my duties now," his guide told him apologetically. "Will you be all right on your own?"

Raistlin assured her he would be fine. She told him where to find the dining hall and said that he was free to see the wonders of the rest of the temple.

"There are only a few areas which are prohibited," she said. "The chambers of the Highlords, which are in the tower, and the council chamber."

"What about the dungeons?" Raistlin asked.

The guide frowned. "Why would you want to go there?"

"I am a servant of Morgion," said Raistlin in his soft voice. "I am commanded to bring my god new followers. I find that those rotting in prison cells tend to be receptive to his message."

The guide grimaced in disgust. Most dark pilgrims loathed Morgion and his priests and their methods of preying upon the sick, luring them with false promises of renewed health to draw them into a hideous bargain from which not even death would free them. Raistlin's guide said caustically that if he wanted to visit the dungeons, he could do so. She cautioned him not to get lost.

"The Nightlord and the other dignitaries will be gathering here an hour prior to the time of the council meeting. You should be here if you want to join them."

Raistlin said that nothing would make him happier, and he promised to be back two hours before he was wanted. His guide left him, and he found his way down from the upper level of the temple to the lower. He counted the stairs as he descended and marked his mental map accordingly.

Raistlin found his friends in a holding cell. He did not approach, but observed them from a distance. The passageways in the dungeons were narrow and twisted and shadowy. Torches in iron baskets set at intervals on the walls shed puddles of light on the floor. The stench was frightful, a combination of blood, decaying flesh (corpses were often left chained to the walls for days before being removed), and filth.

A bored hobgoblin jailer sat tilted back in a chair, amusing himself by throwing his knife at rats. He held his knife in his hand, and whenever a rat skittered out of the shadows, he would hurl the knife at it. If he hit the rat, he would scratch a mark upon the stone wall. If he missed, he would scowl and grumble and make another mark in a different place on the wall. His aim was poor and, judging by the number of marks for their side, the rats were winning.

Absorbed in his contest, the hobgoblin paid no attention to his prisoners. There was no reason he should. They were obviously not going anywhere, and even if they managed to escape, they would lose their way in the convoluted tangle of planar-shifting tunnels, or tumble into a pool of acid, or fall victim to one of the other traps placed in the corridors.

In the dim light, Raistlin could see Caramon slumped on a bench at the far end of the holding cell. He was pretending to be asleep and, not being a very good actor, was doing a poor job of it. Tika, at the opposite end, held Tas's head in her lap. Tas was still unconscious, though, by his moaning, he was at least alive. Berem sat on a bench, his vacant eyes staring into the darkness. His head was cocked, as though he were listening to a loved one's voice. He spoke softly in reply.

"I'm coming, Jasla. Don't leave me."

Raistlin toyed with the idea of freeing Berem. He discarded it almost immediately. Now was not the time. Takhisis was watching. Better to wait until nightfall, when her attention was focused on the battle for power among her Highlords.

The only problem with that plan was that Berem was likely to be discovered long before night fell. The false goat-hair beard he wore to conceal his features was starting to slip off. His laced shirt front gaped open slightly, and Raistlin could see a faint gleam of green light from the emerald in his chest. If Raistlin could see it, so could the hobgoblin jailer. All he had to do was look away from his contest with the rats . . .

"You are in danger, Caramon," Raistlin warned silently. "Open your eyes!"

And that moment, as though Caramon had heard his brother's voice, he opened his eyes and saw the glint of green. Caramon yawned and heaved himself to his feet, stretching his arms as though stiff from sitting.

He glanced at the jailer. The hobgoblin was watching a rat that was trying to make up its mind if it would be safe enough to emerge from its hole in the wall. Caramon sauntered nonchalantly over to Berem and, keeping one eye on the hobgoblin, swiftly drew the lacings to Berem's shirt front closed. The glint of light from the emerald vanished. Caramon was about to try to stick the false beard back in place when the hobgoblin hurled his knife, missed, and swore. The knife clanged against the wall. The rat, chittering in glee, made a dash for it. Caramon sat down hurriedly, crossing his arms over his chest and feigning sleep.

Raistlin fixed his gaze, his thoughts on Caramon. "You can do this, my brother. I have often called you a fool, but you are not. You are smarter than you think. Stand on your own. You don't need me. You don't need Tanis. I will create the diversion. And you will act."

Caramon sat bolt upright on the bench.

"Raist?" he called out. "Raist? Where are you?"

Tika had been patting Tas's cheek, trying to rouse him. Caramon's shout made her jump. She stared at him reproachfully. "Stop it, Caramon!" she said wearily, her eyes filling with tears. "Raistlin is gone. Get that into your head."

Caramon flushed. "I must have been dreaming," he mumbled.

Tika sighed bleakly and went back to trying to rouse Tas.

Caramon slumped down on the bench, but he didn't close his eyes.

"I guess it's up to me," he said with a sigh.

"Jasla's calling," said Berem.

"Yeah," said Caramon. "I know. But you can't go to her now. We have to wait." He laid his hand on Berem's arm, calming, protecting.

Raistlin thought how often he'd been annoyed by that same protective hand. He turned away, retracing his steps along the passage, moving away from the main prison area, deeper into the darkness. He was not certain where he was going, though he had some idea. When he came to the place where the corridor branched off in different directions, he chose the passage that sloped downward, the passage that was darkest, the passage that smelled the worst. The air was dank and fetid. The walls were wet to the touch; the floor, covered with slime.

Torches lit the way, but their light was feeble, as though they, too, struggled to survive in the oppressive dark. Raistlin spoke the word that caused his staff to shine, and the globe of crystal glimmered palely, barely enough for him to see. He moved quietly, treading softly, alert to any sound. Arriving at the top of a staircase, he paused to listen. Voices—the guttural, sibilant voices of draconian guards, drifted up from below.

Hidden in the darkness, Raistlin removed the golden medallion of faith from around his neck and dropped it into a pocket. He took several pouches from around his neck and tied them to the belt of his black robes. Then, dousing the light of his staff, he crept down the stairs.

Rounding a corner, he saw a guard room with several baaz draconians seated at a table with their bozak commander, playing at bones beneath the light of a single torch. Two more baaz stood at attention in front of a stone arch. Beyond the arch was darkness vaster and deeper than the darkness of death.

Raistlin remained on the landing at the bend of the staircase and listened to the draconians talk. What he heard confirmed him his theory. He gave a loud "ahem" and walked loudly down the stairs, his staff thumping on the stone.

The draconians leaped to their feet, drawing their swords. Raistlin came into view and, at the sight of his wizard's robes, the draconians relaxed, though they kept their clawed hands on their sword hilts.

"What do you want, Black Robe?" asked the bozak.

"I have been commanded to renew the spell traps that guard the Foundation Stone," said Raistlin.

He was taking an enormous risk mentioning the Foundation Stone. If he had made the wrong surmise and those draconians were guarding something else, he would soon be fighting for his life.

The bozak commander eyed Raistlin suspiciously.

"You're not the usual wizard," said the bozak. "Where is *he* this night?"

Raistlin heard the inflection on the word; realizing it was a test, he gave a snort. "You must have extremely poor eyesight, Commander, if you mistook Mistress Iolanthe for a man."

The baaz draconians hooted and made rude comments at their commander's expense. The bozak silenced them with a growl and slid his sword back into its sheath.

"Get on with it, then."

Raistlin crossed to the arch that was festooned with cobwebs. He lifted his staff and let the magical light play over the web. He spoke a few words of magic. The strands glistened with a faint radiance that almost immediately died. The draconians went back to their game.

"A good thing I came," said Raistlin. "The magic is starting to fail."

"Where is the witch tonight?" the bozak asked in casual tones that were a little too casual.

"I hear she is dead," said Raistlin. "She tried to assassinate the Emperor."

He saw, out of the corner of his eye, the bozak and the baaz exchange glances. The bozak muttered something about her death being "a waste of a fine female."

Raistlin started to walk through the arch.

"Stop right there, Black Robe," said the bozak. "No one allowed past this point."

"Why not?" asked Raistlin, feigning surprise. "I need to check the other traps."

"Orders," said the bozak.

"What is out there, then?" Raistlin asked curiously.

The bozak shrugged. "Don't know. Don't care."

Guards were not posted to guard nothing. Raistlin was now firmly convinced that the Foundation Stone lay through that arch. He tried to catch a glimpse of the fabled stone, but if it was there, he could not see it.

He looked up at the arch. A strange feeling came over him. His flesh crawled, as when someone steps on your grave. He could not figure out why, except that he had the oddest impression he had seen the archway before.

The stonework of the arch was ancient, far older than the guard room, which appeared to have been recently built. Raistlin could discern the faint outlines of carvings on the marble blocks that formed the arch, and though the carvings were faded and damaged, he recognized them. Each marble block was engraved with a symbol for the gods. Raistlin looked to the keystone, the center point of the arch, and though the lines were faint he could see the symbol of Paladine.

He closed his eyes, and the Temple of Istar filled his vision, beautiful and graceful, white marble shining in the sunlight. He opened his eyes and looked into the twisted darkness of the Temple of Takhisis, and he knew with unerring certainty what lay beyond:

The past and the present.

"What's taking you so damn long?" the bozak demanded.

"I cannot figure out what type of spell Mistress Iolanthe has cast," said Raistlin, frowning in seeming puzzlement. "Tell me, what would happen if someone were to pass through the arch?"

"All holy hell breaks loose," said the bozak with a relish. "Trumpets sound the alarm, or so I hear. I wouldn't know myself. It's never happened. No one has ever gone through that arch."

"These trumpets," said Raistlin. "Can they be heard in all parts of the temple? Even in the council hall?"

The draconian grunted. "From what I'm told, the dead can hear them. The noise will sound like the end of the world."

Raistlin cast a rudimentary spell on the cobwebs, then started to leave. He paused and said as an afterthought, "Do any of you know by chance where they have taken the elf woman they call the Golden General? I am supposed to interrogate her. I thought she would be in the dungeons, but I cannot locate her."

The draconians had no idea. Raistlin sighed and shrugged. Well, he had tried. He climbed back up the stairs, thinking as he went that the trap he had set was so obvious, only a complete moron would stumble into it.

15

The Nightlord. Paying a Debt.

26th Day, Month of Mishamont, Year 352 AC

emple bells rang the hour. The time of the council meeting was drawing near, and Raistlin still had to make his way back to the upper level. Once he was out of sight of the guards, he removed his pouches and concealed them once more beneath his robes. He put on the golden chain and the medallion of faith, transforming himself from wizard to cleric and left the dungeons, counting the stairs to find his way to the upper regions of the temple where the Nightlord's entourage was gathering.

Raistlin joined the group of Spiritors in an antechamber outside the council hall. He kept apart from the others, not wanting to draw attention to himself. He did not speak to anyone, but stood in the shadows, his head bowed, his hood over his face. His limp was pronounced. He leaned heavily on his staff. A few of the Spiritors glanced at him, and one started to approach him.

"He's a follower of Morgion," said another, and the cleric changed his mind.

After that, everyone left Raistlin severely alone.

The Nightlord made his appearance, accompanied by an aide. The Nightlord was clad in a black velvet robe over which he wore vestments shimmering with the five colors of the five heads of the dragon, Takhisis. The Spiritors, dressed in their own ceremonial garb, clustered around him. The Nightlord was in an excellent humor. He greeted each Spiritor in turn; then his flat and empty eyes turned upon Raistlin.

"I am told you are a worshiper of Morgion," said the Nightlord. "It is not often we have one of his followers among us, especially one of such high rank. You are welcome, Spiritor—"

The Nightlord stopped talking. His eyes narrowed. He studied Raistlin.

"Have we met, Spiritor?" the Nightlord asked, and though his tone was pleasant, the expression in his eyes was not. "Something about you seems familiar. Put back your hood. Let me see your face."

"My face is not pleasant to look upon, Nightlord," said Raistlin in a harsh voice, as different from his own as he could make it.

"I am not easily shocked. This very morning I cut off a man's nose and gouged out his eyes," said the Nightlord, smiling. "He was a spy, and that is what I do to spies. Let me see your face, Spiritor."

Raistlin tensed, cursing his luck. He should not have come up here. He should have foreseen the danger that the Nightlord would recognize him. They would not bother taking him to the dungeons. The Nightlord would kill him here, where he stood.

"Take off the hood! Show him your face," said Fistandantilus.

"Shut up!" Raistlin hissed under his breath. Aloud he

said, "My lord, I have sworn an oath to Morgion—"

"Show your face!" The Nightlord took hold of his medallion of faith and began to chant, "Takhisis, hear my prayer . . ."

"He will kill you where you stand! Take off the hood! As you said, we are both in this together. For the moment . . ."

Slowly, reluctantly, Raistlin took hold of the hood and drew it from his head.

One of the Spiritors covered her mouth with her hand and gagged. The others averted their eyes and shrank back from him. The Nightlord looked away not from disgust, but because he had lost interest. He had not unmasked a spy, merely a diseased follower of a loathsome god.

"Cover your face," said the Nightlord, waving his hand. "My apologies to Morgion if I have offended him."

Raistlin drew his hood over his head.

"Once again, I have saved you, young one."

Raistlin pressed his hand against his temple, longing to reach into his skull and rip the voice out of his head.

Fistandantilus chuckled. "You owe me. And you pride yourself on paying your debts."

A hand squeezed Raistlin's heart. His chest hurt. He struggled to breathe and was seized by a fit of coughing that doubled him over. He pressed his hand to his mouth. His fingers were covered in blood. Raistlin cursed inwardly, impotently. He cursed and coughed until he was dizzy, and he sagged back against a wall.

The Spiritors eyed him in alarm. The word *contagion* was on everyone's lips, and they nearly came to blows trying to get away from him. Then the sound of a gong reverberated throughout the temple. The Spiritors forgot Raistlin in their excitement.

"The bell summons us, my lord," said the aide, and he opened the double doors that led from the chamber into the council hall.

The Spiritors crowded around the door, eager to witness the procession of Highlords and the arrival of the Emperor.

"Must you gawk like peasants?" the Nightlord said angrily.

The Spiritors, looking chastened, left the door and returned to the antechamber.

"The Emperor's troops are gathering around his throne," reported the aide from his position at the door. "They are making ready for the Emperor."

"We enter after Ariakas," said the Nightlord. "Line up."

The aide bustled around, forming the Spiritors into two lines. The Nightlord took his place at the end. No one paid attention to Raistlin, who was leaning on his staff, gasping for breath and trying to clear his mind. The thunder of tramping feet, marching in time to the rhythmic thumping of a drum and shouted commands of officers, caused the floor to shake.

"First will come the Procession of Pilgrims," the Nightlord told his Spiritors. "When all of you have assembled on the platform, I will enter and take the place of honor beside Her Dark Majesty."

The soldiers in the hall began to cheer.

"See what is going on," the Nightlord commanded his aide.

"The Emperor has entered the hall," the aide reported.

"Is he wearing the Crown of Power?" the Nightlord asked tersely.

"He wears the armor of a Dragon Highlord," reported the aide, "a cape of royal purple, and the Crown of Power."

The Nightlord's face contorted in anger. His outraged voice sounded shrill above the thunderous ovation. "The crown is a holy artifact. When Queen Takhisis has conquered the world, we will see who wears this crown."

The Spiritors stood in line, expectant, excited, awaiting the signal and the arrival of their Queen. Raistlin fell in at the end. He began to cough. The cleric in front of him whipped around to glare at him.

Ariakas's troops cheered him and kept on cheering. Ariakas appeared to be in no hurry to stop them, for the cheering grew louder and more raucous. The soldiers struck the floor with their spears and banged their swords against their shields and roared his name. The Spiritors were growing tired of waiting. They began to mutter and shift impatiently. The Nightlord scowled and demanded to know what was happening.

"Ariakas is making his reverence to the throne of the Dark Queen," the aide reported from his place at the door. He had to shout to make himself heard.

"Has Her Dark Majesty arrived?" the Nightlord asked.

"No, your lordship. Her throne remains empty."

"Good," said the Nightlord. "We will be there to welcome her."

The Spiritors fidgeted. The Nightlord's foot tapped the floor. Finally, the cheering began to die. A hush settled over the troops. Another gong sounded.

"That is our signal," said the Nightlord. "Make ready."

The Spiritors readjusted their hoods and smoothed their robes. A trumpet sounded and cheers again erupted in the hall, as loud or louder than those that greeted the Emperor. The Nightlord was pleased. He made a gesture, and the line of Spiritors began to move toward the door. From there, they would walk out onto the narrow stone bridge that led from the antechamber to the throne of the

Dark Queen. The first two Spiritors were at the door when the aide suddenly cried out for them to stop.

"Why? What for?" the Nightlord asked, frowning in displeasure.

"The signal was for Highlord Kitiara, your lordship!" the aide said, trembling. "The Blue Lady and her troops are coming into the hall now."

The Nightlord paled with fury. The Spiritors broke ranks and clustered angrily around their leader, all of them clamoring to be heard. The entrance of a draconian wearing the insignia of the Emperor's guard brought sudden, chill silence.

"What do you want?" asked the Nightlord, glowering.

"His Imperial Majesty Ariakas extends his respects to the Nightlord of Queen Takhisis," said the draconian. "The Emperor has sent me to inform your lordship that there has been a change in plans. Your lordship and these honored holy men will enter the hall after the Highlord of the White Dragonarmy, Lord Toede. The Emperor—"

"I will not," said the Nightlord, dangerously calm.

"I beg your lordship's pardon," said the draconian.

"You heard me. I will *not* enter last. In fact, I will not enter at all. You may so inform Ariakas."

"I will inform the *Emperor,*" said the draconian, and with a bow and a disdainful flick of his tail, he departed.

The Nightlord cast a grim glance around at his clerics. "Ariakas insults me and, by insulting me, he insults our Queen. I will not stand for it and neither will she! We will go to the Abbey and give her our prayerful support."

The Spiritors swept out of the room, their robes rustling with righteous indignation. Raistlin started to join them. He took a step then, clutching at his chest, cried out in pain. His staff fell from his limp hand. He stumbled, staggered, and sank to his knees, coughing and spewing up blood. With a groan, he slumped onto his belly and lay on the floor, twitching and writhing in agony.

The Spiritors stopped, staring at him in alarm. Several looked uncertainly at the Nightlord.

"Should we help?" asked one.

"Leave him. Morgion will see to his cleric," said the Nightlord, and he waved his hand dismissively and hastened off.

The Spiritors did not wait to be told twice. Covering their mouths and noses with their black sleeves, they tried to get away from Raistlin as fast as possible.

Once he was certain he was alone, Raistlin rose to his feet. He picked up the Staff of Magius and walked to the door and looked out into the hall.

A narrow bridge of black stone extended some distance ahead of him. At the end was the shadowy alcove and the throne of the Dark Queen. She had not yet made an appearance. Perhaps she was in the Abbey, listening to the complaints of her Nightlord. In the hall, drums beat and soldiers cheered. Another Dragon Highlord was making his grand entrance. Raistlin ventured out onto the bridge. He did not go far. He wanted to see, not be seen.

The bridge had no rails, no barriers. Raistlin peered over the edge, looking down on the heads of the crowd that was far below him. The soldiers surged and heaved and wriggled, reminding him of maggots feeding off rotting flesh. The platforms on which the Dragon Highlords had their thrones rose high above the floor. Narrow, stone bridges extended from the antechambers of each Highlord to the throne. Thus, the Highlords were spared the need of walking among the masses.

Ariakas's throne reared above all the others. His throne was in the place of honor, directly beneath the Dark Queen's alcove.

The Emperor's throne was made of onyx and was plain and unadorned. Takhisis's throne, by contrast, was hideously beautiful. The back of the throne was formed of the gracefully curving necks and heads of five dragons, two on the right, two on the left, and one in the center. The arms of the throne were the dragon's legs; the seat, the dragon's breast. The throne was made entirely of jewels: emeralds, rubies, sapphires, pearls, and black diamonds.

From his vantage point on the bridge, Raistlin could see two of the other Highlords: the handsome and disdainful face of Salah-Kahn and the ugly, cunning face of the half-ogre Lucien of Takar. The white throne was empty. Ariakas had been shouting for Lord Toede, Highlord of the White, but no one by that name was answering.

The same Toede who had been Fewmaster in Solace. The same Toede whose search for the blue crystal staff had plunged Raistlin and his friends into danger and started them on the bright and shining, dark and tortuous paths they walked.

Raistlin could not see Kitiara from where he stood. She must be seated on the throne to Ariakas's right. Raistlin advanced along the bridge. He no longer worried about anyone below seeing him. The domed ceiling of the hall was wreathed in smoke from the breath of the dragons, who were watching from their alcoves high above and from the hundreds of torches mounted on the walls and the fires burning in iron braziers. In his black robes, Raistlin was just another shadow in a hall of shadows.

Takhisis would be watching him, as she was watching with avid interest everything that was going on. The air in the hall reeked of smoke and steel, leather and intrigue. Certainly Ariakas must have smelled the stench. And yet he sat on his throne alone, isolated, apart, supremely confident and invincible. He had no armed guards, only the Crown of Power. Let his underlings ring themselves round with steel. Ariakas feared nothing and no one. He had the backing of his Queen.

"But does he?" Raistlin wondered.

A ruler is supposed to appear confident. Even arrogance has its place upon the throne. But no god can forgive hubris. The last living man who had worn the crown had suffered from that malady. The Kingpriest of Istar had believed himself to be as powerful as any god. The gods of Krynn had shown him power; they had sent a fiery mountain crashing down upon his head. Ariakas had made the mistake of thinking too well of himself.

Raistlin was finally in a position where he could see Kitiara.

And with her was Tanis Half-Elven.

16

CROWN OF LOVE, CROWN OF POWER.

26th Day, Month of Mishamont, Year 352 AC

aistlin had not anticipated finding Tanis there, and he was annoyed. The presence of the half-elf could seriously disrupt his plans. Tanis was not standing at Kit's side; no one was allowed on the platform with the Highlord. But he was as close to her as he could manage, however, standing on the step leading to the throne.

Raistlin's lip curled. Tanis had come to Neraka to save the woman he loved. But did he know, even at that moment, which woman that was?

The council meeting proceeded. Raistlin, high above the thrones of the Highlords, could hear Ariakas's deep bellow, but much of what he was saying was swallowed by the vastness of the chamber. From what he could gather, Highlord Toede was not there because he had been slain by kender. And that news prompted a sound Raistlin could hear clearly—Kitiara's scornful laughter.

Ariakas was furious. He rose to his feet and started to descend the platform. Kitiara did not move. Her soldiers grabbed their weapons. Raistlin was amused to see Tanis take a protective step toward Kit, who remained seated on her throne, regarding Ariakas with a look of unutterable scorn. The other two Highlords were on their feet, watching with interest, neither offering any support, both probably hoping Ariakas and Kit would kill each other.

Raistlin walked to the edge of the bridge and looked down on Ariakas, who was directly beneath him. That was the moment to strike. No one was paying any attention to him. Everyone was watching the Highlords. Raistlin readied his magic.

Then he went blind. Darkness obliterated his sight, filled his mind, his heart, his lungs. He froze in place, for he was standing on the edge of the bridge. A wrong step would carry him over. He could always use the magic of his staff, which would allow him to float like a feather through the air, but everyone in the hall would see him, including Ariakas, unless they were all blind as he was at the moment. Reading his thoughts, an unseen hand tore his staff from his grasp and smote him in the back. His heart lurching in terror, he pitched forward. He landed, hard, on his knees, and though his wrists tingled and his knees were bruised, he shook with relief, for he had not plunged over the edge.

He reached out a shaking hand and felt nothing in front of him except air and realized how close he had come. He longed to crawl to safety, but he had lost all sense of direction and he feared that he might yet fall. The hand was pounding him, grinding him, crushing him into the stone. Then suddenly, when it seemed his heart would burst, the hand released him, the darkness lifted from his eyes. Raistlin scrambled back until he bumped into something solid, the Dark Queen's throne.

Raistlin turned to face her not because he wanted to, but because she compelled him. And that was her mistake.

She was a shadow, and for Raistlin the shadows held no terror.

He looked down to see his sister and the rest groveling in fear. Kitiara cowered on her throne. Tanis Half-Elven had been driven to his knees. Ariakas knelt before his Queen. They were nothing, and she was everything. Takhisis had her foot on their necks. Once she was assured of their submissiveness, once she was certain that they knew she owned them, she lifted her foot and permitted them to rise.

Her gaze flicked over Raistlin, and he knew himself forgotten. He was nothing, a nonentity, a grain of sand, a speck of dust, a drop of water, a flake of ash. Her attention was focused on those who held the power, those who were important to her: her Highlords and the struggle that would end with the most powerful among them ascending to the throne and dealing the death blow to the forces of Light.

Raistlin blended into the darkness, became the darkness. He watched and waited for his chance.

Takhisis began to orate. Kitiara looked pleased; Ariakas, baleful. Raistlin could not hear what the Queen was saying. She was talking to those who mattered. He watched the proceedings, feeling as though he were watching a play from the last seat in the very last row.

Kitiara left her throne and, motioning to Tanis, descended the stairs and advanced onto the floor of the hall. The soldiers fell back to give her room. Tanis walked behind her like a whipped dog brought to heel.

A platform reared up like a striking snake from the middle of the hall. Kitiara climbed the spiky stairs that were difficult to traverse, apparently, for Tanis, coming after her, kept slipping, much to the amusement of the onlookers. Following the analogy of a play, Tanis was the understudy called on to perform at the last moment. He had not rehearsed, did not know his lines.

Kitiara made a grand gesture, and Lord Soth entered, his awful presence overpowering all the other actors in the piece. The death knight carried in his arms a body wrapped in white cloth. He laid the shrouded figure at Kitiara's feet; then he vanished, a dramatic exit.

Kitiara reached down and unwound the cloth. The light shone on golden hair. Raistlin moved closer to the edge of the bridge for a better view as Laurana struggled to fight her way out of the winding sheet. Tanis instinctively reached out to help her. Kitiara stopped him with a look. When he obeyed her, she rewarded him with that crooked smile.

Raistlin watched with interest. Together at last were the three who had started it all. The three who symbolized the struggle. The Darkness and the Light and the soul that wavered in between.

Laurana stood tall and proud in her silver armor, and she was all that Raistlin remembered of beauty. He looked down on her, and he sighed softly and pressed his lips together grimly. He knew loss in that moment, but he also knew she had never been his to lose.

Tanis looked at Laurana, and Raistlin saw that the wavering soul had finally made the choice. Or perhaps Tanis's soul had made the choice long before, and his heart had just now caught up. Love's light illuminated the two of them, shutting out Kitiara, leaving her alone in the darkness.

Kit understood and the knowledge was bitter. Raistlin saw her crooked smile twist and harden.

"So you *are* capable of love, my sister," said Raistlin. And he knew then that he would have his chance.

Kitiara ordered Tanis to lay his sword at the foot of the Emperor, swear fealty to Ariakas. Tanis obeyed. What else could he do when the woman he loved was a prisoner of the woman he had once imagined he loved?

It was strange that Laurana, the prisoner, was the only one of the three who was truly free. She loved Tanis with her entire being. Her love had brought her to this place of darkness, and her light shone more brightly still. Her love was her own, and if Tanis did not return it, that no longer mattered. Love strengthened her, ennobled her. Her love for one opened her heart to love for all.

Kitiara, by contrast, was tangled in a web of her own passions, always reaching for the prize that hung out of reach. Love to her meant power over one, and that meant power over all.

Tanis climbed the stairs leading to the throne of Ariakas, and Raistlin saw the half-elf's eyes go to the crown. Tanis's gaze fixed on it. His lips moved, unconsciously repeating the words, *Whoever wears the crown rules!* His expression hardened; his hand clenched on the hilt of the sword.

Raistlin understood Tanis's plan as clearly as if he and the half-elf had spent years working on it. In a sense, perhaps they had. The two of them had always been close in a way none of their friends had ever understood. Darkness speaking to dark, perhaps.

And what of Takhisis? Did the Queen know that the half-elf, shaved clean of the beard that had once hidden his shame, climbed the stairs toward destiny, prepared to sacrifice his life for the sake of others? Did she know that in the heart of her darkness, down in her dungeons, a kender and a barmaid and a warrior were grimly prepared to do the same? Did Takhisis realize that the wizard wearing the black robes that marked his allegiance to self-serving ambition would be ready to sacrifice his life for the freedom to walk whatever path he chose?

Raistlin raised his hand. The words to the spell he had memorized the night before blazed in his mind like the words he'd written in blood on the lambskin.

Tanis climbed the stairs, his hand clutching his sword's hilt. Raistlin recognized the sword. Alhana Starbreeze had given it to Tanis in Silvanesti. The sword was Wyrmsbane, the mate to the sword Tanis had received from the dead elf king Kith-Kanan in Pax Tharkas. Raistlin remembered that the weapon was magical, though he could not remember at that moment what magic the sword possessed.

It didn't matter. The sword's magic would not be powerful enough to pierce the magical field generated by the Crown of Power. When his sword struck that field, the blast would blow him apart. Ariakas would remain safe behind the shield; not so much as a splatter of blood smearing his gleaming armor.

Tanis reached the top of the stairs, and he started to draw his sword. He was nervous; his hands shook.

Ariakas stood up from the throne, planting his powerful legs and crossing his bulging arms over his chest. He was not looking at Tanis. He was staring across the hall at Kitiara, who had her own arms crossed and was staring defiantly back. Multicolored light flared from the crown and shimmered around Ariakas, making it seem as though he were being guarded by a shield of rainbows.

Tanis slid his sword from the sheath and, at the sound, Ariakas's attention snapped back to the half-elf. He looked down his nose at him, sneered at him, trying to intimidate him. Tanis didn't notice. He was staring at the crown, his eyes wide with dismay. He had just realized his plan to kill Ariakas must fail.

Raistlin's spell burned on his lips; the magic burned in his blood. He had no time for Tanis's eternal wavering.

"Strike, Tanis!" Raistlin urged. "Do not fear the magic! I will aid you!"

Tanis looked startled and he glanced toward the direction of the sound that he must have heard more with his heart than with his ears, for Raistlin had spoken softly.

Ariakas was starting to grow impatient. A man of action, he was bored with the ceremony. He considered the council meeting a waste of time that could be spent more profitably pursuing the war. He gave a snarl and made a peremptory gesture, indicating Tanis was to swear his fealty and get on with it.

Still, Tanis hesitated.

"Strike, Tanis! Swiftly!" Raistlin urged.

Tanis stared straight at Raistlin, but whether he could see him or not, whether he would act or not, Raistlin could not tell. Tanis started to lay the sword down on the floor; then, resolve hardening his expression, he shifted his stance and aimed a blow at Ariakas.

Raistlin and Caramon had often fought together, combining sorcery and steel. As Tanis's sword arm started to rise, Raistlin cast his spell.

"Bentuk-nir daya sihir, colang semua pesona dalam. Perubahan ke sihir-nir!" Raistlin cried and, drawing a rune in the air, he hurled the spell at Ariakas.

The magic flowed through Raistlin and burst from him, crackling out of his fingertips, blazing through the air. The magic struck the rainbow shield, dispelling it. Tanis's sword met no obstacle. Wyrmsbane pierced

Ariakas's black, dragon-scale breastplate, sliced through flesh and muscle and bone, and sank deep into his chest.

Ariakas roared, more in astonishment than in pain. The agony of dying and the terrible knowledge that he was dying would come to him with his next and final breath. Raistlin did not linger to see the end. He did not care who would win the Crown of Power. For the moment, the Dark Queen was intent upon the struggle. He had to make good his escape.

But the powerful spell he had cast had weakened him. He stifled a cough in the sleeve of his robes and, grabbing the staff, ran along the bridge, heading back toward the antechamber. He had almost reached the entrance when a mass of draconian guards blocked his way.

"The foul assassin!" Raistlin gasped, gesturing. "A wizard. I tried to stop him—"

The draconian didn't wait, but shoved Raistlin aside, slamming him back into the walls. Soldiers flowed around him, dashing down the bridge.

They would soon realize they had been duped, and they would be back. Raistlin, coughing, fumbled in his pouch and took out the dragon orb. He barely had breath enough left to chant the words.

The next thing he knew, he was standing in front of Caramon's cell. The door was open. The cell was empty. A charred patch on the floor was all that remained of a bozak draconian. A pile of greasy ash denoted the demise of a baaz draconian. Caramon and Berem, Tika and Tas were gone. Raistlin heard guttural voices shouting that the prisoners had escaped.

But where had they gone?

Raistlin swore under his breath and looked around for some clue. At the end of the corridor, an iron door had been torn off its hinges.

Jasla was calling, and Berem had answered.

Raistlin leaned on the staff and drew in a ragged breath. He could breathe easier; his strength was returning. He was about to go in pursuit of Berem when a hand snaked out of the shadows. Cold fingers closed painfully over his wrist. Long nails scraped his skin and dug into his flesh.

"Not so fast, young magus," said Fistandantilus. "We have unfinished business, you and I."

The voice was real and close, no longer in his head. Raistlin could feel the old man's breath warm on his cheek. The breath came from a living body, not a live corpse.

The hand held him fast. The bony fingers with their long, yellowed nails tightened their grip. Raistlin could not see the face, for it was hidden in the shadows. He had no need to see it. He knew the face as well or better than he knew his own. In some ways, the face was his own.

"Only one of us can be the master," said Fistandantilus.

The green bloodstone mottled with red striations glistened in the light of the Staff of Magius.

17
The last battle. The bloodstone.
26th Day, Month of Mishamont, Year 352 AC

Raistlin was caught completely off-guard. A second before, he had been triumphing in his victory over Ariakas, and between the space of one shuddering breath and another, he was held fast in the grip of his most implacable foe, a wizard Raistlin had duped and cheated and sought to destroy.

Raistlin stared, mesmerized, at the bloodstone pendant dangling from the bony hand. When Fistandantilus had been a living man, he had murdered countless young mages, sucking out their lives with the bloodstone and giving the life-force to himself.

In desperation, Raistlin cast the only spell that came to his terrified mind—an elementary spell, one of the first he had ever learned.

"Kair tangus miopiar!"

His hand flared with fire. Raistlin realized the moment he spoke that the spell would be useless against Fistandantilus. The magical flames could only harm the living. He was despairing, cursing himself, when, to his amazement, Fistandantilus snarled and snatched his hand away.

"You *are* flesh and blood!" Raistlin gasped, and he was heartened. He was fighting a live enemy, one that might be strong, but also one who could be killed.

Falling back, Raistlin clasped the Staff of Magius in both hands and raised it in front of him, using it as both shield and weapon. He remembered the times Caramon had insisted his twin learn to defend himself with the staff and how he had always tried to get out of it.

"I will soon be *your* flesh and *your* blood," said Fistandantilus, his fleshless lips parting in a ghastly smile. "A reward from my Queen."

"*Your* Queen!" Raistlin almost laughed. "A Queen you plotted to overthrow."

"All is forgiven between us," said Fistandantilus. "On one condition—that I destroy you. Did you honestly think your actions, your plans, would escape my notice? In return for your demise, I will become you—or rather, your young body will house me."

He cast a disparaging glance over Raistlin's thin frame and sniffed. "Not the best body I have inhabited, but one that is powerful in magic. And with my knowledge and wisdom, you will become more powerful still. I hope that will be a final comfort to you in your last moments."

Raistlin lashed out with the Staff of Magius, aiming a blow at the wizard's hooded head. But he was not particularly skilled as a fighter, not like Caramon. His strike was clumsy and slow. Fistandantilus ducked. He caught hold of the staff, and jerked it out of Raistlin's hands.

The staff's magic crackled. Fistandantilus cried in rage and flung the staff halfway down the corridor. Raistlin heard the crystal globe crack as the staff struck the stone floor. The glow of magic dimmed.

Raistlin glanced back over his shoulder and marked where the staff lay. He fell back a step, his hand fumbling beneath his robes for the pouches that held the dragon orb and his spell components. Fistandantilus saw what he intended. He pointed at the pouches and spoke words of magic. Like iron to lodestone, the pouches flew out of Raistlin's hands and into the hands of the old man.

"Bat dung and rose petals!" Fistandantilus cast the pouches disdainfully to the floor. "When I am you, you will have no need of such ingredients. The Master of Past and Present will craft magnificent magic. Too bad you will not be there to see it."

Fistandantilus extended his hands, fingers spread, and began to chant, "*Kalith karan, tobanis-kar . . .*"

Raistlin recognized the spell and hurled himself to the floor. Blazing arrows of fire shot from the old man's fingertips and sizzled over Raistlin's head. The scorching heat burned his hair. The Staff of Magius lay just beyond reach. The crystal globe had cracked, but the magical light continued to shine and he saw, in its light, something sparkle.

He was about to try to make a grab for it when he heard footsteps behind him—Fistandantilus coming to finish him off. Raistlin gave a moan and tried to rise, only to collapse onto the floor again.

Fistandantilus laughed, amused at his struggles. "When I am in your body, Majere, I will hunt down and slay your imbecile brother, who is now trying to fight his way to the Foundation Stone. Caramon will think, in his final, despairing moments, that his beloved twin was his murderer. But then that's nothing new to poor Caramon, is it? He's already seen you kill him!"

Fistandantilus began chanting a spell. Raistlin did not recognize the words; he had no idea what the spell would do. Something horrible, that was certain. He moaned again and glanced surreptitiously behind him. When Fistandantilus was near, Raistlin lashed out with his feet, striking the old man in the shins and sending him crashing to the floor. The spell ended in a garbled cry and a thud.

Raistlin made a lunge and a grab for the small, sparkling object. His hand closed over the dragon orb, and he scrambled to his feet.

A trumpet blast echoed through the corridor.

Fistandantilus did not bother to rise. He sat on the floor, slapped his hands on his knees, and grinned up at him. "Some moron has tripped your spell trap."

The old man gathered his black robes around him and pushed himself to his feet. He took a step toward Raistlin, who opened his palm. The dragon orb's colors swirled and glowed, illuminating the corridor.

"Well, go ahead, young magus," said Fistandantilus. "You have the orb. Use it. Call upon the power of the dragons to smash me to a bloody pulp."

Raistlin looked at the orb, at the colors swirling inside. His mouth twisted, and he looked away.

Fistandantilus smiled grimly. "You don't dare use it. You are too weak. You fear the orb will take hold of you and you'll end up a drooling idiot like poor Lorac."

He lifted the bloodstone pendant. "I promise, Majere, I won't let that happen. Your end will be swift, though not exactly painless. And now, much as I have enjoyed our little contest, my Queen needs my services elsewhere."

Fistandantilus began to chant.

Raistlin closed his fist over the orb. The bright light welled out between his fingers: five rays, five different colors, slanting off in different directions. Raistlin raised his hand.

"Cease your spell-casting, old man, or I will hurl the orb to the floor. The orb is made of crystal. It can be broken."

Fistandantilus frowned. His chanting ceased. He held up the bloodstone pendant and made a squeezing motion with his hand.

Raistlin's heart quivered and bounded in his chest. He gasped, unable to breathe. Fistandantilus tightened his grip, and Raistlin's heart stopped beating. He could not breathe. Black spots burst before his eyes, and he felt himself falling.

Fistandantilus relaxed his grip a fraction.

Raistlin's heart gave a painful lurch, and he was able to draw in a breath. Fistandantilus squeezed his hand again, and Raistlin cried out in agony and fell to the floor. He lay on his back, staring up at Fistandantilus. The old man knelt down beside Raistlin and pressed the bloodstone against Raistlin's heart.

Fear, raw and bitter, gripped Raistlin. His mouth went dry; his arm muscles clenched; sickening, hot liquid burned his throat. His fear wrung him, drained him, leaving him confused and shaken. He was not afraid of death. Weak and frail, he had fought death from the moment of his birth. Death held no terror for him; even now, it would be easier to simply shut his eyes and let the easeful darkness wash over him.

He did not fear dying. He did fear oblivion.

He would be consumed by Fistandantilus. His soul devoured, swallowed up, and digested. His body would go on living, but he would not. And no one would know the difference. In the end, it would be as if he had never been.

"Farewell, Raistlin Majere . . ."

Raistlin was swimming in the ocean, trying to keep afloat, but he was trapped in the Maelstrom and there was no escape; the blood-red water was dragging him down, dragging him under.

"Caramon! Where are you?" Raistlin cried. "Caramon, I need you!"

He felt an arm clasp hold of him, and for a moment relief flooded through him. Then he realized that the arm was not the muscular arm of his twin. It was the bony arm of Fistandantilus, clutching his victim closer, preparing to suck out his life. Fistandantilus pried open Raistlin's fingers and took hold of the dragon orb. He held it up before him and laughed.

Raistlin saw to his horror his own face laughing at him. The eyes were his eyes, the pupils the shape of hourglasses. The hand that held the dragon orb was his hand. The light of the staff, which was fast dimming, glimmered on golden skin. The delicate bones, the maze of blue veins, were all his.

He was losing himself, dwindling away to nothingness.

Rage blazed inside Raistlin. He was too weak to use his magic. The spells writhed like snakes in his mind and slithered away, and he could not catch them. But he had another weapon—the weapon a mage could use when all other weapons had failed him.

Raistlin gave a flick of his wrist, and the little silver knife he wore on the thong around his forearm slid into his palm. His hand closed spasmodically over the hilt and, with his dying strength, he wrapped his arm around Fistandantilus and pulled him close and thrust the knife into him. Raistlin felt the knife pierce flesh, and he felt it scrape horribly against bone. He had struck a rib. He jerked the knife free. Blood, warm and sticky, gummed his fingers.

Fistandantilus flinched and gave a puzzled grunt,

wondering at first what was wrong. Then the pain hit him, and he realized what had happened. His face that was Raistlin's face contorted. The hourglass eyes darkened with pain and fury. Raistlin had not dealt his foe a mortal blow, but he had gained precious time.

His strength was almost gone. He had one more chance, and it would be his last. Unwittingly, Fistandantilus helped him, twisting his body in an effort to try to seize the knife. Raistlin stabbed and the blade sank deep. Fistandantilus gave a cry, only it was Raistlin's voice that screamed. Raistlin saw his own face contort in agony. He shuddered and closed his eyes and thrust the knife in deeper. He gave the blade a twist.

Fistandantilus fell, writhing, to the floor. Raistlin let go of the knife; his hand was too weak and shaking to hold on to it. The knife remained buried up to the hilt in the black robes.

Raistlin gasped for air and watched himself die. He realized suddenly he had only a few moments to act. He grabbed the bloodstone that still lay on his breast and slammed it down on the heart of the dying wizard.

An eerie feeling come over Raistlin, a feeling that he had done this before. The feeling was strong and unnerving. He ignored it and kept the stone pressed to the heart, and he felt his own strength, his own being returning to him and with it, the knowledge, the wisdom, the power of the archmagus.

Fistandantilus opened his mouth in an attempt to cast a spell. He coughed, choked, and blood, not magic, flowed from his lips. He gave a shudder. His body went rigid. The blood bubbled on his lips. The hourglass eyes fixed in his head, and he lay still. His hand went flaccid; the dragon orb rolled onto the floor. The hourglass eyes, dark with enmity and rage, stared up at Raistlin. He looked down on himself, dead, and Raistlin wondered, suddenly, fearfully, if he was the one who had died, and if it was Fistandantilus who was gazing down at him.

Alarmed at the thought, he snatched the bloodstone from the body, and the flow of knowledge ended abruptly. He did not know what he had gleaned; his head was littered with strange spells and arcane knowledge. He was reminded of the confusion in the library in the wretched Tower of High Sorcery in Neraka.

He rose, shakily, to his feet, and he was suddenly aware that he was not alone. By the light of the Staff of Magius, once more burning brightly, he could see on the wall a shadow—five heads of the Dark Queen.

Well done, Fistandantilus!

Raistlin caught his breath and cautiously looked up.

Raistlin Majere is dead! You have slain him!

The shadowy eyes of the shadowy heads stared at something in his hand. He looked down to see that he was holding the bloodstone pendant.

"Yes, my Queen," he said. "Raistlin Majere is dead. I have killed him."

Good! Now make haste to the Foundation Stone. You are the final guardian.

The heads vanished. The Dark Queen, intent upon other dangers, disappeared.

"Not even the gods can tell the difference," Raistlin murmured.

He looked at the bloodstone pendant. As the wizard's dark soul flooded into his, Raistlin had glimpsed unspeakable acts, countless murders, and other crimes too terrible to name. He closed his hand over the pendant, then flung it into one of the acid pools. He watched the acid devour the pendant, as the pendant had almost devoured him. He seemed to hear it hiss in anger.

Raistlin held up the dragon orb. He watched the colors swirl in the light, and he chanted the words and disappeared from the tunnels, leaving the body of Raistlin Majere behind.

18

Two brothers.

26th Day, Month of Mishamont, Year 352 AC

aistlin stood before a broken column, encrusted with jewels that glittered temptingly, luring the unwary to their doom. He murmured the words to a spell he had not known he knew, and he traced a rune in the air. The figure of a woman appeared inside the stone. The woman was young, with a sweet and winsome face, pale with grief and sorrow, soft with yearning. The woman's eyes searched the darkness.

He saw her lips move, heard her ghostly, anguished cry.

"Berem comes, Jasla," Raistlin said.

He was careful to avoid stepping in the underground stream, which was crawling and snapping and roiling with baby dragons. Climbing a rock ledge that ran along the foul water, he came to a place some distance from the stone, where he could keep watch. He spoke the word, *"Dulak,"* and the staff's light went out.

Raistlin waited in the darkness for the person who had

been dumb enough—or perhaps courageous enough—to walk into his spell trap. Raistlin knew who that person was, the other half of himself. He heard the sounds of two people sloshing through the dragon-snapping, blood-stained water. He knew them in spite of the darkness.

One was Caramon, a good man, a good brother, better than he deserved. The other was Berem Everman. The emerald glimmered and, in answer, the jewels in the Foundation Stone began to glitter with a myriad of colors.

Caramon walked protectively at Berem's side. His sword was in his hand, and it was stained with blood. His black armor was dented; his arms and legs were bleeding. He had a bloody gash on his head. His jovial face was pale, haggard, drawn with pain. Sorrow had marked him. The darkness had changed; the darkness had changed him.

A brother lost.

Raistlin looked into the future and saw the end. He saw a sister's love and forgiveness, her brother redeemed.

A brother found.

He saw the temple fall. The stone splitting as the Dark Queen shrieked in rage and struggled to keep her grip on the world. He saw a green dragon, waiting for his command, waiting to take him to the Tower of Palanthas. The Tower's gates would open at last.

"*Shirak,*" said Raistlin, and the magical light of the Staff of Magius banished the darkness.

19

The End of a Journey.

26th Day, Month of Mishamont, Year 352 AC

he Temple's darkness is lit to day-like brilliance with the power of my magic. Caramon, sword in hand, can only stand beside me and watch in awe as foe after foe falls to my spells. Lightning crackles from my fingertips, flame flares from my hands, phantasms appear—so terrifyingly real that they can kill by fear alone.

Goblins die screaming, pierced by the lances of legions of knights who fill the cavern with their war chants at my bidding, then disappear at my command. The baby dragons flee in terror back to the dark and secret places of their hatching, draconians wither in the flames. Dark clerics, who swarmed down the stairs at their Queen's last bidding, are impaled upon a flight of shimmering spears, their last prayers changing to wailing curses of agony.

Finally comes the Black Robes, the eldest of the Order, to destroy me—the young upstart. But they find to their dismay that—old as they are—I am in some mysterious way older still. My power is phenomenal. They know within an instant that I cannot be defeated. The air is filled with the sounds of chanting, and one by one, they disappear as swiftly as they came, many bowing to me in profound respect as they depart upon the wings of wish spells. . . .

They bow to me.

Raistlin Majere. Master of Past and Present.

I, Magus.

AFTERWORD

ragons of Autumn Twilight, first published in 1984, celebrates its twenty-fifth anniversary in 2009. Since then, the *Dragonlance Chronicles* have been continuously in print. They have sold more than thirty million copies worldwide and been translated into almost every language.

We have become friends with so many people around the world, people of all races, creeds, and nationalities, who have been brought together through a love of reading. We would like to thank the many fans worldwide for their help and support and encouragement. We want to give special thanks to the group on the Internet message boards of the Dragonlance Nexus, who have rallied around to provide background research and information.

Perhaps our proudest moment was to be involved with the production of the animated film *Dragons of Autumn Twilight*. We would like to thank the people who worked on the movie, which has been released on DVD from Paramount Pictures: producers Arthur Cohen and Steve Stabler, director Will Meugniot, writer George Strayton, coexecutive producers Cindi Rice and John Frank Rosenblum, and composer Karl Preusser who wrote the fabulous original musical score. All the actors did a wonderful job, but we would especially like to thank Jason Marsden, who did the voice of Tasslehoff and who was so kind to give his time and talent to the fans and to us.

Our thoughts go to our friends and members of the very first Dragonlance team: Jeff Grubb, Michael Williams, Doug Niles, and Harold Johnson; our first editor, who took a huge chance on us, Jean Blashfield Black; the amazing art staff of TSR, Inc.—Larry Elmore, Jeff Easely, Clyde Caldwell, Keith Parkinson; our former publisher, Mary Kirchoff; and our former executive editors, Peter Archer and Brian Thomsen. Finally, we would like to give special thanks and heartfelt gratitude to our friend and editor for all these many years, Pat McGilligan.

And to all of you who have read and loved these books. May dragons fly ever in your dreams.

—Margaret Weis and Tracy Hickman

RICHARD LEE BYERS

BROTHERHOOD OF THE GRIFFON

NOBODY DARED TO CROSS CHESSENTA . . .

. . . WHEN THE RED DRAGON WAS KING.

"This is Thay as it's never been shown before . . . Dark, sinister, foreboding and downright disturbing!"
—Alaundo, Candlekeep.com on Richard Byers's *Unclean*

ALSO AVAILABLE AS E-BOOKS!

DUNGEONS & DRAGONS®

FROM THE RUINS OF FALLEN EMPIRES, A NEW AGE OF HEROES ARISES

It is a time of magic and monsters, a time when the world struggles against a rising tide of shadow. Only a few scattered points of light glow with stubborn determination in the deepening darkness.

It is a time where everything is new in an ancient and mysterious world.

BE THERE AS THE FIRST ADVENTURES UNFOLD.

THE MARK OF NERATH
Bill Slavicsek
August 2010

THE SEAL OF KARGA KUL
Alex Irvine
December 2010

The first two novels in a new line set in the evolving world of the DUNGEONS & DRAGONS® game setting. If you haven't played . . . or read D&D® in a while, your reintroduction starts in August!

ALSO AVAILABLE AS E-BOOKS!